HAUNTED HEART

Annice laughed as happy tears moistened her eyes. "Now you're talking with your common sense. Life isn't given as we want it to be, Luke. It comes as it is. So we'll be married and I can be happy again. Oh, I love you."

His arms went around her and his lips crushed hers. His breath was hot against her face. His mouth on hers was hot honey as he drew the honey from her lips and mouth. He kissed her savagely then and could not stop. His life's blood rushed to her and he had to have her no matter what it cost.

As they moved toward the bedroom, he groaned. It was going to cost her, not him. If she or someone couldn't help Marlon, she would be the loser. He was crazy with wanting her, crazy with not wanting to hurt her, and she could see the conflict in his eyes.

"It will be all right, my darling," she assured him. "This is the right choice for us."

HAUNTED HEART

Francine Craft

BET Publications, LLC
http://www.bet.com
http://www.arabesquebooks.com

ARABESQUE BOOKS are published by

BET Publications, LLC
c/o BET BOOKS
One BET Plaza
1900 W Place NE
Washington, DC 20018-1211

All Kensington Titles, Imprints, and Distributed Lines are available at special quantity discounts for bulk purchases for sales promotions, premiums, fund-raising, and educational or institutional use. Special book excerpts or customized printings can also be created to fit specific needs. For details, write or phone the office of the Kensington special sales manager: Kensington Publishing Corp., 850 Third Avenue, New York, NY 10022, attn: Special Sales Department, Phone: 1-800-221-2647.

BET Books is a trademark of Black Entertainment Television, Inc. ARABESQUE, the ARABESQUE logo, and the BET BOOKS logo are trademarks and registered trademarks.

First Printing: December 2002
10 9 8 7 6 5 4 3 2 1

Printed in the United States of America

DEDICATION

This book is dedicated to Myles, my love.
May we always be there for each other.

And to Billy and Betty, who know a lot about love.

ACKNOWLEDGMENTS

Many thanks to Dr. Maude Adams for her expert and kind help.

A world of appreciation to my editor, Chandra Taylor, for her patience and wonderful slant on life.

Prologue

Annice Steele came awake around midnight, cold, trembling, yet light perspiration filmed her body. Another dream of Luke—passionate, enthralling. Her very soul stirred. Sitting up, piling bed pillows behind her head, she drew up her knees and hugged them.

Luke. She could see his earth-brown, close-cropped hair, feel his sinewy, walnut-brown body pressed close to hers. "No," she cried out. He was gone and let it be that way, if that was the way he wanted it.

Her face in the triple dresser mirror was bereft. The tan skin seemed dull and the offblack hair was tangled.

She had gotten out of the hospital yesterday. The doctor had told her to rest a few days, and she refused to think about why she had been there. Physically, she felt little pain, but the pain in her soul wracked her with grief unlike any she had ever felt before.

If only she could cry. But she couldn't cry. As a psychologist, she was well familiar with the five stages of grief necessary to heal from loss of something hoped for, but not gained. She had known incredible ecstasy with Luke. Now she was paying for it.

Leaning over, she switched on the lamp beside the bed and the large diamond engagement ring on her finger caught fire. "No," she whispered again. Luke had given her the ring two years ago, kissing it onto her ring finger. Oval shaped, magnificent, she had protested that it was too expensive and he had scoffed. "Why have money if I can't make a woman who means more to me than anything happy?"

She slipped the ring up and down on her finger but did not take it off. She wondered why she had worn it to the hospital.

How could it happen? They were together, madly in love, then it was over. She had been on special study in London and had come home for a brief visit because she missed him.

"I'm sorry, love," he had said. "I don't think we can work as a couple. Neesie, know that I love you, and I'll always love you, but I won't marry you."

She had heard the regret and the pain in his voice. "But *why*?" she had pleaded. "You owe it to me to tell me why."

He had taken her hand and held it like a Dutch uncle, not a lover. It was as if he were consoling a child. "One day perhaps I can tell you, but I can't now. Believe me, this is for the best."

"Are you in love with someone else?"

"I don't want to answer that."

"I never thought you could be cruel," she'd cried.

"One day you'll know I'm being kind. I won't stay and torment you. Take care of yourself, my love, and I'll be in touch from time to time."

Hurt and furious, she had stormed, "No, don't stay in touch. It's better if we break clean. Have fun with your life, Luke."

She had twisted the ring from her finger and handed it to him. He had taken her hand and slipped it back on, kissed her fingers again. What manner of madness was this? she wondered.

"Keep it for the day you will know what this is all about."

Numb, she had done as he asked.

"Neesie," he had reached for her, tears in his eyes. They had been in her living room, and she had gone to the door, opened it. "Leave now, Luke," she'd said then, "before I make a fool of myself."

His smile was lopsided, sad. "That's the one thing you could never be. I wish we could talk about this, but it isn't possible. People make mistakes, my love. . . ."

"Don't call me your love. It's too bizarre."

"I have to ask you to understand what you cannot possibly understand."

His sinewy frame filled the doorway. His sad expression made her want to comfort him, and this made her angrier. She still ached for him; he no longer wanted her.

He had reached out and gently touched her face. "One day you'll know I did the best I know how to do. Trust me, Neesie. . . ."

Tears wracked her voice as she choked, "Don't ask me to trust you any longer, Luke. From the time I've known you, I would put my life in your hands and I wouldn't be even a little afraid. Now, no, I don't trust you. I never will again."

"Please," he'd said softly. "One day when I can tell you the truth, you'll understand."

"Just *go!*"

She had hoped he wouldn't leave just then, but he had. She had wanted to watch him walk down the hall to the elevators, but she'd slammed the door shut and gone to the windows. It was growing dark. Rain clouds behind December city lights had been a fit background for her grief.

Now she got out of bed and padded over to the windows, remembering. Bad call. It was misting rain the way it had threatened the Sunday night Luke went away. She sighed deeply. They had not seen each other again. He had written her cards wishing her well, but he had not called.

Luke had bowed out of her life six months ago and the hurt never seemed to stop. Now, the bitterness was still like gall. She had to do something to end it.

Getting out of bed, she pulled on yellow slacks and a brown cashmere sweater, then slipped into her loden, cloth brown coat and pulled on cashmere-lined leather gloves. Wrapping a woolen scarf around her head and standing up, she slid on her boots and went outside.

She was crazy and she knew that now. It was midnight and she could be in deep trouble before she'd gone the eight blocks she intended to walk to Washington, D.C.'s Tidal Basin.

Out of the hospital that day, she'd come home to find another card from Luke:

> *I wish you all the best.*
> *Luke*

Little enough to write. Nursing her wounds, furious, hurting beyond belief, she had known then what she had to do. Why hadn't she gone in the daytime? No, she wanted to be around as few people as possible.

A light mist surrounded her as a blue and white police car headed in the opposite direction slowed.

"Any trouble, ma'am?" the policeman's friendly voice asked. His female partner looked at her sympathetically.

"I'm fine," she said. "There's just something I have to do at the Tidal Basin."

"Well, look, my partner and I would be happy to take you there."

"No, please. I'm all right."

"Okay. Well, you take care now, you hear?"

"Yes officers, I'll take care. Thank you very much."

She passed the row of first-class popular restaurants on the waterfront, passed the marina and the seafood markets, went under the aqueduct and onto the Tidal Basin. Why hadn't she done this before? And she had an immediate answer. The pain had been so great at first that numbed, she could make no decision, take no action, but now this new pain had galvanized her into action.

Standing at last at the side of the Tidal Basin, opposite the brightly lit Jefferson Monument, she pulled off her gloves, tucked them into her pocket and stroked the ring, watching as it glittered in the streetlights. She slid it from her finger, angry because she wanted to kiss it. Drawing back her arm she prepared to fling the ring into the water.

At the last minute, she changed her mind about sending it far out. Instead she simply let it fall and watched the light ripples on the water's surface. There, that was the end of Luke and her. In time, she could be happy again.

The police car that had passed her earlier parked in a pathway and both partners got out. ''Ma'am, we couldn't help but wonder if you need help,'' the female officer said.

Forcing gaiety, Annice said, ''I told you I'd be all right. There was just something I had to get rid of.''

The officers looked at her steadily. ''Are you leaving now?''

''Yes. There's no reason to stay. I wasn't going to kill myself.''

''Well a lot happens,'' the female officer said. ''Let us take you home.''

Light-headed, Annice thought then about what could have happened with her walking alone at midnight.

''Please,'' the male officer said. ''Let us take you home.''

''Why thank you.''

A few minutes later they pulled up in front of her apartment complex, and she invited them in, desperately needing company. She had close kin, friends. Why hadn't she called one or some of them? She was twenty-nine and she knew this was the kind of pain that cut one off from others.

The two officers stayed a half hour drinking café latte and eating raspberry tarts. She wanted them to stay longer but didn't ask. *I can rest now*. She had been hanging on to Luke, not facing the fact that he no longer wanted her. With the dropping of the ring, he was now out of her life forever. A wave of anguish and disappointment swept over her. She felt as desolate as ever. It was going to take a long time to get over him.

Chapter 1

Walking that morning near the administration building on the campus of Casey's School for Troubled Youth near Minden, Maryland, Annice Steele breathed in the fresh, early September air. Passing her hand over her long, off-black, chemically straightened hair, she touched her tan skin and sighed. She could heal here. Heal from the hellish psychic blow that her once-beloved had dealt her.

Red brick buildings were nestled in shrubbery and tree-lined walkways. Most of the students were on-campus residents; some had stayed the summer. Annice smiled. This was going to be a lovely year. She liked making a difference. Dr. Will Casey, the school's founder and superintendent, had leaned on her to come and work at least a year. He was a psychiatrist who had mentored her, and she couldn't see herself refusing him. A broad smile tugged at the corners of her mouth.

She had been walking in a happy daze when she saw the tall figure ahead of her pause and look back. He was broad-shouldered, with cinnamon-colored skin, narrow-hipped with earth-brown hair, cut close, and a gentle, mocking smile. He waited while she moved toward him. This was no dream; it was a nightmare.

"Annice," he said, walking back to meet her halfway. "How are you?"

His brown, gray-flecked eyes roved her body in remembrance.

She could barely speak her throat was so tight. "I'm well, Luke. And you?"

His lopsided grin was charming. "I've been better. I've been worse. Have you gotten my cards? I haven't wanted to inundate you."

"I got them. It isn't something you have to do, you know. You made your choice. I can live with it."

"Then you're one up on me."

Luke swallowed hard. She looked so wonderful. He loved her hair any way she wore it, and the tan skin was smooth, flawless. With half closed eyes, he caught the essence of her slightly overweight spectacular form. Deeply curved, broad hips, narrow top, just the opposite of his own form. Just looking at her made his heart turn over, his loins hurt.

Her throat was dry as she asked him, "What are you doing here?"

He looked at her thoughtfully. "You wouldn't have had time to know. Dr. Casey had a heart attack day before yesterday. He's got to have some time off. I'm on sabbatical, so I volunteered to take over until he recovers. . . ."

Blood rushed to her head. *No*! she screamed inside. *I can't take this*. She looked at him angrily. "You should have notified me."

"There wasn't time. Too many other things to be taken care of. Besides, it's too late for you to back out. That's what you're talking about, isn't it?"

Her voice seemed trapped deep in her throat as she answered. "You're damned right that's what I'm talking about."

"Neesie?"

She didn't answer him.

"If you knew my story, you'd forgive me. Forgive me anyway. Trust me."

Annice's laugh was scornful. "Once bitten by a rattlesnake, would I press one to my bosom at any future time?"

"I'm not a rattlesnake, just a man whose heart is torn up over leaving you."

"I don't want your explanations."

"I keep saying it and you don't want to hear it, but one day. . . ."

"One day the world is going to end. I can't stay, Luke. You must know that. What we had was too deep. I nearly . . ."

"You nearly?" he asked.

"Never mind. It's water over the dam." She certainly wasn't going to tell him she had nearly gone under. And she thought bitterly: *Psychologist, heal thyself.*

He spoke slowly. "I know how much you hurt, but I beg you to understand, this had to be. I still love you. I'll always love you."

"Spare me the consolation conversation, Luke. I'll stay until you can replace me. I know a new psychologist who will be happy to come here. She hasn't landed anything she wants yet."

He listened carefully before he said, "When I've talked with Dr. Casey, he's been excited that you'll be at his school. He thinks the world of your work with troubled youth. He's been delighted thinking you'll carry on with him."

"And I was delighted to be working with him, but you know how impossible this is. When will he be coming back?"

Luke was silent a long moment. "It may be a few months before he can return even part time. He's counting on you."

She looked at him angrily. "You keep asking me to understand. Will you understand where I'm coming from?"

"Please stay. You owe this to yourself. I know you've studied in London as well as the United States, but the work you'll be doing here will be some of the most important you'll ever do. You know that. We've got some tough cases, and they need your help. They and you deserve the best."

He had reached her where she lived. She cared about her work with young people. Casey's School for Troubled Youth had eighty boys and forty-five girls, many of them headed for destruction. And she could reach and help most of them. The young psychologist she had wanted to send was not in Annice's class; she was green, unseasoned. Annice was young, but she had finished high school at sixteen and had an excellent head start.

He looked at her gravely. "He was always there for you. Don't let him down. I know what I'm asking. If you want it that way, I'll stay away from you as much as possible. Being around you tears me up, too, but Dr. Will has to come first."

She relaxed then, blinking back a few tears. She wouldn't look at him. She looked instead at nearby yellow and bronze chrysanthemums lining lush evergreens. From the corner of her eye, she saw a gangling seventeen-year-old pass at an angle and called, "Marlon. What a surprise. Weren't you going to speak?"

"Yeah, sure." Marlon Jones came to them. "Hello, Neesie." Awkwardly, he shook the hand she offered, but held himself stiffly as she hugged him.

"Hello yourself. Looks like you've grown a few inches. You're no longer at Ellisville?"

Marlon looked down and frowned. "I pulled out and came here with Luke." His voice sounded choked, guttural. What was going on here? she wondered, frowning. The man and the boy seemed uncomfortable and Marlon didn't look well. Now Luke's jaw was set the way it got when he wasn't going to talk about something.

"It's good seeing you," she told Marlon, who looked like a seventeen-year-old version of his thirty-four-year-old brother, Luke. Marlon was so plainly anxious to leave.

"Yeah, sure," the boy said. "Look, Luke, I'm going back to the dorm for a little bit, then I'm going to the cave with Julius."

Luke nodded to Annice. "Julius came from Ellisville to be with Marlon. They're still buddies."

She nodded. "I remember Marlon."

"See ya," Marlon said as he left.

Annice stood bemused, "And I always thought Marlon wanted to put as much distance between you and him as possible. Something about the urgency of separation and becoming a man. He's staying in the dorm and not with you?"

"No. Not with me. I'm in Doc Casey's house."

"He left Ellisville to be with you. He liked it so well. . . ."

Luke shrugged. "The best laid plans of mice and men oft go astray."

She loved the sound of his voice that was losing its strained timbre and coming back to its natural baritone as they stood there.

"Could I buy you a soda at the snack bar?" He looked at her for a moment, then shook his head. "Okay, forget I said it. I will put distance between us, Neesie. I swear I will. But if you need anything at all. . . ."

She looked at him directly, her eyes brimming with tears. "Let's not make it harder on each other. We had our own little world of trust and dreams and you chose to put it away. You say you hurt, too, but it was your choice. I can't think of anything you could tell me that would make it easier."

He looked at her levelly. Brilliant, warm sunlight warmed them both.

"We'll make it," he said. "Neesie, we have to make it."

He glanced at her hands. He wondered what she'd done with the engagement ring he'd given her; she'd been so happy with it. She was going to have to do the farewells first, he couldn't. Her shapely body was like a magnet drawing him. Her somber face held him entranced. He wanted to stay with her, *be* inside her. That was never going to end. They were here together and they never should have been, but they were. The *one day* he had spoken to her about wasn't here yet. Would it ever be? And how were they going to weather this?

Chapter 2

The next day was Saturday and as uncomfortable as she was, Annice looked forward to the first Heartwarmer gathering, founded by Dr. Casey to keep faculty and students in touch.

The gym where the affair would be held was festive with balloons and crepe paper streamers of coral, green and white. She was early and found Velma and Arnold Johnson already there. The Johnsons were at Casey's School because she had recruited them. Velma was girls' dorm matron, Arnold, boys' major. The couple was from her home in Crystal Lake, Virginia, and they lived in a cottage adjacent to the girls' dormitory.

Velma rushed to her side as she came in, demanding, "Why haven't we seen you? Oh, I know it's only been one day, but . . ."

"I've had so much I have to do. I'm sorry, love," Annice said and hugged her.

"Give her some breathing space," Arnold said to his wife as he came up.

Annice smiled. "Accept my apologies, please, for not getting in touch sooner."

Velma cocked her head to one side. Velma Johnson had salt-and-pepper hair, a slender, wiry middle-aged body and a broad face. Arnold was portly with dark brown skin and twinkling eyes.

"Did you know Luke would be taking over?" Velma asked.

Annice shook her head. "There wasn't time to let me know."

"How're you dealing with it?"

How like Velma to put it on the line, Annice thought, but then they were friends of very long standing. Both were well aware of Annice's devastation over the breakup. But they didn't know the whole story, Annice thought bitterly. She was the only one who knew the story and even she didn't know the whole of it.

Aware that she hadn't answered Velma's question, Annice told her, "I'm taking it somehow. We get over things."

Velma caught her hand and squeezed it. "Some things take time, a lot of time."

"Leave it be, hon," Arnold said gently, patting his wife's back.

Velma gave her a sympathetic look. "Trust me," she said ruefully, "to rush in where angels fear to tread."

"I can't expect you to read my mind, and time has passed." Annice looked at her friend, reflecting on the deep bond between them. The Johnsons were also very good friends of her parents.

"Well, nobody said the handsome and oh-so-personable Dr. Jones would be easy to slough."

"Seems to me I heard the name *Jones*."

"Oh dear," Velma said, turning to face Luke. "Your hearing is too good."

And Luke did look handsome in a heather-brown suit, a pale yellow shirt and a wide, diagonally striped brown, yellow and rust tie. Looking at him, Annice felt sick with longing she valiantly fought down. Raising heavy black eyebrows, Luke looked at Annice with haunted eyes.

The band from D.C. was warming up, playing slow, sensuous music. A voluptuous young girl had taken the microphone, singing, "Where did you go?" How fitting, Annice thought.

Luke looked at Annice again, his eyes hooded. Her body never quit mesmerizing him, her face was something he had fashioned in his dream. But it was the woman's depth and sensitivity that held him, her way of going to the heart of matters, her lively grace and her forthrightness.

He hadn't meant to ask her, but he found himself doing just that. "Would you dance with me?"

"What? Oh Luke, maybe we shouldn't. . . ."

"I know we shouldn't, but grant me this and I'll try not to bother you too much again."

As she went into his arms by a cluster of silver balloons, her heart drummed in her breast and she felt dizzy with desire she could hardly control.

"The band is good to say they're such a young outfit."

"Yes." What could they talk about? The song asked plaintively, "Where did you go after you left me?" and the music washed over them both with honeyed cadence.

Holding her, Luke felt wild desire sweep him. How long would it take to be by her side again? Hold her? And what if he was never able to work it through? He groaned and Annice asked, "What's wrong?"

"Us. We're what's wrong. We're in one hell of a bind, locked-in on campus here together, bound by what we both owe Will Casey. I'm beginning to get a bit of a feel for what we're going to have to do. Be friendly, but you and I can never be just friends. Best friends, yes, but not just friends."

"We're adults, Luke. Grown up. If it won't work, I'll leave, help you find someone else."

"You're the best, the classiest game in town. Trust me,

I need you here, Neesie. You'll forgive me when you know what's going on."

The song ended. The dance floor was rapidly filling up. Luke and Annice stood at the fringes. She wanted to get away from him and with the same blind insistence, she wanted to stay.

A slender woman with dark blond hair, pale skin, and green eyes came to them. She smiled deeply at Luke, but with Annice the smile didn't quite reach her eyes.

"Well, Dr. Jones, I hope I can inveigle at least one dance with you."

Luke answered her indirectly, "Dean Claire Manton, let me introduce you to Dr. Annice Steele. She's our psychologist and she goes back a long way with Dr. Casey."

Annice extended her hand and accepted the none-too-firm handshake from the coolly lovely dean.

"I'm happy to meet you," Annice said gently. She didn't like this woman and she knew it had to do with the other's proprietary air toward Luke.

"Well, the pleasure's all mine, *if* Dr. Jones will dance with me. Otherwise, my heart will be broken and I'll take no joy in anything." She smiled and blushed. "I knew there was someone with your name in Luke's life, but I never met you. Luke and I go back to childhood. I've always loved him."

Annice inhaled a harsh breath. The dean came on strong.

Luke looked a bit uncomfortable as he said, "Come on, Claire. Be real."

"Mix! Blend with the music! Get to moving!" The joyous soprano voice of Della Curtis made Annice smile as the woman came up with her son, Calvin. A stout woman of indeterminate age, she wore her dark red hair in a feather bob and smiles played perpetually around her generous mouth. She owned an inn out from Minden and lived with her son, who attended Casey's School.

"How are you, Dr. Steele?" the boy asked. She was often impressed with his impeccable manners.

"I'm fine, Calvin," Annice told him. "And how are you?"

He shrugged. "I'm making it, learning about being an innkeeper. Now it's September and I'll be going to school." He attended Casey's, according to his mother, because he was overly bashful and couldn't seem to get it together. She spoke of sending him to Minden's high school the next year. He was a junior.

The boy was lanky, with a dreamy, brown-eyed smile that always touched Annice's heart. She and Della went back to high school days.

"Scoot!" Della told her son. "Flirt with the girls, but don't get carried away. I want you around at least until you finish college."

"Aw, Mom," the boy protested. Grinning suddenly, he looked at two boys who walked toward them. Marlon and a boy she didn't know. Marlon quickly introduced the boy as Julius Thorne.

"His old man's a judge," Marlon said. "Figure that."

"That's nothing on you," Julius said. "Your brother's a school superintendent."

"Guys, let's not brag," Calvin said evenly. "My mom's an innkeeper. Best of the bunch."

Della threw back her head and laughed. "There's nothing wrong with any of you that a little humility wouldn't cure."

"Are you a medical doctor?" Julius asked Annice.

"A psychologist."

"Oh." He seemed disappointed and more than a little uncomfortable.

"I said it before. Scoot! The three of you meet and mingle and have fun." Della's never-ending store of goodwill spilled over.

As Annice stood talking with Della, two girls came over. The lushly proportioned, dark brown girl with her badly straightened hair and wide smile took the lead.

"You're going to be our psychologist?" she questioned cheerfully.

"I am." Annice's mouth held her own wide smile. For some reason she liked this girl on sight. "How can I help you?"

"My name is Belle Madison and this is Carole Cates."

"I'm glad to meet you both. I'm Annice Steele."

She shook hands with both girls. "Belle lives in Minden and helps me sometime," Della said. "She's a wonderful helper. None better."

"Oh, thank you. I enjoy helping you."

Carole was pale yellow-rose, with brown hair and eyes, and she seemed to delight in just being alive. What psychological help did she need? To Annice's surprise, the girl said, "Maybe I can help *you.* I get jealous of Belle getting to help all the good people."

Her musical voice lilted. She was a physically beautiful girl and she seemed to be well aware of it. She had a model-slender form and laughing eyes. "We can certainly talk about it," Annice assured her. "Come to see me when you have time."

"If she can take the time from boy hunting," Belle said good-naturedly. She hugged a laughing Carole. "My buddy, the pants chaser." Carole's expression didn't change.

"Give her a break." Annice found herself wanting to protect Carole.

With hooted laughter, Belle said, "You just don't know."

Refreshments were served at nine-thirty. Delicious fried chicken, potato salad and barbecued potato chips, hot, buttered rolls, pineapple punch and a variety of really delicious cookies.

Luke came over to where Annice stood alone.

"Eat with me. I hate eating by myself and I'll walk you home when you're ready to go."

"Luke, don't. I'm hungry and I won't have you spoiling my appetite. I don't need you to walk me home. Thanks to you, I've got to get used to being alone. I may even learn to like it."

A flicker of pain crossed his face as she thought, he wasn't going to have his cake and eat it too.

She moved away with her paper platter of food toward the warmly welcoming Johnsons. Velma saw the expression on Luke's face as Annice walked away and her sympathetic heart went out to Luke.

"Lord," she said, "I hope something works out for those two or they're not going to make it."

Annice tried to keep her eyes from following Claire and Luke on the dance floor. Did he really hold her that close or did *she* press in to him? Well, Luke wasn't hers anymore. He had sworn off, so he was free to press his magnificent body to anybody he chose. He was free. She could still kill him for the pain he had caused her.

The affair broke up at eleven and Annice started to slip out unnoticed, but Velma came to her.

"Let us walk you home." She shrugged. "But if Luke wanted to dance with you, he'll probably want to do the honors."

"Nobody need do the honors. It's so close I'll walk over on my own."

"You always were an independent woman, even as a child," Arnold said. Velma agreed. "I'd be proud to have you and your sibs as my children."

Velma looked sad and her husband took her hand. "We've made it just fine, honey," he said. "We've been blessed."

"I'm not complaining." She turned to Annice. "Don't you love this campus?"

"I do. It's beautiful."

Velma looked at her sharply. "Is it going to be too hard on you?"

"Luke?"

"Yes."

"It isn't easy. I'll do my best."

They walked her to the door and she walked outside in

the moonlight along the stone-bordered walkway on the short distance to her cottage. The campus was well lit, but certain parts lay in darkness because of the dense shrubbery and trees.

Walking along, she felt a sense of ease. The fog inside her head since seeing Luke had begun to lift. They had talked. They had danced together and she wasn't dead from heartbreak. It pleased her to know she could take it, but they were going to have to talk.

Her cottage lay ahead. Most single teachers and staff lived in faculty apartments. She was pleased to have a house fashioned of French gray clapboards with sparkling white trim. Bronze and yellow chrysanthemums nestled close to the front and the sides of the house. As she got closer to the cottage, she reached into her bag for her keys when she heard the jangling of many keys and a man cleared his throat loudly behind her. Who? She nearly jumped out of her skin as she looked around.

"Evening, ma'am," a bass voice said. "Don't let me scare you."

Annice laughed from sheer relief.

She paused and the man stopped beside her. "You must be new. I know all the people left over from last year."

"Yes, I'm new." Annice held out her hand. "I'm Annice Steele." She didn't give him her title.

"And I'm Bill Sullivan, one of two security guards who roam the school after dark. Pleased to meet you."

"I'm pleased to meet you. I feel safer now."

The guard laughed. "This place is about as safe as it gets. Never had any trouble for the three years I've been here. Young male pranks, a few girls slipping off campus. Nothing much. I hope you'll be happy here." The guard rubbed his fingers over his face. He liked this woman. Her physical attractiveness didn't hurt either. A big, good-looking man, dark brown with strong white teeth, Bill Sullivan had a working wife and three children, but he was married, not dead.

* * *

Inside her house, Annice listened to the quiet sounds. There was a big, Black Forest cuckoo clock in the living room. She hadn't been here a full day yet. Bill Sullivan had graciously taken her keys from her, let her in and she had thanked him. Safe? Was she safe here? Certainly she was safe in the way people meant when they spoke of safety. But Luke was here and she felt her very person was in danger.

She had a chance to look around and she liked what she saw. The house was roomy, well furnished and well decorated. The living room was dark English rose and cream, her bedroom French blue and white. *If I manage to survive seeing Luke, I'm going to like it here.*

Undressing slowly, she pulled on a white silk crepe nightgown, put cream on her face, spread on a thin layer of almond oil and got into bed. Resolutely, she refused to acknowledge Luke's face as it swam before her. She couldn't deny the jealousy she had felt as he danced with the dean, Claire Manton. Annice told herself she didn't care. His life was his own. But she couldn't help wondering if Claire Manton was a woman in his life that he'd left Annice for. No, she told herself, he was too straightforward for that. She wasn't going to speculate on why he'd left her. She had been telling herself these past months that she was healing fast. Well, seeing Luke today had certainly sent that to hell in a handbasket.

Turning off the bedside lamp, she snuggled under the light blanket. Nights were beginning to be cool in this part of the country. She had slept long and fitfully when the dream came of standing at D.C.'s Tidal Basin and watching ripples in the water that sparkled from lamplight. "No," she cried. "No. Please!"

She woke up sweating and threw the covers back. Another nightmare! The radial clock gave 2 A.M. Then she was aware of fear cooling her blood. She had heard a noise near her bedroom window. She listened carefully in the dark room and it seemed she could hear her heart racing.

Talking with Della and the Johnsons had just about given her a map of the school campus. Annice's cottage stood alone, not far from the gym. Several acres of woodland lay behind her house. Luke lived in Dr. Casey's house, which was located at the other end of the campus. She was not a fearful person, and she tried not to be foolhardy. Yet she felt fear now. She listened again. Someone was outside her window.

Swinging her long, shapely legs over the side of the bed, she got up, padded to the closet and got a robe. Slipping into the robe, she slid her feet into mules and got a flashlight from the night table. *Don't be a heroine. Don't be a fool!*

She raised the window higher and shined the light outside. A black-cloaked figure sprang out and ran swiftly, but she had heard hard breathing, which meant he had been very close. Her heart hammering, she pulled the window nearly down. Apparently the security guard was elsewhere. But he had said they were safe, that nothing had ever happened here. Well, she thought angrily, there was always a first time.

She pulled the window down the rest of the way and sat heavily on the side of the bed, still in her robe. Should she call Luke? Cutting on the bed light, she picked up a slender phone book from the night table to see if it listed a way to get in touch with the guard. There were no instructions. She wouldn't call Luke. What if he were out spooning with Claire Manton? Someone had been watching her, breathing hard enough for her to hear him at the window. What did the intruder have planned? It was the beginning of her second day at Casey's School and already she had undergone more trauma than she usually underwent in a couple of years.

Breathing heavily, he sat in a corner, his hands clenched. He had a secret he could share with no one. Streetlights lit the area except for one dark corner, and he sat down on his haunches in that darkness. When had he begun stalking unusually attractive women? Not all women, just certain ones. He liked the proud, the independent ones, the ones who could look at you with eyes that said, "I want you!" Floozies, all of them.

He sighed deeply. There was no one he could share his secret with. No friend. No kin. It had shocked and scared him out of his wits the first time, then he had felt proud. He was the stronger, strongest. Other boys and men couldn't touch him and he gloried in that.

So far, the ultimate—death—had only happened once and it had been splendid. Power had filled him full to bursting when he was accustomed to feeling powerless. He felt like shouting it to anyone who'd listen. I've got a secret! The only problem was that after nearly a year, the thrill was fading. He shrugged. He didn't need to worry. Another opportunity would come along, another surge of pure, malignant power would fill him and it would happen again. He had never been more certain of anything than he was of that.

The woman had been scared tonight when she'd come to her window. Her voice had quavered when she'd asked if anyone was there. He grinned, imagining his gun jammed against her chest, the violent jerk when he pulled the trigger.

Revenge was sweet. He didn't give a damn who said it wasn't.

Chapter 3

Annice woke late the next morning. She got up, dressed in faded jeans, a black cotton pullover and a downy jacket, and sat in the front porch swing for a few moments. A slight shudder shook her as she thought about whoever had run away from her window. She would speak with Bill Sullivan, the security guard, when she saw him, or she would look him up.

The Johnsons wanted to show her Pirate's Cave this afternoon. The cave was famous in that part of the area for its beautiful stalactites like giant icicles and its white clay floors and walls. Located on the back side of school property, it was private and only those connected with the school were welcome.

She rose from the swing and began to look around her spacious front yard. Gingerly she walked to the outside space under her window and peered intently into the shadows of the big evergreen. Maybe it would be necessary to cut down that big oak. Annice shook her head. It was a fabulous tree, over a hundred and fifty years old, with upthrusting, gnarled roots.

There was no doubt in her mind that someone had been there. Her blood cooled again as she thought about it. Suddenly she saw a metal badge of some sort just under the window. Moving in, she picked it up and looked at it carefully. There was the lettering on it: *Minden County Sheriff's Department*.

She frowned. What on earth . . .? The telephone's ringing cut into her thoughts. She relaxed as Velma's pleasant voice came onto the line of her cell phone. Going inside, she was tense, walking as she talked.

"I hate disappointing you," Velma said. "Remember Arnold and I were going to show you Pirate's Cave, but he's under the weather."

"Oh, I'm sorry. Some other time then."

She envisioned Velma smiling as she said, "Oh, I've made other arrangements. *Luke* is going to show you the cave."

Annice's voice caught in her throat. "You didn't have to do that. Any time will do."

"No, I promise you, it's beautiful, and you're going to be a busy lady later on. Della showed it to us. I think you should see it as soon as you can."

Annice thought a moment. She needed to tell Luke about what had happened last night, and they had to talk, too. Pursing her mouth, she breathed deeply to stop the anxiety that coursed through her.

"Same time?" she asked Velma.

"Yes. You're not mad at me for asking Luke to take you?"

"Of course not. If I'm going to work here this year, and it looks like I am, then I'm going to have to get used to occasionally being in Luke's presence."

"That's my girl. Who knows. . . ."

"Don't make any plans for the two of us," Annice said softly. "We all have to accept our losses." There, that sounded almost real. Only her heart knew it was the biggest lie.

She hung up the phone and stood rubbing her forearms. Out in the kitchen, she squeezed fresh orange juice and ate a mango and a raisin bagel with cream cheese spread on it. Her coffee was excellent Colombian supreme with cream and natural sugar. Glancing at the wall clock, she saw it was nearly ten o'clock. She had slept late because she had slept so little before early morning rolled in.

Carrying the last of the bagels with her out of the kitchen, she looked at the sheriff's badge lying on the table by the phone and picked it up, studied it. She saw then that smaller letters read *Volunteer*. Putting it back down as if it were hot, she went into her room to dress. As she drew her bath, she tried not to think at all. This wasn't denial or running away, it was simply survival.

She took a leisurely bath and dressed in white jeans, a navy T-shirt and navy loafers. Her face in the mirror looked somber, drawn. She didn't feel so hopeful now about being able to be around Luke with any degree of comfort. But Dr. Casey had done too much for her to let him down. He needed all the friends he could get to carry on his work while he was ill and when he was recovering.

Luke came promptly at eleven. She sat on the porch, waiting for him.

His face lit up when he saw her. "Good morning," he said. "You look lovely, but then you always do."

"Thanks. You certainly look well." He wore stonewashed blue jeans, a black T-shirt and a heavy woolen hunting jacket. Her breath caught at her memories of his splendid physique. Thinking of his rippling biceps made her long to reach out and stroke them.

"Would you like some coffee? Tea? Whatever?" she asked.

He cocked his head to one side. "You know I'm a coffee man. And load on the cream and sugar. I live dangerously."

"You're right about that. I have to admit I still take a little cream in my coffee, even if I do use a natural sweetener. But I've made other changes. Maybe I can coast with it for a couple or more years. Come with me into the kitchen, won't you?"

"Certainly."

They sat at the table and she had another cup of coffee with him. When they had finished, she told him what had happened the night before. His face was drawn, angry when she finished.

"I ran into the security guard on the way home last night. He thinks it's the safest place on earth."

He shook his head. "This has become a world where we can't vouch for safety anymore. It isn't just in this country. Then the world never has been the safe haven we like to believe it is. Neesie, I'm sorry."

She got up and got the badge from the phone table and brought it back to him. He studied it for a long while, turning it over in his big hands.

"Let me handle this. Dr. Casey is very friendly with the sheriff, and I know Lieutenant Jon Ryson at Minden's Police Department. Lieutenant Ryson and the sheriff work together. Thank you for telling me. I'll get on it today."

She had to smile. Luke and she had often spoken of the fact that they were both take-charge people.

"I'll see that Sullivan watches you tonight. You saw the person, you say?"

"Yes, but he or she wore a cloak or something like a cape. I couldn't tell you what size. I was too startled—and shaken."

"Maybe you had better spend a few nights with the Johnsons. Or in one of the faculty apartments."

"Probably not necessary. I have a permit to carry a gun. Once a man I testified against for molesting young girls came after me. He was sent up. I just hope it's not him."

"My God. I wish I'd been able to be there for you when it happened. I'm sorry."

She looked at him levelly. "You had your own fish to fry, Lucas. I'm sorry too."

"I've really missed you."

Afterward, she was never sure just how it happened. They were standing by the telephone table and she felt a little dizzy with anxiety. She swayed toward him, her heart thudding, and she was in his arms, held tightly.

"Neesie," he groaned.

"Luke, don't!" she whispered. But his lips were on hers so hard it hurt and his sinewy body outlined her own. He held the back of her head in his big hand and the other hand pressed the side of her waist and upper hip. For a wild moment, she gave herself up to him, melding with him. He cupped her face then and his tongue found hers and took the sweetness from it. Sliding her jeans down, he stroked her back thighs and she began to surrender.

Then, with tears in her voice, she harshly told him, "No, Luke, this isn't going to happen. You left me. We'll stay apart. I hate halfway things. My life isn't going to be like that."

"I'm sorry. It won't happen again."

Luke was a proud man and she could trust him to honor what he promised her. It was herself she had to deal with. She had blindly leaned against him, still seeking his warmth and his love. She wouldn't do that again.

Pirate's Cave lived up to Annice's expectations. Part of a very high hill, it was partially grown up in evergreens and trees. Inside, the ivory-colored stalactites were awesome. There were several benches and a quartz grotto lay midway into the cave. Annice found the white clay floors and walls everything they were said to be. There was a back entrance that led to fenced-in land on a highway.

"In the ten days we've been here," Luke explained, "Marlon has set up to paint here. The electrician wired the front part of the cave for lights and some of it filters to the back."

At first, they explored the cave and marveled at its beauty. They moved about as if nothing had happened between them, but Annice still felt the splendor of his kiss on her lips, their open mouths extracting honey. Thank God they'd been able to stop. Now they sat on a stone bench, bodies shielded from the cold stone by their heavy clothes.

"Once it was believed that there were gold coins buried here somewhere," he said. "It seems pirates really had a hideout here, but the whole place has long been cleaned up."

"Luke, about us . . ." she began.

He took her hand. "Don't tremble, Neesie. I'm swearing my hands off. It wouldn't be fair to us otherwise. Trust me."

She nodded. "I trust you. It's myself I don't trust."

"Then trust yourself. The onus lies with me. I hate having to be away from you. I'm just praying you don't find someone else before I can work this through."

"Oh? What is it, Luke, that you can't confide in me? I'm as good as gold where you're concerned."

"That's the problem. You'd hurt yourself to help me, and I won't have that. I love you and I'm going to keep telling you that. I can't *not* tell you. But my rage to hold you, kiss you, be inside you is temporarily suspended."

Annice's laughter was pained. "We talk a good fight, you and I," she said. "I want us to swear that there'll be no more kisses like this morning. We've got to help Will Casey the best way we know how. We've got to put aside what lies between us. Put your hands over mine and swear it, Luke."

He did as she asked and couldn't stop the surges of passion that swept him as his hands covered hers.

"I'm working like hell to get this straightened out," he said, "but I don't know when, or even if . . ."

His face was tormented as she knew her own must have been. "I'll stand with you as best I can," she said.

"Neesie, don't!" He wiped his brow with the back of his hand. "Just help me keep Doc Casey's show on the road. I won't let you hurt yourself trying to help me."

* * *

Monday morning, Luke couldn't shake that conversation from his memory. In his big, well-appointed office in the administration building, he looked out the window toward the cave in the near distance. He had just turned to go back to Dr. Casey's mahogany and leather desk when his brother came in.

"You know, kid," he said fondly, "I'd swear you grow an inch every day or so."

Marlon smiled wanly and Luke frowned. "What's wrong?"

They both had the same cinnamon-colored skin, the earth-brown hair, but Luke was sinewy and Marlon was far slimmer, like the boy he still was.

"Are you getting set up? Do you like the place?"

Marlon shrugged and a shadow crossed his face. "Yeah, it's OK. Luke?"

"Yeah?"

"I need to go back, just for a short while."

"Back? You mean to Ellisville? Why on earth would you want to go back?"

Marlon hunched his shoulders. Both still stood. When Marlon spoke, his voice was little more than a croak. "I keep dreaming. . . . Hell, they're *nightmares.*"

"About Sylvie?"

"About Sylvie. God, Luke, if only I could remember what happened."

Luke's face was bleak now, but his brother's face was bleaker. "I've told you from the beginning you need to talk with someone."

"Well, I can't talk to Annice, for sure. I feel too close to her and I couldn't open up. Give me a few months, Luke, please. I'm still scared I might have done it. What happens then? I loved, I still love Sylvie, always will. Why would I hurt her?"

"You can't get out of this bind without help. Let Annice

refer you to someone in D.C. They've got some of the world's best psychiatrists and psychologists.''

"Give me a little time, and I swear I will talk to her. Maybe I will remember just what happened. I was to meet Sylvie again at the garden house, bringing a drawing I'd just done. Instead, I found her. . . . I've told you and the cops all this.''

"You found her. You remember that much,'' Luke said quietly. "You told me you don't remember anything after finding her dead. But we know you must have gone to your car to get to the nearest telephone and you ran into a deep ditch and hurt your head; you had already blacked out.''

"Yes,'' Marlon said. He shuddered and acid tears filmed his eyes. "I'd never hurt her.''

"You weren't indicted. A lot of other people agree that you didn't do it.''

"And a lot of people think I *did* do it. You remember, Luke, one detective said he thought I killed her and getting away in a panic, had the accident, struck my head and went under, or, as he put it, *said* I went under.''

Luke came to his brother, hugged him. "I believe you,'' he said. "I believe in you. One day, you're going to bring yourself to talk to someone and it will all be out in the open.''

"But what if I did it? I couldn't live with myself.''

Luke patted the boy's shoulder. "Marlon, don't. Once we know the truth, we can face it, no matter what.''

Reluctantly, Luke came away from that subject. *What if he is guilty? he thought. What if he did kill her? Lord, I've got to believe in him.*

"How are you fixed for art supplies?'' Luke asked, needing to change the subject.

"I've got plenty. If I couldn't paint, I don't know what I'd do.''

"But you can paint. Marlon, it's only been a few days, but do you like rooming with Julius instead of living with me?''

"Yeah, that's cool. Julius is a heller, but I enjoyed being his buddy at Ellisville, and I'm glad he transferred to be with me. I know we had trouble, and I was jealous of him liking Sylvie so much, but we got over that."

Luke looked at him closely. The way he saw it, somebody had to be well aware of Marlon and Sylvie's movements. Who knew them better than Julius? Julius's father was a well-known judge who had bought his son out of trouble more than a few times.

"Perhaps you could lean on Julius to shape up a little more."

Marlon laughed drily. "I've got news for you. He's a half year older than me; he thinks that gives him the right to run my life as well as his."

"Well, don't let him lead you astray."

"You don't think Julius killed her?"

Luke was silent until Marlon prodded him. "Luke?"

"I guess anything is a possibility. I said I believe in you and I do, but I want to know the truth and I want to know it soon."

In a barely audible voice Marlon said, "So do I."

Annice walked from her house briskly. Nothing else had happened. The security guard had made his presence known by keying in her front porch and she had been grateful. She liked the big, amiable man.

It was bright this morning and the campus spread out before her. The buildings were mostly of neat red brick, none more than four stories high. On her end of the campus, there was her neat cottage, the gym, which also held the art and music studies, and the dining room, as well as an infirmary with a part-time doctor and nurse. Beautifully landscaped with tall evergreens and flowers of the season, it was a physical and a scholastic tribute to its founder, Dr. Will Casey.

In the middle of the campus, the dormitories for girls and for boys stood, then the administration building with its classrooms and offices. On the opposite end of the campus, the Casey home added a touch of elegance. Fashioned of the same red brick as the other buildings, it had rose gardens that were a favorite of Dr. Casey, who loved beauty. On the other side there were several cottages for married faculty members.

As she neared the administration building, Annice looked ahead to where the Johnsons' cottage sat and she looked last at Dean Claire Manton's cottage. White and freshly painted, it was larger than the other cottages and boasted fewer flowers and shrubbery. She wondered how long Claire Manton had been there.

She had interned in psychology here a few years back. Thinking about the campus took her mind away from what had happened Saturday night. She put her hands into the huge pockets of her beige corduroy jumper with navy cotton pullover and touched the cloth over her thighs. Luke's hands had begun to roam her thighs in the cave and she had stopped him. She sighed. This wasn't going to be easy.

Going into the administration building, she rode the elevator to the fourth floor and Luke's office. She found him in the waiting room talking to his secretary. His face lit up when he saw her.

"Ah, welcome," he said. "I'm glad you're early." He introduced her to his small, pert and attractive secretary, Lisa Dabney. "She's not the Ms. type," he said to Annice. "She insists on being called Mrs."

"Not a problem," Annice drawled.

The two women shook hands and liked each other on sight.

"I would have met you at Saturday night's Heartwarmer," Lisa said, "but my husband was a bit busy. I'm glad to meet you now."

"And I'm delighted to meet you."

Luke stood smiling, stroking his face. "Well, it works out then. I'm going to share Lisa with you, Annice. I warn you, she's a crackerjack secretary."

"You're kind," Lisa told him.

He grinned at the small woman. "That is, if you're willing to put up with another difficult soul."

"I think this is going to work out just fine." Lisa's small, heartshaped face glowed. "Don't either one of you think about my having to work for both. I'm a high-octane woman. My husband complains that he can't keep up with me."

Luke took Annice's arm and steered her toward his inner office. Once there, he said over his shoulder to Lisa, "Please hold my calls."

He seemed different, Annice thought. More reserved, even if he had seemed happy to see her.

"How was your night?" he asked.

"It was OK. I was aware of the guard stopping by keying in my house box. Thank you for taking this seriously. It would have been easy for you to just dismiss it as a prank."

"I'd never do that." He wet his lips, wanting to touch her, hold her. She sat, unaware of the turmoil inside him.

"We're going to make it," he told her evenly.

"I certainly hope so."

"I thought of inviting faculty over to Casey House tonight," he said, "but it's Marlon's birthday and I'm taking him to Caleb's in Minden for a feast. The boy eats like he's just started growing." He grinned.

She spoke without thinking, before she could stop herself. "I always enjoyed it when we took Marlon out on his birthday."

He nodded. "We had good times, all the time."

He wasn't going to ask her now and it nettled and hurt her, although she knew she was being unreasonable. She had thought of him that he couldn't have his cake and eat it too. The same held true for her.

He paced back and forth, his hands behind his back.

"Dr. Casey paces like that," she said.

"Yeah, I expect I got it from him. But my father used to pace too."

"Were you close to him?"

"Very. To my mother, too."

Annice nodded. "You're doing a good job raising Marlon." Her words hit him where he lived. He wasn't doing a good enough job, he thought, to keep him out of trouble.

"You can wear out the rug," she said. "I'm going to sit down." He sat down and Annice sat in a chair across from him, reflecting that she always wanted to know whether parents and children were close. She had been adopted by the famous Singing Steeles, and although Annice adored her adoptive parents, she longed to know her biological ones.

"Even worried, you look great," he said, finally settling down.

"So do you."

"Tell me your plans for psyche-doctoring our students."

Annice smiled at the thought. Nothing pleased her more than helping to straighten out a life, get it running well. And yet, she grimly reflected, her own life had gone offtrack. "Believe me, I have plans. Big plans. When I get through, these kids are going to take advantage of the best that's in them. They're going to offer the world the best they have. And they're going to know what it's like to succeed. Group therapy. One on one. Groups of boys, groups of girls. And both."

His eyes on her were hooded, warm, and she felt she was right. He was reserved. He hadn't responded at all to her comment about the three of them going out to dinner on Marlon's birthday.

"What I think," he said, "is that you're right that we can make it through this. Let's not pull away too hard, but we can't get too close. We've had the world on a string and maybe one day we can have it again." But even saying it, he seemed cool to her, guarded. Had she pushed him away too hard?

Luke balled his fist and slid the side of it along the thick glass top of the desk. The more he thought about it, the more he wanted Annice to talk with Marlon. But psychic doctors didn't treat friends just as medical doctors didn't treat those close to them. His heart hurt for his brother, but the hurt was nothing compared to the agony Annice and he now knew.

She began to rise. "I think I'll be getting to my digs. I like Dr. Casey's office."

"You've visited him before?"

"I have. Remember I interned here."

"I know."

He got up and walked her to the door where they were greeted by the sound of Claire Manton's tinkling laughter.

"Good morning, Dr. Jones," she said, a soft smile lighting her face. "I hope I'm not barging in on anything." She looked somewhat sly. "And how are you, Ms. Steele?"

"Well, thank you. And you?"

"*Very* well."

Luke stood in the doorway. He couldn't quite decide whether to walk Annice to the door or stop at Claire Manton's side. He decided on the latter. He had to let Annice know that it was a serious thing they had undertaken. They would be civil, kind, but all love and lust was off limits for the time being.

Annice said good-bye to Lisa and went out into the hallway, aware that Luke and Claire had gone back into his office and closed the door. As she closed the door to the inner office, she heard Lisa say into the intercom, "I'll be happy to hold all your calls, Dr. Jones."

Annice drew a sharp breath, an edge of anger filling her. The late Harry Stack Sullivan, the eminent psychiatrist, had posited that deep anxiety served to bring on deep anger. And she was certainly anxious. Luke had to tell her something, had to confide in her. She didn't know how she would bear it otherwise. Then she pulled herself up and took several deep breaths. She was a hardy woman who knew how to ride with the tide. But she wouldn't lie to herself. She didn't know how she was going to get through this hellish turn of affairs.

Chapter 4

By October, Annice's life had settled down nicely. It bothered her, though, that Luke stuck to their vow of limited interaction. He was courteous, pleasant, warm. She couldn't fathom how he did it because she was waspish on occasion and tears often came to her eyes because she missed their old times together. Being less close to him left her more time to brood over finding her biological parents.

She was a bit glum as she looked around her group therapy room, then glanced at her Movado watch, a gift from Luke. In ten minutes the kids would come tromping in—ebullient, contentious, interested and interesting.

Annice had twelve groups of ten people and one more-advanced group of five. Each group met twice weekly and she saw others on an individual basis. She had her hands full and often thought about her hormones-on-legs charges.

She got up and paced a bit, thinking about how Luke paced. She got a warm feeling now thinking about the weekly verbal and written reports she gave him. He seemed warmer then, friendlier. She shrugged. No use fretting over losses; you had to go on with your life. Luke had said that one day he would be able to tell her what was going on. But when?

Marlon and Julius Thorne came in.

"Morning, Dr. Steele," Marlon drawled.

"Yeah, morning," Julius murmured. A really big kid, Julius had deep chocolate-colored skin, a shaved head and a lackadaisical manner. He could be cold and cutting in a flash when things didn't go his way. She wished Marlon had a different kind of best friend.

"Good morning, Marlon, Julius."

"How come he gets first dibs on your greeting?" Julius rumbled. "I'm six months older."

Annice shook her head. "Don't be competitive, Julius. It hardly ever gets you anything."

"Tell that to the Redskins and the New York Yankees," Julius shot back. "My old man always says when he gets to heaven, he's going to take St. Peter's place."

"Listen to me at least occasionally," she told him. "I have your best interests at heart."

Della's son, Calvin, came in then, rushed and anxious. For a skinny kid, he had good muscles. He paused in front of Annice. "Gee, you look great in that outfit, Dr. Steele."

"Why, thank you." Annice glanced down at her gray-blue woolen dress that fastened with big buttons in a curved line down her side. Three-quarter sleeves showed off her richly smooth tan forearms and the wide silver bracelet that Luke had given her.

Marlon and Julius looked from Calvin to Annice with a sly grin on their faces. They were always on the lookout for male-female interaction, especially teachers and students.

They sat in chairs in a circle as Carole and Belle drifted in. "It was a great show here until the campus twins happened by," Julius said loudly. "See one and you get the other."

"Julius, I don't want that kind of hostile display in here," Annice told him. "*Talk* about your hostility to Belle. Don't put it into words directed at her; that's action."

Julius slouched down in his seat. "I feel like some action." He poked Marlon in his ribs. "Think we could find us some action?"

"Don't be difficult," Annice said. "It gets you nowhere."

Julius slouched down in his chair and stretched out his legs. Carole sat as if she were on cloud nine. Belle was a love, Annice thought, but she liked to psychically rumble. Annice thought she probably needed to separate the two. Carole and Julius flirted heavily and were beginning to be an item. Belle, who was Carole's best friend, couldn't stand him and he returned the favor.

"Who wants to tell me some of the rules we need to remember to govern our work in here?"

Carole raised her hand. "First one is *respect*. Be sure to respect ourselves and our fellow group members. Everybody, really. It's so important."

Annice nodded. Marlon's hand shot up. Julius gave him a hard look and he stammered, "I'll let somebody else tell you. I listed five last session."

Acknowledging Belle's upraised hand, Annice looked sharply at Julius. She wasn't going to sit idly by and let him run Marlon's life.

Belle mumbled, "Never let what goes on between us in this room be bandied about to others outside the room. That is, I don't tell Carole's business and nobody else's—you know, the things we talk about about ourselves, and others don't talk about what I say." The girl was so down on herself. She was the opposite of the flippant, flirtatious Carole.

"Wonderful," Annice told her. "Now, this is going to be one of the hardest rules to abide by, but it, too, is most important. Group participants will and should say things they don't want to hear repeated."

"Another one," Calvin piped up, "is *helping* your fellow group members in any way you can." Julius rolled his eyes at him and Calvin shriveled as Annice frowned.

"Julius," Annice said, looking at the big boy levelly,

"try to be cooperative. It gets you more than being competitive, more than acting hostile."

Julius didn't answer but drew his legs in. And to her surprise, he mumbled that he wanted to state another rule. "Stand on our own feet." Then he added. "I do that in spades."

"I don't meant to criticize, but sometimes you overdo it."

"It's the way my old man taught me."

"I see," Annice said.

A slender youth who always had little to say brought up the rear. "Limit competition—although we compete sometimes—and go all out with collaboration."

"Great. Comments?"

"Yeah. I want to talk about this," Julius said. "You mean I ought not to try to outdo my buddy here in getting good grades?"

"Julius," Annice said gravely, "getting good grades is a part of being who you are, of giving yourself what you deserve. That's not competition."

Belle got up and got a glass of water from the long table in a corner. As she came back to her seat, sipping the water, paying little attention, Julius's left foot shot out and she tripped over it, spilling water on the carpeted floor and a little on Julius.

He looked up through narrowed eyes. "A born klutz. Big girl, can't you even walk straight?"

"You did that on purpose," Belle raved. "I could *kill* you for this."

That flash of anger seemed to come out of nowhere. Annice drew a quick breath and said calmly, "Sit down, Belle." She got up and got a roll of paper towels from the table, brought it back and blotted up the water, throwing the wet pads of paper toweling into the big, gray wastecan.

Belle had tears in her eyes. She had expected anger from Annice. She came to Annice's side and said roughly, "Here,

you'll ruin that pretty dress. You should have let me do it."
But Annice had blotted it all up.

With the group seated again and calmer, except for Belle,
they settled in.

"Now," she said to Belle, "we see what I mean about
talking things through. Now, Belle, talk to your fellow group
member. Tell him . . ."

"Well, I sure don't think she should have said she could
kill him," Marlon shot out. He gripped the sides of his seat.

"Simmer down, bro," Julius murmured. He bore a look
that Annice couldn't fathom. Was it a look setting up a bond
between Marlon and him?

"I'll simmer down when I get good and damned ready,"
Marlon said loudly. "You don't own me."

"Hey dude, cool it." Julius's face had gone hard. "People
talk about killing people every day. And sometimes they *do*
it. Don't you know that?"

Marlon jumped up and only the person sitting in the chair
next to him kept the chair from going over. His face was a
study in anxiety and anger as he fled the room.

"Never"—Annice said angrily to Julius—"never pull a
stunt like that in here again. We talk things through. We
don't taunt and belittle and trip our fellow group members."

"Is it all right if we do it to people outside the group?"
Julius laughed loudly. He started up. "I got to see about
my buddy."

"No, you sit there. I'll see about Marlon and I want you
to cool down."

Carol and Julius flirted openly now. It was as if she were
turned on by Julius's behavior.

Annice found Marlon at the end of the hall. She had been
afraid he would go into the men's room and she couldn't
handily reach him. He stood at the hall window looking out
and his shoulders heaved. She put her hand on his shoulder.
"Marlon, why are you so upset? You didn't do anything
wrong."

He needed a hug and she hugged him lightly. He clung to her for a few moments, then pulled away. "I'm sorry."

"About what? Impassioned emotions come up in therapy. We're here to learn to keep our emotions in check as best we can, not to act them out. Was leaving the best you could do?"

"Yeah. It was." His voice trembled now and she saw naked fear in his eyes. Anxiety. And anger. And something else: a terror that went beyond fear.

She had to say it. "Marlon, I think you need to be less close to Julius. Be friends, sure, but you need other friends. Calvin is fond of you, looks up to you. Why not move closer to him?"

He shrugged. "Julius is OK. He just gets lost sometimes."

Chapter 5

A little over four weeks after Dr. Casey's heart attack, Luke received word that he could visit with him. Delighted and worried, he told Annice that Dr. Casey had asked her to come with him.

Now, with both Annice and Luke sitting on the same side at his bedside, Will Casey grinned delightedly. His doctor came in, walked over to stand above Luke. "I'm sorry I couldn't let you see him before, but I've been concerned about letting him get too involved with anything for a while."

"We nearly lost me," Dr. Casey said, then chortled as he smiled at Luke and Annice.

"We weren't going to lose you if I have anything to say about it," the doctor said.

"Oh yes, I'm forgetting my manners," Dr. Casey said. "Drs. Annice Steele and Luke Jones, Dr. Robert Porter." He indicated each with a wave of his hand. "I'm awfully grateful to you, Doc Porter."

Dr. Porter gravely shook hands with Luke and Annice. "I'm glad to know you both. Doc Casey certainly speaks glowingly of you both, but I've got to warn you not to tire him.''

Luke smiled. ''That won't happen. We're too anxious to get him back on his feet, up and about.''

A shadow crossed Dr. Porter's face. ''We'll talk about that later. Now, please don't keep him occupied too long.''

''We'll take good çare of him,'' Luke said.

When Dr. Porter left, Dr. Casey looked at Luke and Annice and smiled. ''Are you two together again?''

Annice was the one who answered after a moment, ''I'm afraid not. It's Luke's ball game now. I'm still in the dark.''

''I see.'' Dr. Casey looked from one to the other. ''What have you to say for yourself, Lucas?''

Annice was surprised at the misery that crossed Luke's face. ''It's just not something I can talk about night now, Doc Casey. But I do hope to work it out with Neesie.'' She felt better each time he promised this, but the question hung in the air: *When?*

''Make sure you do. I don't think I've ever seen two people more in love, more suited for each other. Not even my beloved late wife and me.'' He shifted his pillow about. ''Now, since we're pressed for time, I'll ask you how Marlon is doing.''

''He likes Casey's School and he's doing well. Of course, he's hardly had a chance to buckle down, but he's painting. A friend of his came up from Ellisville. He'll spend a year at Casey's.''

''A good friend is always good to have.''

''I wish you were there to help me understand Marlon's friend, Julius Thorne. I can't quite make up my mind about him,'' Annice said.

''Thorne?'' Dr. Casey said thoughtfully. ''Anybody I know? That's a common enough name.''

''He's New Orleans's Judge Thorne's son.''

''Ah yes. The almighty Judge Thorne. I can see where his son might be a handful. The whole family's high and mighty.''

"Well, he hasn't been in any real trouble, but I think the judge was smart to put him in a special school. He has trouble controlling his impulses. But then he's really here to be close to Marlon."

Luke tapped the back of his hand to his forehead. "I'm forgetting something. Marlon did a portrait of your late wife when he knew I was visiting you. Excuse me while I get it out of the car."

He got up and touched Annice's shoulder. He felt drawn to do it, and he saw Dr. Casey's eyes light up.

When the door closed behind Luke, Dr. Casey studied Annice closely.

"And how have you been? You look splendid. You always were a beautiful human. Don't be too hard on Lucas. He's one of the finest. Give him time, space."

"I don't have any choice."

"Believe in him. He loves you very much. And you love him."

"Yes."

"And *I* love you both."

Annice's smile widened. "As we both love you. Dr. Casey, you're such a wonderful man. You helped me so much in accepting being an adopted person and making the best of it. You know how much I love my adoptive parents. It's just that I . . ."

She was surprised to feel the sting of tears.

He nodded and reached for her hand. She got up and put her hand in his. "The Steeles are marvelous, good people," he told her. "You all have meant the world to each other. But there is something in us all that craves knowing the origins of our lives. Keep looking. Many people have found their biological parents. You will, too."

"Yet when I begin to look, I feel so ungrateful, and I stop."

"The Steeles know how much you love them. And how are they, that great family of five? Singing? Loving?"

"They're all great. From time to time, Mama and Papa

Steele sing with Ashley, and she's on top of the world. She's sending you several albums as soon as you get home. They all send their love to you when I talk with them.''

His face clouded then. ''Oh yes, when I leave here, I won't be coming back to Casey's School for a while. I'll stay with my daughter, Marlene, in D.C.''

''Oh?'' Questions rushed to her lips, but she held them back. ''I'll have Ashley send them there.''

''And I'll enjoy the albums, the way I always do with Ashley's spirituals and gospel songs. So, she has a new husband. She deserves better than she got the first time around.''

''I'm with you there. Dr. Casey, be sure you don't talk too much. I enjoy just being here with you. We don't have to talk.''

''As do I enjoy being with you. I'll take it easy all right. I guess I should be retiring.'' He flashed her a bright smile. ''There are no words to tell you how delighted I am that you agreed to come to my school. I'm so disappointed not to be working with you.''

''I'm glad to be there. I'm becoming so attached to the students, and I feel I can help them.''

''I know you can. Today's kids are in such a bind. Busy parents. Busy lives. Too many things to do in not enough time. I think the kids in the special schools are lucky. They get more individual attention and the pace is slower.''

''I wish you could be there.''

''I'm sure Luke is doing an excellent job filling in for me.''

''He's an educator, not a psychiatrist.''

''Psychology minor. I trust him implicitly. I'd consider any child of mine fortunate to have him as a guide.''

Dr. Casey released her hand. ''It's hell working with him with things the way they are, isn't it?''

''I won't lie, it *is*.''

''Hang on a little longer, and you'll never know how

much I owe you for coming to the school. If I know Luke, he'll be resolving this problem as soon as he can."

Luke came back then, carrying a tissue-wrapped package. "I'll open it for you." He tore the wrapping from the two-foot by three-foot portrait framed in stained oak. Dr. Casey's eyes filled with tears as he beheld his beloved late wife.

The woman in the portrait, dark mahogany colored, with clear brown eyes and an oval face, was marvelously rendered.

"He did it from one of your photos?" Dr. Casey asked Luke.

"Yes."

"Take him many hugs from me. Make sure he knows how much I . . . Look in the drawer of this table."

Luke did as Doc Casey asked, then asked him, "Is it the paper and the pen you want?"

"Yes."

Luke handed him the items and picked up an *Ebony* magazine for him to write on.

In shaking letters, Dr. Casey penned the words *Thank you with all my heart. The portrait is beautiful and loved.*

They saw then that he was crying and they watched over him until he stopped. Then he said gravely, "Those acid tears do my heart more good than all the medicines in the world. Now, tell me what you've got going on that's grand."

"Well," Luke said, "Annice is doing her usual superb job. The woman's a wonder."

Annice chuckled, "Thank you."

"She's set up group therapy sessions along the path you fashioned. The therapy is going swimmingly. Until the cold weather sets in, we'll meet outdoors frequently. Scholastic projections are all in place, and I don't think I've ever seen so many kids trying—really trying. Some, however, seem to be already heading to fall by the wayside. They're the ones I'm worried about. I'll be glad to see you return."

"Luke?" Dr. Casey usually called him *Lucas*. Only when he wanted to say something profound did he call him *Luke*.

"Yes, Will?" They were men on equal footing now.

"I might as well tell you now. The doctor forbids me coming back for at least a year."

Luke's head jerked up. "Oh?"

"I know it will be taking a year out of your life. That is, if I can ever come back."

"Think on the bright side. Doing something you love is always good for you. As for taking a year out of my life, I surely wish everything was going as smoothly for me as the school is going."

"Trouble?"

Luke nodded. "In spades. Something I can't even talk about just now."

Dr. Casey looked again from one to the other.

"So, enough about that," Luke said. "I'm keeping a written and an audio report on our daily activities and I'm saving them until a time when you can be bothered with such things."

Dr. Casey's face lit up. "I'm really looking forward to that. I told Neesie while you were out that I'll be staying with my daughter here in the District when I get out of here."

"I see."

"I know you're surprised, but I think that's for the best. I'm sorry to throw cold water on your plans, but you'll never know how much I appreciate your taking over the school in my absence."

"I'm glad to do it, Doc, but there is a problem. It isn't easy on Annice working with me with our relationship in the bind it's in."

"How long do you expect this bind to last?"

"I wish I knew." Luke looked so miserable, Annice's heart hurt for him.

Dr. Porter came back then and checked Dr. Casey's temperature and blood pressure.

"They're both up a little," Dr. Porter said blandly. "You're the first nonfamily members I've let him see. Unfortunately, I'll have to ask you to cut it short. He needs a lot of rest.''

The doctor left then, and they heard voices outside the door. A man's gruff voice and a woman's angry one.

Annice went to the bed and kissed Dr. Casey's face, then smoothed his eyebrows. Luke shook hands and pressed Dr. Casey's shoulders. They left reluctantly, but moved swiftly to cooperate with Dr. Porter.

Out in the hallway, Annice and Luke were surprised to see Claire Manton, dressed to the nines and arguing with Dr. Porter.

''Just five minutes,'' she was saying sharply. ''Surely that little time won't hurt. I'm the dean of his school and he'll have things to say to me, as *I* have things to say to him.''

''Your name again, please?''

''Manton. Claire Manton. As I said I'm his dean and I have—''

''Well, Miss Manton, I'm sorry, but I cannot let you see him.''

''But others have seen him.''

''I can't argue that. It was under different circumstances. He's tired now.''

''I'm sure he'd want to see me.''

''Claire.'' Luke spoke evenly, but his expression was stern.

''Oh, Dr. Jones, can you help me explain my case to the doctor here?''

''Come away, Claire. Come with us now. We can't be arguing outside Dr. Casey's door.'' He spoke to her as with a recalcitrant child, and to their surprise, she walked away down the corridor with them.

As they neared the entrance, she turned around. ''I'm sure my staying just a little while would have done him good. Of course, he's my father's friend, but I would say we've grown close since I've been at the school.''

''Then if you're close,'' Luke said flatly, ''be good to him. Forgo trying to see him.''

Claire looked around again and shrugged. Luke looked really angry then. "You're not to see him today. Do I make that plain?" His unspoken words were that there would be hell to pay if she did.

She felt his anger wash over her then, and she slumped meekly. "Yes, Dr. Jones, you make that plain. I'll do as you wish." Her eyes on him were adoring.

Chapter 6

Seeing Dr. Casey in the hospital made Annice feel down the rest of that day and the mood carried over into Monday. He didn't look as well as she would have liked him to. Now, at her desk in the group therapy room, she pondered what it meant to her. So he wasn't coming back to Casey's School any time soon. That left her here with Luke, and what was Luke feeling?

This was her free period, and she spent it writing out thoughts about her charges. She opened the shallow front drawer of her desk and looked in. She was running out of ballpoint pens and pads. Maybe she could borrow a few from the art teacher. She pushed the drawer in and got up. She wanted to check with teachers on two pupils, Marlon and Belle. Neither was doing very well in the group. Both were depressed and indifferent. A talk with the art teacher for Marlon and the music teacher for Belle should be helpful.

The art and the music departments were located in the gymnasium. Going to the coat closet, she got her burgundy reefer and a white- and- burgundy-striped scarf and set out.

Ed Norris, a swarthy young man with black hair and eyes,

was the art teacher. She found him in the hall and asked about Marlon. He frowned. "He seemed to start the year with a great heart, and he was involved in a frenzy of painting. Good stuff. In such a short while, he's gone off-track. Lately he's only done one really good painting—a portrait of Dr. Casey's late wife."

"Yes, we took it to him yesterday. It *is* good."

"How is Doc coming along?"

"It's hard to tell. I wish he was better."

"And he'll be back when?

"His doctor doesn't know. He's a careful man and he takes care of himself, but we both know he works too hard."

"I guess we all do sometimes. Getting back to Marlon. Please stay here a moment." He raised his hand. "I'm going to get one of his later paintings and bring it out that side door. Can you wait?"

"I can."

He left and Annice moved about as she waited. She jumped as someone touched her arm.

Merry laughter filled her ears. She turned to find Belle grinning. She returned the girl's smile. "You're laughing," Annice said, "and I haven't heard you laugh in a week or so."

Belle shrugged. "Things on my mind. Can I talk to you?"

"Of course. When?"

"Today or tomorrow. I'll stop by to say when I can."

"The busy Miss Belle. How's your music coming along?"

"Oh, that's why I'm grinning. Miss Camper thinks she can get me into the Duke Ellington School in D.C. next fall."

"Why, that's wonderful." She touched Belle's arm. "I know you can do it. Just give it your best shot."

"You know I'm gonna do just that, but . . ."

"But?"

"Well, you look at me and I guess you see a real dog. It ain't gonna be easy over there with all those spiffy city kids."

"Belle, stop it!" Annice said sharply. "I've been planning to talk with you, but other things have come up. Who does your hair? That may sound like a foolish question, but my method has a meaning."

"*I* do it. My mama does it sometime. I don't guess either one of us is good at it. My mama's got *good* hair."

"No such animal," Annice shot back. "*All* hair is good hair, if it's properly taken care of. You could lose a few pounds. I'm not trying to hurt your feelings by being critical, but I happen to think you're a *very* attractive girl."

Belle laughed a short harsh sound, more like a hoot.

"Who you kidding, Dr. Steele? I was born seventeen years ago, and my mama says I get uglier all the time."

Annice continued as if she hadn't heard her. Didn't the girl know that on the few days when she'd left off her baggy pants and worn a skirt, her legs were spectacular? And under that extra weight, Annice was certain there was a good figure. Or maybe she thought that didn't matter. Maybe she and her mother both felt the portwine birthmark on a section of the left side of her face said it all.

"Where you think I'm going to get money for a hairdresser? And I bet you think I need better clothes."

Annice nodded. "I need help around the house. I'm a bug for doing my own housework. I'll pay you well."

Belle threw her arms around Annice and hugged her tightly. For a moment, she looked radiant, then her face fell. "My mama ain't gonna like this one bit, but my dad'll be mighty happy. He always said I got a guardian angel somewhere. Looks like he's right."

"Why don't you let me talk to your mother?"

Belle laughed again and looked a little uncomfortable. "Mama doesn't like company and she won't come here. She doesn't even come to hear me sing. My dad comes."

"I could talk to her via phone."

Belle got excited.

"Oh gee, golly. I've been saying from the beginning of the year you're a special, sweet woman."

"Why, thank you, and I think you're one sweet girl."

As Ed Norris walked toward them, Belle walked on to the music room and went in, calling back over her shoulder, "Come hear me sing when you get time."

"That'll be in a few minutes," Annice called back.

Ed Norris turned the back of the painting over and Annice gasped. The painting was of a young girl propped up on the trunk of a huge, moss-draped oak. Her offblack hair flowed over her shoulders and her head lolled forward. Was she asleep? Then Annice saw with a start. "Is this girl dead?"

Ed Norris pursed his lips. "*I* certainly think so. I asked Marlon about it and I couldn't get more than a shrug. The girl doesn't seem to be anybody here at Casey. He wouldn't talk about it. This is the third painting he's done of what I take to be a dead girl. He finished this last week. I don't want him to think I ratted him out by tattling to you, but he needs help. He used to talk with me. Now, he doesn't any longer."

"I'm afraid he isn't talking to me either."

"I think he's in trouble."

"Yes. Keep trying and I'll keep trying."

"Will do." Thoughtfully, he tucked the painting under his arm and went back through the side door that opened into his office.

Lou Emma Camper, the young, caramel-colored voice teacher, was delighted to see Annice. "You're coming to hear my best student."

"That's why I'm here, but I always want to know how things are going for you."

"Just fine, Doc."

"Call me Annice, or Neesie."

"I'm Lou Emma. Lord, but this girl has a glorious voice. I hope I can get her on the right track."

"I hope so, too."

With Annice there, Belle glowed. Lou Emma ran Belle through a set of trills and turned on background music for a few minutes. Tambourines, guitars and a piano's music filled the air. After a few minutes Lou Emma snapped it off.

"Now, I'm going to accompany you. I don't do it often, so you better be good."

"You know I always do my best."

"I know. You're a love of a girl. Wish I had one like you."

"You're not old enough."

"Well, whatever," Lou Emma said. Annice stood thinking she, too, would like a daughter like Belle to work with.

Positioned, her hands clasped in front of her, Belle began to sing. Starting with a near-whisper, she gradually built volume. "Goin' home" was the spiritual she sang, and her honeyed voice caressed every note, drew full substance and added a glory of its own.

Annice felt tears come into her eyes as she sat there. Belle deserved the best life had to offer.

Back at the administration building, Annice stopped by Luke's office and found Lisa Dabney making a pot of coffee.

"I'm supposed to be your secretary, too. Boss, you haven't given me a whole lot to do."

"I know, but I'm stacking up chapters on my book. You're going to need overtime." She smiled.

"Oh, no you don't. I've got the energy of several deer. I never met a boss I couldn't keep up with."

"I'm going to take you up on that. Is Dr. Jones in?"

"You've got it. He's alone, waiting for a fresh cup of coffee."

Annice felt wistful. Luke loved her coffee, and once upon a time, she never missed a chance to make it for him. Colombian Supreme was his favorite, and chocolate raspberry.

She knocked and at his invitation went in.

"Busy?" she asked.

"Never too busy to talk with you. Have a seat. What's on your mind, Neesie?" She sat down and told him about her conversation with Ed Norris and the painting that they both took to be a dead girl. Luke nodded and gripped a ballpoint pen, sighing.

"I know. He's painted a couple at his dorm. They're of a girl he once knew—and loved."

"Oh? What happened?"

"She was murdered."

"Oh, my God. Luke, you never told me."

"I haven't been able to talk about it. I didn't and don't want you getting involved."

"It happened when I was away in London?"

"Yes."

"Is there a story behind this?"

"There's always a story behind a murder, even if we never ferret it out."

"She was his girlfriend? He's so young."

"He's eighteen now. He was seventeen then. Talk about Romeo and Juliet. They were in love, Neesie. She was the daughter of close friends of mine." Annice saw his knuckles blanch on the pen then as he thought: *They have nothing to say to me now*. It hurt to lose friends you'd known since college. But he didn't have time to think about them, because Marlon had to be his first priority. His brother was like a son to him, and was he losing his brother?

Discomfited, Annice went back to the group therapy room. Her free period was nearly up. In a few minutes the room would resound with the shuffling and merry feet of teenagers. She opened the shallow front desk drawer and pulled out a sheet of white paper that hadn't been there when she left.

There were large, block-printed words cut from magazines and newspapers. The message was so startling. One line proclaimed: *Angel face*! And one line just below taunted, *Devil body*!

She stared at the sheet of paper. What in hell? The bell rang for classes to change and this particular group session to begin. Benumbed, she pushed the drawer shut, locked it and awaited her charges. She wished she had more time to study this and think about it, but there was no time. She was surrounded by kids trying to settle down and grope for answers to the demons that bedeviled them.

She worked as best she could, but the words on the paper filled her mind with angry loathing. She flushed hot and cold and felt befuddled. Who had put it there? And why?

She had another group session after the one she'd had just after finding the sheet of paper. After that group left, she called Luke and asked if he could come over.

Once there, he locked the door and they studied the sheet of paper. He looked distraught, bereft, far beyond what she would have expected. Shocked, he finally said hoarsely, as if the words were torn from him, "They found a paper like this by Sylvie Love's body."

Small rivulets of cold sweat ran down her body as she shivered. What was the meaning of this?

"Sylvie Love lived with her parents in Ellisville, went to the high school in Ellisville, as you know Marlon did. Sylvie's parents teach at the Ellisville School."

"I remember your talking about them, but I never met them."

"They hate Marlon and by association me." He looked terrible.

"The badge someone dropped in your yard. Your feeling someone was outside watching you. I've asked for Jon Ryson's help with this. He contacted the sheriff's office. They'll have jurisdiction. It may not add up to much, but I don't believe in waiting until someone is hurt to jump on top of a situation."

She sat behind the desk with her palms turned up. He leaned over and his big hands covered hers. "Neesie," he said softly, ardently. Then he whispered something.

"What did you say?"

"I said *my love*."

* * *

Back in his office, Luke stood at the windows looking out. It seemed he could see all the way back to Ellisville. The sheet of paper with the hateful words bore down on him.

Marlon was there. And Marlon was here. Could he conceivably hurt Neesie, and why? He had always seemed to love her, but he wouldn't let her probe his mind.

Fear chilled him then; Marlon was his brother, but if he hurt Neesie . . .

He would talk with Marlon after school. With a leaden heart, he turned to his tasks at hand.

Chapter 7

That night, Luke went to Marlon's dorm room where he found Marlon and Julius wrestling in horseplay. They stood as he came in, with Marlon saying, "Luke, what's up?" and Julius muttering, "Evening, Dr. Jones."

Julius took a photo from a big manila envelope. "See my Dad's new wagon?" He passed Luke an eight-by-ten color photo of a gorgeous white Jaguar.

"My old man's new wheels. Aren't they great?"

"The best," Luke said, smiling.

"He told me I'll be getting whatever wheels my heart desires when I graduate. I'm thinking Rolls Royce."

"You don't come cheap," Luke said, laughing. He began to settle down, talk cars for a moment with Julius. Then Luke hesitated a moment before he said, "Julius, I wonder if I can talk with Marlon alone a short while."

Julius stopped in mid-sentence, flushed. "Sure." He got up and sauntered out, but you could tell he didn't like being interrupted.

Luke was silent for a few moments. When he told Marlon

about the sheet of paper in Annice's drawer, Marlon started and clenched his hands. "How come you're telling me?"

"I thought you'd want to know."

Marlon sat on the edge of the bed as if he had to be careful not to fall. "I'm sorry, Luke. I don't need to act like such a jerk. What does it mean? Do you know? Does this make you think even more *I* had something to do with it?"

Standing there, Luke rocked on his heels. "I've told you before, Marlon. I've got to believe in you. I don't think you're a killer."

"Thanks, man," Marlon said huskily. "Sometimes it seems to me I'll never be free of people thinking I killed Sylvie."

"That's where you're wrong. There wasn't sufficient evidence to convict you. I know how you loved her. I think I know you."

Marlon clenched his hands tightly. "The fact is I can't remember much that happened after Sylvie died in that garden house. I had a painting with me I knew she was going to be crazy about. I called it *Girl in Shadows*." He hesitated a long while, then continued. "After I found her dead, I guess I rushed out to my car and left to get help. I'd forgotten my cell phone. I ran into a deep ditch and got knocked out. I don't remember anything after I saw her lying there. The doctors thought I might be brain damaged."

"But thank God you weren't."

"Sometimes I wonder."

"Marlon, don't." Luke put his arm across Marlon's shoulder. "I'm sorry."

The boy was crying now, hard tears, sobbing. "Luke, doesn't it ever get any better? Am I always going to close my eyes and see Sylvie's face tormented in death? She laughed—a lot. Why can't I see her laughing anymore?"

Luke hugged him, but Marlon shook his head. "We made love the day before. It was so beautiful. God, why didn't they kill me instead?"

"Stop it!" Luke said sharply. "You were badly hurt.

Don't beat yourself up, my brother. Sylvie wouldn't have wanted you to. Do you still have some of the sleeping tablets your doctor prescribed?''

"Yes, but I don't take them. I don't deserve to sleep."

"You deserve the best there is. Take a couple and talk to the doctor about getting more." He started to tell Marlon about the badge that had been found earlier in Annice's yard, but decided against it. The poor guy was having a hard enough time.

"Listen," Marlon said suddenly, "I've got to go back, Luke. I've got to try to make myself remember."

Luke thought a moment. "I'm beginning to think you should. Can you hold on a week or so longer?"

"Yeah. I've held on all this time, but it's getting harder."

"I've got meetings next week with two foundation trustees regarding funding for the school. It's something that can't be put off because my main contact in one is going to spend a few months in South Africa."

"I can wait. I want you to go with me."

"And I'm glad you do."

"Thank you." His voice was hoarse, tormented.

What Marlon had told him, he had heard before, but then the boy had been numb, cool in the first days after Sylvie's death. Now he was sick with rage and deepening loss. Sylvie had been the first and only girl he'd loved.

"How about coming home with me?"

Marlon shook his head. "I'll be all right, Luke. I'll take the tablets and see Doc Welles tomorrow. Don't worry about me."

"I can't help it. I hate seeing you suffer."

"It's OK. Who in hell could have put a sheet of paper in Neesie's desk drawer with the same words on it that they found on Sylvie's body?"

"You tell me."

As Marlon thought, his blood ran cold. He and Julius both knew about the paper found on Sylvie's body. The words *Angel face, Devil body* weren't all that commonly paired. He had suffered blackouts after the accident. Had he killed Sylvie and run away? There were so many things now he didn't remember. In a fugue state, *had* he cut out words from magazines and newspapers and put them on paper? Had he then left such a paper beside Sylvie's body and put one in Annice's desk drawer?

He wanted Luke to leave now. If he hadn't done it, had Julius? They were best friends, but Julius had a mean streak and Julius had told him he had a crush on Sylvie. He believed the world was his oyster and he intended to get his share. He couldn't rat on his best friend, but he had seen Julius coming down the hall along just outside the therapy room door. Marlon had been with several other students when they went into the room. Julius had turned and followed them in. Julius had never said whether he liked or disliked Annice.

"You're sure you'll be all right now?" Luke asked.

"Yeah. I'm bushed. I painted a lot this afternoon. Julius was out running track."

"You know, Marlon, you need other friends, too, besides Julius."

To Luke's surprise, Marlon answered, "I know I do. Sometimes Julius pisses me off, but I guess he's OK. I'm gonna go to bed, bro."

Luke sat on the side of the bed and hugged Marlon. "If you need anything, just call me."

Marlon sat up as Luke left the room. He hoped Julius didn't come back anytime soon. And no, he wouldn't take the sleeping tablets. Bad enough that he had these blackouts, he had enough problems without medication further messing up his brain waves.

Luke passed the front desk of Marlon's dormitory and went out into the cold, windy night. He'd give anything to take away Marlon's blackouts, his torment. His heart felt heavy and his shoulders ached. At home, on impulse, he dialed Annice's number. She answered on the first ring.

"It's a strange request," he told her, "but I wonder if you would come over to my house—Dr. Casey's house? I'll come and walk you over."

"It's barely dark. I'll walk myself over."

"Don't be flippant, Neesie, something strange seems to be going on. Until we get to the bottom of it. . . . Pick you up in a half hour."

"Agreed."

He paced the living room, willing his mind to blankness. He kept glancing at his watch. He would set out in about twenty minutes. It was a ten-minute or so walk from Annice's cottage.

He wanted a strong cup of coffee and Lord, how he missed Annice making it for him. He paused before separate photos of her, Dr. Casey and himself and picked them up, one by one, peering at them. Closing his eyes, her fragrant body was with him then. He was going to tell her tonight. She had to know *why* they were no longer together.

He went to the hall coat closet, got a beige Burberry raincoat and put it on. Annice had given it to him the past Christmas. The doorbell rang and he frowned. He needed no company other than Annice tonight. Striding impatiently to the door, he flung it open. Annice stood there.

"Neesie, what the hell? Why didn't you wait for me to come for you?"

"It's such a short distance. I'm not going to run scared, Luke. I'm just not."

"Once in a while, there's a time to run scared." He pulled her into the house and caught her gloved hands, squeezed them. A surge of anger hit him that she wasn't taking the badge, the person in a black cloak she had seen running and now the sheet of paper in the drawer seriously enough.

She took off her gloves and he helped her with her coat. He hung it in the closet thinking it was the burgundy wool coat that he had helped her pick out.

"Can I get you something to drink?" he asked.

"No. I was just finishing herbal tea and a spot of brandy when you called."

They sat on the couch with a sofa pillow's distance between them. How to tell her? Was he making a mistake? Well, if it was a mistake, it was too bad because he felt he had to confide in her.

He took her hands in his and rubbed them. Her lovely face was so dear. Being with her made his loins flame with passion and his heart thunder in his chest. How to begin?

"I'm going to tell you something I wish I could have told you months ago."

She caught her breath sharply, saying, "Yes?"

Slowly he told her about Marlon, about Sylvie Love being murdered after meeting Marlon in a rendezvous. "There was not enough evidence to convict Marlon, but he was considered a suspect. Some of his skin was found under her nails. He claims she lightly scratched his back and his back *was* scratched. When he came to he could remember Sylvie dead, but nothing else."

"Oh, my God, Luke. How could you not tell me?"

"You were in London, studying hard, trying to get your work done."

"Does he still have memory trouble?"

"Yes."

"Maybe I can help him."

When he didn't answer, she told him, "Not telling me because I was studying isn't good enough. Why?"

He put a fist into his palm and pressed hard. "I didn't want you involved. I won't ruin your life with my problems."

"We were in love, Luke. We *are* in love. Your problems are *my* problems."

"Bless you. I know you want it that way."

"And you don't?"

He was silent a very long while before he said, "Somewhere inside myself I'm afraid for Marlon. His loss of memory scares the hell out of me. What if he did kill her?"

"Do you think he did?"

"I'm trying not to think too much about it. He's my brother. Marlon has a hot temper. If they quarreled . . ."

"But I want to help."

He breathed a harsh breath. "One detective felt that was just a fluke, that he killed her, then set out. Other DNA was found, but they couldn't match it. They could and did match his. His fingerprints."

Annice nodded. "I'm too close to you both to treat him, but I could get him a referral to the best psychologist, psychiatrist, psychoanalyst."

"That's the hell of it. He refuses to talk to anyone who could help him. He wants to remember on his own. He's scared, Neesie. I think he's afraid he killed her."

Annice placed her hand on Luke's face and stroked it. "I'm so sorry, Luke, but you should have told me. I could have helped somehow."

"No one can help us if we don't help ourselves."

"You're right there, but sometimes it isn't possible. Of course, I only met Sylvie a couple of times, but I liked her. She seemed to be a lovely young woman."

Luke smiled wryly. "She reminded me so much of you. Both of you fairly tall, beautiful, full of life."

Her face was earnest as she asked him, "Now that you've told me, where do we go from here?"

He cleared his throat. "I want you to go back to Ellisville with Marlon and me."

"Why?"

"He's haunted, Neesie. He feels if he could go back, perhaps he could remember." He hunched his shoulders, "but I need you to go back for my support. You'll never know how much I've needed you."

"I think it was worse for me. Talk about a *haunted* heart. Luke, there have been times I wasn't sure I could go on living. I wanted to, I planned to run away when I found you here taking Dr. Casey's place. It was all I could do to stay. Then I saw you still cared, whatever else, you still *cared*."

"I'll always care. Will you go with us? It'll only be for a couple of days."

Annice sat with her hands folded in her lap. Finally she spoke. "I'll go. I can get a substitute to fill in for me."

"It won't be necessary. We'll fly down on Friday night and come back early Monday morning. He thinks he'll know something quickly."

"I only hope he's right. These things can take a very long time."

He took her in his arms and felt her heart thudding against his.

"Annice?"

"Yes, love."

"If only you knew what I've been through."

"I know what you put *me* through, and I'm angry about it."

"Can you understand why? If Marlon *did* kill her . . . He refuses to talk to anyone who could help him remember. What's going on?"

Staunchly she said, "I can take it, Luke, no matter what it is. I want to be with you, help you, walk by your side. Promise me you'll count on me in whatever else happens in your life."

"I promise. Thank you for saying you'll go back to Ellisville with us."

"Thank you for finally telling me." Then her face looked very sad as she told him, "I've got things of my own to tell you, things I'm not proud of."

His head jerked up. Was there somebody else?

"I've got a tough hide," he said. "For the rest of our lives, I'm going to be there for you."

"And I'll be there for you."

"What is it you want to tell me?"

She shook her head. "I can't talk about it yet. Sometime, I hope soon, I will."

He got up and pulled her to her feet, his rockhard body outlined against her very soft and silken one. She smiled, remembering his super buns and how she teased him about them, making him flush.

Slowly he stroked her back, going down to her hips before he caught her face in his big hands and brought her soft lips to his firmer ones. "I want to make love to you so bad," he said.

"I want that, too," she said softly, "but I can't. Not now. There are unspoken, hurtful things still between us, on *my* part now. Trust me. Soon."

"I hate to scare you, but I think I'm going to die right here on the spot. I've got wicked loins where you're concerned, and they're crazy to get a workout."

Annice laughed delightedly, then she sobered. She pulled a bit away. "I know we're happy to be almost back. . . ."

"What do you mean almost?"

"It will take your hearing what I have to say to bring us closer to being back."

"I don't care what you tell me, love, I won't let you go again."

"Thank you. I hope you're right. I want to think more about Marlon."

"And I'm happy you do, but at least I want to hold you, kiss you."

"You are holding me. Your kisses set me on fire. What more do you want?"

Luke laughed a small, throaty laugh. "I want you under me, moving the way only you can move. I want to feel the silken wonder of you thrilling my very soul. I want to feel your love wash over me and send me up in flames. I want to hear your cries, know you want me inside you. I *want* you, Neesie, all of you."

His words were shaking her up, making her blood race swiftly, then slow to a torpid feeling she could barely survive.

"We need to talk, Luke. We need to talk more. There are so many unresolved things."

"You know I'll wait, but we *are* talking. You and I have always talked with our bodies as well as our lips. Believe me,

I'm thinking of everything. Marlon. The volunteer badge. Someone running away from your window. The paper with the hateful words in your desk drawer. The sheriff will send someone to talk with you tomorrow and I've gotten Jon Ryson to come out and see what he can make of it.''

"Jon Ryson? Police lieutenant with Minden's finest?"
"Yes."
"I've met his wife. She's a radio talk show host."
"I know. He's top-notch."

His index finger traced her jawline as she blew softly onto his face. "I know now," she said sadly, "why I did the things I did when you left me. You're so great, and I could never hope to fill the emptiness you left in me with someone else."

Slowly he took the diary from his lockbox on the closet shelf, sat on the edge of the bed and opened it. He closed it for a moment and looked at the soot-black cover. Black for death. Gold lettering and gold-edged shiny paper. Black was the color of death the world over. White, too, but black was more so. Black was the absence of color as death was the absence of life.

He sighed and turned a few pages. He had begun keeping the diary with Sylvie's murder. There, he'd said it. Usually he set down the words *Sylvie's death,* but murder was an honorable word. It meant power. Strength. Holding the book with his right hand, he flexed the fingers of his left. He had long fingers. Powerful fingers. One day he would use their strength to pull a trigger again. He laughed shortly. You didn't need much strength to pull a trigger. But he did need strength to batter the body the way he had. He smirked. Yes, he had a whole list of killings he just might do.

The full details of Sylvie's death lay here in the book. But he had had to guess at the carnage he had created because with the trouble in his head, he had lashed out, hurling, pitching, beating, crying. He could never believe his own strength, his own glory.

He had come to find the beautiful Sylvie lifeless, so he had killed her. That made him happy. That joyful face was stilled; but the face was still beautiful even when purple from lack of oxygen. The lush body's beauty had been beaten out of it. He was quick to anger. Then there was his secret. She shouldn't have been so good looking, shouldn't have reminded him so much of someone who'd helped to break his heart. He read the Old Testament. An eye for an eye. Yes, he would kill again. One death at a time and time to savor the thrill.

The words swam a bit before him. It was like this when he was getting a spell like the one he'd gotten while quarreling with Sylvie. Power. Glory. And death! When would it happen again? He smiled narrowly. He didn't know when, but he knew it would happen again. It was his secret and it fulfilled his life too much for it not to happen again.

Chapter 8

Luke walked Annice home, came in and looked around, found nothing amiss. After a few minutes he told her, "I've also asked Jordan Clymer to come out and check your security. We've got to play it safe. I told you I'm talking to Lieutenant Jon Ryson and the sheriff. They'll want to talk to you."

She shrugged. "Probably some kid being hateful. They like to get on grown-ups' nerves. Julius knew about the paper found by Sylvie's body. He's such a goof."

"I hope so." He squeezed her shoulder. "Good night, Neesie. Sleep well."

She was disappointed that he didn't kiss her, and she walked over the house after he left, not wanting to go to bed. "Calico!" she called and waited for the cat to come to her. Where was Calico? The cat played in the yard all day on sunny days and mostly stayed on the porch on rainy ones. But her major berth was Annice's lap when night came.

Sitting on the couch, she wondered where the cat could be. Going to the front door, she opened it and looked around.

No Calico. Frowning, she repeated her movements at the back door.

She felt restless, but very pleased. As soon as she could tell him her story. . . . He would be hurt, but she had forgiven him. Couldn't he forgive her? Men were difficult.

She decided she would take a long shower in the morning instead of her usual night bath. Undressing, she chose a peach-pink, flannel-lined satin nightgown with sheer cutouts on the yoke. Then slipping into her matching robe and slippers, she thought of something she wanted to do. Yes, work a bit on her book in progress. She went to a file drawer in her den and took out a fairly large stack of pages. Sitting on the sofa in the living room, she went through them. Her working title was *Making a Great Life for Teenaged Girls.*

She leafed through the pages, thinking about the often hectic life female teenagers lived. Marlon certainly wasn't a girl, but he'd had his share of troubles. Poor kid. She'd held her thoughts back since she talked to Luke tonight. He should have told her. She'd never back away from anything where he was concerned. Could she persuade Marlon to talk with her? She intended to try.

She continued leafing through the first draft of ten chapters and studying them, but her mind kept going back to Luke. She had wanted to go into his arms, make love to him. She hurt with wanting.

Getting a blue pencil from the end-table drawer, she began to correct her copy. She felt like writing more and hoped her words would help girls like Belle and Carole.

Engrossed in her work, she heard the clock strike twelve and paid little attention. Her thoughts were racing now and she considered her ideas excellent. She had a hard day ahead and needed to go to bed, but she was on a roll, thinking she might even write more copy. She read so intensely that she heard little until it dawned on her that there were scratching sounds at the front door. Listening carefully, she put the papers aside, got up and went to the door. She heard frantic scratching now and opened the door, leaving the chain on.

Calico leaped in and across the room, not pausing at her side. The cat was soaking wet and had bald spots on her back. "Calico," she said softly, "what happened to you?"

The cat seemed to pay her no attention, but jumped to the top of a bookcase, arching her back and spitting. Then she sprang down and went under a table.

"Calico?" The cat didn't move, but cowered under the table.

Going into the kitchen, Annice warmed a cup of milk and took it back to the cat. She set the bowl on the floor and gently coaxed her. "Here, kitty, kitty."

Nearly fifteen minutes passed before Calico slunk out from under the table and gingerly came to her, but the cat pulled back when she tried to stroke her.

"I wish you could tell me what happened."

Calico looked at her with injured eyes as outrage surged in Annice's breast. Who would do this to a beloved animal?

In her office the next morning, Annice reflected on the night before. She had only gotten three hours of sleep and had finally been able to lure Calico into a padded basket in her bedroom. The cat had still shrunk from contact with her and she had reluctantly left her. She would take her to the vet that afternoon.

Now she sat alone, thinking of Luke. Didn't he know she would stick by him through anything? She couldn't see Marlon as a murderer, but what if he were? She wanted to help him, talk with him, but Luke had said he refused to talk about the murder. And he wanted to go back to see if he could remember things he was unable to remember now. She would go with them, glad to be part of Luke's life again.

A light tap sounded and at her invitation, Velma Johnson came in with a white paper bag.

"Good morning. Goodies I brought you."

"For which I thank you. I woke up too late to get a proper breakfast."

Velma smiled. "Two blueberry muffins and a slice of ham I baked yesterday. Enjoy."

"You bet."

Velma squinted. "You look a bit tired. Up late?"

"Yes, working on the book." She drew a deep breath, then told her about Calico. Velma's outrage matched her own. "We've got some real sickos around. Do you want me to take her to the vet in Minden?"

"Thanks, sweetie, but I want to talk to the vet myself."

"Well, if there's anything I can do to help. My take on Minden and its outlying places has been that it's much like Crystal Lake, pretty safe. Now, is that changing?"

Annice shrugged. "I hope this proves to be an isolated incident."

Velma had remained standing. She bent and stroked Annice's shoulder. "I've got to run. Later on, I'm baking Arnold a cake."

"What's the occasion?"

Velma laughed. "I love him and he demands proof."

"I hope Luke's and my love lasts the way yours and Arnold's has," Annice said wistfully.

"It will. When are you two going to work things out?"

"We're on our way. We talked last night and we'll be talking again. I hope that brings it all back together again."

"You have my blessings. Arnold asks about you and Luke all the time. He'll be happy. You don't mind my telling him?"

"As if you could keep a secret from him."

"That's about right." A shadow crossed her face, as she bent and hugged Annice.

"Bye, love. Let me know when everything's copasetic."

"I wouldn't miss it for anything."

When Velma had gone, Annice waited for Belle and Carole to come in for a session. She didn't have to wait long.

Both girls seemed downcast. Annice pulled up chairs into a circle and they began.

"Why the down-slanted faces?" Annice asked.

"Belle always has to have her way," Carole blurted out.

"Belle?"

"I don't like her being so fast. She's my friend and I want to protect her."

"Of course you do, as I'm sure she wants to protect you."

Belle hooted. "I don't need protecting. I can take care of myself."

"As if I can't," Carole cut in.

"Ladies. I'm sure you can both protect yourselves, but what brought this about? Can you say?"

Belle drew a deep breath, looked at Carole. "I got to tell. I want you to stop before you get in trouble."

Annice looked from one to the other. "Suppose you tell your side of it, Belle."

"Well." Belle hesitated as she looked at Carole and blurted out, "somebody's got to take care of you. Your mama don't care what you do. Your dad's dead and your mama's boyfriends come on to you. I *care* about you, girl."

Carole looked uncomfortable as Annice glanced at her watch. "I want to bring this out in the open and talk about it as soon and as much as possible. Can we get right down to brass tacks?"

"She's slipping out at night," Belle blurted out.

"Oh?"

"Yeah. Julius is rotten. He's going to get her into trouble. Now, she likes Marlon, too."

Annice drew a sharp breath. "Marlon and Julius are friends."

"I know that," Belle said. "She's playing Marlon to make Julius jealous."

"I like Marlon—a lot," Carole said softly, then added, "and he likes me. He says I remind him of someone."

"I see," Annice said softly. Did Carole remind him of Sylvie Love?

The three were silent for a moment before Annice spoke. "You shouldn't be slipping out, Carole. I'm sure you know that. Where do you go?"

Carole sighed. "Julius has so much money to spend. We go to Caleb's and sometimes to D.C.—and about."

"About?"

"Motels," Belle said flatly.

Carole huffed, "Remind me to never tell you anything else again!" Tears stood in her eyes.

Annice looked at the girl who, if Annice were a little older, could be her child. Both were joyous, carefree, caring; but whereas Annice had always been mature, painstaking, Carole was wild, undisciplined.

Belle squirmed for a moment, then looked uncomfortable. "Ah, Dr. Steele?"

"Yes, Belle."

"Well." Belle wrung her hands. "My mama won't agree to let me help you. She says she don't want me in nobody's kitchen except hers and Miz' Della's."

Annice's look was quizzical, but she said only, "I understand. I'm sorry. I looked forward to having you help me."

Belle looked at Carole, grinned. "Go on, ask her," she said to Carole.

Carole nodded. "I want to help you. Will you let me?" Her face looked anxious.

Annice hesitated only a moment. "That would be great, Carole. Thank you for wanting to help me."

"You're welcome. I can start any time you want me to."

"How about this afternoon. Your last class is at two-thirty. I had a key made for Belle. I'll let you have it. I'm really pleased."

"Me, too," Carole said, blushing.

Annice turned to Belle. "Would you let me talk with Carole a few minutes?"

"Sure." Belle sprang up and went out.

For a few minutes, Annice said nothing to Carole, merely studied her. Physically, she was such a lovely girl who could be beautiful if she carried herself in a more confident manner. Finally Annice spoke.

"Carole?"

"Ma'am."

"I'm going to have to ask you to stop sneaking out at night. You know it's wrong and you could get into deep trouble. There are many bad things going on these days. . . ."

"It's Julius," Carole said heavily. "He wants to go and I love him, Dr. Steele."

Annice nodded. "I would hope," she said, "you love yourself more."

"He's the first boy that ever said he wanted to marry me."

Annice looked somber. "You're seventeen. Plenty of time to get a great many proposals." She didn't respond to Annice's statement regarding loving herself more. Annice thought she'd go further. "Is it true your mother's boyfriends hit on you?"

"Yes ma'am. Every one of them."

"Your parents are not together, then."

Tears came to Carole's eyes. "My dad died of throat cancer when I was eight." Her face looked woebegone, and her voice went ragged. *"I still miss him."*

"I'm terribly sorry," Annice said. She got up from her chair, reached down and hugged Carole.

For a moment, the girl clung to her, then drew away.

"You might want to see Julius a little less often, and for heaven's sake, Carole, learn to say *no* to him. It will be to your advantage. If he loves you, he'll be proud you did."

Carole wrung her hands. "I'll try. He likes to tell me what to do."

"Don't let him control you. Control yourself and the situation."

"I'll sure try. Julius is so rich, I think he's spoiled."

"You bet he is. So, Julius is rich; you're not altogether poor. You're a very attractive girl and you're smart, talented.

What do you want to do with your life? We haven't talked much. We're just getting started.''

The girl rocked back and forth in her chair, grinning. ''I want to be a runway and an underwear model.''

''As in Victoria's Secret?''

''Oh yes. Yes!''

''All the more reason for you to learn to keep your wits about you where boys are concerned. In the modeling field, you'll come across a lot of attempted control, domination. You've got to learn to be strong.''

''I'm going to try real hard. Julius likes other girls anyway. He's a player.''

''So many boys and men are these days. Don't let them play you.''

Carole breathed hard. ''Thank you, Dr. Steele, for helping me, and thank you for letting me help you.''

Getting up and going to her desk, Annice unlocked her top drawer and got a key from her purse. ''Start with the refrigerator and the stove, then dust,'' she began. Then she asked, ''Have you done much cleaning?''

''Our house. I do all the cleaning and I'm good, better than Belle.''

''Great. I'm going to take my cat to the vet and I should be back by four. So I'll see you there.''

Carole looked joyous now, purposeful.

Thinking about Calico's injuries made Annice's blood boil. She couldn't wait to get her pet to the veterinarian.

''I hope we're not beginning a wave of this damned foolishness,'' Dr. Thalia Murphy, the vet, told Annice. ''When did it happen? This makes me so mad.''

''I'm glad they didn't kill her, whoever it was.'' Annice stayed close by Calico. The cat was still skittish, recoiling from physical contact. ''I'm going to have to put her under,'' the vet said. ''Take X rays. I know Calico. Someone or some devil or monster would have to tie her down to do this. She'd scratch him or her raw otherwise.''

"Yes, I would think so. She was soaking wet when she came in.''

Thalia Murphy shook her head. "No telling when it happened. I think I can work miracles with your pet—with the Lord's help.''

"Thank you,'' Annice said as the vet took the cat into the examination room.

Out in the waiting room, Annice leafed through a pet magazine, then picked up a *Jet*. A lissome model holding a cat was on the cover. Luke was away in D.C. this morning. She hadn't called and told him about the cat, thinking she would see him at his office. His secretary told her he'd been called away to D.C. unexpectedly.

"Dr. Jones said to tell you to feel free to call him.''

"Thanks. I have his number.''

Lisa Dabney had laughed. "You're such an easy boss to work for,'' to which Annice had replied, "You'll take that back. In less than a month I'll be unloading on you.''

Annice looked in the direction of the examination room. Calico would be under sedation by now. The poor darling.

Sitting there, she dozed off until a bell tinkled and a small woman cuddling a beautiful red-beige chow came in and sat down. The woman picked up and hugged the dog and kissed her face. The dog looked mournful.

"The doc's in, isn't she?'' the woman asked.

"Yes, she is.''

"Shoney here is having a tough time from an upset stomach. She's been vomiting.''

"Too bad. It's so heartrending when animals get sick. They can't tell you what's ailing them.''

"You're so right.''

The vet came to the door. "Be with you in a minute, Elaine,'' she said to the woman. Then to Annice, "Except for the fur so grossly pulled out and the fact it'll take a while to grow back, I think Calico is in good shape. She wasn't burned the way these animals often are. Consider yourself and Calico lucky. I took X rays. No broken bones. I want to keep her overnight.''

"Fine. Do you need me for anything else?"

"No, I don't think so. She's still under. I'll tell her good-bye for you when she comes out.''

Chapter 9

When Annice got home, she found Luke already there with three other men he introduced as Jordan Clymer, an attractive light brown-skinned man who owned a security agency, Sheriff Ralph Keyes, a grizzled veteran of police work, and Lieutenant Jon Ryson, a hunk who was with the Minden Police Department.

She and Luke had talked a long time about Calico and he had been angry. He was as fond of the cat as she was.

Annice invited the men to be seated while she went out into the kitchen to prepare their drinks of choice. As she bustled about, pouring snacks into bowls and placing them on trays and fixing the drinks, she read a note addressed to her. That would be from Carole, she thought. Opening it, she saw the brief note:

Dr. Steele, I finished everything you mentioned. I'm going to like helping you.

Carole.

Luke spoke from the doorway. "Do you need help?"

"Not really, but thank you." She smiled warmly at him.

"How did you leave Calico? I assume the vet's keeping her overnight."

"Uh-huh. She's pathetic with all that hair pulled out. I'm so glad it isn't worse."

"So am I."

He came to her, nuzzled her neck as thrills ran through her. She wanted to kiss him so bad. He felt her tremble and smiled as his big hands partially encircled her waist.

"Luke?"

"Yes, sweetheart?"

She expelled a harsh breath. "We've got to get something worked out. We can't go on this way."

He nodded. "I talked with you, but I've got something else to say. And I'm waiting on tenterhooks until you tell me what you have to say."

"All right, but I've got to think this through, figure out a way to say it so you won't be hurt."

"Just blurt it out. I can take it."

She shook her head. "No, I'm sure I should think this through."

"OK, you bore with me. I'll bear with you—if I can keep myself from swallowing you whole."

"Greedy!"

"You've got it."

Back in the living room, sipping their beverages of choice and eating the Ritz crackers, cheese, and assorted nuts and crisp cereals, Annice noticed the volunteer badge from the sheriff's office and the piece of paper with the *Angel face, Devil body* pasted on it. The sheriff picked up the badge and said slowly, "Then there's the person you saw running in the black cloak.

"We get a lot of volunteers we value. Young boys really get to help us and occasionally a young girl, but it's mostly interested grown-up citizens. The badge could belong to anybody."

Jon Ryson nodded. "Whoever did it knew enough about pasting letters so they couldn't be traced." He shuddered, thinking about threatening notes that had once been sent to harass his wife.

"Yeah," the sheriff said. "Now Dr. Jones tells me your cat had tufts of its hair pulled out and was wet, bedraggled when she came home. Scared as hell. I'm glad you're smart enough not to just attribute this to a kid's pranks. It could be, but something's setting up a pattern here, I think."

"You're probably right," Jon Ryson said.

"I'm going to keep an eye on your house and the school," the sheriff said. "We're short-handed, but I'll manage if I have to do it myself. Dr. Casey and his school have brought a world of honor to our community and I owe it to them. I checked. You've got a couple of security guards who seem to be on the ball as far as I can tell."

"We're grateful," Luke said. He told them then about the same words that were on the paper having been left beside Sylvie Love's body. The sheriff's jaw fell. "Well, hell, this puts a completely different slant on it."

The sheriff bent forward toward Jon Ryson, "What d'you make of it, Jon?"

"I make of it that it's serious, going beyond the prank stage. Have you any idea if it could be somebody you know?"

Unbidden, a picture of Marlon rose in Annice's mind. He was still friendly, but he shied away from her now. She didn't want it to be Marlon. Julius, with his deep pockets and his feeling the world was his oyster? She didn't think it was either one, but she knew few others at Casey's School.

"We'll keep in touch with you, too," Jon Ryson finally said. "I'll drop by from time to time and you'll see our cars on campus. You're lucky. Things are a little slow in town."

When the sheriff and Lieutenant Ryson had left, Jordan Clymer walked with Luke and Annice about the house and the premises.

"You've got a pretty good system here," Jordan said. "I'd like to set up more vision space for you from inside."

"Anything you wish," Annice agreed.

"Do your best," Luke said hoarsely. "I don't intend to have her hurt."

"We're pretty good at what we do. I'll come by tomorrow morning. I'll meet you here around noon, if that's OK. You'll be away from counseling for lunch." He said evenly.

After Jordan Clymer left, Annice changed into a cream-colored jumpsuit and a gold chain belt low on her waist.

"Wicked woman," Luke said, "You're trying to entice me."

He came to her, put his thumb under her jaw and kissed her, his tongue going deeply into her mouth.

Annice chuckled. "When it comes to you and me and enticement, I don't try, I'm the expert."

"And I'm such a pushover?" His voice was husky now. "Have you had a chance to eat anything?"

"Afraid I filled up on snacks. What about you?"

"I went wild at the Campus Grill. If you can believe it, they put together a mean crab cake."

She closed her eyes and leaned against him. Fire leapt in her body and her spine tingled. His arms went around her, holding her close. Her softness was turning him on, driving him mad. He moaned in the back of his throat. They had to wait, but he missed her so.

He picked her up. "No," she said, "I won't make love to you until you hear what I want to tell you."

"And maybe not even then," he said as alarm bells went off in her head.

"Why do you say that?"

He walked with her in his arms the short distance to the sofa, then put her down and cuddled her as one might cuddle a small child.

"Neesie?"

"Yes, love."

"I'm not going to make love to you until this thing with Marlon is worked out."

Her breath came short. "You think he might be guilty then?"

"I don't want to think it, but Marlon can be volatile. He's a good kid, but he's been under stress since our parents died in that plane crash four years ago. I never saw anyone take something so hard. He was their idol, coming along late the way he did."

"The sixteen years between you two is pretty wide."

"Yeah, but from the beginning he's been my boy. I wanted all the training I could get, so I didn't marry early and have kids. I feel like he's my own kid."

She shook her head. "I can't see Marlon harming anyone."

"You haven't seen him lose his temper. That's been going on ever since our parents died."

"No, I haven't, but it takes a lot more than losing temper to make a person a killer. There are signs."

He shifted slightly. "I'm glad you see it that way. I'm hoping with all my heart he isn't guilty."

She felt his hard, hard body moving over hers and gloried in the feeling.

"A couple of days, then I can tell you my story," she said. "I'm working it through my system."

"Neesie, I've got to tell you, I can't marry you with this thing hanging over me. It wouldn't be fair to you. No matter what, I'm going to stand by my brother who's so much like my own child. You've got a lot of people in your corner, but I'm all he has."

Hot tears came to her eyes. "I can help, Luke. That's what I'm here for. You know how I love Marlon."

"And he knows, too," he said grimly. "But you've got to admit he's holding back with you, like he thinks you might see something he doesn't want you to see."

He brought her to him and wrapped his arms about her. Unlimited passion surged through her body as she kissed his face, nibbling at his ear. He was temple-sensitive and she stroked him there. She was in flames now, loving him, needing him. She damned the time they had been apart and, to a lesser extent now, still were.

He blew lightly on her face, a line from temple to mouth, then his tongue found hers and they did a practiced, expert dance of seduction. Honey flowed from their open mouths and he delighted in her minty breath. His breath was hotly seeking, impassioned. "Oh, Luke, my darling," she said softly.

"My love," he whispered, his hot breath warming her face. "God knows, I don't want to deny you. But then you have something to tell me. I promise you this, whatever it is won't make a difference to me. Until I find out more about Marlon, I'll keep holding you, kissing you, wanting you, but I won't marry you until this is over."

They drew apart with Luke holding himself above her on his elbows.

She was silent a long moment before she said, "The man at my window, the badge, the paper, then"—she paused and Luke finished for her—"Calico."

"Yes. The vet thinks she'll be all right within a few months."

"I'm glad."

"You should have seen the way she arched her back and shied away from me, as if *I* were the enemy."

"We're thinking of teenaged boys here, but we have security guards and other guards filling in for them. And the countryside is well populated. Minden is a growing place and different sorts of people are coming in from all over. We don't know what we've got on our hands."

She touched his face. "I've been shaking since I found that paper in my desk drawer, and you told me about Sylvie Love."

Luke hugged her then, rolling over onto his side on the wide couch.

He was silent a long moment. "Lord, I wonder where this will all lead."

"We'll stick together, Luke," she said fiercely. "All right, you don't see that we can get married with this hanging over us."

"Yes, we'll stick together. We belong together. We always have. We always will."

It was late, but Luke stopped by Marlon's dorm and found him sprawled at his desk studying. Did a shadow of annoyance cross his face?

"I'll make this brief," Luke said. "Why didn't you tell me you and Julius did volunteer work with the sheriff's office this summer?"

Marlon's look of annoyance was plain. "I guess I just want to be on my own without you baby-sitting me."

Luke told him then about the badge and the man in the cloak in Annice's yard. He didn't miss Marlon's catching his breath, or the hoarseness when he answered.

"I *lost* that badge," he said. "We were supposed to turn them in. Julius leaned on me for us to keep them, and I did. But like I said, I lost it or someone stole it."

Luke said nothing, but he saw the frightened look that lay on Marlon's face.

"I swear I'm telling the truth."

"OK," Luke said. "Be sure you are."

Chapter 10

Luke, Annice and Marlon flew down to Ellisville, Louisiana, the following Friday morning. The town was twenty miles from Baton Rouge, and the ride was uneventful. They would stay at a plush motor lodge out from Ellisville. As they passed through the Baton Rouge airport, Marlon said he wanted a soda. None of them had eaten the food on the plane.

"Not a bad idea," Luke said as they headed for a food court and took seats.

After the waiter had taken their orders for sandwiches and sodas, Marlon spoke up hesitantly as he glanced at Luke. "There's something I want to do and I'm not sure you'll approve."

Luke looked at him sharply. "Try me."

Marlon cleared his throat. "I want to spend a night at the garden house where Sylvie was—murdered."

Luke frowned. "Why? Have you thought this over?"

"A whole lot. Listen, it may sound dumb but I want to *feel* Sylvie's presence. I think it may help me remember.

It's a deep hunch. . . ." His voice trailed off. He looked miserable.

Annice leaned forward in thought. "It might not be a bad idea." Then she stopped. She wanted to help, but this was Luke and his brother's ballgame. This was the reason Luke had delayed their marriage.

Luke looked at her appreciatively. "To my surprise, I'm thinking along the same lines."

Marlon bit his lip. "I've got a key. Nobody ever asked for it. I guess they didn't know Sylvie had had another one made. The only thing is we've got to ask Mr. and Mrs. Love to give me permission."

"You bet." Luke blew a stream of air as the waiter brought their hot tea and ham, turkey and cheese club sandwiches. "They'd have your butt in jail for trespassing in a hurry. They were crushed and bitter. I'm not sure they'll even talk to us."

"We've got to try," Marlon urged.

Luke nodded, and they ate in silence. In a little while they finished and Luke began to get up. "OK. Listen, let's go pick up our rental car."

Twenty minutes later, headed past the Ellisville School Luke had lately headed, they neared the Love home, which was located on the near side of Ellisville. The garden house where Sylvie had been killed lay far on the other side. She and Marlon had driven back and forth, taken bikes. They were always together.

The attractive white clapboard house was lit up so that meant the Loves were home. They were two of the few teachers at Ellisville who didn't live on campus. They had been town residents all their lives. Both had begun teaching at the private Ellisville Junior College when they were just out of college.

The door opened and Allen Love, a stocky, dark brown man stood there.

"Yes," he said only and seemed to hang on to the door for support. "Surely you don't expect me to ask you in."

He glared at Marlon and shifted nervously from foot to foot.

"You'll never know how sorry I am," Luke told him. He had recruited both parents for Ellisville School. "We need to ask you a favor."

Now Allen Love's glare shifted from Marlon to Luke. "I can't imagine granting you any favor. My girl's *dead*." His eyes nearly closed as he looked again at Marlon. "And I still think you killed her."

Marlon's voice seemed to come from deep inside him. "I never would. I loved her so much."

"Yeah, well, love and hate get together sometimes."

"Not for Sylvie and me."

"Tell Mr. Love what you want," Luke prodded gently.

"Honey," someone called from the living room. "Who is it?"

"I don't think you want to know."

The very fair skinned, brown-haired Clarissa came to the archway, and her eyes went wide, but she said nothing as she came to her husband's side.

"In a word, I'd say he wants to relive his crime," Allen said. "You're lucky I don't get my gun and kill you."

His voice and body trembling, Marlon stood his ground. "I want to spend some time in the garden house where Sylvie died. I'm hoping it can help me to remember. I keep being on the edge of remembering, but it just doesn't come."

Clarissa Love moved to stand a bit behind her husband and she put her hand on his back, as if to steady him.

"Yeah," Allen said, "my guess is you don't really want to remember. Your ass would be in prison or executed if you remembered."

"I don't care," Marlon said, his voice breaking even more. "I don't care what happens to me, please just give me permission to spend some time there. I've got a key Sylvie had made."

Allen shook his head. "Wouldn't do you a damned bit

of good. We had the locks changed, just in case you decided
to go in there again.''

Tears ran down Marlon's face. "Please don't do this.
Sylvie was everything to me. Everything! Help me to remember so we can all know what happened.''

Allen Love's guard went down all at once. This boy had
spent almost as much time in this house as he'd spent in
his own. They and Luke Jones had been fast friends, delighted that their kin loved each other, looking forward to
their marrying, having kids. But Marlon and Luke's parents
had been right in saying they were too young to marry. As
much as he hurt, Allen knew what he had to do.

"All right," Allen finally said. He turned to his wife,
"Honey, get the key and we'll see what comes of this.''

With a startled look, Clarissa Love turned and left the
room. No one spoke until she came back and handed Allen
the key. He held it out to Marlon who took it, gratitude
flooding him.

"You think hard," Allen said. "Do what you have to do.
Maybe you *can* give us some peace of mind. But listen to
me. When you bring the key back, put it in an envelope and
slide it under the door. I don't want to see your killing face
again.''

"Thank you," Marlon said humbly, and in silence the
three walked to the rental car and got in.

It was late when Luke and Annice checked into the beautifully constructed and landscaped lodge. They had driven
Marlon to the garden house because he was anxious to spend
a night there. They would bring him his meals.

Annice went to the window wall and looked out at the
fountain that tumbled water and spilled into the big, concrete
basin below. Each suite of rooms had a separate section
fenced in with bamboo. Evergreens lined the walkway. It
was warm for November.

Luke had been superintendent of The Ellisville School

for Troubled Youth. He had resigned when Marlon was accused of killing Sylvie Love less than a year before.

Luke had his back to her. "Come see how lovely this is," Annice said. "I remember passing by when they were building this place. Remember when I used to come and visit you?"

He nodded. She went to him, took his hand. "You're thinking about Marlon, aren't you?"

"Yes. I can't help hurting for him."

"I hurt for him, too. Luke, I can help you and Marlon. I'm sure of it."

"Can you be sure he didn't kill Sylvie?"

"He doesn't fit the profile of a killer."

"Other people haven't either, yet they killed. Psychiatrists and psychologists have sent people home from mental institutions saying they were nonviolent and they were wrong. I don't have to tell you the outcome of this."

Annice looked at him thoughtfully. "We make mistakes, but we come out ahead most times."

Looking at him, she felt she was bleeding inside. She needed to tell him her story so she could at least make love to him, be by his side. Marriage wasn't everything. They belonged together.

"Hadn't we better turn in?" he asked. "Tomorrow, which is now today, I want to visit the school and I want to talk with Detective Duchamp."

"Oh?"

"Yeah, he had some doubts about Marlon's guilt, said they came from his gut. It was those doubts in part that set Marlon free. The district attorney was his arch enemy. Years ago, he had a younger sister murdered."

He took her in his arms then, buried his face in her throat as they stood there. She was going to tell him. Now.

"Luke?"

"Yeah, sweetheart?"

"Let's sit down. I've got things crowding my chest, knocking my breath away."

They sat on the sofa and he drew her to him. "Get started."

The long months hadn't eased the pain. It was still raw, rending. Acid tears stung her eyes and her voice was so choked she could barely talk.

"Neesie, what is it?" She let it spill.

"I was pregnant, Luke, when you left me."

Shock rippled through his body. "Why didn't you tell me? What happened?"

"There wasn't time, although I don't think I'd have told you. You had left me."

"Now you know why." Impatient, he asked again, "What happened?"

"I had a spontaneous abortion a few weeks after I found out I was pregnant. I kept getting sick in the morning. My doctor confirmed the pregnancy."

Luke crushed her to him, his voice harsh with emotion. "Oh, my poor darling. You know I would have come to you."

"I didn't want you to come. I think I hated you."

He kissed her face. "How could you not hate me? Yet I did what I thought was best, my darling. But had I known ..."

"There's more. It hit me hard. I wanted your baby, and it took me a long time to get better. I wonder if I'll ever entirely heal. Luke?"

"Yes?"

"One winter night when I was feeling stronger, I took your ring, walked in the bitter cold to the Tidal Basin. I wanted to fling the ring in with all my might. Instead, I quietly dropped it in. It sank so quickly, with only a few ripples. That was the low point of my life. I wanted to follow the ring into the cold water."

His arms were crushing her now as if he would meld them together.

"Oh, my precious darling." His tears fell on her hair, ran

down her face to mingle with her own. "If only I had known."

She had a growing sense of comfort in his arms as he hugged her, stroked her back. "Neesie, my own love. I've got so much to answer for."

"You couldn't know," she said in a small voice. "You were wrestling with something that was tearing you up."

"Yes, but I kept seeing your face, your body. I was tormented staying away from you, but I wanted to give you a chance to live your life without being burdened with my problems—and Marlon's. I should have written, something, but I wanted to drive you away, free you from me.

"Neesie, I love you with everything that's in me. I can't ask you to forgive me, because I know I did the best thing for you."

Stroking her soft body under its winter garments, his mind ran rife with passion. He rose mightily against her, lust and love and passion intermingled. He wished he could make love to her, but it couldn't be.

Sick with desire for him, she whispered, "Make love to me, Luke. Please."

With a half strangled cry, he got up and held out his hand, helping her to her feet.

In his bedroom, they undressed hurriedly. So far to go, so little time.

When they were both naked in the soft lamplight, he drew her to him, his body surging against hers. "I love you," he whispered, "so much that I can hardly bear it."

With a whimpered cry, she took one of his hands from her body and kissed it, tonguing the palm, the way he had often done to her. "And I love you," she told him. "Don't you know you're my *life*? Without you, I'm empty and I don't want to be empty."

He lifted her to the bed and lay her down, devouring her silken body with his eyes that were cloudy with passion. Where to start? As she lay on her back, he lay down beside her, cupping her face with his big hands, sealing them both off from the world. Then he kissed her and it seemed she would go under with passion. Heat leapt about her body like wildfires as his hands came away from her face. Their tongues intertwined, drawing honey, delighting in honey drawn from each other.

"Oh God," he whispered. Moaning in his throat, he sucked her breasts ardently, licking the nipples gently as she bucked beneath him. He was taking it slowly and it was killing him, but he was determined. As she willed herself to be still, he began with her scalp, tonguing kisses that would cover every inch of her body.

It had been so long, but he would make it longer.

"Now, sweetheart, now!" she commanded. "I don't want to wait anymore."

Drawing a sheath from the night table, he began to slip it on when her soft, deft fingers helped him and he had to clench his teeth to keep from going over.

Sheath on and smoothed, he lay passive for a few minutes. Finally, she asked, "Why are we waiting?"

He grinned at her. "You know why we're waiting. I want to be able to give you at least a few minutes of pleasure. Try me sooner, and you've got no chance at all."

She became passive then, her shining eyes feasting on his beloved face. When she would have stroked his erection, his hand stayed hers and held it tightly. Then he spread her legs and slid into the nectared honey-sheath of her body and throbbed for a minute before he began to move gloriously and expertly.

With the first thrust, Annice gasped for breath and thrills went the length of her body. She had long ago found out that his tender spots were behind his left ear and his temple and she daringly touched each place with her tongue. "Better not go there," he said huskily. "You're determined to cheat yourself out of a decent length of time making love."

"Nothing lasts forever," she said gently. Then laughing, "Give me all you've got. I can take it."

She lifted her legs over his back and he slipped into a

deeper place and both closed their eyes with rapture. He couldn't last. It had been too long. He felt himself burst into fire as explosions gripped his loins and lingered there.

Annice lay beneath him, moaning softly, then suddenly a small enraptured scream escaped her throat and he put his hand over her mouth, so she could be free to scream again, as much as she wanted to. Inside her body, raw flames licked and fed on ecstasy. She was trembling and trembling, shaking wildly until the tremors that were in her body were like heaven itself. She went limp and he rolled over on his side.

"You were spectacular," she said softly.

"Thank you. I know *you* were. Neesie, I don't know if we've done the right thing. We can be friends without making love, although it would be hell for me. For your sake I'd do it."

"Hush!" She placed her hand over his mouth. "We won't marry if you think that's best, but I *need* you. My heart and body need you. My *soul* needs you."

They were quiet then, reliving the enthralled siege they'd just gone through. Annice got big, white terrycloth robes from the bathroom and brought them back.

"What're you getting up for?" he asked. "The play isn't over yet. You want plenty, and I'm bound to satisfy your needs."

"Perfect, but I'm pretty hungry. That sandwich and drink we had in the airport terminal have long fled."

She went to the refrigerator. They had asked to have ham and cheese, fried chicken, and champagne stocked in the refrigerator. Bags of nuts and potato chips, bottles of olives and pickles lay on the table. Luke helped her open and pour the snacks into bowls. She sliced the cheese and ham and set them out and made toast for sandwiches.

When it was done, they ate heartily at the small table by the refrigerator. Her robe fell away from her exposed breasts, and Luke drew in a sharp breath, rising slowly again.

He went to the spot where champagne sat cooling in an ice bucket.

"You ordered champagne," Annice said.

He nodded. "I wanted to let you know how happy I am that we're lovers again, although I . . ."

"Blame me," Annice said. "You keep trying to do the honorable thing. I want you, however I can get you. I'm sorry about the ring, Luke. I lost my head, and my soul was rubbed raw with losing your baby."

Luke clenched his fists. "If only I could have been there."

They were silent then for long moments until Annice said sadly, "We have to go on from here."

"You're right. I adore you."

"And I adore you."

They sipped the champagne slowly, bubbles going up their noses. Their eyes played wicked games with each other.

"Don't worry about the ring, my love. I know how you felt. There's nothing I wouldn't give for it not to have happened. The ring doesn't matter. Only the pain you must have felt at losing the baby."

Tears filled her eyes as she pressed his hand. Getting up, she turned on the Bose radio and played with the dials until soft dance music filled the room. She held out her arms to him. "Dance with me, lover?"

"Anything you want."

They had not quite finished their flutes of champagne, so they drank as they danced, then set the glasses down and danced slowly with their arms about each other.

"We're quite a pair," he said. "Both with haunted hearts. And Marlon with his smashed-to-bits heart. May God help us all."

"Yes," she said gently, keenly aware of him rising against her, hard and hot. She could deny him nothing.

A Luther Vandross love song rode on the night air. Annice switched off the night light, opened the blinds and pulled them back so the glittering lights from the courtyard came in. The fountain spilled and rainbow lights played in and out of the water.

She lay on the bed and he began kissing her. "This will be the way I wanted it to be before," he said.

"I loved every minute of it."

"And there were so few minutes."

"I'm not complaining."

"When I'm finished this time, you'll be ecstatic."

"I already am."

"My darling love," he murmured as Luther Vandross's music swept over them. Slipping on a latex sheath he began with her buttery scalp again and kissed her slowly, lingering, tantalizing her so that she cried out and again his hand covered her mouth. Those cries were music to his very soul. The ripe brown mounds that were her breasts enthralled him, and her nipples contracting and puckering beneath his onslaught fed his heart. He felt he could consume her and he narrowed his eyes, feasting on her gorgeous body in the shadow of the outside lights.

When he reached her core, his tongue went wild and she drew in her breath sharply at the pure joy that swept over her. Down her thighs and legs, his tongue kept patterning kisses until they reached her feet and he put first one, then the other to his face. Nuzzling them.

The simple gesture nearly took her breath away. He loved her. *All* of her. As she loved all of him.

They were beatific as the music gently aroused them even more.

He pulled her on top of him then and gloried in her hair coming down on his face. He suckled her breasts again, his mouth reaching up for them. Then with a gentle, smooth thrust he entered her once more, pausing a little, then going straight to the G-spot as he pulled her down onto his erection.

"Luke," she moaned. "This is heaven."

"You're right," he agreed. "It *is* heaven."

They were long this time and slow, and both thought they were very good together. She still wore Shalimar bath oil, just a hint of it at the throat, behind her ears and on her wrists. It was his favorite scent.

"You smell wonderful," he told her.

"I'm glad you like my perfume." He named it and she smiled.

Stroking her breasts with his hands as they moved together, he rolled her over and entered her, lifting her hips with his hands.

"You're driving me crazy," she told him.

"I aim to satisfy," he said, chuckling. "I aim to please you in every way."

She didn't want to go into dangerous, dark waters again, but she had to say it. "No, Luke, you satisfy me in every way, except that we're not altogether together."

He shook his head. "Count your blessings."

She didn't answer, but clung to him again. She glanced at the luminous dial of the radio. Two o'clock in the morning. Her body felt wonderfully alive and her heart felt lighter than it had in a very long time.

They finished together, stroke by stroke, moan by moan. It was a long time coming, but the final ecstasy swept over them both and no Fourth of July fireworks were ever more gorgeous, no music more profound.

"Welcome back," he told her, and she responded, "Welcome back to my arms. I'll never let you go again."

Chapter 11

Alone in the garden house, Marlon opened the blinds and
looked out on the bare, uncultivated scene. A short distance
away, a forest stood proudly. A light rain misted as he stared
at the site where the old Love home had burned to the ground
many years ago. In all these years, much of the debris had
not been cleared. He felt numb, failing, yet he was glad he'd
had the courage to come back. Then he realized it wasn't
numbness he felt, but a quiet, steady rage. If *he* had done
this deadly deed, he hated himself, and he wanted to destroy
whoever else might have done it.

It was night now. It had been morning, nearly noon, when
he found her. With sickening clarity he remembered her
broken body and the expression of horror on her darling
face. Tonight he had watched Annice and Luke pull away
and onto the highway. Did Annice believe him? How could
he ask when he didn't know if he could believe himself?
Anger raced in his stomach. The garden house was just as
it had been when he'd found her, except that the blinds were
drawn.

One of the things that had made it so hard for him was

that he and Sylvie had quarreled in a restaurant in town a week before she'd been killed. She had asked Marlon if he didn't think they should see other people as well. They were so young.

Caught up, surprised, Marlon had thundered, "No damn way. I'm in love with you. I don't want anyone else."

She had smiled at him. "I love you. You know that, but we need to know if there are other people out there better suited to us."

"Yeah, well," he had sputtered. His best friend, Julius, had sauntered over. "Lo, Sylvie. How're things going?"

Sylvie had smiled, openly flirting with Julius, a lanky seventeen-year-old.

Beside himself, Marlon cooled it and said evenly, "We were having a private conversation, dude. You can understand that."

The handsome Julius nodded, his eyes never leaving Sylvie's face as he saluted his friend and said, "Bye, dude. See you around, Syl." He saluted her too.

Marlon had watched Sylvie watch the youth move away and he had been angry at himself for loving her so much that he didn't want to share her. He had gripped her hand and exploded. "I want you to be all mine, Sylvie."

"You're jealous," she'd said thoughtfully, "and it's not a healthy thing. Let's just think about it. OK?"

"Sure," he'd reluctantly said, aware that others in the restaurant had been keenly aware of the scene.

The rest of the week, she had not brought the subject up again, but he hadn't forgotten. She had been warmer, tenderer, more ardent. "You're my big, big baby," she'd said, "and you and I are going to have to talk about a lot of things."

But that hadn't happened. He or someone had stilled her lips forever.

Sylvie. Heart of his heart. Her textbooks on marketing were scattered on the bookshelves, with a pile of marketing titles on the floor. Sylvie had been nineteen, two years older

than the high school junior Marlon. She had been a sopho-
more marketing major at a nearby college in Baton Rouge
after having finished high school at an early age.

Laughing, she had often told him, "You're going to be
one of the world's best and well-known artists, and I'm
going to devote my life to seeing that you get everything
you and your talent deserve."

He'd laughed with her. "I want to teach youngsters
more than anything. If I can bring true beauty into just
one life . . ."

She'd looked at him, her eyes shining. "You've already
done that. You brought beauty into *my* life, Marlon. And
you and that beauty are always going to be there."

They'd held each other tightly then and he'd nuzzled in
the curve of her throat. Sighing, he shook himself. He was
beginning to hurt too much. Maybe he shouldn't have come
back. As he brought himself to the present, he moaned from
a stab of pain.

He was looking at the exact spot Sylvie had lain when
he found her, her blood from the bullet wounds in her chest
spread around her like melted red roses. In all this time, he
had not been able to shake her horrified expression from his
mind. Now, he wanted to run wild and free, to get away
from this madness.

They had gone to the garden house around nine that Saturday morning, meaning to study. He had driven his Volkswa-
gen and she had bicycled. She had packed a picnic hamper
and he had brought sparkling cider. Neither drank alcoholic
beverages. Suddenly, with the soft glances they gave each
other, he had a startling vision of a portrait he wanted to do
immediately. Getting out a sketching pad, he quickly
sketched her as she kept smiling. Then he found there were
colors he needed and didn't have.

"Are you doing watercolor or oil?" she'd asked.

"Both. Watercolor first, because that's quickest. This will
be *good*, I promise you."

"It couldn't be otherwise with you doing it. What will you call it? Or maybe you won't know until it's done."

Grinning, he'd put his fist under her chin. "I know, all right. It's going to be *Girl in Love*."

She'd looked pleased. "Too bad I can't paint. We're in love all right. I ache with it sometimes but I still wonder if we shouldn't cool it." He hugged her tightly, mollified.

They'd made love briefly, with him rushing to go home and come back with the colors he wanted. He'd left on top of the world, flying. And he'd come back to a nearly unimaginable hell. She had been lying near the door and the door was firmly shut. A single white sheet of paper lay by her with letters cut from magazines. *Angel face*, and just under that, *Devil body*.

Police had found fingerprints and DNA but could not match them save for Marlon's and Sylvie's. Then there came the incredible part. He had knelt to take her pulse and found none. Crazed with pain, he had pressed the side of his face to her bloody chest, seeking a heartbeat. Her blood had smeared him as he took her in his arms. Quickly realizing he had to get help, he told himself she couldn't be dead. He had stood up and that was the last thing he remembered. How he got outside, got to his car and started off, going out the gate space that led to the house, he couldn't remember. A very short distance out on the highway, he had run into a deep ditch, plummeting downward. He had been thrown from the car, his head hit a small boulder and he had lost consciousness. He remembered nothing after taking Sylvie in his arms, trying to wipe the blood from her precious body, trying to make sure she didn't die.

There were no signs of bloodstains on the floor; they had been bleached out by her parents.

"All right," he said sadly to himself. "Remember, Marlon. Remember!"

He got up and paced then, the way Luke so often paced. Did Luke really believe him innocent? Did *he* believe himself innocent? He had to know what had happened. But if he couldn't remember here, when and where could he remember?

"Sylvie," he whispered. "Help me remember."

But the room was quiet as a tomb and nothing came. He lay on the tan leather couch, his body stiff with pain. Without expecting to, he fell asleep and she was in the dream. She came to where he lay on the couch in the garden house, stood above him and whispered, "Marlon, my love. You are my life as I believe I am yours. *Keep trying to remember. I swear I'll help you. I'll never let you go.*"

He came awake with a start, murmured her name again. He sat up with bitter tears rolling down his face for only a minute or so, then his eyes stung with acid tears and he could cry no more.

He felt mesmerized by the spot where she had fallen. So he had failed her again. If he hadn't been so anxious to paint the picture in his head, he would have stayed with her and she would still be alive.

"Sylvie," he whispered yet again. "Please forgive me for not being here with you. I could have kept it from happening if it was someone else." He shuddered. "And if *I* did it, I want to be with you. But I've got to know what happened."

He stopped thinking for a few minutes, but his mind grew crowded with ugly visions of nightmare death. He was alone here and the emptiness he felt was truly frightening. But she had just said, "I'll never let you go."

Toward morning as he dozed, sitting up, he seemed to be aware of a presence with him, communicating with him. It seemed he *would* remember. Flashes of eerie, white light surrounded him and he was going back again to that time. There seemed an edge of awareness glimmering in his mind and his memory was firm and steady. He gave a small, joyous cry, and the light faded. Everything was dark and he remembered no more of that past morning than he ever had.

Bending forward, he held his head in his hands as he sat on the sagging couch. He wanted to pray, but he couldn't.

And he thought bleakly, if he had killed her, he wouldn't be able to pray.

Luke and Annice picked him up around eight-thirty that morning.

"How'd it go?" Luke asked.

"Nothing. Zilch. I didn't remember."

"I'm sorry," Luke said.

"So am I." Faint tears stood in Annice's eyes.

"We can come back another time." Luke licked dry lips. He had hoped Marlon would be able to resolve this and they could go on with their lives, but he would stand by him, no matter what.

Luke cleared his throat. "We'd better get something to eat, then return the key to the Loves."

"Let's take the key first," Marlon suggested. "Maybe I can eat a little if I'm past that hurdle."

Luke got out with Marlon at the Loves where they found a note on the door. *MARLON, PLEASE KNOCK.*

Marlon felt his heart lift with hope. Had they changed their minds? He used the brass knocker and soon Allen Love opened the door, a broad scowl on his face.

"Yes, well," he said, and held out a lovely twenty-two carat gold bangle.

"I believe you gave this to Sylvie the last Christmas you were hanging around her. I couldn't face you before you left, and I sure as hell didn't want it going with her to her grave."

He thrust the bracelet at Marlon whose hands shook violently. Luke took the bracelet. "Thank you," he said.

"Don't thank me. I hope I never see either of you again."

Stepping back inside, Allen Love closed the door in their faces and they turned to go back to the car.

No sooner had they started out than Marlon said slowly. "Do something for me, will you? I want to visit Sylvie's grave."

Ellisville had only two cemeteries, each allied with a

church, and Luke quickly found the one where Sylvie was buried.

The kindly old minister whom they knew was inspecting the church before the Sunday sermon and he came out and greeted them warmly.

"I'd guess you want to visit Sylvie Love's grave. It was a terrible loss," the minister said sadly, then to Marlon, "How are you, lad? I remember the two of you together."

"I could be better," Marlon said softly.

"I imagine you hurt a great deal."

"Yes."

"I'm very sorry about what happened. Have you visited her grave before? I haven't seen you there."

Marlon shook his head. "At first I couldn't. Then I moved away. This is my first time back."

"I see."

The minister walked with Marlon, Luke, and Annice to Sylvie's flower-strewn grave. There was a new white marble tombstone there and a crystal vase of red roses among the other flowers. Marlon's fingers fairly itched to paint this picture. A white marble angel stood atop the tombstone and he fairly retched as he remembered the sheet of paper by Sylvie's body: *Angel face. Devil body.*

"Well, you're welcome to come again when you're in town. Stop by and visit. Dr. Jones, you're sadly missed in this community. Don't be a stranger now."

They shook hands again all around and Marlon found himself wondering if this benevolent, courteous man believed him innocent.

Chapter 12

By the time the holiday season was upon them, that part of the year between Thanksgiving and Christmas, Annice felt largely settled and on her way to greatly helping Belle and Carole. Marlon brooded and still let no one come too close to him. He was sorely disappointed over his failing to remember the details of leaving the spot where Sylvie had been slain. But the biggest surprise of all was Julius, who suddenly seemed to seek Annice's attention.

He came through the office doorway now. "Got a minute, doc?"

"I have."

He sat down and stretched his long legs out before him. "You don't like me much, do you?"

"Why do you say that?"

Julius threw his head back, laughing. "My old man's got a friend who's a shrink and he teases him all the time about answering a question with a question. So you be careful—I know your game."

"Others have accused us of doing this. Julius, let me ask *you* a question. How much do you like yourself?"

He seemed taken aback. "You better believe a whole lot. I'm my old man's child. That says it all. He'd die for me."

"But how much do *you* like yourself?"

This time, he pondered her question for a minute. "Is this one of those trick questions?"

"No. It's just that sometimes you have a giant chip on your shoulder. When we have quick tempers, we're often feeling helpless, with not so good self-esteem."

He sat up and leaned forward. "My old man thinks the world of me."

"I'm glad to know that, but that's only one facet of self-esteem. I'm going to ask you to reflect on how much you like and love yourself. Don't be afraid. You don't have to put up a front with me."

He thought a long moment before he answered her, and he flushed in doing so. She couldn't be sure, but she thought she saw tears come to his eyes and he got very tense. "Damn it, doc. . . ." he began and jumped up. "Listen I gotta be going. I forgot something back at the dorm." He got up, nearly knocking his chair over.

She persisted. "I'd like to talk with you again sometime. I think I can help you. Julius, I know you're close to your father, but what about your mother? Are you close to her?"

"Sort of," he said and was out the door.

He had no brothers and sisters. She wondered because he was Marlon's friend and because Julius had been in the Ellisville School when Sylvie was killed. Sylvie would let him into the cottage expecting no danger. It was a wild card, but a card nevertheless.

She hadn't had time to get Julius's case folder, but she was certain of one thing, that like most of the youth at Casey's School, Julius didn't like or love himself.

A light knock sounded and Luke stuck his head in the door. The lovemaking of the past weekend warmed each of them, made them shy with one another. Luke's loins tensed with pleasure looking at Annice. The dark rose silk and wool outfit she wore set off her skin and hair. Soft sparks caught and held between them.

He came in. "I saw Julius. He seemed in a great rush."

"We talked—a bit. I think I hit a sore spot. I asked him if he liked himself."

Luke whistled and grinned. "Hell, that's a sore spot with a whole lot of people. Self-esteem isn't an article in overwhelming supply."

He sat down. "What's on your mind?"

"I was thinking of Marlon and his disappointment over the trip. Luke, Julius was close to them both. He's a flirt and he pushed the envelope. He's got a hot, nasty temper. Could *he* have killed Sylvie?"

Luke looked startled, expelled a harsh breath, pondering her question. "Well, I guess he could have," he said slowly. "He was never a suspect. There was the evidence linking Marlon, just not enough." He rubbed his chin. "As you know, Marlon has a sharp temper, too, and has ever since our parents were killed in that air crash. I wish Marlon would talk with you."

"Give him time. He might when he sees he's up against a brick wall. I think he was really counting on the trip back to Ellisville to give him relief."

"Instead, it seems to have made it worse."

"Yes."

"What are your plans for tonight?" he asked.

"Well, I'll be working on my book. But this afternoon after school I'm going over to Della's. . . . She's invited me over for a New Orleans southern dinner."

"Oh? Without me?" he teased.

"Honey, this is about girl talk."

"Very well. I guess it's just as well. Neesie?"

"Yes?"

"We're not going overboard, you and I. It isn't smart. My brother is in a bad way, and I don't plan to make demands on you I can't fulfill."

She looked at him, her heart hurting. Would they ever be

really together again? She wanted to marry him, bear his children. As if he'd read her thoughts, he got up and went to her, touched her hair and face. "My darling," he said softly. "I love you so."

The vibes between them were sweetly electric when Belle knocked and came in. Luke said he had to go.

"Gee, you look spiffy today, Dr. Jones." Belle was never loath to compliment when she liked something. "Charcoal coat, pearl-gray pants. Love those red suspenders and that pearl-gray shirt, and the red tie ain't bad."

Luke smiled and thanked her.

When he had left, Annice turned to Belle. "Have a seat if you want to talk with me about something."

"I sure do. Miss Della is letting me help her even more and I'm loving it, although I sure wish I could be helping you. The money I'm getting, I'm buying my little sister and brother and my mama a lot of things."

Annice got up and got Belle's folder from a steel filing case, came back and sat down, made a few notes.

"All this stuff you write," Belle said, laughing, "does it help you to keep us in mind?"

"It does," Annice said, "and things become clearer when you write them down. Don't worry, you have a keyword representing you where you're referred to. The deep stuff I keep in here under lock and key. What my secretary types are odds and ends. I respect your privacy, Belle."

"You're a great lady, doc," Belle said heartily. "I don't think I thought about respect two times a year before you came along. Now I think about it all the time."

"That's good. It means a lot. Belle, you spoke about helping your brother and sister and your mother. Be sure you spend lots of time helping yourself. Take good care of yourself."

Belle looked startled. "Oh, I'll make it. I'm strong. My mama always said I'm strong."

"Still . . ."

"Yes, ma'am. I'll do like you say and take care of myself,

but gee, I like to do things for other people. If I don't make it as a diva, maybe I'll be lucky enough to be a psychologist one day.''

Annice smiled. "Given your strength and smarts, I think you can.''

Belle sighed then. "Right now, I'd like to be able to help Carole. She's not shaping up.''

"Still sneaking out with Julius?''

"And flirting with the security guard, one of them.''

"Bill Sullivan?'' Belle nodded. "I thought he was married.''

"He is, but my friend doesn't care if he's got *twenty* wives. He's coming on to her and she's coming on right back to him.'' She laughed shortly. "And Julius is m-a-d.''

"Nice mess. I'll talk with her.''

"Thank you. Do it soon. Everybody knows Julius has got a temper and he can be mean. She's got a bruise on her arm now I'm wondering where it came from.''

Annice shook her head. "Abuse is a nasty thing. I hate it.''

"You're right. I'd like to see some man hit me.'' Her head went to one side. "My daddy's never laid a hand on me or any of us, but you know my mama is a beater. She sends us outside to get switches for her to use on us. I guess you could say she's a whipper.''

"I'm sorry about that.''

"I know you are. You're like that. I wish I had a mama like you. But you know my mama would kill me if she heard me say that.''

"It's all right.''

Belle left shortly after and Annice got up and put the file back in the file case. Belle had a heart of gold and she wanted to help her get what she deserved. Carole would be helping her the next day. She made a mental note to talk to her at the house; it would be more intimate there. She prayed that she could reach her.

* * *

At Della's house that afternoon, Annice rang the chimes and waited. In a minute or so, a beaming Della greeted her. "Girlfriend, what a delight to see you. I've got a surprise."

"You're full of surprises," Annice bantered.

As she walked a short distance inside, big hands came across her eyes and she was blinded for a minute or so. She felt her body being turned. The hands came away and she faced a grinning Luke.

"But I thought. . ." Annice began.

Della smiled broadly. "You thought I'd pass up a chance for a hunk like this to have a girl talk? Uh-uh. I never miss an opportunity to rap with a king."

"Oh *you*," Annice said delightedly, pleased to see Luke, who hugged her tightly and kissed the tip of her nose.

Della's house was a big barn of a place, connected to her Minden's Inn. It was light, spacious, airy, done in colorful Spanish decor. "We're going to eat right away because I'm starved," Della said. "What about you two?"

"Ravenous," Luke said heartily.

"Likewise starved," Annice said as they came to the dining room. Calvin poked his head in the door. "Any time I serve is OK with me."

Della flashed him a smile. "My hero. Calvin's going to serve us. He insists on it."

"It's practice for having my own inn in California one day," Calvin told them.

Seated at the informally appointed round table, with its boldly patterned and colorful dinnerware, Calvin served as they began with shrimp cocktails.

Looking from one to the other, after a moment, Della said, "Gee, I hope in the very near future, you two will be fully back together. I'm keeping my fingers crossed, and praying."

"I'm praying, too," Luke murmured. "Let's toast to that hope."

They held up their crystal glasses of chablis as Luke's husky voice gave the toast.

"To times that were the best I've ever known. Let them come again."

Three glasses touched and the crystal rang. Annice felt her heart squeeze and flutter. They began with shrimp and crab gumbo over rice, then roast turkey and spiral-sliced ham, wild yams, brown rice, summer squash, asparagus, and a huge garden salad.

"I don't know when I've seen food look so pretty," Luke complimented their hostess.

Calvin, dressed in blue Dockers and a white shirt, with a big white apron wrapped around him, did the honors. "I'm accepting all and any compliments," he told them. "Forgive my apron. I'm pretty good at spilling food on myself."

"You're coming along nicely," his mother told him.

Dessert was chocolate mousse with raspberries and golden pound cake.

Calvin smiled broadly as he served the dessert. "Can you believe I made the cake and the mousse?"

Laughing, putting on her tough-girl act, Annice grinned at him. "Get out!"

"He did, you know," Della said. "I'm so proud of him."

When the meal was finished and dishes were cleared, they heard Calvin moving about in the kitchen. "Anybody in a hurry to go to the living room or elsewhere?" Della asked.

"I'm loving it right here," Annice assured her. "My stomach's in heaven. It's positively thanking you and your son."

They were sitting and sipping the wine when Calvin came back in. "Mom, I'm going out a bit. Think I'll look for buried treasure in Pirate's Cave."

Della nodded. "Just don't expect to find any gold. It was supposedly buried a long time ago. And don't stay out too late. You've got your homework to do."

The sun was setting as a Christmas carol came on.

"Lord, we're hardly free of Thanksgiving," Della said,

"and they're pushing us into Christmas. At least they only play a few a day."

"I love Christmas carols." Annice hunched her shoulders. "I cried when I first heard Leontyne Price sing 'O, Holy Night.' "

"She's gorgeous," Luke said.

They heard the front door slam and the house seemed to Annice to settle down with the absence of its juvenile inhabitant.

Della leaned far back in her chair. "Everybody stuffed to the gills?"

"Aye, aye," Luke said.

For a moment or so Annice felt tranquil, at ease. "You'd better believe it."

"How's Calico?" Della asked. "And has anything else happened?"

Annice shook her head. "Calico's coming along nicely. And, no, nothing else has happened. I hope nothing else *does* happen."

Luke glanced at her sharply. She hadn't told him that the night before she had imagined someone following her home from school. Tracking her in the woods near the sidewalk. She had rushed then and was pleased to see Bill Sullivan coming up the sidewalk. He was always suave, pleasant with her, courteous and respectful. She was glad to know he was out in the night, protecting the campus.

"My bashful son has a message for you, Neesie."

"Oh?"

"He wants you to know he appreciates his brief talks with you."

"We've only talked a couple of times. He has trouble opening up."

"Yes. Give it time. He's got another year at Casey's School. If you're still here helping him, I expect great results. Not that there's much out of order now."

Della cleared her throat. They listened to a classical music station and "Meditation," from Massenet's *Thais* came on. They fell silent until it was over.

"Brings back memories," Annice said. "At Hampton, we used to sit in the music room in a building on the waterfront and a music professor would play his favorite songs for us. 'Meditation' was one of them. It's still marvelous."

"Do you know Calvin actually likes classical music? Isn't that great? Now, he's into hip-hop and rock and roll, but he also likes the classics. My son, the wonder kid."

"You've done an exceptional job with him," Luke told her.

"Poor baby. I try. At first, he was devastated when his father left. . . ."

Annice nodded. "I surely remember that."

Della's eyes on her friend were bleak. "I couldn't even talk to you, Neesie, about what happened. The love of my life just taking off with someone else, so much younger than he is. He was so close to Calvin. Maybe I got careless, feeling that we were joined at the hip."

"Don't blame yourself," Annice said. "You've gone through hell."

"I must be pretty good at parenting. Calvin got over it in record time, and he's been my junior rock for a few years now. I'm going to talk with him about having more sessions with you."

"Don't push him too hard," Annice said. "He's very good in group therapy. Helping. Caring. He told me one day if he didn't want to be an innkeeper, he'd want to be a psychologist."

"Is Calvin interested in girls?" Luke asked.

Della pondered his question. "Not that much, but he keeps saying later. He's so bashful. He's got a roomful of pinups, and nope, he doesn't seem to have anything against girls."

"I'd be glad to mentor him." Luke's eyes on Della were sympathetic.

"Oh, I'd love that, and he'd love it, I'm sure."

"I'll get started the second semester."

They moved into the living room where Della switched off the radio and turned on the stereo. Dreamy music from the incomparable Luther Vandross serenaded them.

Suddenly Della seemed dispirited. "I worry about my son," she said. "He didn't deserve his father's leaving, but he's pulled through so beautifully, and I'm proud of him."

Annice sat wondering if she should tell Luke about the feeling yesterday that she was being followed. No, he'd worry, and she wasn't going to live like a prisoner. Still, it spooked her, and goose bumps lined her arms as she thought about it.

"What is it?" Luke asked.

"Nothing." His eyes narrowed. He knew something was wrong.

Sitting in the deep chairs in a circle, Annice was pleasantly reminded of her group therapy sessions.

Della sat up straight in her chair. "You know, I may be a bit premature bringing this up, but I've got a young nephew who's an undercover police officer in D.C. I think he talks to me more than he should, but he's thinking of getting out. He tells me"—she turned to Luke—"he tells me that one of your security guards might be involved in a drug ring, the favorite drug of today's youth, Ecstasy."

Luke groaned. "I wonder if it's Bill Sullivan."

"Yeah, that's the name. He said he wanted me to know how to protect Calvin. Calvin seems to like the guy; he takes up time with him. That's why it would be invaluable if *you* would mentor him, Luke. I only heard about this yesterday, so I'm not late in passing the news along."

"For which I thank you."

Annice glanced at her watch. It was six-thirty. "I hate leaving so early," she said, "but I'm back with my book, working when I can sandwich it in. I hate leaving good company." She flashed Luke a flirtatious smile. "I've got my car. One of my best friends saw fit to lie to me that we were having a girlfriend tête-à-tête and sneaks a male hunk past me."

"Don't tell me you're not pleased," Della said. "Your face lit up like a sky full of stars when you looked at him. How I wish it could be the way it was before with you two."

Chapter 13

As Annice neared her home, she was surprised to see the living room lights on. She put the car in the garage and went in to find Carole sitting in the living room on the sofa. The girl stood up as Annice opened the door.

"Dr. Steele, please don't be mad at me."

"What's wrong, Carole?" She hurried to her side.

Carole's breath shallowed. "I hope you don't mind, I came over to straighten out that hall closet and I just stayed. Mrs. Johnson knows where I am. She told me it was OK."

"What is it? Come and sit down."

They sat on the sofa and Carole raised her flared sweater sleeve to expose a deep bruise.

"What happened? Julius?"

Carole nodded. "We were arguing. He slapped me, then gripped my arm until I cried."

Annice felt her gorge rise. "You've got to break up with him. Do you know why he did it?"

Carole nodded. "You know how I flirt. I don't mean any harm. He accused me of coming on to Marlon, said I was trying to leave him and he wasn't going to let me. He accused me, too, of flirting with the security guard, Officer Sullivan. I'm starting to be scared of Julius."

"You should be afraid of him. I think he's dangerous."

"Could you talk to him?"

"I'm certainly going to try. Have you had your dinner?"

"I ate at the cafeteria. I'm not hungry. I guess I'll go now."

"No, you won't. Not by yourself. I'll drive you over."

"It's just a little ways. Besides, you'll be coming back by yourself."

"I can take care of myself. Obviously, you can't. Sometimes anyway."

Carole began to tremble. "I hate being such a coward."

"You're not a coward, my dear. You've just never been trained to take care of yourself. Carole?"

"Yes ma'am?"

"You like Marlon a lot, don't you?"

"How did you know?"

Annice shrugged. "Just a hunch. I think he likes you."

"Oh, do you think so?" Carole asked. "He's so quiet. He said he and Julius have been friends for two or three years."

"Yes, but there's a wedge between them now," Annice said. "You."

Carole shook her head. "I don't want to come between them."

"It isn't your fault. You're all so young. People grow out of relationships, just as they grow into them. You're going to have to make up your mind which boy you want."

Carole looked down at her feet. "I really like Marlon the way I used to like Julius and don't anymore."

"That's understandable. And what about Officer Sullivan?"

Carole giggled. "Oh that. He's a hunk and all the girls like him. He's got a wife and three children. If he got married early, he could be my father."

Annice smiled. "You might want to remember that when you're flirting with him."

"I will. I'm sorry."

"Don't be sorry because you're telling me about it. Just know that it's not the right thing to do. Don't play fast and loose with boys and men. It isn't to your advantage."

"I know, really I do, but something gets into me. I'm sorry."

Annice patted the girl's knee. "Stop saying you're sorry and change your behavior. Do you think you can do that?"

"I think I can. Dr. Steele, do I have a chance with Marlon?" The girl sounded so wistful as she asked, "Am I good enough for him?"

"Good enough?" Annice sighed, exasperated. "Carole, look at me."

Bashfully, Carole met Annice's compelling gaze. "Yes ma'am."

"*God made you.* He made us all. How can you not be good enough? But you've got to believe in yourself."

Tears came streaming down Carole's face as she sobbed, her shoulders hunched. Annice reached over and drew the girl to her, stroking her back. "Go on," she said. "Cry it out. Change begins with feelings. Love yourself, Carole. Like yourself, but more than that, *respect* yourself. When you lead men on, you're not paying yourself proper respect. Can you understand that?"

"Yes." Carole's voice was faint, her head bowed. "Nobody's ever respected me before. My mama calls me all kinds of names when she gets mad, and she's no angel."

Annice nodded, then sighed. "Parents don't always do what they should do for their kids. But sometimes they came up on the negative side and don't know any better. I think I can help you, at least some, maybe a lot. Can you come in for counseling more often? Do you want to?"

"Oh yes. I'd like that more than anything. Julius doesn't like my talking to you. He says his father has a friend who's a psychiatrist, and he's the craziest man he knows. Sometimes I think Julius is crazy."

"Never mind Julius. We've got to get your life worked through. You're a beautiful, smart young girl and you should be enjoying life, not fighting it. Do you hear from your mother often?"

Carole shrugged. "She calls and tells me I'm a dumb hussy."

Annice thought bleakly: fulfilling prophecy.

"Do you ever ask her not to talk that way to you?"

Carole's laugh was short, ugly. "Once I did and she hit me across the mouth with the back of her hand. I bled. I've never asked her again."

"I'm sorry, but you're seventeen. Less than a year and you'll be adult, agewise, that is. You want to do modeling, don't you?"

"Yes, something like Victoria's Secret or *Ebony*'s Fashion Fair."

"I think you'll make a great model. But what I'd really like to see you do is get your life together, be good to yourself, and as I said, respect yourself."

"I hope I can. I've been into so much."

Annice reached out and touched her cheek. "I left out something. You have to forgive yourself as God forgives you, and forgive others. You don't have to forget, but you do need to forgive."

"I'm really going to try."

"Good. What about your father? You didn't have much to say when I asked about him earlier."

"He's dead like I told you. I want to talk with you about him later. Mom dates a lot of men. When I got her to send me here, I was sneaking out, shoplifting. Her boyfriend at that time . . ." She paused a long time and looked outraged. "Well, I slept with my jeans on to stop him from coming into my room and molesting me while she was sleeping. I guess she was glad enough to get rid of me."

Annice nodded. "How do you feel about your other relatives?"

"There's just my uncle; my father's brother. He writes and sends me money, but he doesn't visit. Mama took most of the money when I was home, says she's the one who really deserves it."

Annice sat with half-closed eyes. Belle and Carole were both girls she'd like to adopt and she knew there would be others. Her heart expanded with hope. Dear God, to be able to help set a life straight, to bring joy and ease suffering. She wanted others to know the kind of love she and Luke shared, even if the light had dimmed for now. In spite of this, she thought how blessed she and Luke were to have known childhoods like they had known, to have found each other.

"Thank you, and I guess I'd better go."

She looked at Annice shyly. "I hope you don't mind. Sometimes I pretend you're my mother."

"Do you know something? I'm very glad you came and stayed. I think we're going to go far." Her eyes shone with plans to help Carole. "Now, I'll get my coat and let's go."

Carole's eyes shone with hope and fear.

A little while later, Annice pulled into her driveway and drove into the garage, but she sat in the car a while longer. Frowning, she wondered at the coolness in her blood and licked her dry lips. *There was someone in the woods.* She was sure of it. There was the loud croaking sound like a crow. Or was it a human croaking like a bird? For a few minutes, everything was still in a pristine, overcast night. Then the croaking started again, low and soft, but piercing and steady. A crow's courting call?

Her mind rested on Luke. She wished she had invited him over. Their time in Ellisville in the lodge had been glorious. But then, they had had so many glorious times together. She wanted to belong to him as she wanted him to belong to her. But Marlon and his guilt or his innocence stood in her way.

What if Julius were the killer? He would know how to get to Sylvie. Through watching, he would know when Marlon left the garden house. Julius slapped and bruised young women. Had he killed one?

As she lowered the garage door and locked it, the sounds of croaking filled her ears, frightening her because some inner voices told her it was not a bird, but a human bird of prey, a nighthawk. She hated being fearful. It was no way to live. She would call Luke before she went to bed. She smiled at the thought of hearing his voice.

By the time she reached the living room door, the telephone had begun to ring. She picked it up to hear Luke's voice. "I hope you're not tied up. Jon Ryson and Sheriff Keyes are here. They want to talk with us."

Annice breathed a sigh of relief. "I'm free. Come right along."

They were there shortly; now she wouldn't have to be alone.

"How's it going?" The older Sheriff Keyes led off as they settled down.

"I keep thinking I hear things," Annice said. "Much of it is probably my imagination."

Jon Ryson nodded. "But that may not be the case. You know what they say: Just because you're paranoid doesn't mean there's nobody following you."

Annice chuckled. "If I'm not paranoid, I'm getting there."

"You've had a couple of things happen," Sheriff Keyes offered. "If somebody put a sheet of paper in my desk with the wording you found, I'd be concerned, especially if the same kind of thing had been found beside a murder victim."

"That's true," Annice said hollowly.

Luke looked at her closely, his heart aching for her. She looked so vulnerable—his precious, strong and strong-willed

Annice. Whoever meant to hurt her was going to have to come through him.

"We have some information that will interest you both," Sheriff Keyes said. "Remember the badge you found, the volunteer's badge?"

"Yes." Annice shifted nervously.

"I was on leave for much of the summer. One of our deputy sheriffs runs the volunteer program and he's been away lately so there's been little communication between us. I told him about the badge and we went over a list of volunteers. Now, I don't know how much this means, but a couple of boys—buddies my deputy says—signed on from Casey's School late this summer. Seems they were bored and wanted something exciting to do. They only worked a month or so. A deputy who supervised them said they were good workers and bright kids. We've got their names— Julius Thorne and Marlon Jones."

Luke's head jerked up. "You know Marlon's my brother?"

"Yeah." Sheriff Keyes looked intensely at Luke. He passed his index finger under his collar. "You know they do say that most crimes, big and little, are committed by someone we know very well. Not that this is necessarily the case."

"I surely hope not." Luke was quiet, his eyes narrowed.

"Have you heard anything suspicious lately?" Jon Ryson asked her.

She nodded. "In the garage this evening, I thought I heard someone in the woods croaking like a crow or like some bird . . ."

"A crow?" Jon Ryson continued questioning.

She laughed shortly. "I'm not that familiar with birds. It wasn't a pleasant sound, and for some reason I was frightened. Maybe it *was* a bird."

"And maybe not," Jon said. "Except for hoot owls, I know of few birds that sound off at night. I just thought if it were somebody behaving like a bird and we knew what species, we might know more about the person doing it. Does that make sense?''

"Crows are a symbol of death,'' Annice said quietly as Luke's head snapped up.

Jon Ryson looked at her quietly. "Yes, they're said to be.''

"I've been in touch with Detective Duchamp in Ellisville,'' Sheriff Keyes said abruptly. "He's puzzled by the similar sheets of paper.''

"That was very kind of you,'' Luke said.

The sheriff shrugged. "I don't take criminal shenanigans lightly. I believe in nipping things in the bud.'' Now he nodded at Annice. "You're the last person I want to see any harm come to.''

"Thank you,'' Annice told him, grateful for how he was handling the case, if indeed it was yet a case. One volunteer's badge, one sheet of paper with offensive words printed on it, strange sounds in the night, loud croaking—none of these constituted a case. A shudder passed through her tense body. Would there be a case? She felt her breath coming faster.

Jon Ryson took up the questioning. "How do you like your new security system?''

"Very much. I think it makes me feel quite a bit safer. I guess I'm spooked now and can expect to hear things.''

"I'll tell you what,'' Sheriff Keyes told her, "don't let anything be too small to call me or Detective Ryson about. He's here because he and Dr. Jones are friends. I'm here because this is my turf, and I mean to defend it.''

Annice smiled widely. "For which I can't thank you enough. Would anybody like something to drink?''

After discussing a choice of drinks, they all chose dandelion wine that Annice had made the year before. As they sipped, they praised the bouquet.

Luke grinned at her. "You've got a lot of arrows to your bow.''

"You just never know,'' she murmured.

Draining his glass and accepting a refill, Sheriff Keyes

hunkered down. "What kind of relationship do you have with your brother?" he asked Luke.

"Once, wonderful," Luke answered. "Now, there's trouble. We're not as close."

"Do you know why? Was it the girl's death in Ellisville?"

Luke thought a long moment. It was the last thing he wanted to discuss. "He's drawn away from me since our parents died. Sylvie's death only made it worse. He's drawn away from everybody except Julius. Now, it seems they're falling out."

"Do you know why they'd be falling out?"

"A girl Julius is keen on likes Marlon. She's flirting with him and Julius is green-eyed."

"That would do it? They were both at Ellisville. What was the romantic score there?"

"Julius liked Sylvie a lot, the girl who was killed. I don't know if he was actually coming on to her, but he liked her. Marlon was angry with him about her."

"Yet they came here together in the summer, not too long after her death."

"Yes, they did. From the time they met, they've been very close, but as I said, now they seem to be falling out."

"Strange, don't you think, that they could withstand trouble over the girl in Ellisville, but not here?"

Luke's shoulders hunched. "It could be they would have fallen out in Ellisville if Sylvie hadn't been killed."

Jon Ryson was quite pensive, his intelligent eyes reflecting how he put things together and came out ahead. "How do you get along with Julius Thorne?" he asked Annice.

"Not all that well. He's courteous enough, but he's a showoff, a tease. He does things like sticking out his leg and tripping a girl carrying a glass of water in group therapy." She hadn't realized how nettled she was at Julius since he did that.

Now Sheriff Keyes said what he had wanted to say to Luke since he came in. "Marlon was accused of killing Sylvie Love. I talked with you, then with Detective

Duchamp. Marlon doesn't seem to remember anything after walking away from her body. Is that right?''

"That's what he says."

"Do you believe him?"

"He's my brother."

"A part of you believes. A part of you doesn't believe."

Luke pondered the statement. "I guess that's about right."

"Did he have any kind of therapy for this trauma?" Jon Ryson asked.

Luke shook his head. "As you know, Dr. Steele is a psychologist. He refuses to talk. He keeps saying later, which could mean never."

"And he doesn't really open up to you either," Sheriff Keyes said. "A lot of people can't talk to a therapist, but they can to a minister or a friend."

"That's true." Annice was getting edgy just talking about Marlon.

Sheriff Keyes balled up his fists and bent his arms. "Well, I've got a heller of a day tomorrow, so I'd best be going. I've certainly enjoyed talking with you and Dr. Jones, Dr. Steele. I promise you we'll be on top of this. Count on us."

Jon Ryson chuckled. "I've got the same kind of day facing me, so I'll be going too. You've got our cards. Call anytime and don't let anything be too small to tell us about or ask us about."

Luke and Annice promised they would and the two lawmen left.

Luke and Annice stood in the doorway, cold wind whipping past them. "We're going to be candidates for pneumonia," Annice murmured.

"Then you can nurse me. I'd like that. Neesie, did you know Claire was once a registered nurse?"

"No," Annice murmured tartly, "but I can stand not knowing a lot of things about Claire."

Luke threw back his head, laughing. "You're beautiful when you're jealous, even knowing you don't have anything to be jealous about."

"You never know. You two go back to childhood."

"And we grew up and put away childish things. She decided she didn't want to be a nurse, never practiced and went back to school. This is her first job in education."

"How lucky for you. Even life throws you two together."

"No, honey, *we're* the ones life has thrown together."

"You won't let me help you with Marlon."

"*Marlon* won't let you help. I refuse to let you ruin your life. He doesn't remember, Neesie. What if he's guilty?"

Annice's answer was straightforward. "Life throws us hard curves, Luke, and we have to deal with them or go under. You know that. Why do you refuse to accept it?"

Luke pulled her back and shut the door. She slid into his arms effortlessly, her soft, tender body melding into his harder one. Electricity whipped around them. He felt his very soul on fire for her, and swirling waters of desire threatened to sweep her under. His mouth crushed hers, hurting her until she moaned.

"Are you going to take this through?" she asked him.

"Make love, you mean."

"We did in Ellisville. Do you consider that a mistake?"

"You know damned well I don't, but I can't keep taking advantage of our love. I have faith, Neesie, that this will be over. We'll find out one way or the other. But I can't, I *won't* burden you with Marlon's problems."

Chapter 14

After Luke left, a keyed-up Annice sat on the sofa with Calico on her lap. "You're going on a diet, kiddo. That's for sure." She stroked the cat's fur, which still had bald spots, while Calico purred and climbed up on the back of the sofa and stretched out.

"Independence plus," Annice told the cat. "That's you. Why can't you stay in my lap?"

Calico meowed as if she understood. Stretching and yawning, Annice got up and went into the room she had fashioned into a den. She got the folder from a file that contained notes for her book. She had worked on her guide for teenagers for over two years because she wanted it to be a book teenagers could relate to.

There was something else she wanted. Years ago, she had clipped an article dealing with a dysfunction called *limbic rage* from a women's magazine. She and Dr. Casey had discussed the article and both had remained interested in the condition. The limbic area of the brain grew inflamed and the person afflicted gathered enormous strength. A small woman could send a stuffed chair sailing across a room when in the throes of this malady.

Not much was known about it, but it came on suddenly and with truly awful anger. She would call Dr. Casey and Monday she would put in calls to several hospitals. The way angry fire had leapt from Marlon's eyes from time to time bothered her. But she also thought that he seemed to contain himself.

She dialed a number and Dr. Casey answered. When she identified herself, his greeting was effusive.

"I don't see enough of you," he said. "You and Luke must come to visit more often."

"I promise I will," she murmured. Then she asked him about limbic rage.

"Well," he told her, "after you called it to my attention, I got interested. I have a lot of material I've amassed on it. It's a fascinating topic. Why does this come up now?"

Hesitantly, she marshaled her thoughts, then spoke slowly. "Marlon has flares of temper that seem to me more than temper. It's as if he's in the grip of rage itself. He leaves the room when it happens, so I don't know the aftermath."

"I see. Have you any idea how long this has been going on?"

"It certainly wasn't the case a couple of years back. The times I visited them in Ellisville, I saw no signs of it. It's only since he's been here that I've been aware."

"Would you like me to send you some of the best material I have? And Neesie, I see limbic rage as being such that he couldn't control himself well enough to leave the room under his own control."

"Yes, I would like more material. We know limbic rage gives phenomenal physical strength. Sylvie Love was badly beaten about her body, but not her face. Would the person with limbic rage have enough presence of mind to make such a decision?"

"I think so. Part of the brain still works. There are stages.

He or she could have a milder form. You don't think Marlon has limbic rage?''

''I wonder. He also has a hot-headed friend I've mentioned to you.''

''Julius Thorne, my judge friend's son?''

''Yes.''

Dr. Casey chuckled. ''Don't get carried away now. We've got vicious tempers around, always have had. It's getting worse, but it doesn't have to be limbic rage.''

''You're right, of course. I'll be coming to visit soon. Luke and I.''

''Be sure you do. And I'll get that material in the mail to you tomorrow.''

Hanging up and going back into the living room, Annice stood in front of the sofa. ''You're a card,'' she said to Calico, hands on her hips. ''Here you are, stretched out like the Queen of Sheba when you could be in my lap.''

Calico raised one sleepy eye wider than usual, the green pupil glowing, then closed it.

Annice laughed. ''Ignore me. See if I care. Keep on ignoring me when your milk is due in a few minutes.''

Calico purred.

Going into the kitchen, Annice heated milk in a pan and poured it into Calico's bowl. She heard the thump of Calico hitting the floor and smiled. The difficult cat nevertheless had her heart. As Calico came through the swinging door, she squatted by her and stroked her fur.

''I'd like to do bad things to whoever did this to you.'' The cat looked at her with loving eyes and slurped the liquid.

The ringing telephone took her into the living room. It was Luke.

''Are you OK?'' he asked.

''Except for a cat who doesn't love me the way I love her, I'd say I'm doing OK.''

''She loves you. I'm sure of it. How could anyone not love you the way I do?''

''You're kind,'' she told him. ''How are you?''

"I'm fine. Any more croaking or other strange sounds? I don't particularly like your being at one end of the campus and me at the other."

"I feel OK with the new security system. Even if I hear someone breathing, I'm in here and they're out there."

His voice got husky. "I fell asleep on my couch and I dreamed of you. Fantasyland. Caesar and Cleopatra had nothing on us. Thank you for that few minutes of glory. Neesie, that's why I want you with me, so I can look after you. I've got to work this Marlon thing through. Get to the bottom of it."

She told him then about limbic rage and he was silent a long while. "I've never heard of it. As for Marlon's temper, he began acting strangely shortly after our parents were killed. I guess anything's possible, especially since he doesn't want to talk to anyone. The poor guy's hurting like hell, and you and I are apart. What's going to be the end of it?"

"I wish I knew. Luke, my parents are coming over tomorrow. A pop visit. And Dr. Casey thinks we're neglecting him."

"I'll be glad to see Caroline and Frank. And we have to go and see Will Casey. Neesie, about this limbic rage thing, don't forget to give me some of your material on it. I'm open to any suggestions about Marlon. The problem is, he's not open to suggestions these days."

"I wish he'd let me reach out to him."

"So do I. I don't know what to make of the two boys having volunteered when they came here last summer and saying nothing about it."

"Young people don't keep things in mind very long."

"I don't think Marlon would do anything to you. He's very fond of you."

"I'd say *was*."

"What could change that?"

"He could change. His brain could change. You have to take limbic rage seriously."

"I do. Speaking of Marlon, go with me to Pirate's Cave tomorrow."

"OK. Any particular reason?"

"Just checking it out. Marlon's painting there and I like to see his new work. He's crazy about the cave, although I'm not crazy about his reason. He says it feels as dark and bleak toward the back as he does. He's leaving his paintings on exhibit there. I tell him it's tempting thieves. He merely shrugged and said he'd paint more to replace any stolen ones."

"That's the mood he's in these days. What time would you like to set out?"

"Eightish. That will give you time to get back and prepare for your folks' coming. Neesie?"

"Yes, love?"

"We used to be after each other like Cupid and Aphrodite. If I seem less passionate, that's not the case. I want to work things out with us. I can't, I won't marry you until things with Marlon are resolved. And I keep hoping, praying. . . . Were we wrong to make love in Ellisville? I needed you so much."

"And I needed you. We weren't wrong, my darling. Marriage isn't everything. I don't agree with you about not getting married, but I understand all too well. I just wish you and, yes, Marlon trusted me more."

"It isn't a matter of trust. I'd trust you with my life. It's a matter of what's best for you."

"Shouldn't I be the one to decide that?"

"You're in love, the way I'm in love. Your psychic vision isn't always clear."

"What makes you think yours is?"

He chuckled. "Very well, it's clear where you're concerned. I'll go to bed and call up more wonderful fantasies."

"And I'll be competing with you with fantasies of my own."

Luke lay awake for long moments after he went to bed. He had gone through a stack of papers he'd brought home with him, but he had difficulty focusing on them. Annice's face kept rising before him. Her beautiful, lively, caring face that he loved so much. He licked his lips at the thought of her body beneath his, on top of him, at his side. As he felt her soft, tan, imagined flesh against his far harder flesh, he groaned aloud. It couldn't be a mistake that they'd made love in Ellisville. Was it a mistake that he intended to protect her, to see to it that she had a free life, unburdened by Marlon's problems?

He drifted to sleep in the darkened room after saying a fervent prayer that things would work out for him and Annice.

Annice found herself unable to concentrate on her book or the limbic rage material. She undressed slowly. She could stay up late because tomorrow was Saturday. In her bedroom, she switched on the big-screen TV set and settled down to watch a movie. Tonight there was a screening of *Black Orpheus*, an old movie she had seen frequently. A woman was being pursued in that movie and finally met her death. No, she didn't want to watch that.

Going to the window, she raised it a quarter of the way up. She climbed into bed and hit the remote switch, leaving the room in darkness. The windows had been secured. She wouldn't hear any breathing outside again.

She wasn't sleepy, but she thought she needed to go to sleep so she could be fresh for her outing with Luke the next morning. Reaching into her night-table drawer, she took out an organdie bag of lavender and sniffed it. A delicious aroma filled her nostrils. Putting it near the edge of her pillow, she lay back and was soon asleep. Dreams came immediately of Luke's muscular arms about her. Held tightly, she felt tears in her eyes as the precious wonder of him struck her to her core.

Then she heard it. The same harsh, croaking sound she had heard as she walked along from work earlier and when she drove Carole to her dorm. It sounded sinister then; it sounded sinister now. There were trills and variations on a theme. *Damn it,* she thought, and this time acid tears rose in her eyes. Her heart thudded with anxiety. Should she call Luke? No, there was nothing going on, except some croaking, some silly croaking that waxed and waned and didn't sound like any bird she had ever been witness to. But her flesh was cold and her blood had chilled. She had trouble getting her breath. She was reminded again that crows were said to be symbols of death.

She lay there a long time in the darkness, then as abruptly as the croaking had begun, it stopped. She thought about getting up and fixing a glass of hot Ovaltine and decided against it. But finally she did get up, checked her security panel in the small room beside the living room and got back into bed. Looking at her radial dial a half hour later, she reflected that she'd heard nothing else and she drifted into a disturbed sleep.

Early next morning in Pirate's Cave, Annice and Luke were surprised at how much work Marlon had done on the cave. An electrician had helped him set up lights for a large front corner. His easel and a supply of paints were set out, with a variety of brushes and other painting paraphernalia. A second large easel held sketches of Sylvie. There was a big aluminum lockbox to store his materials.

Luke hugged her briefly, feeling flooding him. The physical feeling alone was enough to drive him crazy, but the emotional yearning was even harder to take. Would this ever be over? he wondered.

"No more problems last night?" he asked her.

She shook her head and didn't tell him about the continued croaking. She shivered as an imaginary goose went over her grave. "I'll tell you what," he said. "Let's go into the woods back of your house. Perhaps someone has dropped something else that can give us a clue."

"Good idea." She felt cold even with the warm coat, and back in this corner of the cave, it was fairly warm.

"We won't stay too long," he said, "especially since your folks are coming."

They examined the paintings carefully. "Why would he choose the cave to paint in?" Luke wondered aloud. "But then Marlon has always been a bit strange. I think it goes with his artistic temperament."

"He likes being alone."

"Tell me about it. He used to leave the house when he became a teenager, go deep into the woods and stay there much of the day in the summer. It used to drive my mother wild."

"I can imagine. He's gifted. I want all the best for him. I'm so sorry this has happened." The thought flashed across her mind that Marlon liked the woods and there were the frightening sounds coming from the woods behind her house.

"So am I. Neesie," Luke said, "are you sure nothing else happened last night?"

She hesitated. "Why do you ask?"

"Because I know you so well. You're tense, keyed up. I know you as well as I know myself."

She told him then about the croaking and he swore. "Let's not stay here. Let's go to the woods now, see what we find. I think the earlier the better."

"OK, but let's look at the sketches a little longer. Marlon's sketches and paintings talk to me. Things have just got to be all right for him."

"Very well, we'll study the sketches a while longer."

As they stood before the easel, Annice said, "He's left room for other sketches or paintings. I wonder what he has in mind."

Luke shrugged. "It's hard to tell."

Sylvie Love's likeness, her delicate wistfulness, looked back at them. She had been a live wire, Luke thought, like Annice and like the girl, Carole. Beautiful women, independent women who knew their minds and went after what they wanted.

Suddenly Annice thought of something and asked, "Luke,

the bracelet the Loves gave back to Marlon. What do you think he'll do with it?''

Luke pondered her question before he spoke. "I don't know. I wanted to ask him, but I thought better of it. I wanted to put it in my safe, but I thought he probably wanted to keep it close to him.''

"Probably. Well, I certainly hope people are kind and no one ruins his playhouse in here. Probably because the guards walk through, we haven't had the homeless or vagrants hanging out here, but it could begin happening at any time.''

"Well, let's hope it doesn't. My heart really goes out to the homeless. Twenty-five or more percent of them mentally ill, others alcoholic and still others just down on their luck, the way *any* of us could be. Neesie, I thank God every day for you and what I have, even if we're not where we want to be.''

They left then and fifteen minutes later in the woods behind her house, they walked, gloved hand in gloved hand, along a woodland path parallel with the barbed-and-block-wire fence.

Looking carefully as they walked, they saw an empty and crumpled cigarette package in a large area opposite Annice's bedroom windows. Luke picked it up, asking Annice, "Have you a bag of some sort in your knapsack?''

"Why yes." She unsnapped the knapsack and took out a plastic bag. "What do you intend to do with it?''

"I'm being a frustrated criminal investigator. You never know what fingerprints and DNA will turn up on material these days. I'm going to turn this over to Jon Ryson and Sheriff Keyes.''

"That's a good idea.''

Sunlight struck through the forest and midway they were warmer than they had been. "I'm glad to see Calico mending so fast,'' he said.

Annice laughed and reminded him of the incident the night before when Calico had ignored her until she prepared her warm milk.

"Like owner, like pet. Maybe you need a dog. You could have both."

"I know, but Calico is so dear to me. She seems to read my mind. Maybe she wouldn't get along with a dog."

"I've been considering buying you a parrot. Would you like one? I'm told African gray parrots do stupendous things with their voices. They're nearly human."

"I'd like to think about it. What's kept me from getting one is I hear they're awfully jealous of *their* human. If someone else comes by, they cut up."

"Hell, put them in their cage, throw a cover over the cage and you're home free."

Annice laughed. "You've got the answer to everything." She kissed his cheek and his eyes nearly closed.

"Except the most important answer," he said somberly.

"Luke!" she said suddenly.

"What is it?"

"I heard something."

They both listened and heard the sound of pounding feet crashing through the dry underbrush, running away. Luke's big body pitched forward to run.

"No, don't," Annice said with alarm. "You don't know them. They could hurt you." She clung to his arm.

"I guess you're right, but I wish I could hurt the bastard."

"That may not be the same person who was here last night. Could it have been a bird?"

"I doubt it."

They walked then to the other side of the forest over to where two homeless old men sat at the side of the road. They climbed under the wire and faced the men.

"Good morning, gentlemen," Luke greeted them. They returned his greeting. "Did you see someone come out of the woods a short while ago?"

One man nodded. "Sure did."

Luke's heart leaped with hope. "Can you tell me what he looked like?"

The man removed his woolen cap, scratched his head and

beside his mouth as he thought. "Strange-looking dude, I tell you. Wrapped in a black cloak, black hat pulled down and stranger yet, he had on a mask. He was running hell-for-leather. We sure didn't try t'stop him. He do you some harm?"

Luke shook his head. "We're not sure." He took out his wallet and pulled a twenty-dollar bill from a compartment, handing it to the man. "I hope this can help you both."

The man took the bill with alacrity. "Lord, thank you, sir. We been wondering where we'd get our next meal. Soup kitchen gave out. My stomach's driving me crazy and I know my boy here is the same way."

The younger man nodded, smiled.

After a moment of deep thought, Luke pulled another twenty from his wallet and handed it to the man. Tears stood in the old man's eyes. "This here's my only son, Tom. I'm Hubert Tate. And I thank you from the bottom of my heart. It's been a long time since anybody was this kind to us."

Listening to the man, it struck Luke that he had at least a fair education. The cadence of his voice was faintly musical. The son remained silent, giving no clue that he heard the conversation. Annice thought she detected mental and/or emotional illness.

Luke and Annice extended their hands. The father and the son shook hands with both.

The old man's voice was choked as he said, "He was robbed and beaten up a few months back. He's never felt well since."

"I'm sorry," Luke said.

"I've been around here almost a year now, since the boy got hurt. I *see* what I look at. I know you're something big in the school back there. I've seen you drive in and out."

"Where do you stay?"

"In an old, abandoned house about a mile away. We don't require much. I love my boy and I know he loves me. I've got to help him all I can. You go now and may God be with you."

"May he be with you and your son," Luke intoned. "You take care."

On the way back through the woods to her house, Annice asked, "Who do you think it could have been dressed in black? Mr. Tate said he was tall, but not as tall as you. With the cloak and the mask, he couldn't tell anything else. He ran into another patch of woods, so there's no telling where he was going."

When they reached the back yard of her house, Luke paused and clenched his teeth before saying, "I want to go home and call Sheriff Keyes or Jon." Then he said, "Later, show them this cigarette package and tell them what we know. It's little enough, but it doesn't always take a whole lot. Maybe we'll get lucky. And Annice, when *anything* else happens, for God's sake tell me. Don't be a hurt heroine."

Chapter 15

As they rounded the side of the house, they heard voices and hastened their footsteps to find a bundled-up Carole and Belle sitting on the front steps, grinning. Both had several big department store bags. Luke smiled and spoke to the girls, who giggled. As Luke walked away, Carole said, "I would kill for the likes of him."

Belle sighed. "He's one of a bunch you'd kill for. Besides, he's taken." She rolled her eyes toward Annice, who smiled and said only, "What brings you two by?"

Carole spoke up. "We went into Minden and got the things you and I talked about for Belle. Under that raggedy cap, I want you to see the haircut the hairdresser gave her. We were getting ready to leave because we weren't sure you hadn't gone away somewhere. And we wanted to know if you needed any help."

"Hm-m-m, my parents are coming this afternoon, and you could help me a little. I've pretty much got things under control, so we could also spend a while getting Belle fixed up."

"I don't know as I want to be fixed up," Belle hooted. "I kind of like myself the way I am."

They stood on the porch, and Annice reached out and touched Belle's powder-soft, dark brown cheek. "Work with Carole and me and we'll make you a star."

Belle laughed. "Double dare you to try."

Inside the house, Belle took off her hat to display her new hairdo.

"Gorgeous!" Annice exclaimed.

Belle flushed and looked down at the floor.

"Lift that chin," Annice commanded.

"Today, we're going to make you a queen," Carole declared.

They took off their outer garments and put the packages in Annice's bedroom, then set out to do minimal housecleaning. "What time are your parents coming?" Belle asked.

"Late afternoon. We've got plenty of time. Why don't we have some hot chocolate and marshmallows first?"

"You've got my vote," Carole said, and Belle grunted her approval.

In the kitchen, the two girls sat around the round table as Annice prepared the hot chocolate.

"This is great chocolate," Belle said. "It warms me where I live."

Carole looked at her friend and twitted her. "*Any* food warms you where you live."

"Don't knock it," Belle told her friend. "You don't eat enough to feed a bird." In a falsetto voice, she mocked Carole, "Got to stay skinny for Julius. He likes thin broads." She turned to Annice. "Julius told me he thought you were in great shape."

"Oh?" Annice said.

"You are in great shape," Carole spoke up. "But Julius likes women too thin. He likes the bird-skinny models."

Belle ran her fingers over her lush black hair. "Let's don't talk about Julius. I don't want to ruin my day."

The girls didn't want further food, so they set about vacuuming and dusting. There wasn't much to be done. Carole had polished the silver several days before.

When they were through, Carole put her hands on her hips. "Now we begin the metamorphosis."

Belle thumped her friend's shoulder. "Mighty big words for a skinny little girl."

"It's a word Julius likes."

"I notice," Annice said, "you're talking a lot about Julius today. Weren't you going to slough him?"

Carole reddened. "Yeah. He's being nice now."

"Ain't gonna last," Belle said. "He always gets sweet after he's popped you."

Carole looked uncomfortable, so Annice mildly warned her. "Think about it, Carole. I mean about letting him go. Life's too short for this kind of heartache. You can do far better."

Belle mocked Julius again. "I'm the judge's son and my daddy owns and runs the world."

Carole looked even more uncomfortable. "Let's get started on Belle," Annice said.

They took garments from the bags and laid them out on the bed. Three new skirts, three new sweaters, two blouses. One skirt and one sweater were matching burgundy, the others were mixed colors.

"Take off those rags you're wearing," Carole ordered.

"They're my choice," Belle scoffed, reaching for the new skirt.

Carole tapped Belle's hand away from the garment. "Not yet. I've got something else to do." She went into her tote bag and pulled out a cosmetics kit. "Sit!" she commanded.

Drawing a short pink plastic cape from the bag, she then took a pallette of makeup from another bag. Belle sat meekly, breathing shallowly with anticipation.

"My mama says only fast women wear makeup," Belle told them.

"Do you believe that?" Annice asked.

"Not really. My mama's old-fashioned. My dad wants

me to wear it if I want to." Very wistfully the girl said, "My daddy's a real sweet man."

"He certainly sounds that way," Annice offered.

At the mention of a father, Carole's looked woebegone as she continued to work with Belle's face.

With special covering makeup, then dark brown cream makeup base, no powder, lighter brown eye makeup and a touch of burgundy, the portwine birthmark was largely concealed. The girl's skin was beautiful. Black eyebrow pencil and black mascara. Burgundy lip gloss. As Carole stepped back to admire her handiwork, Annice sat in admiration. Belle looked from one to the other of them, but she couldn't hide her joy.

Carole brushed back the thickly lustrous, half-kinky black hair, then brushed back the short sides. "I give you," she said, "my miracle."

Belle looked down again and it was moments before Annice saw the glimmer of tears in her eyes.

"No," Carole demanded. "No crying. You can't ruin my work. Stop it now."

Belle grinned then.

"You see," Annice said sharply. "It's like I told you. Underneath all that indifference, you're a good-looking, a beautiful, young woman with a heavenly voice."

Calico came into the room and jumped onto the bed beside Annice.

"What's wrong with her back fur?" Belle asked.

"Someone attacked her, pulled it out," Annice answered.

"Crazy people," Belle muttered. "Here kitty." But Calico crept closer to Annice.

"It's made her shy," Annice told Belle. "I hope she gets over it."

"She will. Somebody hurt our cat a couple of years ago. He's plenty fine now." Belle's head lifted with hope.

"Now, stand up, glamour girl, and try on your outfits." Annice saw then that Belle had lost fifteen or twenty pounds; the baggy clothes she wore had camouflaged the loss.

The slim burgundy skirt enhanced a neat waistline and rounded hips, and the burgundy sweater molded the high, thrusting breasts. Carole slipped a goldtone rope about Belle's neck and stood back.

"Holey-moley!" Carole teased. "You've got it going on, girl."

Belle swatted her friend away. "You're just flattering me." Her eyes had gotten dewy again.

The skirt was a flattering above-the-knee style that beautifully displayed Belle's stunning legs, now reflected in the room's three-way mirror.

"Carole," Annice said, "I think you might think about exchanging being a model for a career as makeup artist to the stars. You've got a very deft touch."

Carole thanked her and looked at the array of makeup Annice had left out that morning. "If you like my work," she said, "let me do your face next."

"OK."

Belle sat on the bed as Annice seated herself at the makeup table where Carole immediately went to work on her. Calico not only snuggled up to Belle, but she purred and Belle laughed aloud. "This little cat's gonna get well," she said heartily.

Under Carole's deft touch, Annice's makeup was soon finished, and she saw that she had not overpraised the girl.

"Uh-oh," Carole said suddenly. "I forgot something."

"What?" Annice asked.

"The plant outdoors you wanted to come into the house for a bit. I forgot it." She wheeled suddenly. "I'll go bring it in now. You and Belle finish looking at her new things."

Calico jumped off the bed and padded out. Annice felt a surge of affection for her animal. The vet felt that in a few more months the hair would be largely grown back in. She was such a great cat. If there were such a thing as reincarnation, Annice thought now, Calico would have been a regal queen.

Belle stood before Annice now in a scarlet sweater and

a black wool skirt that wonderfully flattered her skin. This time, *she* picked up a short goldtone necklace and slipped it around her throat.

"I told you," Annice said. "Now do you believe me?"

"Well, I don't want to brag, but I look kind of all right."

"More than all right."

Then they heard Carole calling frantically, "Calico! Calico!" before she came back into the room, meeting the other two at the door. Carole wrung her hands frantically. "She streaked past me as I held the door open to bring the plant in. I saw her go under the fence and she wouldn't come back."

Chapter 16

Annice and the girls made phone calls on her phone and her cell phone. They alerted the dormitories, asking that anyone who saw Calico would please bring her home.

"We could stay with you," Belle offered. "Won't you need help with your folks?"

"Well, ah, Julius and I are going to play bid whist," Carole cut in. Then she shrugged. "Let him find somebody else to play with."

"No, really, I'm fine. You two have made my day, and my Mom's a bundle of energy. It's Saturday. Go and get in some happy time."

"You two have already made me happy," Belle said, "but after we look for Calico, I'm going to get a pass and go to a movie."

Annice called Luke then and told him. "I'll be over shortly," he said.

By the time he got there, Caroline and Frank Steele had come, loaded down with homemade preserves and jellies and baked goods.

They fondly fell on Luke. "You're as handsome as ever," Caroline said, kissing him on the cheek.

"But you get more beautiful," Luke gallantly told her. Caroline's skin warmed and her smile was beatific.

Frank and Luke shook hands and hugged.

"You shouldn't have brought so much," Annice said as she and Luke helped them unload the car. "I wanted this to be a rest period for you two."

Caroline laughed. "We rest all the time. Eleni is traveling with Ashley at the moment, so we've got nothing but time."

Annice smiled at both parents. "I heard from Ashley yesterday. She certainly is on top of her world. But I miss her."

"We miss her, too," Frank grumbled. "But she's really enjoying herself."

"Are she and Derrick as in love as ever?" Annice asked wistfully as Luke's eyes met hers and he smiled warmly, reassuringly.

"I think you know the answer to that. But she and Derrick have nothing you and Luke don't have. My two girls were lucky. I'm sorry my son was so badly hurt."

Caroline looked at her daughter closely. "You look bothered, love."

Annice nodded. "My cat got out and I can't find her."

Caroline patted her shoulder. "Dear Calico. Give her time. Every cat we've ever had has disappeared for days on end. It seems to be the nature of cats we've liked. But, oh yes, Calico was hurt and that's what you're worried about."

"Yes, it is."

"It probably won't happen again. We once had a cat come back injured. That never happened again."

"I hope you're right," Annice said ruefully, then asked, "What's in the box?"

"Open it," Caroline said.

Annice did so and found a mahogany wooden box inside the cardboard box. Inside the padded, silk-lined wooden box was a pair of large, exquisite silver candlesticks. They all exclaimed at that soft and gleaming beauty.

"I polished them," Caroline said, "because I wanted to display them at their best. Listen sweetheart, your sister said to be sure to tell you that these candlesticks are one-hundred-fifty years old and were part of a count's estate. She's told you about the flea markets they have in Berlin, like no other."

"Um-m-m, where they bring family heirlooms to sell? Yes, she has. I'm going to call her a bit later."

"Good," Frank said, "we can all talk with her."

Looking around, admiring the arrangement of her daughter's house, Caroline finally spoke up. "How's Marlon? I thought he'd be here."

"He's coming later." Luke looked bothered for a long time.

"Anything wrong?" Frank asked him, but he shook his head.

"I imagine you don't want to talk about this," Caroline finally asked, "but how is Marlon taking the girl's death?"

"Hard," Luke answered without hesitation. "He's still spinning in midair. He only remembers finding her. After that, total darkness. I haven't talked about it with you, because I've only recently talked to Annice. I'm sorry, I just couldn't. I guess I'm just terrified that he slipped up somehow during a quarrel—he and Sylvie could wrangle. I'm afraid he may have been guilty. My heart tells me *no*, but my head says there was some evidence there."

"But they never arrested him?" Frank asked.

"They did, but they had to let him go for lack of evidence. They called it a crime of passion, said whoever did it was enraged. I've told Annice I know my brother has a temper, but whoever did it had gone over to being a *monster*. This is what makes it so hard for me to take. The Marlon I know would never do such a thing, but do I know my brother anymore?"

Annice and Caroline went into the kitchen then and prepared to serve dinner. There was little Annice had to cook—brown rice and asparagus. Caroline had brought a rack of lamb, a baked hen and a spiral honey-baked ham. Caroline prepared the green tossed salad and hollandaise sauce for the asparagus.

Caroline giggled as she held a white paper bag behind her. "Care to guess?"

"You know I'm no good at guessing games. Show me."

Caroline opened the bag, withdrew one perfect, lightly browned Parker House roll and held it up.

"Oh, you love of a woman, you didn't."

"Oh, you love of a daughter, I did it just because I know they're your favorite."

"Twenty more pounds, here I come, and with these, I won't regret a single pound."

Caroline put the bag on the table and put her head a little to the side. "You're holding up well weightwise, dear. A little over, but I find that attractive. What does Luke think?"

"He absolutely loves it. He always says he's a meat and potatoes man. Meat on his woman and potatoes in the pot. He loves white potatoes in any way, shape and form. I've got apple cider on hand and cinnamon sticks. Plus, I made some eggnog."

"Everything sounds so good." Caroline went to stand before a calendar. "December tenth," she said slowly. "Are you ready for Christmas?"

"I certainly am. I've got a great set of two fruitcakes aging with brandy."

"I hope I'm due one of those. So many people don't like fruitcake."

"To each his own. I'll take their share."

In the living room, Luke and Frank sat on the sofa watching the beginning of a football game, talking intermittently.

"I'm so proud of what Neesie tells me you're doing with Doc Casey's school. Anything new?"

A big smile spread across Luke's face. "I guess Neesie's told you about the Programmed for Success venture."

Frank nodded. "You and the others work with each kid and move heaven and earth to turn him or her around to being what he or she will most enjoy being."

Luke felt a thrill of accomplishment and hoped-for accomplishment flood him. "That's a great way of putting it. Already I'm seeing growth and pride in what the kids—the youth—are doing."

"You're cutting a hard edge to bring into being diamonds, I'd say, but if there is ever any help you need, I'm with you. Caroline *and* I are with you."

"Thank you. I can't tell you how much I appreciate that. I could use you both as occasional voice coaches and teachers to help our music teacher."

"Just tell me when, and Luke, I'm damned glad you and Neesie have found your way back to each other, at least some of the way. In the very near future, may it be *all* the way. Neesie has been hurting."

"Thank you," Luke said huskily. "I've hated hurting her, but I felt it was necessary."

The doorbell chimed then and Luke answered to find Velma and Arnold Johnson standing there, with Marlon a little behind them. Luke invited them in and took their coats. Hearing their voices, Annice rushed in and hugged all three. She rubbed Velma's hands. "Such cold hands," she teased her.

"But she's got a mighty warm heart, I tell you," Arnold proclaimed, as his wife smiled broadly.

"Absolutely the best," Annice said, then turned to Marlon. "I'm so glad you came. Would you like some hot cider? Eggnog?" She noted again that he had lost weight since they'd come back from Ellisville.

His voice was little more than a croak, and he was very tense. "Ah, cider, and could I taste the eggnog? Yours is my favorite."

"You sure know how to pull my strings."

Caroline came in and there were more hugs all around. The phone rang and Annice answered. It was Claire, who asked to speak with Luke. He strode over and picked up. After a minute, he said, "That's not going to be possible just now, Claire. I'm tied up here. Will be for several hours."

He listened again. "I left Mark to fill in for me. Have you called him? I'm sure you can handle it. Good-bye."

Replacing the phone, he came back to them. "Claire's a great friend, but she is easily rattled. A couple of students have gone off campus without permission. She wants to track them down. Mark feels they should be given a few hours to come back on their own. Kids that age are testing their wings, and the harder you press, the higher they try to fly." He looked at Marlon, who flushed and looked down.

In a few minutes, the phone rang again. This time it was Mark Whitley. Luke spoke briefly and ended by saying, "You've got my complete confidence, Mark. Do what you think best."

When the food was ready, they each drank a small glass of apple cider, stirring it with a cinnamon stick. After studying him a few moments, Caroline asked Marlon in a voice warm with sympathy. "Honey, what's wrong?"

Marlon shrugged. Luke and Annice didn't expect him to answer, but he did. "I'm having trouble with my friend, Julius. He thinks I'm trying to take his girl."

"Carole?" Annice asked. So many of the boys courted several girls.

"Yeah."

"And are you?" Luke asked levelly.

Marlon shrugged again. "I won't lie and deny it. I like her, a lot, but I'm not trying to horn in on him. She likes me, too."

Both boys have come to like Sylvie. She closed her eyes. *Don't think about Sylvie.* But she found it impossible not to think about Sylvie.

Marlon asked to and set the table. Annice had candles to fit the candlesticks, and had chosen a centerpiece of gladioli and broadleaf fern. Marlon stepped back to admire his handi-work.

"You're not just an artist with your painting, but also in other ways," Caroline complimented him. "Marlon, you're going to make some woman a fine husband."

He shot her a look that was a little frightened before he said huskily, "That's a very long time away." His expression was sad.

Annice had selected her best gold- and dark blue-bordered Royal Doulton china and Waterford crystal. The silver was heavy and of a simple design.

They began with white wine and shrimp cocktails and continued through a meal brimming with superb food, joy and goodwill. Then they took their plates of dessert into the living room to eat with eggnog.

Annice found herself frowning. "What's wrong, dear?" Caroline asked.

Annice sighed. "I guess I'm thinking about Calico. She always seemed so happy when I had company and when I put her food before her."

Frank exploded. "I hate the thought of you being threatened, Neesie. Missing cats, volunteer badges, sheets of paper with cryptic messages pasted on them. It makes me feel so helpless."

Luke nodded. "I feel helpless, too. Could Julius be behind this?"

"I guess anybody could be," Marlon said lamely. "I know he's being a beast to me right now. I'm not trying to take his girl."

"She's so pretty, but she's a slippery one," Velma said. "I'd like to see her choose you instead of Julius. At least she'd have someone who cares about her."

Marlon looked uncomfortable.

Caroline clenched her hands. "Like your father, I, too, get so mad at the thought of someone threatening you."

Annice leaned over and patted her mother's hand. "I know you both do. Don't worry. I'll be all right." But her arms were flecked with goose bumps as she thought, *Goose*

*going over my grave again. That's been happening a lot
lately.*

"I've never felt so helpless in my life," Luke declared,
remembering the strange figure in black the day before. They
hadn't told Frank and Caroline about that.

Marlon seemed to get more panicky by the minute. Frank
cleared his throat and frowned deeply. "I guess I'm old-
fashioned," he said. "Eye for an eye and a tooth for a tooth
sometimes. That girl in Ellisville. I'd like to see whoever
took that poor girl out taken out himself."

At this, Marlon seemed to have trouble getting his breath.
His anger seemed palpable. He stood up, nearly knocking
over his eggnog glass. "I'm not feeling well," he said. "I'm
going to have to go." Not looking at any of them, he put
his food on the coffee table, grabbed his coat from the closet
and bolted from the room.

In silence, the other members of the group looked at each
other.

"Now what in the world is wrong with him?" Caroline
asked. "Marlon doesn't drink, does he? He's looked a bit
uncomfortable all evening, but he was more or less all right."

"I don't know what's wrong with him," Luke said, frowning. "He's never liked liquor."

"Well," Frank rumbled, "I'd say he's under the influence
of something that's not agreeing with him."

Annice sat thinking that Marlon had come unglued when
Frank had made the statement about wanting to see the one
who had killed Sylvie taken out. She felt chills go up her
spine and more goose bumps proliferate on her arms. Her
eyes stung with anxiety.

December 10. He unlocked his diary and got a pen from
his red flannel shirt pocket. Everything was going so well.
They had come after him yesterday in the woods, but he
had gotten away safely. The world was full of stupid people.

The hussy Sylvie was dead. She had looked at him with star-filled eyes, ripe from making love to Marlon.

He'd like to kill them all, every one of them who sparkled and shone with life and yes, damn it, lust. He'd gotten away with Sylvie. He would get away with the ones to come. He was smart, clever, and he hid his tracks well.

He hugged his secret to his heart. He hadn't known he would kill her. He only wanted to frighten and hurt her. No, that was a lie. He hated every woman like her. He would always get away and his secret would be safe.

And his secret? He had fits of rage that came on him suddenly, gripping him, until he saw blinding waves of red. He was strong then, powerful, the way he was normally kind of weak, ineffective. He had felt that way from time to time for over a year and Sylvie was his first murder. To kill, how sweet the sound. That was the real power. He didn't see the rage that gripped him as fearsome. It was his friend. Before the rage came to him from time to time, he had often felt so bad he wanted to die. Now, someone else was dying in his place.

He knew of at least two more women he intended to kill. He grinned. There would be others. He couldn't stop now, it was too exciting. The woman they called Annice. He didn't call her doctor when he was alone. Yeah, Neesie, he would see that her time came. She was proud, independent, in love with life. She had the power he had formerly lacked until the rage came into his life. He didn't ask or wonder what caused the rage. He was just happy to let it happen.

Frowning, he thought, too, that when he'd killed Sylvie, he had been full of the rage, but it hadn't lasted long. He was himself, and he was not himself, but also a second powerful other. Now, he thought he knew something else, that he didn't have to have the rage to kill. He was proficient at the beginning. Sylvie's murder had been his first, but he didn't want to think about that. He focused on the ones to come. He saw himself as Bluebeard, as Jack the Ripper, as all the godlike men he had read about who had killed and gloried in it. And they hadn't been caught.

He grinned again now and breathed deeply. He had already chosen his next victim and it wouldn't be long. He flexed his fingers. They were great for pulling a trigger and for the horrific body beatings he inflicted. He went to a mirror and looked at himself, liking what he saw now. He wished he knew when the blessed rage would hit, but he didn't. So far, it had never come at an inopportune time. He trembled a bit thinking it might one day flare when he was ill prepared.

The rage gave him strength and was his friend. This year, for the first time in a very long time, he felt the power he needed to keep going.

Caroline and Frank left late Sunday afternoon. Caroline drew Annice to her bosom. "You're so precious to me, Neesie. You take care and I can come to stay with you. Frank can take care of our place. Or we both can come and leave the house to Minnie and King."

"I'll be all right, Mama. I'm very careful and we have help with this, the way I've told you. My security system. Security guards. The sheriff comes by often, or one of his men does, and there's the wonderful Lieutenant Jon Ryson of the Minden Police Department. Please don't worry."

"Honey, of course I'm worried. It shivers my bones that the same type of paper was in your desk drawer that was found by Sylvie Love's unfortunate body. I'm worried sick. Lord, I sure hope it isn't Marlon. I've liked that boy so much."

Annice shook her head. "I don't think it's Marlon, but I don't know." She started to tell Caroline about the man in the black cloak, but didn't. No need to worry her more.

Going back inside after Frank and Caroline had left, Annice called Dr. Casey.

"Neesie, how good to hear from you. Did you get the material on limbic rage?"

"Not yet. I'll probably get it tomorrow. Is there anything extra you can tell me about it?"

"Well, first of all, what brings limbic rage to mind?"

She told him then about Marlon's spells of barely suppressed anger and Julius's high temper. But it was Marlon she wondered more about. Julius acted his anger out more. With Marlon, it was as if he had demons inside him, now rearing up.

"Well, limbic rage is nothing to play with. An operation can help in many cases. As I told you, the limbic center of the brain simply goes haywire, giving superhuman strength."

Annice's breath came too fast. She was remembering what Luke had told her about Sylvie's horribly beaten body. "As if a demon had taken over."

"It's sad," he said. "It seizes the person, but they are aware of what's going on. They just can't stop themselves."

"There are tests that can be given?"

"Oh yes. We've got PET scans now that can tell us what we're looking for. Once there was little hope; the person virtually self-destructed. Now there are a few things that can be done. Medications that are sometimes effective. I'll be glad when you go through the material. I think it can give you answers. But the best article—better than in the medical journals—I've seen was in a women's magazine ten or fifteen years ago. I enclosed a copy of that."

"I already have that article and you're a love."

"No, you are, and I'm coming out there soon. I talked with Luke this morning. Neesie, the program you two are undertaking, Programmed for Success, has hit the ground running. You're taking blighted lives and putting them on the glory path. I'm so proud of both of you. Now, if I can just get you two altogether back again, I'll be happier still."

"It *will* happen," Annice said staunchly. "It has to happen."

Chapter 17

Monday morning Annice dressed with extreme care, choosing a dark navy silk rep dress with large gold coin buttons and a gold rope. Navy butter-leather pumps would make her legs look even more shapely. She laid the garments and her shoes on the chaise longue and grinned, quite proud of her legs. It was funny. Both she and her adopted sister, Ashley, had similarly shaped legs and she often spoke of it. Ashley always pursed her lips and said, "But you are my sister, sweetie, in every way. It doesn't matter that we had different biological parents."

She showered and ate a light breakfast of a raisin bagel with cream cheese and a big glass of freshly squeezed orange juice, eating the pulp of the orange she had just squeezed before putting another into the juicer. It was going to be a great day; she could just feel it. Mel Sunderlin, who headed the Sunderlin Foundation in New York City, was due to meet with Luke all that morning and much of the afternoon. Annice would meet with them around ten-thirty.

"Don't be surprised if he keeps you on past your allotted two hours," Luke had told her. "He has an eye for a pretty face. Be nice to him. It's his family's foundation and if we can get his support, we've got it made.'' He hesitated, studying her. ''You look a bit sad. Are you thinking about Calico?''

She had nodded. He had offered to spend the night, but she had declined. ''I'll be OK. Why help me get such an expensive security system if I'm going to run scared?''

He had placed a finger under her chin. ''You've got guts, my good woman. They don't come feistier than you. I'm proud of you, love, all the way through.'' He had held her then a very long time, and she had felt his heart thrumming along with her own heart. A gentle, honeyed liquid heat had permeated her body and she had gone limp.

He had smiled with half closed eyes. ''Shall I go? Shall I stay?''

''Go man,'' she had said. ''You know you've got that presentation to make to Mel Sunderlin.''

He had shrugged. ''And so I have. I intend to be in my office by seven in the morning to get everything in order. Lisa will be there early. How is she working out as your secretary? I could give you more time.''

''She's working out splendidly. I've always kept my own notes. My handwriting's pretty good.'' She chuckled. ''I keep threatening to inundate her, and later I will have a few more things. But she's such a whiz. She works so quickly and there are no errors to speak of.''

Luke had nodded. ''Sunderlin's meeting with Claire and me the early part of the afternoon. Lunch is twelve-thirty to two. You're invited. In fact, lunch is a command performance. You don't have to sit in with Claire if you don't want to.''

''Fine. If you don't leave, it's going to be morning.''

He had laughed then. ''You're right, but I don't want to leave.''

''I'll be fine.''

''Even if you will be, I want to cuddle, snuggle, whatever you want to call it.''

"And I suppose I don't?"

"Do you?"

She had stretched out her arm with a finger pointed toward the door. "Go, man!" she ordered. He had kissed her again, stroking her back and her hips, kissing her face with tongue kisses. And he had left.

Now it was morning as she sat at the kitchen table, swinging her legs, her blue satin robe loosened around the lace-trimmed navy lingerie she wore.

She had dreamed dreams of Calico, but she could not remember what. She crossed her legs and idly watched her blue satin mules that Luke liked so much. He was a lover. No doubt about it. With her, he frequently proclaimed, all roads led to love.

"Don't you mean *sex*?" she often chided him.

He frequently grew still when she said it, and explained his feelings. "Neesie, I'm a sexual being. Not everyone is. I respect my sexuality and that of others. It's a gift from God, when it's properly used. It initially brings the children that are our heritage. When it's based on love, it binds us in ways that few things can be said to bind us. Inside you, I feel glory, and by your side, I feel a bond with God and His Heavens and the earth we inhabit. You are a part of me, as I am a part of you."

Her eyes had brimmed with tears. "That's beautiful," she had said. "No wonder I love you so."

She sat up straighter, finishing her orange juice. Luke was so precious to her. Were they ever going to be married?

A sharp pinpoint of pain struck her breast. Where was Calico?

Mel Sunderlin was tall—two inches shorter than Luke's six feet three inches—a dark brown fit man who looked sophisticated and pleasant. You knew to watch him move that he owned his share of his world. His handshake was firm, engaging.

"Dr. Steele. I've heard a lot about you, all of it good."

Annice found herself blushing. Luke looked at her sharply. He was not a jealous man, most of the time, but he liked being the alpha male so far as she was concerned.

"Dr. Jones has told me a lot about you," Annice complimented. "All of it good."

Mel Sunderlin threw his head back. Oh, this one was a charmer. And pretty to boot. He was a man who liked women, most of them. He often felt there were few ugly women, just those who didn't know how to properly turn on their beauty.

They sat at a round table in Luke's office and discussed Programmed for Success, the development program for Casey's School that Luke had created and quickly dubbed PfS and Mel Sunderlin had followed through on.

"You know," Sunderlin said early, "I was so anxious to get started in this foundation that I could only wait to get my master's. Then when I see people accomplish what you two and others are accomplishing, I get envious."

Luke leaned forward, his eyes warm and friendly. "I'd say, my friend, that you need envy no one."

Sunderlin smiled broadly. "Thank you." He turned to Annice. "Does that tell you why I regard him so highly? But then, I'd have to stand in line to give him the accolades he deserves. He did wonders with the school in Ellisville." His face got grave then. "Dr. Steele . . ."

"Please call me Annice."

"Annice it is. Certainly I have rarely met someone I felt close to so quickly. And I am Mel to you as I already am to Luke. Take your time and tell me what you want to accomplish as your share of this program."

She began slowly. "I want to change lives—from blighted to shining hope."

"A tall order," Mel said, nodding.

"I know, but only by thinking big thoughts can we achieve big things."

"How do you propose to achieve this? Along with others, of course."

"Yes, along with others, and along with the youths themselves. I love people, Mel, and I love children. I grew up proud and strong and full of hope, and I am intent on passing this onto others. If there *are* bad children, it is because they are blighted in their lives; mistreated, if you will. I think *respect* is the most underrated word in the English language or any other language. My goal is to help youth and children respect themselves, their lives and their earth."

Mel Sunderlin looked at her closely, and Luke's eyes shone with pride.

"Of course," she continued, "there are youth who are mentally and emotionally hurt, sometimes crippled. It is terribly difficult, but they can, at least be helped. I know it takes time, effort, money, imagination, and I think it can be done."

Mel pursed his lips, "And people like you and Luke and others will do it. I went to Dr. Casey's house for a visit yesterday. He thinks the world of both of you. He has led a wonderful school and he is delighted to be able to turn it over to you both for a while. Luke, you will want to find your own school to head again and Dr. Casey has told me of the deep bond between you two. It will be the Casey's School's loss when you move on, but I compliment you in advance for what you are accomplishing, I'm sure, and what you will accomplish."

They both warmly thanked him and he continued. "Should either one of you tire of such an enormous burden, I would hope you will turn to our foundation. It would please me greatly to have you on our board."

Again, they thanked him. Both had prepared special case files for him to take with him and study. He took four files. Marlon. Carole. Belle. Julius. He leafed through Carole's first, then asked, "Tell me what your goals are for this student."

"She's a lovely girl," Annice said. "Bright, capable,

winning, but she has low self-esteem as so many of the students have. I'm working with her one on one and . . .''

"Time consuming, isn't it? How do you find the time?"

"I make the time. Fortunately, most of the students develop beautifully with special sessions of group therapy. They help each other and not all of them need one-on-one therapy."

"But as you say, most are lacking in self-esteem. How does group therapy help?"

Annice thought a moment. "I have worked with Dr. Casey and with doctors abroad, mostly in London, to formulate special group sessions . . ."

"May I know a little about what those sessions entail?"

"I think I said it at the beginning. I feel this as other teachers here feel it. *Respect* is our foundation and our cornerstone. Then *love* for ourselves, for others and our world. Mel, these are the basics, without which we can get nowhere. Without these two attributes, our lives are like a heart that is badly damaged and unable to function.

"Most of our children have been abused in some way or fashion. They need daily—yea hourly—conditioning in understanding, in feeling that they are important, that they matter, that they're an integral part of this world. They talk out the anger, which is most often based on hurt, and they soothe and assuage their own and the pain of others. It works well, helping others while helping ourselves. I would be happy to send you case histories showing the progress we hoped to make and what we made at the end of this school year."

Mel leaned back and looked from one to the other. "I know I will lean heavily in favor of funding Casey's School, but there are others I must deal with who have their favorites to fund. You have reason, however, to feel very hopeful."

"Thank you," Annice told him.

Luke smiled broadly. "That makes our year."

Then Annice said, "I want to call your attention to three more students whose case histories you have in your packet.

The first is Julius Thorne, whose father is a judge, so lack of money isn't the only way to be headed for trouble. Belle Madison is another student. She's a junior and possesses a truly gorgeous mezzo-soprano voice. We're near to getting her a scholarship to D.C.'s Ellington School for the Arts.''

She smiled then. ''And there's Marlon.'' She nodded toward Luke. ''He's here to be with his brother. Because of something personal, he's having a hard time this year, but heretofore he's been developing nicely. So, you see, we don't back away from troubled youth.''

Mel Sunderlin nodded. ''Programmed for Success. PFS. I like it. No, I regard it highly. I *respect* it. I hope you will do a book, or perhaps you will do a book together.''

''I'm working on one now,'' Annice said.

''Splendid,'' Mel Sunderlin told her. ''Whenever it comes out, please see that I get a copy.''

''I'll be sure to.''

''With all I have mapped out, I don't foresee an early time when I'll be finishing a book I started year before last,'' Luke said.

''I know the feeling,'' Mel said. He glanced at his watch. ''It looks,'' he said ruefully, ''like my time with you is ending, Annice. It's difficult to tell you how very much I've enjoyed talking with you.''

They broke for lunch then and found Claire in the waiting room of Luke's office. She stood at a window and swiftly came to them. She gave Mel Sunderlin a dazzling smile. ''I'm sure you'll want to continue your conversation with Dr. Steele. I'll walk with Dr. Jones.''

Mel smiled easily as if he knew every step of her plots and plans toward Luke Jones. ''My pleasure,'' was all he said as he offered his arm to Annice.

By the time Annice neared home that afternoon, she was in high spirits. After lunch, the two men had met with Claire for a briefer meeting, then with other faculty members and students. Mel Sunderlin praised them profusely. Luke called her back to sit in with him just before the wrap-up meeting. Before she left Luke and Sunderlin alone, Sunderlin told her, ''I am leaning in your favor, as I said. I am so delighted to have met you.'' He held her hand a bit longer than necessary. Luke looked from one to the other, bemused, eyes half closed. She was glad to see him seem so happy again, even if the green-eyed monster was bedeviling him again.

Late that afternoon, walking along the wide sidewalk as she neared her house, she thought of when she had recently walked here with the woods beside her and had been spooked by the feeling that someone moved in sync with her footsteps. She shuddered a bit. It was daylight and in the setting sun's benevolence, everything seemed serene. It got dark quickly after sunset. A dog barked in the distance. A child's frustrated screams rent the air, and Annice looked down the walk and saw a woman and a child who was soon quieted. She smiled sadly. She and Luke would have had a child by now.

As she got to the house, she looked over into her side yard and saw a big burlap bag. She hadn't left anything like that lying around. Perhaps the man who did her yard had done some clippings and bagged them, although he usually didn't come by without telling her. Oh well, she'd get her clothes off and see what it was a bit later.

Letting herself in through the front door, she reset her alarms for night and went to her bedroom. She walked around the house humming, then singing one of Ashley's spirituals, ''He's Got the Whole World in His Hands.'' She missed Ash, who was so busy they didn't talk as often as they once had. She had a concert in Carnegie Hall tonight. Maybe she'd call her afterward to congratulate her on her continuing excellence.

She undressed and got into pale yellow silk lounging pajamas that flattered her tan skin. Going to the three-way mirror, she peered at herself intently. She didn't look as haunted as she had looked before she and Luke had partially gotten back together. No, she thought, she merely looked anxious. She was being stalked. It wasn't just her imagination. Luke and Jon Ryson and Sheriff Keyes were proof of that. The man in the black cloak running was proof of that. And most of all, the white sheet of paper with the words *Angel Face, Devil Body* was proof that she, indeed, had something to fear.

She was not a fearful woman, and she hated being threatened. Had Sylvie Love been stalked?

Lunch had been heavy, so she prepared yogurt with fresh pineapple chunks and a grilled cheese sandwich. Feeling a bit hungry, she ate the food slowly. Then she remembered the burlap bag. In so short a time it had grown dark. She switched on the side yard lights and went outside. Picking up the bag, she noted that it was not knotted, just tossed carelessly into the yard.

With full light shining on her, she looked inside the bag and screamed. The next scream froze in her throat. Lights showed her what she would have given everything not to see. Calico's severed head, Calico's severed tail and Calico's charred-to-a-crisp body. She couldn't stop shaking and with a heaving stomach she stepped aside to retch. After a little while there was nothing left to throw up. She picked up the big bag, carried it into the kitchen and put it on the floor near the door. She sat down then and the tears came, hot and burning and full of grief.

"Oh, my poor darling," she whispered. "My poor Calico."

Luke seemed to be there almost as soon as she called him. He held her close and stroked her. "This makes me mad as well," he said. But he was thinking that all the courses both had had in psychology taught that people who tortured animals more often than not wound up killing people. Was the dead cat a warning? He wanted to protect her from all evil and for a minute he felt helpless. Then a surge of power flooded him. He would do what he could and that should prove to be considerable.

She wanted to bury the cat that night, but Luke pointed out that they needed to call Sheriff Keyes and Jon Ryson. The sheriff was away for the day, but Lieutenant Ryson came quickly.

"It just gets a little nastier each time," Jon Ryson said. His eyes on Annice were warm, sympathetic. "Sheriff Keyes is going to hate to have missed this."

When the doorbell rang, Annice got it. Marlon stood there. "I . . . uh, just wanted to ask you a couple of questions," he said. "It's about talking to you about—about, well, everything that's happened. I didn't know you'd have company."

"It's all right."

"I hear Luke. Could I just go back to the kitchen?"

Thinking quickly, Annice told him he could. Marlon swung the door and looked at the two men who stood over the cat's body on the burlap bag.

"My God," the boy said and seemed to have a hard time getting his breath. "What happened?"

"That's what we'd like to know," Lieutenant Ryson growled as he squatted beside Calico's lifeless body.

"I don't like cats much, but this is awful," Marlon croaked. His skin had gone ashen. Then he said to Annice, "I'm sorry. I know how much you loved her."

To save her life, Annice couldn't answer. Finally, Marlon said, "Well, with everything going on, I'm not going to stay. Neesie, please give me a call when you get a chance. I'd really appreciate it."

He seemed stiff, unyielding, Annice thought. Why had he come by? He was eighteen now. Fast onto being a man, and where was he headed? The figure in the black cloak could have been him, but why would he stalk her? She had loved him as part of his brother's life and for his stunning talent. Was he betraying that love?

Once Marlon had left, Annice, Luke, and Jon Ryson hunkered down in the kitchen drinking strong, black coffee.

"I'll take Calico with me to the medical examiner's office. It's early enough," Jon said. "I'll be in touch tomorrow."

Luke insisted on staying the night. "You're in no condition to stay alone."

"It's a little campus with a big appetite for gossip," she protested. "Luke, I'm more enraged than I am afraid. Please don't worry about me."

"You're damned right I'm worried." He came to her, held her close and stroked her. "I'm a moral man, Neesie," he told her. "But I will not sacrifice my love and my life to appease gossiping tongues. I'm going to heat you some Ovaltine and put you to bed."

She undressed as he heated the warm drink and brought it to her. "Go ahead and cry," he said, putting the cup and saucer on the nightstand. "Scream. Beat the pillows. That bastard is out there somewhere."

"I at least wanted to bury her."

"Afraid you can't now. They're going to do a partial autopsy, at least on the little flesh they have left. We can bury her when they're through. It's a low-down, dirty shame, the kind of thing a juvenile would do. He's my brother, Neesie, and I love him, really love him, but I keep wondering. Marlon said he came by to see you, to talk with you. He seemed out of it, cold. Is my brother on drugs? Alcohol? I never smell any on his breath. What's going on with him?"

"I don't know, Luke," she said slowly. "I just don't know. Do you think Marlon could be doing this? Or know who is?"

"I don't know what to think." He bent forward and wrapped her in his arms, held her. "We're going to get to the bottom of this, sweetheart. I won't have you hurt. I'll kill before I see you hurt."

He sat on the edge of the bed then, his fist under his chin. "What about sleeping tablets? Have you got any?"

"Yes, in the medicine cabinet."

He got the tablets and a glass of water. Her throat was so tight she could barely swallow, but she forced herself to drink the water, then the warm milk. She sat propped on pillows, tense, as if she had to be prepared to run. The sleeping tablet was very effective, and in less than a half hour she had fallen asleep.

The first dream came easily. Calico sat on her lap in a chair in the side yard just where the burlap bag had been. She stroked the cat lightly. Calico didn't like being ruffled or harshly touched. She picked her up and held her against her heart. Dear animal. Then she smiled as she traced the cat's face and body with her forefinger. "Soon, we're going to call you a *fat* cat, my pet. You're fast getting there. Diet city, here we come."

Then before her eyes, Calico began to change forms. Once when she had been a student, medical journals had carried pictures of a cat changing from mentally healthy to schizo-phrenic — wild eyed, with spiky fur and a splayed body. This was how Calico looked now as she lunged for her.

"No!"

In a frenzy, she tried to get up, but Luke's big body held her. "Wake up, sweetheart. You're having a nightmare."

Annice looked around, imagining her face nearly as wild as the dream and the beloved cat's had been. She told Luke the dream and his eyes on her were tender.

"I think," she said, "this means I see whoever is doing this as psychotic, which is no surprise. Go to bed, Luke. I can handle my nightmares. You've got to get some rest."

But she sadly thought that she didn't truly *feel* she could handle her nightmares and it felt wonderful to come awake with Luke holding her, watching over her the way she would watch over him if he were in trouble.

Chapter 18

When Annice came groggily awake the next morning, Luke was calling her name. She glanced at the clock. Seven.

"I've fixed you a bit of breakfast. I know you don't feel like eating, but it will help."

"Oh sweetheart, you didn't need to do that."

"I wanted to. Rouse yourself. Wash your face. I'm serving you breakfast in bed."

She stumbled up, half sick with a vicious headache. In the bathroom, she ran cold water over her face, took two aspirins, then showered and did her makeup.

After a few minutes, Luke came back in. "I'm not even going to ask how you feel. I think I know."

"I can tell you this. I feel better with you here."

"I'm glad."

She got back in bed, sat up, and he stood the bed tray over her lap. She tentatively put a bit of cream in her coffee cup, a packet of natural sugar and poured the coffee from a ceramic pot. He had done waffles with strips of bacon cooked in, one of her favorite meals. Pouring blueberry syrup over the waffles and sticking a fork in the scrambled eggs and shrimp, she smiled wanly at him.

"You don't have to talk," he said.

"OK, but when I'm finished, I need to talk with you about Marlon. I *want* to talk."

He went back and got a tray for himself and they ate in companionable silence. She was hungrier than she had expected to be.

Once they had finished and he had taken the trays back to the kitchen, she sat on the side of the bed.

Luke sat in a rocker by the bed. "I don't want you to go to work today," he said. "I know how tender you are. Cry. Mope around. Begin to grieve. I can only stay a little while longer, but I'll call to check on you. I'll have the aide monitor your sessions. Your kids are pretty well behaved. I say your kids, but they're the school's kids. They're just interested in what they're doing in there and they give less trouble."

"I respect them," she murmured. "They know that. And I demand that they respect themselves, others and me."

A small grin tugged at the corners of Luke's mouth. She sighed. He was such an attractive man. Heat rose in her body and she felt drawn to him, grew warm with wanting him.

"I just wanted to talk a bit about Marlon," she said. "When he was over for dinner with my parents and the Johnsons, and left so suddenly, I couldn't help but think about limbic rage. Of course he could just have a trigger temper."

"Marlon wasn't like that before our parents died. He's changed. He's secretive, on edge."

"The hell of it is," Annice said, "that if he does prove to have limbic rage, it's treatable. Medication. An operation if it's serious enough. It affects the limbic region of the brain, but there is so much hope."

"Too late now to make him undergo treatment, but I wouldn't have, I don't think. God, Neesie, what am I going to do about my brother?"

"I don't know, Luke," she said slowly. "He's said now he wants to talk with me, and I'm going to press him for a starting time."

"That's a good idea. Make it soon." Yes, she thought, the sooner they could work through Marlon's troubles, the sooner they could be completely together again. They both ached with wanting that.

On the radio, Christmas music swirled around them. It was going to be a sadder Christmas without Calico. The cat always seemed to enjoy her presents and the extra attention she got. Normally independent, she clung to Annice when others were around. Annice thought grimly that she hadn't clung when she'd run out past Carole a few days before.

Luke showered and dressed. He sat on the edge of the bed before he left. Gathering her in his arms, he kissed her fondly, holding back the ardor he felt. She needed sympathy now, but sympathy was mixed with wanting her in every way.

It was ten and Annice had dressed in gray sweats with a gray band around her hair when Carole called.

"Dr. Steele, I ran into Dr. Jones and he told me what happened to Calico. I feel so guilty." The girl sounded choked.

"Don't take guilt for this on your shoulders," Annice soothed her. "It couldn't be helped. I know you're sorry, and I don't blame you."

"Thank you." Carole hesitated a long moment. "I could buy you another cat, take it out of what you pay me."

"That's a wonderful thought, but I don't want a cat for a while."

"Dr. Steele?"

"Yes, Carole?"

"I want to come by. I can get a pass from the office. I wouldn't stay long. They say you aren't coming in. I need to talk with you."

"Oh? Has something come up?"

"You might say that. Will it be all right? I'd come now."

"Of course you can. Don't forget to get a pass."

"Oh, I won't."

Hanging up the phone, Annice reflected that her hands were cold in the warm room. What was going on in Carole's world?

The girl seemed sick with fear when Annice opened the door to her. She fairly stumbled in. "I won't stay long," she said again.

"Take your time. My dear, what's wrong? Let me have your coat."

When Carole had given Annice her coat, she dug into her backpack and handed Annice a sheet of paper. On the white sheet of paper were pasted the remembered hellish words: *Angel face. Devil body.*

"What on earth?" Annice began. "How did you get this? And when?"

Carole breathed raggedly. "I left my backpack on the floor beside the chair I wanted to sit in in your group session room. I was staking out that chair. When I came back, I went into my bag to get a pen and I found this."

"Was anyone else in the room?"

"No, not when I left the backpack."

"And it scares you."

"Marlon came in and I showed it to him. He's mad with me for going back to Julius. I wasn't bothered at first. I thought it was just a prank. Then he said a girl he knew was murdered and someone left a sheet of paper like this beside her."

"It seems cruel of him to tell you that, but maybe he was trying to help."

"Is it true?" Carole demanded. "Did it happen the way he said it did?"

Annice took the girl in her arms. "Carole, I'm afraid it's all too true. Dear God, how I wish it weren't." She said nothing to Carole of the similar paper she had found in her drawer.

"What will become of me?"

"Nothing is going to happen to you," Annice consoled her. "Come and spend a few nights with me. I'll want you to talk to the police about this and I'll get Bill Sullivan, the security guard, to take you when he comes on duty this afternoon."

Carole shook her head. "No, ma'am. You see, he's mad with me too. I flirt, Dr. Steele. You've told me about it. I don't put out anymore, but I still flirt. I don't know why. He was coming on to me and I came back on to him. But I wouldn't sleep with him. He called me a tease and stopped speaking to me. I don't think he'd take me."

Annice studied the girl. "He would if I asked him. But I'm going to give you a number to call for the police. Ask for Sheriff Keyes, or I'll give you another number for Lieutenant Jon Ryson."

"Yes, ma'am. Do you think I'm being silly?"

"No. I don't think you're being silly. Do you want to spend a few nights with me?"

"No, ma'am. I'll be all right."

Annice felt a burst of sheer annoyance. She felt certain that Carole didn't want to stay with her because she intended to meet Julius.

"Is Julius still knocking you around?"

It was a moment before Carole answered. "Not really. He gives me a few of what he calls, 'love cuffs.' "

"They're not 'love cuffs,' Carole. They're the mark of an abusive man, a man who doesn't love you the way he says he does."

Carole looked stricken and torn. "I better go back. I hate what happened to Calico. Who would do a thing like that?"

"Someone bitter and enraged and with half or less a heart. I'm glad you came by, and listen, if you change your mind and decide you want to stay a little while with me, just let me know."

"Oh, I will, and I may. You don't like Julius, do you?"

"I don't like Julius's *actions*. Carole, let him alone. He's no good for you. One day, he could hurt you—badly."

Surprisingly, the girl's head jerked up. "I know. My mom's boyfriends mostly beat her up, but she stayed. She says it proves they love her. That isn't true, is it?"

"No, it isn't true. It's controlling, manipulative, dominating, domineering. Do yourself a favor and break clear."

"Well, I like Marlon plenty and he likes me, but he's no prize either. When I told him I was going to keep on with Julius, his eyes caught fire like he was going to kill me. I got scared, then I got real sweet and after a few minutes he turned and left me. We were in Pirate's Cave and we were looking at two paintings he's done of the same girl. It was spooky, Dr. Steele. One of the paintings looked like a dead girl. Was that the girl who was killed?"

"Yes, it was."

Carole slid her sweater sleeve up to look at her watch, then slid it down quickly, but not before Annice saw the deep bruise. Carole blushed.

"Oh, Carole, how can you go on tolerating this?" she wailed.

Carole's grin was sickly. "This time he really didn't mean it. We were just playing around." She finished lamely, "He doesn't know his own strength."

Annice looked at her and shook her head.

Carole gulped. "I've got to go now. Thank you for being such a sweet lady and not blaming me for Calico. You change your mind and I'll get you another cat in a heartbeat."

Annice hugged the girl. "Take care of yourself," she said gently. "Why don't you call me every day for a while? Call around nine or ten at night."

"Oh, Dr. Steele," Carole sputtered, "I get to studying and I get carried away. I may not remember, but if I do, I will. I'm such a bat brain. Julius says I'm all body and face and no mind. He looks at other girls a lot, but he doesn't want me to look at other boys and men."

Annice had not meant to admonish Carole, but she found herself doing just this. Annice looked at Carole levelly. "Get rid of Julius, Carole. You once said you would. Why did you change your mind?''

''I guess I love him. I told you he told me he wants to marry me when we're out of school, maybe sooner.''

''I see. Yet you're afraid of Marlon's temper.''

Carole shrugged. ''You know, it's different. Julius's licks are like an angry child's. Marlon looks like a devil when he's gotten angry with me. . . .''

Her voice trailed off, leaving Annice to wonder. *Angel face. Devil body.* And Marlon's eyes that looked like a devil's to Carole when he got angry.

Velma and Della came by in the late morning.

''I was on campus to see the woman who runs the cafeteria and the grill when I heard about Calico from Luke. Neesie, our school and town are not that kind of place.'' She shook her head. ''But I guess we're getting to be. I don't guess you've talked to the police yet.''

''Yes, they have Calico's body.''

The two women hugged Annice and comforted her.

''After Luke told me, I was on my way here when I ran into Della,'' Velma said. ''So we came together.''

Velma accepted a cup of coffee, but Della demurred. ''Calvin got up early and made coffee and I had two big mugs, so I'm coffee'd out.''

''Calvin is doing really well in therapy, but he is *so* bashful,'' Annice said.

''He's always been that way,'' Della said. ''He's all boy now, but he tries. It isn't his fault that he doesn't always feel comfortable with his peers. He adores Marlon and Julius, and he feels bad that they're not getting along well. He's a great peacemaker.''

''He's a love of a kid,'' Velma brought in. ''Why is he at Casey's School?''

Della shrugged. ''He wanted to come. He thinks Minden

High School is too rough. He's something of a loner at times."

Velma smiled sadly as she told Annice, "I miss seeing Calico jump from that bookcase onto your lap and hearing you groan from all that weight."

"I'll survive," Annice said, "but I'd never groan again if she could come back."

She told the women then about the sheet of paper that had been left in Carole's backpack. Then she told them about the paper lying beside Sylvie Love's body. They knew about the paper she had received. Both women looked shocked.

"Oh, my God," Velma said softly. "You know, sheriff's office cars are on campus more frequently and around my place. And I hear they're getting two more security guards."

"That's true," Annice told them. "Four in all for the time being."

"And not a minute too soon," Della brought up staunchly.

The women left shortly after, with tears in their eyes as they hugged their friend. Their words, "Take care," seemed more meaningful to Annice than ever.

By three o'clock, Annice had grown restless. She got into her coat, gloves and a scarf and set out for Pirate's Cave. She wanted to know what Marlon was doing. He had confided in her that he had fixed up a studio in front of the cave to the left and farther back as you went in. She would wait for him.

All winter the weather had been warmer than usual and the cave was fairly warm. Marlon was young, his immune system functioned well and he probably didn't even notice cooler weather.

As she walked in, a shudder of apprehension ran the length of her body. Marlon sat with his side to her. He had prepared a cozy little place with a big straw mat, a chair and a table and a fairly large easel. Another easel held two pictures of Sylvie Love. It felt strange to look at them. To his right sat the lockable large aluminum box that held the paintings when he wouldn't be there for a couple of days.

She walked over to him, noting that he seemed annoyed. "Hello, Marlon."

"Hello, Neesie."

"You're here early."

"I just got here. Don't mind me if I don't talk much. I feel like sketching." He held his sketch pad on his lap.

"What are you working on now?" He had drawn in only a few strokes, but he continued to draw as they spoke and she saw with dismay that he was sketching a cat.

"Is that Calico you're drawing?"

He didn't answer for a moment. "Yes."

"Any particular reason?"

"Yeah. I'm trying to immortalize her, the way I keep trying to immortalize Sylvie."

Annice stepped forward to hug him, to say to him, "You poor kid," but he held himself aloof.

"I have to keep trying," he choked out. "I can't get used to death."

Annice knew the human mind better than most, so she knew he could say and believe something like he'd just said and kill too.

"You're talking to me," she said. "You're telling me what you feel, or some of it. Did you realize that?"

"Yeah. I want to talk to you, Neesie. It's just that I can't. I freeze and the words don't come. One day I'll open up, really talk to you. I've got to." A glimmer of tears came to his eyes. "I can't hold on much longer."

"What do you mean?"

As he hunched forward, the sketch pad nearly slid off his lap, but he caught it. "I don't know what I mean, but I know I'm going under if I can't make some sense of this. I've got to do so much on my own. I'll get it together. Then I'll talk to you."

"Why that's wonderful, but I can help you get it together . . ."

"No!" he exploded. "I tell you I can only talk when it comes together in my mind first. If I'm doing these crazy things, I don't want to go on living."

This time Annice placed a hand on Marlon's shoulder. "I'm with you, Marlon. I love you. Luke and I both do, as you well know. Trust us. Let us help you. Let me help you probe your mind."

"You can't save me," he said. "If I die, I'll be with my folks."

Annice's head jerked up. "We don't know about the valley of the shadows that is death, Marlon. You may not be with them."

"If I'm not," he said doggedly, "at least I won't know it."

Wisdom and sadness crept into Annice's voice as she told him, "But you may know it. You may."

He looked startled then. "I can't go on this way. I *won't* go on this way."

She had to be blunt. "Are you threatening suicide?"

"What do you think?"

"You will get over this, love. You're strong. We all suffer losses. Talking about it will help—a lot. Marlon, promise me you'll give talking it out a chance," she said urgently. "Live for Luke and me if you can't live for yourself. This would kill your brother."

"Nah. Luke's strong the way I wish I was."

"You've got to promise me you'll give yourself a chance. Will you?"

She hadn't expected him to, but he nodded. "OK, we'll try it your way, but no promises."

"I can make you a promise that you'll feel better. Come to dinner tonight."

"No. I want to be alone. I'm going to make more sketches. I don't much feel like eating."

She glanced around. The stalactites hung in all their beauty. The white clay floor was smoothly worn by time and more than a few footsteps. The lights the school's electrician had put in for Marlon's use added to the place. In the bowels of the very high hill, he could paint and sketch and be a part of nature as he worked. It could help him to heal.

He was one with his work now, and she knew it was time to leave, but he smiled at her lopsidedly and said, "Maybe I'll have dinner another night."

"Any time at all," she said.

As Marlon sketched, Annice went farther back into the cave to look at the giant stalactites located around the corner. She always knew peace here, and she sat on the stone bench someone had placed near them. Marlon didn't look well and that bothered her, but what she really found herself thinking deeply about was his anger—and his hurt.

After a few minutes, she walked back toward the back, then changed her mind and decided to leave. As she passed by Marlon, he said, "I'm such a dork, Neesie. I didn't even tell you I'm sorry about Calico. I know how you loved her."

"It's all right. I understand. I'm leaving now. Don't forget to save some time to study."

He shrugged. "My grades are falling off, but I don't care. I'll stay out a year or so if it's necessary."

"Just give it your best try." She touched his shoulder and he smiled a wan, lusterless smile.

Life and fellow human beings were so difficult to understand, she thought. Did Marlon still love her the way she loved him? Or did he bear some hidden grudge she couldn't know about? He wasn't nearly as warm and they weren't nearly as close as they once had been.

Walking back to her house, she slowed her steps and ambled along. It was nearing sunset and orange-red rays streaked the sky. It had been a beautiful day. Lost in her thoughts, she suddenly became aware that in the light of day someone seemed to walk as she walked, but the dense underbrush made it impossible to see them.

Then she heard it again. A low trill, then a croaking. The

cry of a crow. She quickened her steps and the croaking continued. She jumped as someone broke through the underbrush, parting the wire and coming through. Her heart raced and a shiver of cold fear shook her. It was daylight, she reminded herself, not the still of night when bad things happened.

She stood stock-still. She wasn't going to run. Besides, her legs would barely hold her up.

"Afternoon, Dr. Steele."

"Julius!"

"Yes ma'am." He carried a branch of holly and one of mistletoe.

"Gathering Christmas decorations?" She breathed a huge sigh of relief.

"Right. I intend to hold some mistletoe over my head all day every day until Christmas Day is over."

Annice smiled wanly. "Tell me, did you hear a croaking sound? Bird or human?"

"Croaking?"

"Yes, like a crow."

He paused a moment. "Why no, I came down the fence from that way. I didn't hear any birds and if somebody was trying to sound like a bird, I didn't hear."

Annice cocked her head a little to one side. "Do you know anything about birds?"

He laughed. "Just what most folks know, that they make good eating for cats." He clapped a hand over his mouth. "Lord, I'm sorry. I forgot about Calico."

"It's all right."

"Well, you take care, Dr. Steele. I've got to get over to the dorm and do my decorations."

"Yes, you take care," Annice told him. She turned to watch him as he loped along, secure in his heritage of wealth and privilege. He was lying. He had to have heard that harsh crow's call.

Once he was gone, she walked slowly again.

She managed to turn a ten-minute walk into nearly a half

hour, but she finally reached her house and behind the front evergreens, she heard voices.

A girl's voice—Carole's—said angrily, "That's the way it's going to be and there's nothing you can do about it."

Then a man's angry voice, low, scalding. Bill Sullivan. "I won't let you make a fool out of me, Carole. I'll see you in hell first."

Annice coughed and cleared her throat and walked around the bushes to face the two who stood there. Carole clapped a hand to her mouth. "I'm sorry, Dr. Steele. I thought you'd be out longer. I didn't see you come up."

"Um-m," Annice said, then looking at Bill Sullivan, his face set in anger, she told him, "Those are pretty strong words, Bill."

"I'm sorry that you had to walk up on this, Dr. Steele. It's a quarrel as you can see."

"I'm going to need to see you tomorrow in my office. Can you make it around three?"

"Oh, yes ma'am. But I've got a side to this."

"Carole is still a minor and you're grown up, married, with children. Just see me at three and we'll talk. Now, I'd like to speak with Carole—alone."

"Sure, ma'am," he mumbled and shuffled off.

"Dr. Steele, I came when you weren't here because I wanted to get a head start on the Christmas cleaning and I forgot a book I need to study. You don't mind?"

"Of course I don't mind, but did you let Mr. Sullivan into the house?"

"Oh, no ma'am. We walked out here. I'm sorry you had to hear that."

"Do you want to go inside?"

"No ma'am. I need to be going. I've got a lot to do."

"Carole, are you"—she hesitated—"involved with Mr. Sullivan?"

In the streetlight, Carole shook her head vehemently. "I've been flirting with him, the way I flirt with a lot of men. He's given me a few presents. Expensive ones. I told him I was breaking off. You heard how mad he got.''

''I thought he had more sense. And you, Carole, you've got to stop playing games like this. First thing you know, there'll be someone else cuffing you around.''

Carole's sigh was heartfelt. ''I keep telling myself I've just got to cut it out, but somebody else I like comes along and . . .'' She shrugged.

''Do you like Bill Sullivan?''

''I used to, a lot. Like I've said before, if he had married young, he could be my dad.''

''You told me you miss your father a lot.''

For the longest time the girl didn't answer and when she did, her voice was choked. ''Yes, I miss him a lot.''

''Let me set up an appointment to talk in depth with you very soon. Let's see if I can't help you fight this through.''

''Yes, Dr. Steele, but you needn't worry. I'm letting Bill alone. He's too hot for me to handle.''

''And there's Julius.''

''He keeps talking about getting married. I want to get married, have kids, so I won't be alone.''

''He's not a good candidate for marriage.''

''I can change him, Dr. Steele. He says I can.''

Wryly, Annice thought, *And a snowball can stay frozen in hell.*

Carole left then, her book bag on her arm, and Annice watched her as she had watched Julius. Had he seen Carole and Bill Sullivan together? Did he know about them? She wondered if he were the one whistling like an unknown bird. Would he have identified himself to her if he were? Or did he identify himself to prove his innocence? Her head hurt with pondering and she sat on her front stoop between the huge concrete urns that held fern for much of the year.

She hated the thought of going into a house without Calico.

Chapter 19

The night of the Christmas Heartwarmer came swiftly. Annice found herself working very hard with faculty and students for the big night, and she was early to check last-minute details. Dr. Casey was well enough to be there and to stay a short while.

Standing in the middle of the polished floor of the gym, she felt exhilarated. They had gone all out. Wreaths of red velvet, ferns and pine branches, holly, and poinsettias graced the floors, and silver, gold, red and green balloons hung suspended.

At a wolf whistle, Annice turned to face a laughing Velma Johnson.

"Oh, are you ever the beauty," Velma said.

Annice wore a black velvet full-length gown with a boat neckline. The gown hugged her figure and ended with a trumpet bottom. She wore a rope of marble-size cream cultured pearls and dangling cream pearl earrings.

Now Annice laughed. "I return the compliment," she told the older woman, assessing her lavender jersey gown with its figure-hugging drapes and folds, and her amethyst necklace and earrings. Arnold took Annice's hand and kissed it.

"Be careful," Velma teasingly warned her husband, "when it comes to younger women, I'm jealous."

Arnold grinned. "You've got nothing to fear. I'm a one-woman man."

Della came over. Dressed in bright red panne satin, she looked well and accepted their compliments, returning them graciously.

"Everything looks so lovely," Della said. "I'm telling you I went all out to work with the caterer on this to-do."

"I'm hungry already," Annice said. Her mouth opened in soft astonishment as Carole and Belle came in the door. Carole wore a deep rose fitted dress with gold jewelry and looked as lovely as always. But it was Belle who took Annice's breath away. Dressed in garnet red that set off her dark brown skin, she had chosen obsidian jewelry. The portwine birthmark was nearly covered. But it was Belle's hair that caught Annice's attention. Carole grinned.

"We went this afternoon to try this new cut," Carole said as Belle glowed.

Belle's superthick, kinky-curly hair was cut short, but not too short, and shone with a very light oil.

"There's this hairdresser in Minden who works wonders," Carole said. "I told you about her."

"You did," Annice answered. "Seeing this, I'll make an appointment."

"You look so pretty, Dr. Steele," Belle said. "I'm in seventh heaven with my new look."

"Thank you. You ought to be."

"Yes, you do look like a dream," Carole began when she caught sight of Julius and excused herself.

As the girl walked away, Annice muttered, "Talk about casting pearls before swine."

"What did you say?" Belle asked.

Annice shrugged. "Nothing much."

"Carole's talking about leaving school, marrying Julius. Can you imagine?" Belle asked.

"Let's pray on that one."

Belle nodded, saw some friends and moved away.

A happy-looking Calvin came to Annice.

"You look great, Dr. Steele."

"Thank you. You look pretty scrumptious yourself. I've seldom seen you in a suit." And indeed in his dark brown suit and gold and gray tie, he did look his best.

He was such a well-rounded boy, she thought, rough and tumble, yet there was something fragile about him. He was a success story for divorced parents.

"Your mother's done a wonderful job with you," she told him.

His face lit up. "I'm glad you think so. Mom's super. I love her so much."

His voice went ragged here and a shadow crossed his face. "I'm going to be really successful and try to give her the world. Listen, I gotta go help her now."

A band from D.C. played and a few couples danced. Annice held her breath as Claire Manton came to her.

"Great job you did with decorations," Claire said.

"Thank you. You were on the food committee. I understand it's going to be stupendous."

"I hope so. You look very—nice." Claire's face was cool.

"And you look extravagantly lovely," Annice offered.

"Thank you. Listen, Annice, I haven't had a chance to say how sorry I am about your cat. I'm not much on animals, but I know how it feels to lose anything you're fond of."

"I miss her a lot." She didn't feel like sharing her sorrow with the beautiful Claire, costumed in emerald green that matched her eyes and brought out the splendor of her red-gold hair. Her body was model-thin and supple, held with assurance that she knew her exalted place in this world.

Claire excused herself and walked to Luke as he had started toward Annice. They talked a few minutes before

Luke came away and to Annice where he whistled long and low.

"Talk about superb," he told her with his eyes half closed. "Do I deserve you? In my opinion, we're Beauty and the Beast."

Annice laughed. "Some beast. You're a hunk in that steel-gray suit with your pale gray shirt, your dark and light gray and scarlet tie. If you ever get tired of being a school superintendent, you'd make modeling agencies happy."

"Too old. Too plain."

"I said you're a hunk and I meant it. Don't go modest on me."

"Dance with me."

She went into his arms, loving the feel of his fit body against hers. The band played an oldie, "I Still Remember," and Annice softly hummed the tune.

> I still remember, you in my arms.
> Your voice, your smile
> Are my treasured charms.

"Like that, do you?" Luke asked.
"It's one of my favorites, especially this part."

> Will you return, love?
> I need you so.
> Bring back the joy
> of long, long ago.

Yes, she thought, *bring back the joy of long, long ago, when I knew that by now I would be big with your child. We're together now, but not altogether together. You refuse to let me be what I know I can be to you. I would stick with you no matter what Marlon's trouble is. How can I make you let me help you and him?* She snuggled close to him and her heart hurt with wanting him.

She looked up at a commotion at the door as Dr. Casey

entered the room, and with him was Mel Sunderlin. Dr. Casey was soon surrounded by students and faculty, stood for a short while, then sat down where he was immediately enthroned in a big, stuffed chair set up for him.

"I didn't realize Mel Sunderlin was bringing him," Annice murmured as she hurried to join the others.

Luke frowned. "Neither did I. I thought his daughter was to bring him."

Once Dr. Casey was settled, Mel Sunderlin went to Annice's side where he said in a low voice, "What a beautiful woman you are."

"Why, thank you." Annice blushed. When she saw an opening, she moved toward Will Casey, with Mel following close.

Luke felt a stab of jealousy at the way Mel Sunderlin looked at his, Luke's, woman and he thought sadly, *He's quite a guy. He could give her what I can't, a wedding ring and babies. Still, I could put his lights out when he looks at her that way.*

"Annice!" Dr. Casey exclaimed. "Lots of hugs. You look magnificent. There are so many pretty women here tonight. Can my old heart take it?" He chuckled merrily.

"And you," Annice began, "you're looking very, very well." She admired the leonine mane of silver hair and the fierce black eyes. "You give the young hunks a run for their money."

"Hm-m-m." Will Casey smiled. "A few compliments a day like that, and I'll be well."

The students and faculty crowded around him. Then Annice heard the velvet, bass voice of Mel Sunderlin as he reached for her. "May I have this dance?"

Annice went into his arms smoothly and he drew her close, too close. She tried to draw away a little, but he held fast.

"We weren't expecting you back so soon," she told him.

"Nor was I expecting to come back so soon, but Doc Casey called and said his daughter had other fish to fry and couldn't bring him, and I jumped at the chance. He was going to ask you or Luke Jones.''

"And we would have.''

"Aren't you glad to see me? I came back so soon largely because of you.''

His eyes on hers were very warm and compelling. "I apologize for rushing you, but all life is too short to go slow. I'm going to ask you a question and I'm going to ask you to be honest with me.''

"OK. If I can.''

"Is there something between you and Jones? I didn't want to ask Dr. Casey.''

"Yes. There is something between us,'' she said quietly.

"Something deep? Or something that can be swept away by a willing, determined competitor?''

She paused a long moment. "I don't know how to answer that. Just say that we're close. Extremely close.''

But not close enough, a small, still voice said in her heart. *Not close the way we once were.*

"I see,'' he said and pulled her a bit nearer. This time, she smiled and said, "As much as I enjoy dancing with you, please don't hold me too close. Students watch and they expect an unattainable perfection from faculty. They're always ready to break out and stampede. They need faculty to set a cooler pace.''

He laughed. "Aptly put. I'll be in D.C. a couple of days. May I take you to dinner and dancing at a place of your choosing? That way we can talk and no one can stop us from dancing as close as we wish.''

"I don't think so,'' she began, but he cut across her.

"But I know you're attracted to me and I'm altogether hung up on you, as the kids say. Come on, surely your friend Jones lets you fly the coop once in a while.''

"I just don't think it's the right thing to do.''

He held her a bit away then, searching her face and she grew uncomfortable under his ardent gaze.

"I'm going to ask you another question,'' he said slowly.

"And it's a loaded question. I mean it to be. Is Jones offering you the future you want for yourself? I'm pretty sure *I* can, although you may think me a fool for asking so soon."

A sharp pain went through Annice. *Damn you, Mel Sunderlin,* she thought. *You and your questions that hurt because I don't have answers. Will Marlon's troubles ever end? Will we ever know?*

Out of the corner of her eye, Annice caught sight of Luke dancing with Claire and her eyes met his, lingered a while, then both looked away.

"Well?" Mel said.

"I think I ought to pull up a chair and talk with Dr. Casey for a bit."

"Why? He'll understand if you don't, and besides, he has all the company he can handle."

"He's one of my favorite people."

"I want to be one of your favorite people, the way you're fast becoming one of mine."

The song ended then and Annice, with Mel in pursuit, started toward Luke. She didn't know if he saw her, but he and Claire were laughing. Claire turned her delicate, heart-shaped face to Luke's and they danced off again.

"Is Dean Manton your competition?"

Damn him again. "Not that I know of." *Liar*, she chided herself.

"I think you may be mistaken. If ever I've seen a woman taken with a man. I'd give everything I have for you to look at me the way Dean Manton's looking at Jones."

"Give it a rest," she said sharply. "We're not married."

"I wish I knew the full story, your full story. You're not even wearing an engagement ring. Let me court you the way I want to. You may find you'll like it."

His hot breath fanned her neck as she told him, "I'm just not sure."

"That's all right. Give me time and I'll make you sure."

"Oh, Mel." She thought she sounded like a silly schoolgirl, but this man was serious. She had no doubt that he could give her everything material, but he wasn't Luke.

The food was served early because Dr. Casey would be there for only a short while. Tables groaned under the weight of roast beef, turkey, ham and sushi. Green salads, with avocados and tomatoes, made a colorful array, while the macaroni and cheese and potato salad tasted as good as they looked. Several different kinds of rolls, black bread, and hot buttered biscuits abounded. Eggnog, apple cider, and other drinks lined a separate table.

But it was the array of desserts that let you know it was entertainment for youth with a sweet tooth. Every imaginable kind of cake and pie graced a long table, with Christmas candies and luscious fudge disappearing greedily. "Well." Belle laughed. "I'm stuffing myself, but it takes a lot of energy to do all this dancing."

And Belle was dancing. Several boys surrounded her and vied to be her partner. And tonight, she would sing.

Annice caught up with Lou Emma Camp, the music teacher, and the women admired each other's outfits. Lou Emma wore winter white, which set off her olive skin.

"I thought," Lou Emma said, "I'll have Belle sing before Dr. Casey has to leave."

And a few minutes later, with Lou Emma at the baby grand piano, Belle blessed them all with a marvelous rendition of "O, Holy Night." When she finished the song, she went as close as she could get to Dr. Casey, bowed low and blew him a kiss. He beamed. "The change in you is wondrous," he told her.

Annice didn't see Marlon at first and it worried her. Then she caught sight of him relieving the ticket taker at the door. She went over to him.

"Hull-o, Neesie. Nice party, don't you think?"

"Yes, but you don't seem to be having much fun. Why don't you mingle?"

He shook his head. "I'm not for parties tonight. My head's been putting a savage hurting on me lately."

Alarm bells rang in her head. Limbic rage victims had frequent headaches. Oh Lord, she had to make Marlon see a doctor.

"Listen," she said quickly, "if I asked you to be checked out for something, something physical that I think will make a world of difference, would you do it?"

"I dunno. Maybe."

"At least you'd be free of the headaches, with treatment."

"Talk with you in a couple of days."

"Please *do*." Then she added softly, "Please do. And don't wait. You may be suffering unnecessarily."

"And maybe not. A girl is dead, Neesie, and I may have killed her. How am I going to live with that?"

She hugged him then and he clung to her. They were coming close again, she felt, and there was hope, all the hope in the world. Glancing over at Dr. Casey, she remembered what he said so often, "As long as there's life, there's hope."

Walking away from Marlon, she started to where Luke and Claire stood talking, but Mel Sunderlin stopped her.

"One more dance?" he asked. "We'll be leaving soon."

"All right."

As soon as they began dancing, the urgency grew in his voice. "I haven't wanted a woman badly very often, the way I want you. Think about me. Let yourself dream a bit, the way I'm dreaming about you. You may find you like me. One thing I know is you'll be hearing from me."

Something compelled her to look up then and she met Luke's eyes. He stood with Claire, but they weren't dancing. Then she felt her heart surge with joy as he came toward them, reached them and tapped Mel on the shoulder. "May I cut in?" he asked smoothly.

Mel looked surprised, but Annice's heart danced. Two alpha males competing over one female—Annice. She knew who she wanted to win, but would he let himself?

Mel and Dr. Casey left shortly after that dance, and before

he left, Mel took her hand, pressed it. "Good-bye for now," he murmured.

Dr. Casey sent for Luke and standing with him, Annice heard words that warmed her heart.

"This is one of the best Heartwarmers I've ever known. Luke, Annice, thank you for the outstanding job you've done." He threw a kiss to all of them, complimenting the faculty and blessing the students.

"Surely," Dr. Casey said, "I am the most fortunate man alive."

Chapter 20

In the car in front of Annice's house after the Heartwarmer, Luke turned to her. He had been quiet, introspective
after Dr. Casey and Mel Sunderlin had left.

"I'm coming in," he told her.

"You're welcome. You haven't said a word about how
well the Heartwarmer turned out. And wasn't Belle
radiant?"

"She was a knockout. So are you. And apparently I'm
not the only one who thinks so."

"You're jealous."

"I *am* jealous. I don't usually let anything stand in the
way of something I want. This puts me in a bind. I want
funding from Sunderlin's foundation. He wants my
woman." His voice got deeper. "But no, I'm wrong. I've
had to give up all real claim to you."

"I haven't given up any of my claim to you."

"Don't tease, Neesie. You know what I mean. Let's go
in. We've got to talk."

He helped her bring in mistletoe and holly from the Heartwarmer. Della had also insisted that she bring some of the

delicious leftover food so she wouldn't have to cook the next day. She thought wistfully now that Calico had loved party leftovers and she had fed her bits, but the vet had said she shouldn't have them. Poor Calico. This time she felt sad, but her eyes didn't fill with tears.

Inside, Luke helped her out of her coat and stood looking at her.

"You're a beautiful woman, Neesie. If I don't say it often enough, it's not because I don't know it."

Annice smiled. "It's OK, Luke. I don't need a lot of reassuring."

He hung the coats in the hall closet and came back. He was hurting with wanting her and knowing he could lose her. He was his own man and he was on top of things, a winner, but Sunderlin ran him a dead heat.

"Do you like Sunderlin?" he demanded.

Annice coughed a little as she laughed. "He's a nice man. He isn't you."

"Are you going to see him again?"

"I don't think so. He asked me out. I told him you and I are a couple, but Luke, we only go so far as a couple."

"Don't remind me. Neesie, give me a few months to try to chase this thing with Marlon down. I'm going to start leaning on him to get treatment. If he won't talk with you, then someone else. Maybe Dr. Casey. They like each other."

"That's a wonderful idea, but I'm not setting up a time-table for you."

"I know and I thank you. Do you understand where I'm coming from, that if my brother is a killer, I don't want you involved with him? It will take years for him to get over this, if he ever does. I'm so afraid he'll do himself in if he finds he killed Sylvie Love."

"Look on the bright side, sweetheart. Killers make a certain profile. I don't see it in Marlon."

"Yet you admit he doesn't open up, so you have no way of really knowing."

"No-o-o, but he is beginning to talk with me. I told you about it."

"Yes, and thank you for trying." She was so near and the black velvet gown made her look desirable beyond words. Then he scoffed, hell, in a flour sack she'd turn him on sky high. He came close to her, took her in his arms, pressing her rounded hips in toward his narrow hip area. Then he bent his head and pressed his cheek into the curve of her breasts. With his arm around her, they walked into the bedroom.

"Neesie, my darling," he whispered, "I want to dance with you now the way I wanted to dance with you at the Heartwarmer. I want you, all of you, and I want to give all of myself to you, but I won't let you ruin your life for me."

She pressed her slender fingers over his mouth. "Don't talk. Just dance with me the way you wanted to dance with me at the Heartwarmer, and the way I wanted to dance with you."

He rocked her then with hot, ardent kisses, his tongue probing her mouth relentlessly, searching for and finding honey, and she returned violent kiss for kiss.

"Oh God, Luke," she cried out, flames of desire licking at her body. He was on fire, but he was going to take the time to do this right. He unknotted her pearls and she slipped off her earrings. She turned and he unzipped the black velvet dress, which fell to the floor, and she stood before him in black lace underwear, her brown silken flesh gleaming.

"Oh, my darling," he whispered as he took off her slip, then her bra and bikini panties. She wore no girdle, so she stood naked before him, a bit chilled in the warm room. Chilled in the flesh, but hot with wanting.

She helped him out of his clothes and gasped at his erection. As she began to touch him, he took her hand away. "Don't cheat yourself," he said, laughing. He lifted her then and carried her to the bed, turning back the spread and the top sheet before he did so. The rose sheets complemented the brown of their skin, and she licked her lips a little.

They lay side by side, unmoving, before she leaned over and got a thin latex sheath from the nightstand. "Can you bear to have me slip it on?" she asked.

"I'll think of snow, icebergs, something," he murmured. "Go ahead, just don't stroke too hard. I'm edgy."

"Tell me something I don't know."

Again they lay still for long moments and he quieted. He lay on his back and pulled her on top of him, flicking his tongue over the nipples of her breasts, then sucking them avidly, his hot breath fanning her body.

She felt sick with desire as his tongued kisses roamed her body, making her belly flame with desire. For a moment, he kissed her eyes closed, then tongued the sweep of her long, black lashes. She thought for a few seconds about the fact that she and her adopted sister, Ashley, both had long black lashes and great legs. Funny.

"I get a turn, you know," she said huskily, and he lay on his back and her avid tongue patterned kisses the way his tongue had patterned kisses over her body.

"My man. My hunk," she murmured.

"My woman, my beauty, and my life," he responded.

It hurt then that she wasn't filling with his seed that would bring them at least one child. They needed to be completely naked to each other, body of his body, heart of his heart, soul of his soul. As he wound his way down, she gasped with sheer delight at what he did to her.

He lifted his head from her willing body that had grown so warm beneath his touch. "Do I please you?" he asked. "Because God knows you please me in every way possible."

"Yes. Oh yes." Her voice rang like soft bells.

He spread her legs and entered her then and she put her legs over his back, loving him, wanting him, growing dizzy with excitement. Her hot, nectared sheath enclosed him like a small fist and he groaned with ever-deepening desire.

They moved slowly, in rhythmic unison. He stopped for a few moments from time to time, then catching fires of desire like an emotional and physical conflagration, he drove straight into her, turgid and throbbing, his hands under her hips, his tongue in her mouth, on her breasts, in the hollows of her throat. "Now," she whispered, "I'm on the edge."

He laughed shakily. "Hell, I've been on the edge since we began." And he gave one deep thrust and they moved together into a paradise of beautiful sights and colors and sounds. The radio still played soft, danceable music. Lovers' music. But they heard and saw little save for each other.

He gave one smooth and final thrust as she arched up to him, and she cried out with wild joy. "Luke. Luke. Oh sweetheart!" He was with her in ecstasy and passion rocketing to glory as her body shuddered with deep delight and a passion that matched his own.

"I love you," he said softly. "I will never stop loving you."

Choked with tears, she couldn't answer for the life of her.

They lay on the bed, silent, each stroking the other's body. After a long time, she raised on her elbow. "How do you feel about a glass or two of port wine?" she asked.

"I'll get it."

"No, you rest. You've earned your rest."

He laughed. "What about you? You really responded like magic."

Looking at him, mischievous laughter played about her lips and she stroked his face. "So you like what you got?"

"Honey, *like* isn't the word for it. I could die happy after one of our glorious sessions."

She got up, got her robe from the closet and slipping it on, came back to the bed. She sat down a moment, leaned over and kissed the hollow of his neck. "One of your turn-on points," she teased.

"I'm all turn-on points where you're concerned. Get the wine before I grab you again."

"No, you don't. You rest. You've earned it."

She went to the wet bar in the living room and opened a fresh bottle of port wine, got a tray and two crystal wine-glasses. She took them back into the bedroom and set the tray on the nightstand, pushing aside a vase of red-and-white-striped carnations.

"I should have opened the wine. You're so independent."

"I want you to rest. I have other things for you to do."

She sat on the edge of the bed, sipping her wine and he sat up and joined her. Savoring the fruity flavor of the port, she moved it around in her mouth with her tongue.

"Wine and champagne are drinks for lovers." She smiled at him through lowered lashes.

"Everything is for lovers when they're you and me."

They sipped the wine slowly, in thrall, gazing at each other. Then setting his glass on the night table, he got up, walked over to the dresser and picked up two sprigs of mistletoe and got back in bed, holding the mistletoe over her head.

"This means you owe me a deep, deep kiss. One that doesn't stop for a long time."

She set her glass on the night table and lay beside him, as he held the mistletoe over her head again. He kissed her very softly at first, his lips moving over hers. Then he put the mistletoe on the side of the pillow and kissed her again, harder this time. He couldn't seem to get close enough and suddenly he crushed her to him and kissed her so hard her mouth hurt. It was the most wonderfully exquisite pain she had ever known.

He played her body like a violinist strumming a beloved instrument, then she played him.

"I want to spend the night," he said. "Wake up in your arms. Don't put me out."

"Stay. I want you to stay, but right now it feels like we won't be finished until morning."

He chuckled and stroked her hair and face. It had begun to rain and the raindrops beating against the windows made them feel shut in on each other, washed in splendor. They lay side by side until she swung a leg over onto him and his face got somber, flushed with desire.

They moved in slow motion then, caressing each other

avidly, gasping for breath at the tremulous movements they orchestrated.

"I've kissed every inch of you," he said softly. "Shall I start over?"

"No. I need you inside me."

Leaning over, he got a condom from the night table drawer and slipped it on.

The passion on her face fed his ardor as he rose against her, harder and swifter. Turning her onto her back, he entered her and this time went almost immediately to a deeper place.

Feeling the length of him inside her, she could hardly get her breath at first, then she relaxed and breathed slowly, willing him to last. His fingers brushed her lips and his hot breath fanned her face.

They spent a long and beatific time, the way they had often been in the past. But she thought sadly, they were different now. Close, but not dedicated to a life and children together. Not yet anyway.

He cupped her face in his big hands. "You drive me crazy," he told her. "You're everything I want in a woman."

She smiled. "You're everything I want in a man. Luke?"

"Yes, sweetheart?"

"I love you so much. At times I thought I didn't want to go on without you when you left me."

He thought a moment. "I'm sorry for what I had to put you through, but you have to understand, Neesie. It's for your own good."

"I'll never stop arguing that I want to be altogether with you."

"We'll work it out somehow," he said, "but I won't listen to your arguments about us marrying until the trouble with Marlon is worked through. I have faith, Neesie, that it can be worked through somehow."

"You have hope," she said quietly. "I'm the one who has faith."

He kissed her long and hard again, thrumming inside her ripe, willing body. They belonged together. He worked smoothly then and she clung to him, again gasping for breath at the sheer splendor of their passion. They came together and it seemed a long time with the tremors that shook her body and the explosions ricocheting through his. But it wasn't long enough. They were greedy for each other, enthralled and needing to be together more than anything on earth.

It was late. He got out his black diary and opened it to a blank white page. He had so much to write. Every day he was becoming stronger, more powerful, more self-assured. He had the power of life and death over others, the means of revenge that filled him with awe. True, it had only come with the sudden surges of pure rage and strength beyond his imagining.

He had so much to write. About Sylvie. About future plans. The words jumbled and jangled in his brain. Should he write about his glorious accomplishments in the past? Or about what he would do in the future? One down. How many more to go? Calico didn't count. Stupid cat. He picked up a pen. So much to write, but the words didn't come the way he wanted them to. Why? He was certainly smart enough.

Oh, damn it. Why couldn't he marshal his thoughts? Finally, he grinned and wrote: *I can't wait much longer.*

Chapter 21

The day after Christmas of that same year

Annice woke early. Luke was in D.C. for a Saturday meeting with someone from the Sunderlin Foundation. Christmas the day before had been enjoyable—just Luke, Marlon, Carole and Annice. Carole had stayed on campus for the holidays. Belle had gone home to Minden.

Annice was annoyed that Carole had chosen not to spend the night with her. She had left around seven to go to the dormitory and Annice suspected it had something to do with Julius, who was still on campus, but would go home the next week.

Propping herself up on her elbow, she hugged the covers. It had been such a warm winter, but she had known there to be blizzards in January or February of other warm winters. She was pretty sure that Carole and Julius had planned a rendezvous before he left for New Orleans.

Grinning, Julius had told Annice, ''My old man's busting a gut because I'm not home for Christmas. I've got other fish to fry. I told him, *later*. He'd better be glad I'm coming at all. I'm eighteen now. My own man.'' Then he had added wistfully, ''Still, I hate disappointing him.'' He had said this earlier when Annice had asked him his plans for Christmas.

Carole had promised to be at Annice's house by eleven to help her clean. Carole's help meant Annice didn't need a regular cleaning lady, and Carole used the money to good advantage, buying lovely clothes and beginning to save her money.

Luke had given her a gorgeous diamond dinner ring and she had given him a dark brown leather briefcase. She loved the ring, but it reminded her of the one she had angrily thrown away. Her heart hurt when she thought about that. Would she ever bear Luke's child? Would things ever work for them? She got out of bed.

Going into the bathroom, she brushed her teeth and splashed cold water onto her face. Luke had left shortly after Carole. Surprisingly enough, Marlon had stayed a while longer. He had moved restlessly and looked uncomfortable and more than a little angry.

''Do you want to talk about what's on your mind?'' she'd finally asked him. She would never stop trying.

His sigh had been deep, wretched. ''I wish I could,'' he'd said slowly, then blurted, ''One day, Neesie, maybe sooner than you think. I hate being between you and Luke and I know I'm the reason you two don't marry.''

''I'd marry him tomorrow.''

He looked surprised. ''You would? Even knowing I may have killed someone?''

Her gaze on him was compassionate. ''Why don't you force yourself to talk about it, Marlon? What you feel. We know things about ourselves when we talk that we don't know if we don't talk.''

He had suddenly become wildly restless then, getting up, pacing the floor the way Luke did sometimes. ''Oh God,'' he said. ''I've got to go.'' He went to the closet and snatched his coat off the rack.

''Marlon, wait!''

But he had bolted, banging the door behind him. She had sat up a long time. Luke had called and they talked a little while.

"I saw Claire tonight," he had said. "She came by. I couldn't talk long since I have to be up early."

"What was on her mind?"

"She's happy and sad. She asked me to keep a confidence, so I will."

"Have you and Claire always been such close friends?"

"For many years. You know that."

She hurt then. "Claire's a beautiful woman. Could you be in love with her and not know it?"

"I'm in love with you. And you're a beautiful woman."

"Not as beautiful as Claire."

"To me, you leave them all in the dust. Neesie, jealousy doesn't become you."

Annice laughed softly. "You didn't think that way when Mel Sunderlin was paying me a little too much attention."

"Touché."

"No. It's typical male behavior, typical alpha male behavior, shepherding the females of the herd. Perhaps we both should work to get Mel and Claire together."

"You're kind," he had said, "and I apologize."

Annice went to the kitchen window. It was a dreary day and light snow had been forecast. Now, a few flakes swirled in the air. She groaned. After the delicious dinner she and Carole had prepared, she couldn't face more food, so she brewed fresh Colombian coffee, poured a cup, put in cream and natural sweetener and sipped it slowly. Her robe fell away from her long crossed legs and she stroked the bare top leg in its open-back slipper. She thought again about how much her legs were like Ashley's.

"Brown drumsticks," Luke often said. "I'd like to take a bite. Hell, I could swallow them whole."

"You're hopeless."

"I'm all hope where you're concerned."

Going into the living room, she began to pick up small

articles out of place, gift wrappings, and vacuum, then decided to listen to music until Carole showed up. She was usually early. She smiled a little. If she and Julius had hit the high spots or gone to some lovers' lane or a motel or both, she would be late getting to Annice's.

Suddenly she was annoyed. Why would someone with Carole's smarts and capabilities allow someone like Julius to manhandle her? Annice thought she was no expert on the subject, but Carole seemed to her to have all the makings of a top model. She certainly wanted her to give herself the chance.

When Carole hadn't showed up by eleven-thirty, she called Velma.

"Why no," Velma said slowly. "She came by last night, so happy with the leather jumper you bought her. I gave her permission to go into Minden to see a show with Julius."

"Oh? She didn't mention it. That's not like Carole."

"Well, she promised to call me when she got in, and sure enough, around eleven-thirty, she called. She said she was helping you today and Marlon wanted her to pose for a quick sketch, so she'd be getting up early. Is Marlon getting hung up on her?"

Annice sighed with exasperation. "The Lord only knows what's on Marlon's mind these days. He still goes to Pirate's Cave to paint. He leaves a good supply of art stuff there. I think one day someone's going to surprise him and break into his lockbox, but he won't listen to me or Luke."

Velma chuckled. "He does things *his* way, but my Lord, the boy is gifted. He sketched me the other day and it was *me,* in spades. And he sketches from photos. I wish he could know some peace and quiet. I pray for him."

"So do I."

By noon, Annice switched to soothing pop music and rhythm and blues, then to Ashley's recordings of the spirituals. She was humming and vacuuming when the phone rang. "Ashley," she exclaimed. "Think of the devil . . ."

Her sister laughed. "More like think of angels. You know

we traveled from Brazil on Christmas Day—Derrick, Mama, Dad and I. Brother Whit was at home and Eleni stayed with him. We got in very late and we're paying the price. Still, it was all so wonderful. Neesie, how are you? We've talked about your cat dying and the trouble you're having. Please be careful.''

"I'm always careful, Sis, but no one's going to make a coward out of me. I run my own show.''

"Have you an idea who it might be?''

"No, but the sheriff is on it and he has help from a police lieutenant in Minden who's an expert on this kind of thing.''

"Well, you stay alert and aware.''

"I doubt you know anyone more alert and aware than I am.''

Ashley chuckled. "How's Luke? And are you two any nearer to resolution?''

"Mama's talked to you about us?''

"A little. It has to do with Marlon. I love that boy. He's like Quinn's son to me, a love of a lad.''

"Did Corby go to Brazil with you?''

"No. He and some buddies went to New York with a family he's close to. But getting back to you and Luke. Mama and Dad said Marlon refuses to talk. I don't understand that. He blacked out. They didn't have enough evidence to charge him. Probably he isn't guilty.''

Annice licked suddenly dry lips. "I only wish I knew. But even more, I wish Luke would trust me to stand by him, or with him. He keeps insisting that he isn't going to let Marlon's troubles ruin my life. Oh Ashley, I'm glad you called. Nobody's got a shoulder to cry on like yours.''

"I'm glad. I'll be over before the holidays are ended, unless you plan to come home.''

"No," Annice said quickly. "All possible faculty is needed on campus. Many of the kids have no home to speak of to go to, but we try to make it pleasant for them here.''

They chatted on then about gifts and Christmas and how Annice liked Casey's School and Annice felt her heart grow lighter. For a moment she happily tapped her fingertips on the end table and said in her best merry voice. "Trust me to take care of *me*, Ash. Now let me speak with Mama and Dad, Whit, Eleni, and Corby. That should fill my morning before Carole gets here."

She was on the phone with her family for over an hour. Whit collected mildly naughty jokes and he told her a few. "Nobody appreciates my jokes like you do," he said now. "I miss you, Neesie, and I'm going to see you soon. Give my best to Luke."

"I will." She hung up then. She had wanted Luke to spend the night so badly, but he had seemed restless, bothered. Had he known Claire would come by his house? She couldn't stop the twinges of jealousy she always felt around Claire. If she and Luke were to break up, would he turn to Claire? He said he hadn't when they broke up because he said he wouldn't let Marlon's troubles ruin her life.

Sighing, she got up, put on black jeans and a gray sweatshirt and began to clean. Carole had seemed happy, but something was on her mind. She thought about the day she had come upon Bill Sullivan and her and what he had said.

By the time she had gotten halfway through, it was still drifting snow, but it was growing thicker. It had gotten colder, too; she turned up the thermostat. Thinking that Carole could be at Pirate's Cave with Marlon, watching him paint or posing for him, she decided to walk over to the cave. It wasn't like Carole not to be where she said she'd be, but she was young. There was always a first time. Perhaps she and Julius had taken a run into D.C. early and hadn't gotten back. Bad news Julius, she thought then. Carole had to dump him for her own well being.

Going to the hall closet she pulled on short leather boots, slipped into a heavy coat and got her woolen scarf and matching gloves.

Outside snowflakes swirled around her. She loved snow and there hadn't been much so far. The sidewalks were beginning to be a bit slippery, but her boots had gripper treads.

The cave was a twenty-minute walk from her house if you walked briskly as she did now. Glancing at her watch, she saw that it was one-thirty. She reached the cave and went in, looked around. The lights were on and Marlon's easel sat in its place. Now, there were the paintings of Sylvie and the drawing of her in death.

And something new had been added. A painting of Carole was in the third space. The boy was good, she thought, too good to have his life ruined by limbic rage, if it were limbic rage. He could be made well and it angered her that he had turned his back on himself, refusing to let others help him.

Where was Marlon?

Chills slashed through her and her blood nearly congealed at a high, keening cry. Terror? Pain? She walked quickly back and around a corner that was dimly lit by the front lights. She couldn't take it all in at first, but when her eyes adjusted, Marlon stood up over a girl's body. Carole's. She lay on her back and blood spread over her chest.

"Oh, my God! Marlon, what happened?"

But Marlon stared at her and through her, never seeing her at all. There was blood on his hands and on one side of his face. Then, with another wild cry, he began to lope away.

For a few moments she was paralyzed, then she moved toward his loping figure, but he was too swift for her as he ran full speed out of the cave. She turned back to Carole's body and kneeled, seeking a pulse. Getting none, she reached into her pocket and got her cell phone, called 9-1-1, then the sheriff's office. The sheriff answered the phone.

He listened carefully. "I guess all our worries were on target," he said sadly. "I've had a bad feeling about the troubles you've had, but I told myself that they'd slowed down and were probably over. I'll be there in a few minutes, but 9-1-1 will probably get there first. You afraid to stay?"

"No. I'll go to the front." She didn't want to tell him about Marlon, but the boy was in a bad way. It was getting colder fast and he had on only a light jacket and she thought: *I'm worried about him and the cold and he may have killed his second person.* So she told Sheriff Keyes about finding Marlon there and he said he'd put out a missing persons bulletin.

"On second thought," he said, "don't stay there. Whoever it was may come back. You've been threatened. Go home and wait for me there."

Numb with fear and grief and pain, she longed for Luke. He didn't take his cell phone into special meetings with him, but he always or usually called her when his meeting was over. Now she said softly, "Please call me, Luke." She walked home on unsteady legs, much colder from terror than from the snow.

In her house, shedding her outer garments, she sat down, winded. Where was Marlon headed? Did he have enough money on him to get a taxi? And she scoffed harshly at herself. A lush, beautiful girl probably lay dead, her chest covered with blood. If there was a pulse, Annice had been unable to get it.

As she got up and began to pace, the dam broke inside her and she began to cry harsh, tearing sounds and anguished tears.

She picked up the phone on the first ring, and when Luke called her name, she couldn't speak, only sob. "Neesie, what is it? Tell me. Are you hurt?"

She wiped her eyes with the back of her sleeve. She couldn't for the life of her speak above a whisper. "It's Carole," she sobbed.

"What about Carole?" he demanded.

"She's dead."

"Dead! How? When?"

With her heart leaden in her breast, she found she could talk a little then, but she gasped for breath. "I went to Pirate's Cave. She was to help me this morning and she didn't come. . . . I found her lying dead, I think, in the cave.

Luke, Marlon was there. He was bending over her body. He stood up when I rounded the corner.''

"Marlon?"

"Yes. His eyes were terrible. He looked at me and didn't see me at all."

"What did he say?"

"Nothing. He just looked at me. Luke, he was out of it. It was either drugs or some form of mental illness. Severe limbic rage could do that."

"My God!"

"I called 9-1-1 and the sheriff. They're coming out."

"Neesie?"

"Yes?"

"Lock yourself in carefully. Put on night security. I'll be there as quickly as I possibly can."

"Then your meeting's over?"

"Don't talk about meetings. You're what matters. The roads will be a bit slippery, but you sit tight. I'll be there shortly."

Within a half hour there was a knock on her door, and she looked out the window to see the sheriff's car pulled up in front of her house. A loud rap announced Sheriff Keyes. On trembling legs she went to the door and let him in.

"Afternoon, ma'am. I left a deputy up at the cave. The girl is dead. This is a mean one. Somebody was mad as hell."

She asked him to have a seat and told him about Marlon. He took a pipe without tobacco out of his pocket and clenched it between his teeth, then took it out and held it.

"Are you close to this boy? Any idea what he'd do in a bad situation?"

"I know he's sick. Luke and I have leaned on him to get treatment."

"Think he did it?"

"Oh Lord, I don't know. I hope in spite of the way it looks that he didn't."

"The boy is Dr. Jones's brother, am I right?"

"Yes. I love him as if he were my brother, too."

"It doesn't look good. You think he's crazy. Ah, yes, you mental health people don't like to call people crazy, but sometimes they are."

Annice smiled sadly. "What others call crazy, we call sick. So many can be treated if they'll let themselves be."

"And he so far won't let you treat him?"

"Not me. Not anyone. I'd like to go back to the cave."

"No, Dr. Steele. We found rescue workers there when we arrived. They were loading her onto a stretcher. She was dead all right. Nothing else you can do. You can't help her now. I put out a missing persons bulletin, as I told you. Off his rocker like he is, we'll get plenty of tips. We'll be taking him in, questioning him. Save your strength; you're going to need it."

Wringing her hands, Annice felt her throat constrict. "There's something else. Julius is her boyfriend and he manhandles her, but she didn't pay it much mind because he wanted to marry her."

"That Julius Thorne?"

"Yes, you've got a good memory."

"I remember seeing his name on our volunteer list. Some things we're trained to remember."

"And there's something else."

"Shoot."

"One of our security guards—well, she flirted with him. He's in his thirties, married, three children. . . ."

"Yes?"

"I walked up on them quarreling one afternoon at the side of this house. I couldn't determine what it was about, but he said he'd see her dead and in hell first."

"Well! How old is this guy, and the age of the girl?"

"Bill Sullivan is in his early or middle thirties. We can get his employment form if you need to know. Carole's just turned seventeen."

"I see, and you didn't see fit to call me about this?"

"I talked to her, told her to break off with him. Luke and I talked with him. He told us he valued his job and knew he'd been a fool messing around with 'jailbait' as he called it. I saw no more signs of this."

Sheriff Keyes rubbed his chin. "I hate to bad mouth, but the population of security guards and construction workers is overrepresented in the criminal population."

"I didn't know that. Other than that one transgression, he's always seemed like a fine person. Helpful."

"Yes, he could have *meant* he'd see her in hell. And he was fined once for possession of marijuana, but that was six years ago and he does seem to have cleaned up his act. Dr. Jones anywhere around?"

"He had an early morning meeting in D.C. I talked with him. He's on his way home."

"Good. You and he are going to be able to be a lot of help to me on this one."

"Because of Marlon? We don't know he did it."

He nodded. "You're right. Things aren't always what they seem. Is the boy an artist? Are those his paintings on the easel?"

"Yes, he goes there almost daily. Someone else could have killed her and he found the body."

"Possibly. He's a really talented artist. I think you and Dr. Jones had better get used to the fact that he may have killed her."

Chapter 22

Ralph Keyes had been sheriff for fifteen years and most felt he would retire from the job years later. Straitlaced and no-nonsense, he faced Annice and Luke in the police station hallway. Earlier, when Luke returned, he had called the sheriff and was asked to come in with Annice.

"I'm glad you got back, Dr. Jones," the sheriff said sadly. "This is a nasty business." He smiled at Annice. "Dr. Steele. We'll be questioning three people this afternoon: Julius Thorne, when we can find him. We've already got Mr. Sullivan. And with all the blood on him, I think your brother will be easy to pick up. We've already gotten a number of sighting calls."

Security guard Bill Sullivan sat in a windowless room, waiting to be questioned by Sheriff Keyes and one of his deputies, Teresa Drew. Slumped in his chair, he wondered how he was going to get out of this. When the sheriff's men had come for him, his wife had listened, then called him every name in the book. She said she was going to leave him; he had strayed on her for the last time.

In an adjoining room, Luke and Annice sat quietly. The sheriff wanted to talk with them after the interrogations.

"I can't begin to tell you how helpful I think you'll be to us," the sheriff said now. "Every day, you are with the people we're going to question, so you're likely to know when I tell you what they've said if they're lying or telling us the truth."

Luke's face was gray with strain. "I'm really scared for Marlon," Luke said as he and Annice sat down in the small, windowless interrogation room adjoining the one the sheriff was using.

Annice hadn't been able to stop her heart from thudding. Now she drew deep breaths and breathed out slowly, with a silent *Ha-a-a-a* to steady herself.

She and Luke sat side by side, wretched with sadness.

"Oh God, Luke," Annice finally said, "how could this happen?"

"I keep wondering the same thing."

In the interrogation room, Bill Sullivan's big body held a tense line. Sheriff Keyes led off. "How long have you been a security guard on the Casey's School campus?"

"Five years. I'm the lead officer."

"Hold up a minute. Glad you're here, Lieutenant Ryson."

Jon Ryson shook hands with Sheriff Keyes and gave his apology for being late. He had helped with a baby being delivered on a bus and had gotten mother and child to the hospital.

Sheriff Keyes plodded on. "You had a run-in with Ms. Cates in which you were overheard to tell her you'd see 'her dead and in hell first.' What did you mean?"

Bill Sullivan sat up straighter. "Well—ah—I guess I play around from time to time. You know men. I really liked this girl. I gave her money from time to time, good jewelry. She liked pretty things."

The sheriff pursed his lips. "You don't make a lot of money at Casey's School and you've got a wife and three children to support."

"My wife works. She's a telephone operator supervisor. She makes more than I do."

"Still," Sheriff Keyes pointed out, "living is expensive these days. Even with your wife's salary, three kids take a lot. I ought to know. I've got three."

"Yes sir, but we get by pretty well."

Jon Ryson cut in evenly. "Are you still using and selling marijuana?"

Bill Sullivan caught his breath, then shrugged. "Not selling. Using once in a while. Guess this is going to cost me my job. I promised the school people I wouldn't have anything to do with drugs. But you know how it is . . ." His voice trailed off.

"Did you supply the girl and other students with smokes—marijuana?" the sheriff asked.

"Carole, from time to time. Not too often. She begged for it."

"Were you and Miss Cates having an affair?" Jon Ryson asked.

Bill Sullivan's breath was harsh, labored. He laughed shortly. "I wanted to. She kept telling me she had a boyfriend, a jealous boyfriend, but hell, that didn't stop her from taking my money and my gifts. . . ."

"Did you kill her?" Jon Ryson asked.

"*No*!"

"When did you last see her?" Jon Ryson asked.

"Yesterday afternoon." Bill Sullivan's voice was growing fainter.

"What did you talk about?" Lieutenant Ryson asked.

"I asked her when. I've been getting horny. She was a hot piece and I wanted in. All my money down the drain. She was playing hard to get."

Jon Ryson looked at Sullivan narrowly. "Did you ever think of just letting her go? And how old are you, Mr. Sullivan?"

Bill Sullivan thought a long while. "I'm thirty-five. Thirty-six next March. And no, I didn't think of letting her go. I wanted this girl the way I've never wanted a woman in my life. Man, she set me on fire when I kissed her. . . ."

His face lit up as he talked and his eyes were shifty.

Jon Ryson sat forward. "Can you be specific about why you told her you'd see her dead and in hell first that day Dr. Steele saw you? She took your money, and . . .?"

Bill Sullivan clenched his fists. "She was driving me crazy. God, I've never felt like that in my life before. To tell you the truth, I *felt* like killing her a lot of times. She was playing me for a fool and laughing about it. She was putting out for the boyfriend, but not for me, but she was taking my money, my presents. . . ."

Annice remembered then that Carole had said she wasn't "putting out" for Sullivan.

Jon was smooth now, comforting as he spoke. "Were you perhaps so hurt that she was breaking off with you that you couldn't take her leaving? You hadn't gotten what you came for. Did she tell you she wouldn't see you again?"

"No! Hell no!" Bill Sullivan exploded. "Listen, I gave her a gold bangle bracelet she wanted. Set me back well over a hundred and fifty dollars. She took it and told me I was sweet. That was my Christmas present to her."

"Did she give you a present?" Detective Drew asked.

Bill Sullivan's voice was ragged, angry. "She never gave me nothing except a lot of hot kisses and I felt her up a lot. She seemed to like that. I met her in D.C. a few times when her boyfriend went home for long weekends. I rented a room in D.C.—a hotel room—all three times. She always said her period was on. I knew that couldn't always be the case. Still I waited."

Bill Sullivan seemed to be living out those times and he was agitated, squirming. "Could I have a glass of water?"

"Sure." Jon Ryson got up and poured him a glass of water from a pitcher on a sideboard, brought it back and handed it to him. He gulped it thirstily, took out a handkerchief and mopped his brow. It was hot in the room, and he sweated profusely under his wool flannel, red plaid shirt.

"Do you know how she died?"

"I know how I'd have done it if I'd done it. I'd wring her pretty neck." He looked directly at Jon as if he alone would understand. "Listen . . ." he said.

Jon spoke urgently. "Did you kill her, Officer Sullivan?"

"No. I swear I didn't."

"You had ample reason. She made a fool of you, took your money, laughed at you. Men have killed for less."

Bill Sullivan groaned. "I kept telling myself I was going to cut her loose. Who needed this crap? But I couldn't. God help me, *I couldn't let her go.*"

The man's voice had gone low, wretched, and he was crying tears of agony.

The interrogation lasted well over an hour and the two officers had wrung Officer Sullivan dry. Finally Sheriff Keyes nodded at his cohorts, then said to Officer Sullivan, "You can go home now. We don't have enough evidence to hold you, but we'll be on your back like husks on wheat if you're lying. Don't leave the area at all. We'll be questioning you again, calling you in again."

Bill Sullivan looked up as if he couldn't believe his luck. "Thank you," he choked. "I'm telling you the truth. I know myself and I know I could kill, but I didn't kill Carole. She was headed for harm. She got real pleasure out of hurting boys and men. She didn't give Thorne an easy time, but I guess she loved him the way she just didn't give a damn about me."

"Just a minute," Sheriff Keyes said. "How much do you know about her relationship with Julius Thorne?"

"Plenty," Sullivan blurted out. "Oh, she wouldn't talk much, but she told me she loved him, was going to marry him."

"And how did you feel about that?"

"I got a wife, so it was even-steven. But I'm lying. I didn't want her to get married. I wanted her for myself. A good man can handle several women. Folks in Africa and other countries have got the right idea. Let a man have as many women as he can take care of."

Deputy Sheriff Drew looked daggers at him and said, "Thank God for the United States."

Out in the station house anteroom, Leticia Sullivan waited alone for her husband. The sheriff grinned sourly. Sullivan and she had been in several times for domestic altercations.

"He's all yours," the sheriff told her. "Take him home."

The woman's gaze was cold, malignant. "I'm not sure," she said, "that he's still got a home."

Sitting in the small room, Luke and Annice looked at each other.

"Wonder what's going on with Sullivan," Luke said.

Annice shrugged. "He certainly seemed enraged enough the day I saw them talking."

Luke frowned. "Somehow, I always wondered about him. He seems shifty."

"Operating with hindsight, I'd say we should have fired him when we first knew he was fooling around with her." Annice felt angry, defensive about Carole and her reputation.

"We couldn't prove anything," Luke said. "He could have filed a humongous suit. As far as we know, he just flirted with the girls. No crime there."

The door opened and Sheriff Keyes came in with a quick knock. He closed the door and leaned against it. "They've brought your brother in."

Luke tensed. "How is he?"

"He seems no worse for wear. The officer who brought him in said he came meekly, didn't seem to know what was going on. Does he suffer from blackouts? Does he drink? Do drugs?"

Luke drew a deep breath. "Drugs and alcohol, so far as I know, he doesn't." Luke rubbed his knuckles. "He started having blackouts when our parents were killed in a plane crash over a year ago. The second time I've known him to black out was when his girlfriend was murdered in Ellisville, Louisiana. He was a suspect because he couldn't remember what happened after he saw her lying there. . . ."

"Now we've got a third blackout. He told the officer he'd blacked out, but that he came to himself when the officer picked him up."

"If he was blacked out a shorter time than the periods it happened before, maybe he's getting better."

"Lord, I sure hope so." Luke was sick with worry.

"We're going to question him a while after someone helps him get the blood off his face and hands. We'll take plenty of samples of the blood for DNA testing. We'll check for scratches—for everything. I think it will be best if we talk with him first, then you can speak with him."

"Sure," Luke responded.

Later, Sheriff Keyes reflected that it was at times like this that he hated his job. This young man could have been his child. "Son," the sheriff began, "it's plain to me you're feeling sick, but I've got to ask you a few questions."

"Yes, sir."

"When did you black out? Take your time answering."

Marlon thought a long minute. "When I saw her lying there, I—" His body was wracked in sobs then and his shoulders heaved.

The deputy sheriff got up, put her arms around Marlon and offered him Kleenex, which he clutched. With severe effort, Marlon forced himself to stop crying.

"When you saw Carole Cates lying there?" the sheriff asked.

"Yes, sir."

"Did you see or hear anybody else in the cave?"

"No. No one."

"What made you go back there?"

"Carole had promised to pose for me a little while before going on to help Neesie—Dr. Steele. She hadn't come and I thought she might be hiding back there to jump out at me for fun."

"You two played a lot then?"

"Yes, sir. She was fun. Sweet."

"You seem to have liked her a lot. Did you have a crush on her?"

"I really liked her, but she was Julius's girl. We'd quarreled once before over a girl who was murdered. Sylvie Love. My girl."

Marlon didn't cry then, but his face was a study in grief.

"How did you come to have so much of Carole's blood on you?"

"I don't know. I saw her lying there and I blacked out. I guess I put my face to her bloody chest. I couldn't take it. I had been painting a picture of her from a photograph."

"I see. Do you have a girlfriend now?"

"No."

"Did you want Carole for your girlfriend?"

"I liked her. I've never gotten over Sylvie. I didn't kill her, if that's what you're getting at, but . . ."

"But?" Sheriff Keyes looked at Marlon levelly.

"I don't know what I was going to say. My mind went blank again. Listen, sir, all I can say is I don't *remember* killing either girl, but I blacked out after seeing them. Maybe I blacked out and killed them, too, but I don't remember. I'd give anything if I did remember."

Listening, Sheriff Keyes found himself believing Marlon, but he had been fooled by liars before.

"We're going to be calling Louisiana," the sheriff said. "I'm going to let you clean up a bit more while I do it, then I'll question you again. Your brother and Dr. Steele are here. I want to talk with you some more before you see them."

"I don't want to talk with them, not now. What if I am a killer? Tell them to leave and please lock me up while I clear my mind, try to remember."

Sheriff Keyes nodded to an officer who stood near the door and the officer came and took Marlon's arm and led him away.

Sheriff Keyes went to tell Luke and Annice what Marlon

had said. Luke took Annice in his arms. "Steady, sweet-heart," he said sadly. "He'll change his mind about seeing us."

"Marlon's hurt," Annice said to Luke as he stroked her arm. "He's like a beaten infant who understands nothing that's going on around him. He's crazy with fear. No wonder he doesn't want to see us. Luke?"

"Yes?"

"Marlon's just got to let me or someone talk with him."

"What would you use, truth serum?"

"Not at first. I'm a conservative psychologist. I really believe in the talking cure. It's difficult and it takes time, but I think it works."

"He doesn't even want to *see* us now, let alone talk."

"I'll plead with him."

"And I'll help you."

"We've got to pray the way we've never prayed before."

The sheriff came back in. "I talked with a Detective Duchamps in Ellisville," he said. "Marlon told us what happened there. Detective Duchamps believes Marlon and thinks he really *is* blacking out. What do you think so far?"

Luke shook his head slowly. "I don't know what to think. He's the brother I love and I can't see his killing, but he doubts himself. Sheriff, Marlon draws sketches of people close to him who've died. . . ."

"That explains it. He asked for some paper to sketch on, said he was an artist."

"Can you see your way clear to letting him have it? Maybe one day he'll come to remember from the painting and sketching."

"We're going to have to book him, but he can get out on bail."

Luke's face was a study in despair as the sheriff went out.

The sheriff questioned Marlon for nearly a half hour, then told him he could have paper to sketch on if he would talk to Luke and Annice first.

Marlon looked hesitant. "Why would they even want to see me? It looks like I'm a bad seed."

"A lot has happened to you," the sheriff said. "Give yourself the benefit of the doubt."

Jon Ryson had not spoken during Marlon's interrogation, but he had listened intently, his eyes half closed, a look of deep intelligence and compassion playing about his face. Finally he spoke. "So you think you may have killed Carole Cates?"

"Oh God, I don't know. Why can't I remember?"

"When your parents died and you blacked out the first time, did you ever remember how you felt?" John Ryson asked.

"Yeah," Marlon answered without hesitation. "I had painted them. I paint everybody. After I came to the first time when Sylvie died, I sketched furiously. I was trying to sketch them dead so I'd know they were dead and I'd stop pretending they were still alive."

Jon Ryson nodded. "And with Sylvie Love?"

"In jail, they let me have paper and a pen and watched me while I sketched."

"And did you remember how she died?"

"No. Never. I walked in, saw her dead body and it was like it was this time—my face and my hands and clothes full of blood." His anguished cry was a plea to heaven. "Oh God! Why can't I *remember?*"

Jon Ryson seemed to have brought out powerful feelings that Sheriff Keyes had been unable to bring out.

In a few minutes, a light rap sounded and Sheriff Keyes and Jon Ryson brought Marlon into the room with Luke and Annice. They both stood up. Marlon seemed to hold his breath as he looked from one to the other. Finally he went to Annice and buried his head on her shoulder. "Neesie, please help me," he said brokenly. "If I go through this again, I couldn't stand it and I can't stand hurting other people like this."

Chapter 23

Later that same afternoon, at her house, Annice and Luke sat together on the couch. Sheriff Keyes had asked them to come back when Julius's father, Judge Thorne, arrived.

"You can help me gauge who's telling the truth and who's not," he'd said again.

Now Annice faced a task she dreaded. She had discussed it with Luke. Slowly she began to dial Carole's mother's number. On the fourth ring, a grumpy, high-pitched female voice answered.

"May I speak with Mrs. Cates?"

"You *are* speaking to Mrs. Cates."

Annice cleared her throat. "I call with terribly sad news. I think you'll probably need to sit down."

"If it's about Carole, I've had bad news about that girl before. Shoot."

"Mrs. Cates, Carole was murdered early this morning."

"Like hell! She always got in trouble, but she always got out."

"I'm sorry."

There was a long pause, then Annice said softly, "Mrs. Cates? Are you all right?"

There was hesitation before the woman answered. "I guess you could say I'm all right. Carole's the one who's in trouble. They know who did it?"

"Not yet."

"She was always headed for trouble. I knew something bad had to happen to her. She was so fast. She was after all my boyfriends and lying and saying they were after her. Well, I guess I'm sorry, but something was bound to happen that wasn't good. You shipping her home? I'll need to be burying her."

"I loved your daughter, Mrs. Cates. I'm the psychologist here at Casey's School and she helped me around the house. I thought the world of her."

The woman's laugh was short, mirthless. "You just hadn't come to know her. You didn't say when you're sending her home."

"Not until the medical examiner has made his findings. It may take a while."

"Well whenever. The only child I ever gave birth to and she's been a real disappointment. Well, I guess none of us make our own lives. Things just happen and there's nothing we can do about it."

"She was a beautiful girl."

"Don't say that. Too many men've told her that already. Lord, you don't know what a handful that girl was. Maybe she's better off. She wasn't headed for nothing but grief on this earth. And yeah, she gave me a lot of grief. Maybe she and me can rest in peace now."

"I'll keep in touch. Let me give you my numbers where I can be reached and call, please call, if any of us here at Casey's School can help in any way."

"Why, thank you. I appreciate your offer. And miss, don't you worry too much about Carole Cates. Some people are put on this earth to make things hard for other people the way I guess she was here to make my life a mess."

"I'm sorry." It was all Annice could think of to say. Then, "I'd like to come to her funeral. I and one or two others."

"Well, sure, if her body ever makes it home. My husband left me, but they sent him home for me to bury. She always said she wanted to be buried by his side. I'll call you when I've made all the arrangements to bury her. It'll be a while. I've got a sister sick in Alaska who was fond of Carole. She'll want to come. Give her time to recover. I thank you. I really thank you for being so kind."

They said good-bye then and Annice was left thinking: *You're thanking me for being kind? You and somebody else certainly hadn't been kind to Carole.*

Late that afternoon Judge Thorne came in on a corporate jet from New Orleans and immediately visited the sheriff's office. Seated across from the sheriff, and side by side with Jon Ryson, Julius looked frightened. Luke and Annice surmised that Judge Thorne would be in one of the smaller rooms. The sheriff and Lieutenant Ryson expertly interrogated a trembling Julius.

"You and Miss Cates were pretty close. Were you lovers?" the sheriff asked.

"Yes," Julius said without hesitation.

"Did you maybe get mad and kill her?" the sheriff continued.

"No. I'd never."

"Julius," Jon Ryson began, "we're told you manhandled Carole Cates, roughed her up, bruised her."

"She liked it," Julius said defiantly. "It turned her on."

Jon Ryson felt a ball of anger tighten in his belly. Punks who beat women were on the bottom of any scale he knew.

"I think you mean you got your kicks that way," Ryson shot back. "She was talking about breaking up with you. What happened?"

Julius gloated then. "I asked her to marry me. That leaves me home free."

"And were you serious?" the sheriff asked.

"Maybe. Maybe not." Julius shrugged. "I've got a ring for her."

"So she changed her mind. Does your father know you were going to give her this ring?"

"Hell no! He's going to hit the roof when he finds out." He hunched his shoulders then. "But you know, I may have been going to marry her. She made things real good for me, but she couldn't stop flirting, flirting with other men."

"Marlon?"

"Yeah, Marlon. It's a funny thing. In Ellisville, where I was in school before I came here, Marlon's girl flirted with me. Then my girl flirted with him."

"Were you angry? Did you read her the riot act?"

"You mean . . . oh, did I get after her? I gave that chick hell." He seemed to loosen up then and he smiled. "Marlon Jones and I were once the best of friends."

Jon Ryson cut in quickly. "She flirted with Bill Sullivan, too, didn't she? Did that make you lose it?"

Julius spread his hands wide. "Carole flirted with everybody. A telephone pole. Anything. Anybody. I don't think she could help it."

"Let me put a scenario out to you," Sheriff Keyes said slowly. "Bill Sullivan is a grown man. He was moving in on your turf and she liked it. . . ."

"He's a married man," Julius scoffed, "with three crumb crushers."

"Men with even more children sometimes play around. She could have been in love with him the way young women sometimes fall for older men. You don't like losing, Thorne. You're controlling, manipulative."

"You don't know me."

"But a few others do."

Julius looked at the floor then. "I'd never kill her. Maybe I wouldn't have really married her, but I loved her."

"So much you weren't about to lose her? If you couldn't have her, nobody could?"

"I didn't kill my chick. You're barking up the wrong tree."

"And maybe you're just not telling the truth," Jon Ryson pointed out. "You're strong, Julius, very strong. You've got washboard abs and great, big, rippling muscles. You were in Ellisville when Sylvie Love was killed. Now Carole. You liked both girls. The bodies of both women were badly beaten, but not the face. And they were beaten after they died. Did the two young women do something to you to make you so mad?"

"Nope. You're both barking up the wrong tree. My old man didn't want me questioned without a lawyer, but I said go ahead. Doesn't that tell you I'm not guilty?"

There was a scuffle outside the door before it burst open and the portly Judge Thorne came in with a smaller, waspish, middle-aged man.

"His lawyer's here," Judge Thorne yelled. "How a son of mine would be a big enough fool to let you question him without a lawyer is beyond me. But attorney Sills is here now and I demand that he be allowed to come in."

"Judge Thorne." The sheriff got up, his eyes keen and sad. "Your son is eighteen. He gave us permission to question him without a lawyer because he said he has nothing to hide. Why do you object?"

"His lawyer is here." The judge introduced the round-shouldered, frail-looking man.

"And we're glad," Sheriff Keyes said. "If you'll excuse yourself, we'll proceed with the questioning."

Judge Thorne was escorted out by a young officer and the questioning was again undertaken with Sheriff Keyes rocking back and forth in his chair before he began. "So *you gave the girl a ring* and may or may not have wanted to marry her?"

The lawyer gave a brief gasp. "Don't answer that, Julius. That's a leading question."

Julius was silent, looking down, then he blurted out, "I got nothing to hide. Why don't you let me answer?"

Sheriff Keyes smiled. "You seem to be a forthright young man."

And Julius sat thinking: *Of all the damn-fool luck.* The lawyer would tell his father about him wanting to marry Carole and there would be hell to pay. His father would never let him forget what a fool he was.

Sheriff Keyes warmed up again. "So you fought a lot with Carole?"

"Don't answer that." The lawyer shot forward. "That doesn't mean he killed her."

"I never said it did," Sheriff Keyes said mildly.

"She was beaten," Jon Ryson said. "You were known to like pummeling your friends for fun. Maybe you do it when you get mad, too. You're strong. You could get the best of most people."

The lawyer glared at Sheriff Keyes then at Jon Ryson.

Finally the sheriff said, "Well, it looks like there's not going to be much we can ask you, Julius. This may all just have to come out in a court."

"Where's the evidence you're going to take him to court on?"

"That will come later." Sheriff Keyes breathed deeply. "We're not trying to punish the innocent, only the guilty."

Julius breathed deeply now, his confidence returning. He liked his scrappy little lawyer. He felt grown-up, having a lawyer defend him, work on his side. He liked the idea of doing something and getting off scot-free. He was Judge Thorne's son, and to him all good things should come.

At home that night, Luke saw Annice in and looked around. It was early. He thought about it a while before he asked, "Are you getting over Calico?"

Annice hesitated. "I think so. Why do you ask?"

"Just curious. You two had quite a bond."

"Tell me about it." She laughed shakily. His eyes on her were loving, tender.

"Think you're ready for another companion?"

"Another cat? I don't know."

"You could try another pet. A dog. A parrot. You could try goldfish, a big tank."

"Soon. It's so sweet of you to ask. Carole felt so guilty that she let Calico escape."

"Carole felt guilty about living."

Annice thought a moment. "And talking with her mother today, I think I know why." They sat on the couch and she moved over to him, threw herself into his arms. "Luke, I wanted your baby so bad. I'd be a good mother. I'd raise a healthy child."

Luke's heart tore up. Would he ever be able to make her understand? He thought she would have accepted it by now, that her life would be ruined with the burden of Marlon on her shoulders. He wasn't going to do that to her.

She was curiously angry with him. What if he simply didn't want her and didn't know it? There was always Claire in the background. They had known each other for ages.

Suddenly she felt unbearably tired.

He let his lips brush her cheek and squeezed her shoulders.

"I'm very tired," she said. "I want to go to bed early. We've got hard days ahead."

He looked puzzled. "I thought you'd want me to spend the night. So much has happened."

She shook her head. "My tormenter seems to have let up for the time being, so I'm safe enough. Get some rest, sweetheart, and I'll see you tomorrow."

He got up reluctantly. "You and Claire and I will convene the students left on campus tomorrow morning at ten. We'll talk to them as a whole, then in small groups and individually if they need it. I'm still letting this through my mind. I still don't altogether believe it."

"It's even worse for me. We were getting to be so close. Where would we meet, Luke? We can do it here."

"Doc's house is best. More room. I hate leaving you here alone, love."

"I'll be all right. Go on. Get some rest."

Nearly a half hour after Luke left, Annice sat on the sofa, breathing shallowly. She started to get up when the doorbell rang. She frowned thinking she should have put the night security on. Walking slowly to the door, she turned on the porch light and looked through the viewfinder. Velma and Arnold stood there as she flung the door open and hugged them with relief.

"You're here alone?" Arnold asked.

"Luke just left. What brings you by? I'm so glad to see you."

"We were out walking for fresh air," Velma responded. "When I talked with you earlier, you said you and Luke were going to the sheriff's office."

Velma and Annice sat on the sofa and Arnold settled down in a nearby recliner. She was tired and it took a few minutes for Annice to marshal her thoughts. Finally, she was able to tell them what she and Luke had been a part of at the sheriff's office. When she had finished, they were both silent.

Arnold breathed a harsh sigh and shook his head. "I've talked to people around here all day. Nothing like this has ever happened before."

"Carole may have been a bit flighty, but she had good stuff in her," Velma said. "She surely didn't deserve this." Then, "Is Marlon going to stay in jail? Are you and Luke going to let him do that to himself?"

"He's eighteen. We don't know, he doesn't know if he did it. He's suffering past trauma as well as this. He doesn't trust himself."

She told them then bits and pieces of Marlon's past trauma,

something she had not done before. When she had finished, Velma sighed. "The poor kid, and I call him kid, even if he is a young man now."

Arnold cleared his throat. "Neesie, do you still think about finding your biological parents?"

Annice looked up, startled. "Sometimes." She frowned. "It just seems to me that Mama's face clouds over when I talk about it, even if she does encourage me to do it. I guess I will. I want to do it. Why do you ask?"

"Well," Velma answered, "I know how fond you were of Carole, how you often said you'd like a daughter like her. Of course, you're too young to be her mother, but if you were a few years older and she a few years younger— you were becoming closer to her. She told me she listened to you."

Annice bitterly asked herself the question: Did Carole listen? Did her past pain make it impossible for her to hear or know what was best for her? She was too busy striking out, getting revenge.

"I'm glad if she listened," Annice said quietly, "but I guess I didn't come into her life early enough."

The three people in the room were sad then—reflecting, remembering. Velma stirred, sat up. "Honey, I guess we'd better be going. I don't like your being alone here, Neesie, even if I know how brave you are. Any more trouble?"

"No. Maybe the perpetrator had other fish to fry."

"I would bet on it," Arnold said staunchly. "Neesie, we can wait a bit and you can pack a bag, spend a few days with us. I'm old, but I'm pretty fit. I could protect you both."

Annice smiled. "Thank you so much, but I just sent Luke home. He wanted to spend the night. I've got good security and I'm not afraid once I get in the house. I think whoever it is will be lying low for at least a little while."

"Well, I sure hope you're right. Between drugs and insanity, and no attempt to really treat either one, we've made ourselves quite a world these days."

"You're right," Annice told him.

After the Johnsons left, Annice walked about the house slowly, surprised to find that she wanted to be alone. She had been busy since she'd found Carole dead and Marlon bending over her. Now alone for the first time, she couldn't erase that picture from her mind. The white sheet of paper beside the body heralding *Angel face, Devil body*. But in death, Carole had not looked like an angel. The expression on her face was one of anguish and terror, even in the dimlit cave.

She drew water in the tub, and sprinkled in epsom salts and bergamot bath oil. Letting her clothes fall into a heap, she stepped into the tub. Sliding down, she was in water up to her neck and a welcome sense of torpor filled her. There would be no easy healing from this. The pain with Luke had already left her raw; this was exacerbated grief. The house was quiet. She wanted no music. She thought then how Calico would come into the bathroom with her and lie stretched out on the floor watching her, being her companionable cat self.

She stayed in the tub until the water had cooled too much, then got out and enveloped herself in a huge, white bath towel. Walking to the kitchen, she made herself a cup of valerian tea and drank it. Then slipping into a flannel-lined nightgown, she walked about the house again, looking at familiar items. In the kitchen, she thought, *there's the door Calico had gone through for independence and escape. Am I ready for another cat? Another pet?* She couldn't decide.

In bed she was tired beyond what she had expected and switching off the table lamp, she fell fast asleep in a very little while. Her first sleep was dreamless, but toward morning, a savaged Carole came toward her in the cave. Her blood was everywhere and she held out her hands to Annice, crying, "Help me! Oh God, please help me!"

Annice sat up quickly. Her breath came in gasps and her skin was cold and clammy. She was screaming, "Carole!" and the sounds reverberated throughout the house. Her throat was bone dry. The dream had been terrifying enough, but had she heard something else? She listened intently. No. Nothing.

She didn't want the lights on again. She had put on night security. Now she got up, went to the control panels in the dining room and checked them. They were fine. Her legs felt weak as she thought about the dream.

Going to the back window of her bedroom, she opened the blinds and looked out into the dark. Something drew her, some fear as old as time. She looked into the darkness faintly lighted by front streetlights and a light by the kitchen door.

At first she couldn't believe what she saw—a black-garbed figure, as still as death, stared malignantly at her. A backdrop of holly trees shielded the figure and she certainly couldn't see it plainly, but she *felt* the malice, the danger. She gazed at the figure in front of the holly trees in the thirty or so feet of space between her window and the yard fence; she heard the harsh crowing, then crazy laughter, then a devil's shrill whistling. A light wind carried all that malignancy on the night air.

She felt cold and lifeless, as if her blood had congealed in her body, as she put her hand up to close the blinds. But she stood transfixed, as if by standing still she could conjure up the creature's face, make it known to her and drive it out of her life.

After what seemed eons of time, she drew the blinds and got back in bed. She couldn't think. Should she call Luke? No, with what he was going through seeking funds from foundations, and Marlon, he had his hands full. Parents were going to be looking to him for answers. She felt secure in the house, but she got up again. She had a small flashlight in the night table drawer. She reached in and got it, put it beside the bed. Then, she felt in the nightstand drawer for the small .22 gun Jon Ryson had gotten her. The lock was on. It would only take a second to push it off.

There. She was warming up a bit now. Fortified, she drew deep breaths, filled her lungs with air, then said, "Ah-h-h-h" as she breathed out. Only then did she look at her radial dial that registered two o'clock. She couldn't stop listening as she got back into bed and huddled under the covers, but the sound had stopped completely. Closing her eyes, she fought valiantly to make it through until morning.

Chapter 24

"We are gathered here this morning to mourn the passing of one of our own, dearly beloved Carole Cates."

Annice's voice was hushed with grief. One of the female students sobbed loudly. They were in Dr. Casey's house that Luke had taken over for the year. Students who had stayed on campus for the holidays crowded the living room, parlor, library and dining room. Luke and Claire Manton stood nearby, ready to help.

"The police are working closely with us and I want to warn you to be careful," Luke said. "Carole was murdered yesterday as I'm sure you know. But don't let fear overrule your mind. Be ever watchful."

Annice said other things, lending comfort. Then Luke spoke again to reassure them, and Claire Manton lent what comfort she should. Usually a fashion plate, she was now plainly dressed in chocolate-colored wool.

When the three had finished, the questions began. They answered as best they could.

"I hear they're holding Marlon," one of the male students said.

"He *chose* to stay in jail," Luke answered tersely. "He hasn't been charged."

"Why would he do that? Did he kill her?"

The room was silent for a while before Luke answered. "We don't know the answer to that. We don't know that he did or he didn't. We hope it's the latter."

"Will we be able to see her body?" Calvin's reedy voice sounded strained.

"No," Luke answered. "She'll be sent home from the medical examiner's office. The funeral will be in her hometown."

The students were full of other questions until Luke cut the question session short and suggested that they spend the rest of the time telling what Carole had meant to their lives.

One bass-voiced youth opened up. "She was such a pretty chick," he offered. "Always smiling, alive, on the ball, a winner. She was a star! She always had a smile for me, for everyone. Gee, she was great."

Calvin stood up, trembling, his body swaying as if in a high wind. He braced himself to make a little speech, but his dry throat closed. "I miss you, my friend," he finally said brokenly. "I really miss you."

He hunched down then on the floor and buried his face in his hands.

Most of the students said something kind, flattering, but one girl stood up declaring, "Some say Carole was fast and I don't know about that, but she didn't deserve to die. We all get lost sometimes. I'm sorry, real sorry."

Julius stood up and Annice noticed that his father was with him. The older man looked around him, frowning.

"Carole was my main squeeze, as you all know," Julius said. "She was beginning to be everything to me. We were . . ." He stopped, shrugging, and sat down. His father looked at him sharply.

The meeting took a little over an hour, ending with Luke telling them, "The police will get to the bottom of this. Be of good faith. My door, Dr. Steele's door and Ms. Manton's door will be open to you if you need to talk, and pray as you've never prayed before.''

He led them in the Lord's Prayer and a special prayer. When he finished the room was hushed, still. They had lost a friend, but God was theirs forever.

As the students filed out, Judge Thorne came to Annice and Luke. ''I wish you could lean on the sheriff to let my boy spend what's left of the holidays with me.''

''I can see where he would want to stay here,'' Luke told him.

''*Want* to stay?'' Judge Thorne barked. ''The sheriff forbade him to leave. I'm going to have to ask you to look out for him, Dr. Jones. I'm sitting on an important case, so I can't stay. Killing isn't in Julius. I believe in him all the way, and I hope you do too.''

''We are innocent until we're proven guilty.'' Claire spoke up and was rewarded with a wide smile from Judge Thorne.

''Actually,'' the judge said thoughtfully, ''the girl's death may mean my son's life.''

''What do you mean?'' Annice asked.

''My lawyer tells me he wanted to marry this little . . .'' He broke off, frowning, then resumed. ''If that had happened, his life would have been ruined. Things sometimes happen for the best. It's a shame she had to be murdered though.''

''Yes, it's a terrible shame,'' Annice cut in, disliking Judge Thorne.

''Dad, please.'' Julius had come up.

''Well, it's true,'' Judge Thorne said. ''You'd better worry about your own hide. If you're not careful, they'll have *your* ass in jail.'' He turned to Annice, Luke and Claire, thanking them for their courtesy. ''I'll be going now. I just stopped by to give my regards and ask you to be sure to look out for my son. He's got a head like a rock and hates taking good advice.''

In a short while, the students, Judge Thorne and Claire had left. Luke and Annice were alone. He thought she looked so strained and sought to comfort her. As they stood in the living room, he took her in his arms and held her close. Her body against his was softly firm; her heart beat heavily. He wanted her so. He needed the warmth of her loins and it sent blood surging throughout his body. And her body was heavy with longing to have him inside her.

Luke smiled grimly when he told her, "We want to make love because it's the life in us recoiling from death. Thanatos—death—and Eros—life. God, Neesie, I love you so. Why did this have to happen?"

He loosened his hold on Annice then and she told him, "At least Marlon is ready to talk with me. I've arranged for him to go in for testing for limbic rage tomorrow morning. And, as you know, he's agreed to open out to me. To talk. . . ."

"At least we'll know, one way or another," Luke said. If the outcome was negative, he didn't know how he would stand it.

The doorbell rang then and Luke's housekeeper answered. Belle spoke from the foyer and came forward.

"After you called yesterday," Belle said, "I made my Dad drive me in as soon as he could. Lord, Dr. Steele, Dr. Jones, I still can't believe it. They still don't know who did it?"

"No," Annice said. "It's early."

The housekeeper took Belle's outer garments and Annice smiled at the truly attractive young woman Belle had become.

"You're looking very well," Luke told Belle. "What a metamorphosis."

Belle smiled wanly. "That's me, larva to butterfly. And it's all due to Dr. Steele and Carole." She brushed tears from her eyes with the back of her sleeve. Annice pulled out a drawer of an end table and handed her a box of Kleenex.

The housekeeper came back. "There're a few things I need to talk with you about, Dr. Jones," she said. "It won't take long."

When Annice and Belle were alone, Belle said slowly, "I'm torn up about this. I came back because I wanted to talk to you face-to-face. I know a few things that might help."

"Oh?"

Belle wrung her hands. "The night before I left to go home for Christmas, Carole and I talked a long time. She told me she had talked to you and she was going to follow your advice."

"About?"

"About letting Julius go and flirting and being so fast."

"She told me she was going to marry Julius," Annice said.

Belle shook her head. "She just hadn't made up her mind. Carole wasn't about to let you or anybody tell her what to do. She was slacking off from Julius, so you made a difference. She just wasn't ready to let you know you did."

"Thank you for telling me this."

"Another thing that might be helpful to the police. Carole had three letters on her dresser top addressed to Marlon, Julius and that clown, Bill Sullivan. Bill's letter was in a medium-size manila envelope. The other two envelopes were plain legal size. She asked me to read them. I did."

Annice's breath shallowed. She fervently wished for useful clues.

"The one to Marlon was the shortest. I remember it almost word for word, just that she liked him so much and he had been such a friend. I read the one to Julius. She told him she was breaking off and *she enclosed a beautiful diamond ring* in a little manila envelope."

"And Officer Sullivan's letter?"

"Yeah. It was longer, angrier. She apologized for leading him on saying she didn't always act the way she should. There was a nifty gold bangle bracelet in the envelope. She told him to go back to his wife and be happy because she was turning over a new leaf."

Belle looked at the floor for a long time, remembering.

Tears stood in her eyes. "We hugged and we both cried. She told me the rest of this school session and the next were going to be so different for her. Did you know she had a crush on Marlon?"

"I thought so."

"But she said she wasn't going to shinny up to him. That's the word she used. She was going to take it slow. 'Dr. Steele talks about my psyche all the time,' she told me. 'Well, I'm going to turn my psyche around the way you've all turned me around physically. Are you with me, girl-friend?'"

Belle's voice was hoarse with grief. "I told her I was with her. That we were friends for life."

Annice thought quickly that Julius had said he was *going* to give Carole an engagement ring. Why would he lie?

Annice shook her head for a long while, reflecting on the enigma that had been Carole. Lovely. Changing. Getting on with a different life. And now—*dead.*

Chapter 25

By eight o'clock the next morning at Georgetown University Hospital, Marlon lay prepped and ready for his examination for the presence of limbic rage. As they wheeled him on the gurney into the examination room, Annice walked along.

"Relax," she told him, although she was nearly as anxious as he was.

"Don't worry, I'll be a good patient."

"Dr. Steele?"

Annice turned to find a tall, smiling red-haired man who held out his hand. As they shook hands, he introduced himself. "I'm Dr. John Ware, brain surgeon, and I'll be monitoring Marlon's tests."

"I've heard a lot about your expertise," she said.

He reddened. "Well, I do try rather hard."

"For which I'm grateful. I'll just walk around, visit the cafeteria and go to your library."

"Good deal. This is going to take about three hours and I'll give you the preresults as soon as they're done. It will take about a week for tests to go through channels, but I'll be able to tell you something this morning.''

He moved away and Annice leaned forward toward the glass panels as orderlies were helping Marlon off the gurney onto the testing table and under the machines that would tell his story.

Sighing, she turned away. Call Luke? No, there was nothing to tell yet and he had so much to do. Trips back and forth to New York to the Sunderlin Foundation, other fundraising. And his mind was full of Carole's murder. Strange, she thought how when something like this happened, you went along for brief spells and your life went on as usual. Then it hit you, floored you, and your heart was like lead.

She spent nearly an hour in the cafeteria reading the *Washington Post* and drinking three cups of coffee.

She glanced around her. Doctors, nurses, orderlies, and visitors filed in and out. A table near her emptied four times as she sat. Then, gathering her things, she left for the spacious library.

Settling back into a comfortable chair, she began to read a copy of the *American Journal of Psychiatry*. A librarian who hadn't been at her desk when Annice passed, came to her.

''Ma'am. Do you have an ID?''

Annice nodded and reached into her handbag for her driver's license and her American Psychological Association card. The librarian smiled. ''Enjoy,'' she said quietly and went back to her desk.

Annice went through the magazine, then got up and selected a copy of *Psychology Today*. She didn't want more material on limbic rage. She just wanted to know the results. She forced herself to breathe deeply, but it was hard. Somehow, she just felt in her bones that something was wrong with Marlon. And she and Luke were never going to be right again.

Getting up and going out into the hall, she called Luke on impulse and he answered the first ring.

"How are you, my love?" he asked her.

"Ask me that question a little while later."

"Is my brother being tested even as we speak?"

"Yes. Luke, I'm on edge. I can barely wait. The doctor will be able to give me likely results before we leave."

"That's great, or at least I hope it is. Either way, we'll know."

"Yes. I love you."

"How can you help it? The way I love you demands your response."

"Luke, we're not out of the woods yet, but I love you so much. Try to remember that when you're making up your mind."

She spent the rest of the morning in the library and walking around outside on the beautiful campus. Students milled about, causing her to recall her student days there. Had she ever been that young? It hit her with a rush when she had met Luke, who had been visiting a friend on the weekend. They had known almost immediately that they were for each other and had lit up the sky with their love. She had been a senior and he had been earning his doctorate from Columbia University.

Now everything hinged on Marlon. Everything. She couldn't stop Luke from feeling that if Marlon was guilty, he wasn't going to let her ruin her life by marrying him, Luke, but she knew better. Some loves transcend everything. That was the kind of love she knew.

She felt light-headed by the time she went back to the testing room anteroom and sat down. Dr. Ware came by in a short while and she couldn't read his face until he said, "Good news, Dr. Steele. Marlon has no trace of limbic rage. In fact, I find his brain wonderfully healthy. I should be so fortunate."

She could have wept with relief as she thanked him.

"Thank God, not me. I went in with great trepidation when you told me a bit about his background. Now, with those actions, I'm sure he has some emotional problems, but the ball is in your court for helping him.''

They shook hands again and he turned and went back into the testing room.

In the car, Marlon was silent as Annice drove along the Baltimore-Washington Parkway.

''I'm so glad you don't have limbic rage.''

Marlon shrugged. ''I'm not out of the woods yet. I still don't remember things, no matter how I wrack my brain. Neesie, let's get started right away—this afternoon. I want an end to this. I'm in a panic. It's killing me.''

''Take care,'' Annice said sharply. ''You've got to relax. We can stop by my office and begin. We'll have hour-long sessions twice a day. I may try individual marathon treatment techniques. They've worked when time is so important. What I want from you is that you give it your all.''

''You haven't got a thing to worry about. I promise. Neesie, I'm asking you in advance. Can you forgive me if I killed them?''

The question took Annice unawares. ''Marlon,'' she said finally, ''I love you as if you were my brother. I'll never turn my back on you.''

''OK,'' he said as he nodded his head. He didn't miss the fact that she hadn't said she would forgive him. She had said she loved him and that was going to have to be enough.

As they neared the administration building, they saw Luke walking ahead and Annice honked her horn. He turned around and came back to them.

Annice parked, and she and Marlon both got out of the car quickly and met Luke on the sidewalk.

''Oh Luke,'' she exclaimed. ''Wonderful news.''

''How can you know so soon?''

''A great doctor took it upon himself to let us know.''

The three hugged each other before Marlon's face clouded over. ''There're other things ahead of me.''

''But this is a big step out of the woods,'' Luke said staunchly.

"We're going to get started early this afternoon with Marlon."

Luke's love shone as he looked at his brother. "Give it your all, bro," he said. "Believe in yourself as we believe in you. Whatever happens, I'll never turn my back on you."

Marlon smiled a little. Luke and Annice had used the same phrase.

By two that afternoon, Annice had hung her *In Session* sign on her office door. Marlon lay on an oatmeal-colored couch and Annice sat behind him. It was a favorite stance with many psychiatrists. Most present-day psychologists eschewed this method, but she liked it for difficult cases like Marlon's. When you weren't so aware of another person, you spoke more freely, felt more relaxed. It was a Freudian-based belief.

She set a fresh box of Kleenex on the couch by his hand as he lay there, his eyes closed.

"How about hypnosis?" he asked. "How about truth serum?"

Annice reflected a few moments. "In due time, maybe," she said. "I want to try as much of this as I can. You're afraid of losing control, Marlon. This way, you won't feel in as much danger."

"Luke took me to a psychiatrist in New Orleans after our parents died. I only went twice. He said I was the most resistant person he'd ever seen."

Annice said swiftly, "I wouldn't consider twice enough to make such a judgment. Let's both just *trust* your resistance."

"Hey, I like that. Where do you want me to start?"

"Wherever you want to start."

Marlon was silent for five minutes, his eyes closed, visions that had plagued him for the past two and a half years swarming his brain like angry bees. *I have to remember!*

The words poured out of him then as his tongue tripped over itself. He sat up abruptly. "I see something that isn't coming clear. Two bodies together in a morgue. Dad and Mom. Another body at a later time. Then another body. I want to run. I've got to run. I've done something horrible. If I killed them, I don't remember. . . .''

The tears came then, great gasping sobs of fear and anxiety. The sobs were jerking him around; he couldn't stop and he was losing it. There was no one else here but him and Neesie. What if he killed her too? The thought was too much. It brought him back to reality. His face wet with tears, his countenance bedraggled, he told her, ''For God's sake, Neesie, let's stop now. I feel like I'm dying.''

''You're not dying, but if you want to stop.''

He stiffened. ''No, let's go on. You talked about an individual marathon. Let's go for it!''

They worked for another hour and Marlon was exhausted. Annice closed her eyes and leaned back. Marlon was more relaxed after ventilating so much anger. She glanced at her watch. Three-thirty, and she was late for an errand she wanted to run. It got dark fast in winter.

''Thank you, Neesie,'' Marlon told her as she ended the session. ''I feel better facing what's happened. Will you see me tomorrow?''

''Every day for a couple of hours—psychological hours of fifty minutes. You're off to a great start. Let's keep the momentum going, but don't be surprised at setbacks and don't let them get you down.''

Carrying her purse and a large tote, she walked swiftly to Pirate's Cave, surveying the scene when she reached it. Police yellow tape stretched across the opening. She wasn't supposed to go in, but she felt compelled. There was something she had to find. Police were busy these days and they missed important clues.

Annice smiled sadly. If she hadn't decided to be a psychologist, she would have chosen being a private investigator. Actually there were so many similarities. Both required careful listening, keen vision and hearing. A deep belief in justice.

She ducked under the tape and went inside. Someone had continued to keep the cave lit. Had Marlon come back since the day before? His easel was empty, but the big, locked box that held his painting paraphernalia hadn't been moved. She walked on.

What was she looking for? Going into a darker back room, she took out her flashlight. At first she didn't—couldn't—look at the room to her right, but she forced herself and saw the chalked outline of the space where Carole's body had lain. She needed a larger flashlight to see clearly into the corners.

She was numb now, the way Marlon must be. If she couldn't help him . . . but at least he was trying.

She ran the beam of the flashlight over the walls. Nothing seemed different. Then she remembered a space behind a ledge where Marlon had laughingly told her Carole and Julius left notes for each other. There was the edge of something different there as she carefully searched, and walking over she discovered a nine-by-twelve manila envelope. It was addressed simply to "Bill."

She wouldn't open it, but would turn it over to the sheriff or Jon Ryson. Holding the flashlight she pulled the envelope free and put it in her tote bag. Belle had said there were two other letters. Where were they? As she felt the ridges of some object inside the envelope, she thought it seemed to be the bracelet Belle had spoken of. Bill Sullivan had mentioned giving her a bracelet for Christmas. She put a hand up to her ear as if to ward off the sound of his angry voice as he and Carole had quarreled in Annice's side yard.

It was so quiet here. Some light filtered through the front of the cave. Carole's and Marlon's gay laughter had lain on the air here. Young and tender. Julius and Carole had left notes for each other. Now someone had sealed Carole's fate and she wasn't going to turn over a new leaf after all.

Quiet or not, it was shuddery. Running the flashlight

beams over the stalactites and the walls again, she turned
and went out of the room. Near the front entrance, she paused
at the empty easel, seeing in her mind's eye the paintings
and the sketches of first Sylvie, then Carole. She felt a trace
of fear as she thought she heard something, but no, the
silence lasted as she turned and left the cave. Had Julius's
envelope been left there too? Why had Carole left the envelope for Bill in the same spot she and Julius left envelopes
for each other?

"Carole, you were so young and so hurt," she said softly
as she plodded back to the campus. It took a while, and as
she turned around to look at Pirate's Cave, she thought how
forlorn it seemed now.

A horn blew softly and she jumped. "Can I give you a
lift?" A car had driven up behind her. Lieutenant Ryson.

Smiling, she told him, "I would welcome a ride." He
pulled over to the shoulder of the road and she got into his
private car.

"I've wanted to thank you for the help you and Dr. Jones
have given us," he said.

"We were glad to help. Anything new?"

"Not really. You were visiting the cave?"

"Yes, but I didn't go in," she quickly assured him. She
bit her tongue. What if he had seen her?

"Thank God for small favors. Don't go in. We don't
know what plans the killer has for someone else."

A long finger of icy fear traveled along her spine. "You
think there's still danger to others?"

"Yes, I do. Is Marlon still painting there?"

"He says he can't bring himself to go back just now."

"Good. We want to keep it as undisturbed as we can."

She wanted to tell him about the envelope she'd found
and she would later, but not right now.

"Do you know if Julius is on campus?" he asked.

"I don't, but I could call his dormitory."

"Would you? I want to ask all three people about the
letters that were left."

She took her cell phone from her tote bag.

Julius was in his room when Annice and Jon Ryson reached the dorm. He invited them in and sat on the bottom bunk of his bed.

Jon Ryson didn't waste any time starting to question him about the letter.

Julius shrugged. "Yeah, she gave me my ring back. The chick said she was turning over a new leaf, and that leaf didn't include me. She was talking a lot to you, Dr. Steele. She said knowing you made her want to change." His eyes flashed fire. "You split us up and I don't appreciate that."

"Easy," Jon Ryson told him, "anybody has the privilege of changing his or her mind."

Julius stood with his shoulders haunched.

"Do you still have the letter?" Jon asked.

Julius laughed hollowly, "I've got the ashes."

"So you burned it." Jon's eyes searched the youth.

"To a crisp. I was pretty burned up myself."

"Did she leave it in the cave?" Jon asked.

"No, she handed it to me, along with the box with my ring in it."

"So you had already given her the ring. You said when we questioned you before that you were *going* to give it to her on her birthday. We know she planned to return your ring. . . ."

"OK, I lied. My old man was in town. She did give it back, but not at the cave, in the cafeteria. That was cold. I sure as hell was going to try to cover my tracks."

Julius looked both sad and evil then. "Anything else I can help you with, lieutenant?"

"You must have been pretty angry with her? Steamed?"

Julius laughed tightly. "Burned would be a better word. But I didn't kill her. You don't need to ask. I'll cooperate, man. I'll stay put right here and you can find me anytime day or night. I'm a bit of a slob and I can be a real bastard, but I am *not* a killer."

Jon Ryson asked Annice to go back the short distance

into Minden with him. He wanted her to listen to Bill Sullivan when they brought him in. "I called Dr. Jones who said he's too tied up at the moment and suggested you. Then I'll see him later. I'll see that you get home safely."

Driving to Minden, they were both silent before Lieutenant Ryson said, "I guess you've heard that the first forty-eight hours in a crime case are the most important. Trails get cold pretty quickly. This seems like a crime of passion. Julius swears he didn't do it. So does Bill Sullivan, but they both know about Marlon and the girl in Ellisville and that puts Marlon on the hook. I hate killers. When I can send one up, I'm the happiest man in the world."

To their surprise, Bill Sullivan waited for them in the interrogation room. His eyes shifted when they came in. "You said you wanted to ask me a few more questions."

"Yeah," Jon said. "What about a brown manila envelope you got from Carole? Or did you get one?"

Sullivan's mouth opened and his breath came fast as he licked his lips. He didn't answer for a long while. "I put it behind a ledge in the cave. We quarreled, worse than I've told you. She left, saying she'd come back when the bad smell was gone. I got even madder, but I didn't touch her. I was afraid I'd kill her if I did."

"So you didn't read the letter?"

"No. She told me what was in it. Said it was short and sweet. She was moving on, beyond me. I couldn't take it, but I left the letter in that rock slot behind the ledge. I'd spied on them and knew they exchanged letters there. I wasn't thinking clearly. I wanted to throw a wedge between her and Julius. I thought he might find the letter addressed to me and get mad."

In the small room by the larger interrogation room, Annice sat, quietly tense.

Bill Sullivan was speaking to the sheriff. "She flounced out and left me there. She said later she was going to pose a little while for the boy. She walked out and I hid the envelope. I was going to pick it up later. My wife's been wanting a nice bracelet. I thought I'd get it gift-wrapped and give it to her. Late Christmas present.''

He grinned weakly and spread his hands. ''She flounced out under her own steam and sat out front waiting for Marlon. I left. I never saw her again.''

Sullivan looked wretchedly at Jon Ryson. ''You can't blame me for hiding the fact I met her at the cave. She called me, asked me to meet her. I thought she was finally going to give me what I wanted. I didn't lie. You didn't ask. It don't take much to get a married man in trouble.''

Jon Ryson rubbed his chin and thought before he said, ''Thanks for coming in. You're free to go now. Keep in touch, and I'll be in touch.''

As Bill Sullivan left the room, thoughts of the envelope in her bag scorched Annice's mind. She was withholding evidence! Why? And she knew then. She had expected to find a letter for Marlon. Carole had written a letter to Marlon. Where was it? Probably in yet another hiding place. She had a gut feeling that Marlon was soon going to remember and she didn't want him in jail while he was trying. It was for such a short while. She would look for Marlon's envelope again tomorrow. Take the chance. And when she felt there was no chance of the letter being in the cave, she would give whatever she had found to Jon Ryson.

With a tired smile Lieutenant Ryson thanked her for coming in and they went to the parking lot. ''I'll have you home in a jiffy,'' he said.

Chapter 26

At nine the next morning, Annice walked down the wide corridor to her office. Marlon should be there shortly. She hummed a bit to herself to alleviate the tension she felt, then jumped at the feeling that someone was behind her.

"Dr. Steele." She turned to face Mel Sunderlin, who looked at her carefully. "How are you?" he asked.

"I'm fine. And you?"

He grinned. "Let's put it this way. If I were a whistling man, I'd give you the biggest wolf whistle you've ever drawn. But being myself, I'll just say you look lovely."

"Why thank you." He definitely approved of her navy reefer coat, princess cut and displaying her figure, the long natural angora gloves and the sporty natural tam. A dark red coach leather bag was slung over her shoulder.

"Are you free for dinner tonight, or earlier? At your convenience."

Annice thought a moment. "I'm really sorry, but I've got prior plans."

"I'll even invite Dr. Jones to come along if that's the only way I can get you."

Annice chuckled. "No, that isn't necessary. I'm just taking this opportunity to do some fine-tuning on that book we discussed."

Mel raised his eyebrows. "Oh, a beauty and brilliant too."

"Not really."

"OK. Let's put it this way. I'll be coming back to Casey's School early in January. Begin thinking now of going out with me. I've got to get to know you better. Try me. You might find you like me."

Annice smiled at his derring-do.

"I have your number," he said. "I'll call you later on this week."

"Very well, but don't expect me to be able to go out. I'm a busy woman for a couple of months."

Mel closed his eyes. "Ah, she's putting me off, and I'm not willing to be put off." He touched her arm, and for a moment his eyes held hers before she turned and went up the hall to her office.

She made and drank a second cup of coffee and began to read her notes in Marlon's file. She had hardly gotten settled when Marlon showed up, looking tousled and bothered.

"How much sleep did you get?" she asked him.

"Not much." His voice was hoarse. "I dreamed horrible dreams all night."

"I'm sorry."

"It's OK. Neesie, I keep hoping for what you call a breakthrough. I know it's too early, but what if we don't get even a small one?"

"We'll cross that bridge when we get to it," she said firmly. "Marlon?"

"Yes?"

"You know we're working against time. I just hope that we can get some part of your memory back. That will mean everything. Even if we fail, we've got to try. I want you to be aware, though, that you've got a lot of work ahead of you even once you begin to remember.

"It won't be over even then. Your memory may come back in agonizing bits and pieces or all at once."

"It's OK," he said. "I can take it. I'm willing to work hard. It's just that I feel so little hope."

Annice smiled sadly. "As long as there's life there's hope. Going back to Ellisville probably helped even if you didn't altogether remember. Just keep on probing, trying. Marlon, did you and Carole ever hide notes for each other in the cave?"

He looked grave. "No. That was something she and Julius did." He thought a moment, then scratched his head. "She did say to me lately that I'd better keep looking because she might be hiding a letter from her."

"And have you looked for such a letter?"

He shrugged. "No, I haven't." His breath came faster then. "And I won't be looking. I don't see that I can ever go back into that cave right now."

She put fresh tissues on the couch and sat down. She listened intently, desperately seeking ways to help him remember. A thought chilled her, a frequent thought: What if he remembered that *he* was the murderer? Tears came to her eyes. *Dear God,* she prayed, *let it come out in his favor.*

By one o'clock she was back at the cave. If she could find the letter to Marlon, it possibly contained useful information. Had something set him off that Annice could use to help him? Or it could show a reason why he might be angry enough at Carole. Or it could be unintentional—the murder. A crime of passion. Sylvie.

But no, there had been a white sheet of paper with the fateful words: *Angel face. Devil body.* There was intention there. A planned execution. Someone had hated her, been furious. And someone had hated Sylvie Love and Carole.

She slipped under the police tape. The cave was quiet as it had been quiet the day before. Grimly she thought she would keep looking until there was little hope of finding that letter. Belle had told her it existed and *Carole would not let Belle read it.* She had nearly reached the opening of the room that held the ledges where she had found the first letter when she turned around. She felt an eerie feeling she had not felt the day before.

Marlon's big white chest of painting items sat locked, ready to offer him the materials he needed to paint. What was she looking for at the painting chest? Then it struck her. She missed the painting that had been there of Carole and guessed that the police had taken it.

Pressing her tote bag to her side she slowly began to move toward the room to her left, just opposite the room where Carole had been killed. She forced herself not to look that way.

Then she found the ground rising to meet her, found herself going to her knees, sprawling. Drawing on every reserve of calmness she possessed, she knew she was falling and let herself fall. The tote bag broke her fall. A thin wire stretched across the opening had stopped her. Looking about quickly, she got up and, looking carefully, saw pegs on either side of the archway driven into the dirt, with the wire anchored on either peg. Walking slowly was her salvation. There was a sharp sting of pain where the wire bit into her ankle, but she was otherwise unharmed.

She gasped for breath at a scream and a whirring sound and almost screamed herself as something came at her. Then near hysterical laughter rose in her throat as she saw two bats fly across the room. She rose then on trembling legs and hurriedly left the cave. But she had to find that letter. She chided herself that she had let herself be frightened by a couple of bats, but the fear was too deep, too primeval to ignore.

She would come back tomorrow, she thought, as she walked along to her house, favoring her left ankle a bit. Should she confide in Luke, ask him to help her? She decided against that. He had enough on his plate. As she limped, she planned to come back the day after the next day. She would go into town and get a more powerful flashlight that could search out the crevices. That thought through, she began to relax. She knew, too, that she was skipping a day to lessen her fear.

At home, she went through her side yard and to the back fence. On the other side of that fence a couple of nights back, on the holly trees side, she had imagined or actually seen a figure almost completely draped in black. Had those malignant eyes burned into her? Threatening havoc? Death? She shuddered. Then she saw the black object from the middle of the yard on the holly trees side and went closer. On the small clearing, a long black woolen knit glove lay on the ground. She had an urge to climb through the fence and retrieve it, but decided against it. Luke would be by later and she would ask him to do it.

What a coward she was turning out to be. It was full daylight. What was going on? Anybody could have stretched a wire across the cave room to bring down an enemy, or it could be horseplay between youths playing pranks on each other. But it came unbidden: The wire could have been meant for her and her alone. Someone didn't intend for her to find anything else in that cave.

She soaked her foot and ankle in epsom salts and sprinkled lavender in the foot tub. Trying to alleviate the tension, she dried her feet and gave herself a pedicure. So far it wasn't swelling, but maybe not enough time had elapsed.

Intent on bringing as much of her life back to normal as she could, she drew herself a lukewarm bath and soaked for a while. The whole house smelled of carrier oils, sweet almond and apricot kernel, that kept the French lavender oils from irritating the skin.

Yes, she was on edge. She couldn't help it. Marlon would likely be indicted. His DNA was at the crime scene. His fingerprints. Carole's blood had been on him. Was it conceivable it happened as he said? With Sylvie *and* Carole?

She switched on the stereo and the beautiful soothing sounds of Dvorak's *Eighth Symphony* swept through. It was a favorite of both Annice and Luke.

Putting on a fringed beige woolen caftan, she decided she wouldn't wait for Luke. She put a pan of gourmet New England clam chowder on the stove to heat and rolls in the oven. It was cloudy and a bit darker than usual, she saw as she glanced out the kitchen window.

Getting a loden cloth cloak from the back closet she threw it around her, then bent a clothes hanger to fish the glove from the other side of the fence. Leaving the door open, she began to purposefully walk toward the fence and stopped abruptly. The glove was gone!

OK! OK! She told herself. People went into the woods, which was school property. Anybody could have dropped the glove, then come back to pick it up when she wasn't looking. That must have been it, but she couldn't shake a gnawing sense of danger and her slightly sore ankle brought it even closer to the forefront.

She was sitting on the couch with her foot propped up on a pillow when she heard a car stop outside. In a few minutes, the doorbell rang. She got up gingerly and went to the security front door mirror. It was Luke. She opened the door quickly. He stood still, making no move to come in.

"Are you alone?" he asked.

"Not anymore," she answered, twitting him. "Well, come in."

He came in slowly, looked around. "Did Mel Sunderlin come by? He said he might."

"No, he didn't." Her voice was uptight. What was it going to take to make him know that Sunderlin was a prize catch, but she wasn't fishing?

Luke Jones wasn't used to being jealous. He had faith in himself, but what he knew now with Annice was throwing him for a loop. He was going to have to fish or cut bait.

But right now he felt a deep concern for her as she put her foot back onto the pillow.

"What happened to you?" he asked.

"A misstep," she lied, "off the bottom back step this afternoon." He sat on the edge of the couch and took the foot into his lap. "It's not swollen very much. I was lucky." She'd never tell him about the cave. He'd have a fit.

"Did you soak it?"

"Oh yes."

She looked so precious sitting there in her beige caftan, her eyes wide and dazzling.

"Did you hear from Sunderlin?" he demanded.

"Not since this morning." She smiled. "He invited me out. I said I'd be busy for the next couple of months. After then you'll have your funding, at least in part. End of Mel Sunderlin."

"Son of a bitch," he said. "He doesn't know how to take no for an answer. He knows what a bind his wanting you puts me in."

He was torn up inside with wanting her. He called himself a lustful clown. What could he offer her? He had a brother who might be a killer. She deserved everything life had to offer, not the mixed up life that he could give her.

And looking at him, she felt her heart turn over with love and surging desire. Her body lit up as he went to his knees, took her foot in his hands and massaged it. "Should I do this?" he asked hoarsely.

"I don't think it can hurt."

Taking her foot in his big hands, he kissed her instep, held it to his face. Then he put the foot back on the pillow and put the side of his face into her lap as she sat up.

"Is something wrong, honey?" she asked.

He sat back on his haunches, then got up and sat on the couch beside her.

"Wrong? Yeah, something's wrong, Neesie. I want you for my own so bad it's killing me. My dreams of holding you, of being inside you are driving me crazy. I'm sure

Mel Sunderlin doesn't understand what's going on with me regarding you. Only I know. I've got to have you, but . . .''

Strike while the iron is hot, she thought as delicious thrills coursed over her body. "It's true for both of us," she said softly. "We were meant to be together. Listen Luke, Marlon is coming along, but he has his life to live. We have ours. He's opening out. I believe in him."

"He's my brother. I have to believe in him, but I won't let his problems ruin your life."

"Luke, listen to me," she said urgently. "The only way my life is ruined is that I don't have you for myself. I love you, my darling. I've never wanted anyone else but you. Can't you understand that? What do I have to do to make you know that?"

The dam that he had built against them broke then, and hot, stinging tears rose to his eyes. "When we have grieved Carole's death, Neesie, when this is over, I want you to marry me. I can't go on like this any longer."

Annice laughed as happy tears moistened her eyes. "Now you're talking with your common sense. Life isn't given as we want it to be, Luke. It comes as it is. So we'll be married and I can be happy again. Oh, I love you."

His arms went around her and his lips crushed hers. His breath was hot against her face. His mouth on hers was hot honey as he drew the honey from her lips and mouth. He kissed her savagely then and could not stop. His life's blood rushed to her and he had to have her no matter what it cost.

As they moved toward the bedroom, he groaned. It was going to cost her, not him. If she or someone couldn't help Marlon, she would be the loser. He was crazy with wanting her, crazy with not wanting to hurt her, and she could see the conflict in his eyes.

"It will be all right, my darling," she assured him. "This is the right choice for us."

He swept her up in his arms and took her to her bedroom, unwilling to wait a minute longer. "Is this OK?" he asked. "Do you want me now?"

"Foolish question." She laughed. "I want you always."

Her voice had gone husky and she felt herself melting with delicious desire. She bent and slipped the caftan over her head and stood before him in a lacy, aquamarine bra and bikini pants. He grinned.

"Call the fire trucks."

"No, don't," she said, laughing. "I'm going to put out your fire."

He was free of his clothes in record time, then he stood before her. Taking her in his arms he rose against her and she trembled. She began to move away to take off the bra and panties when his hand stayed her.

"Let me," he said, his eyes narrowed with passion.

His big hands stroked her breasts and her heavily rounded hips and backside.

"You're so beautiful," he murmured, unhooking the bra and pitching it onto a nearby chair. He bent his head to suckle the full breasts, saying, "My God, you have beautiful breasts. You're beautiful all the way through."

Her laugh was full, rich. "You have a beautiful protuberance, too." She was wild with joy. Nothing in her life had meant to her what having him for herself meant.

"We're going to be married, Luke," she murmured. "We're going to be married!"

"Yes, my darling." He bent and helped her slip off her panties, then they walked to the bed as he hugged her close and her feet rode the top of his feet. They laughed like children in full frolic, but what they felt was the very essence of being grown-up.

He stroked her with loving hands as she lay on her back, her eyes glazed over with love for him. Then his fingers began to knead her flesh from her scalp to her breasts, her hips where they lingered, then on to her legs. He kissed the hurt foot and nuzzled it, and fire leaped along her veins, making her blood feel like fevered nectar.

"Luke," she whispered again and again as he turned her over and kneaded the back of her luscious body. He thought of Alaskan ice floes and Northern lights to stay his desire. How could he last? But he had to for her sake.

His tongue on her body raised her to fever pitch. Bit by bit he inched over her until she could have screamed with desire. Then she went languid, waiting for him to begin the deepest ecstasy.

She was a silken brown swan floating—waiting for her lover. She slid her fingertips along his collarbones, then ran her tongue along the clean lines.

His lips and tongue on her body were driving her mad and she moaned with wanting deeper than any she had ever known.

"Now it's my turn," she told him, sitting up, smiling impishly. He lay on his back and closed his eyes, then found he wanted to watch her as she stroked and kneaded him. Her slender fingers roved his body relentlessly before he sat up and drew her to him, her breasts pressed hard against his chest.

He got a comdom from under the pillow and slipped it on.

"I've got to go in now," he said gravely. "If I can't last, you'll have to forgive me and we'll start over."

He entered her then in a blaze of glory, the shaft of him driving gently, then harder until she cried out, "Luke! Oh, my darling!"

He stroked her ardently as he pressed her closer and closer. The length of him inside her filled her with awe as it always did. As he worked her tender body, her breath came fast and she slowed to deeper breaths. Again and again they stopped momentarily, then began again. Neither wanted to let the other go.

Moving expertly, he groaned, "Honey, I can't last any longer." And without a word, she rolled her hips rhythmically under his and he exploded. Under him, she couldn't stop smiling. This was joy. This was hope. This was love. And this was *life!*

Chapter 27

Mac Townsend, Marlon's lawyer, met with Annice, Marlon and Luke in his office in the administration building. A tall, heavyset, dark brown-skinned man with sleepy eyes that belied his brilliance, Mac was famous for his acquittal of borderline murder cases. He faced them now with calm and ease as they sat in a circle of comfortable chairs.

Mac cleared his throat. "I've got bad news, I'm afraid. The D.A. tells me they're pressing for an indictment they think they'll get. Murder One. But I've got a lot of aces up my sleeve."

Annice glanced quickly at Marlon. He was stricken, barely breathing.

Mac leaned over and patted Marlon's hand. "Don't worry, son. I've only lost three cases in my career. I'm not known as the wizard for nothing. And the ones I lost, well, I had fools for clients. They didn't trust me, wouldn't do it *my* way.

"I want the three of you to listen. Trust me. Believe in me. Right now, I'm this boy's ticket to freedom. I'll check with the three of you daily, but for only a short time each time. Know that I'll be working, working like the beaver I am. Questions?''

"How much does it count that he simply doesn't remember?'' Luke asked, glancing at Marlon.

"It counts against him,'' Mac Townsend said bluntly, "but we may be able to use it. I'm not against the insanity plea, but it's a hellish act to set in motion. Most juries won't buy it. I've got jury consultants set up to advise me. Marlon is a handsome, all-American kid and he carries himself well. Few people will believe he's crazy, but we may have to try. It's a rough case and we don't have much to work with.'' He looked levelly at Marlon. "Run it by me again, son. What you remember of both the killings.''

Marlon shuddered and looked wildly around him.

"He gets very upset when he tries to remember,'' Annice said. "I'm working with him to try to help him remember.''

Townsend expelled a harsh breath. "I hope you're using truth serum, or some such treatment. I know what I'd think if I weren't his lawyer.''

Annice shook her head. "No, I'm just using eclectic psychological methods.''

"That includes Freud?''

"Yes, and many others.''

"If you ask me,'' Townsend scoffed, "Freud would have been better off selling couches than using them. What have you got against plain old truth serum?''

"Nothing,'' Annice answered him. "I want to try my way first.''

"We haven't got much time. The hourglass is nearly empty at the top.''

She felt depressed when he said it. "Yes, I know. I've been looking into truth serum. It isn't one hundred percent effective. Nothing is.''

"When will the grand jury be convened?'' Luke asked.

"Probably Tuesday of next week. There're other cases.''

"That soon,'' Annice murmured tiredly. "I'm in contact

with Dr. Casey. Together, we'll get the truth serum administered.''

"Now you're talking. Give me chemicals every time. I just don't believe in this psychiatric-psychological witch doctor mumbo-jumbo.'' He smiled a bit. "No offense to you, Doc Steele.''

Annice nodded. She was less than fond of Attorney Townsend, but he was one of the best his profession had to offer, and Lord, how they needed him.

Mac cleared his throat. "We're coming down to the wire. I don't guess any of us feels like talking. All three of you have my number. I brought you a bombshell about the likely indictment, so you're stunned. Call me anytime, and leave a message if I'm not there. I'll get right back to you. And you, Marlon, I especially want to hear from you. Put me in your back pocket the way I've got you in mine. Now I've got to run. I always bring bad news face to face. Don't kill me. I'm just the messenger.''

Nothing was said in the first few minutes after Mac Townsend left the room. Marlon sat wringing his long-fingered artist's hands without realizing he did so. Luke leaned over and took Annice's hand in his and squeezed, then got up and sat in the chair beside Marlon that Attorney Townsend had just vacated. He rose and hugged Marlon. "We'll get through this,'' he told his brother. "Have faith, bro. Townsend is a damned fine lawyer and . . .''

"Thank you, Luke,'' Marlon said, his voice gone hoarse with despair, "but if I did it . . .''

"Hush,'' Luke scolded. "Don't be so down on yourself.''

Marlon nodded and looked at Annice. "Do we need to meet now, you and I? If you and Doc Casey are going to try the truth serum, what's the point?''

Annice looked at him, her head a little to one side. "I know it's hard, but trust me. I believe in my way with this more than ever now. Let's get started.''

* * *

When Luke had left, Marlon sat for a while, then asked if he could stretch out. It wasn't going well, Annice thought after the first fifteen minutes or so. She knew his mind was on the coming indictment now. Well, so was hers. Suddenly, she told him, "Marlon, it's an old method of getting information and it doesn't always work. You've got to be honest with me. I want you to say the exact word that comes to your mind when I say a word. It's called free association.

"Don't, under any circumstances, hold back or change what's on your mind. We did this at first, and I thought we didn't need it anymore. Now I think we do."

"Shoot!" he said.

"Love."

"Hate."

"Life."

"Death."

"Sex."

"Murder."

Annice flinched a bit. Marlon had always seemed to her so levelheaded about sex and sensuality. Murder? No stopping now. Prior word matching had not gotten this response. Were they going farther from the truth or were they getting closer?

"Woman." She left off again.

"Man."

She paused a moment, then said, "Desire."

He came back quickly. "Murder." Then he got flustered. "Hey, that's the second time I've said that in a few minutes."

"Don't censor yourself at all," she said sharply. "If the word *murder* comes up twenty times in twenty seconds, say it. You owe it to yourself. Maybe we're getting somewhere."

"Yeah, and maybe we're not."

"Be of good faith, Marlon," she said softly. "We are not in this world alone."

"Yeah," he laughed brokenly. "Where is God when I need him?"

The evocative word spell was broken for the moment and Annice asked Marlon to sit up and face her. He looked about to break, he was so tense.

"Marlon," she began. "Something comes to me as I talk with you. You first blacked out not with Sylvie's death, but when Luke told you your parents had been killed in an air crash."

"What're you driving at?"

She held up a hand. "Hear me out," she said gently. She usually let him talk whenever he wanted to, but she had something on her mind. She was seeing something, understanding something she hadn't before and maybe it could help.

"You blacked out with Sylvie when you found her body . . ."

"If *I* didn't kill her."

"And with Carole you blacked out when you found her body."

"Yes."

"I want to suggest that after you see those you love lying dead, or know they're dead, you have to go away from yourself. You can't bear it."

He didn't hesitate. "It sure seems like that, and I have to draw them quickly. Why do I have to do that?"

"And you draw their *dead* images."

"Yes."

"Do you know why?"

A sudden huge sob shook him. She let him sob until he quieted. "If I draw them, I know they're dead. It's the only way I can really know."

"Or accept."

"Yes."

"Marlon, we don't lose the people we love. They live on in us."

His eyes opened wide as tears hung from his lashes. He seemed to breathe more deeply now.

"Were you angry with them—I mean your parents? Sylvie? Carole?"

"Angry?"

"Think back. Let yourself go."

"I want to lie down again."

As he lay on the couch, he was so deep into himself that he seemed miles away from her. Finally he spoke. "Yes, I was angry. Crazy mad."

When he was silent again, she asked him, "Can you talk about that anger?" Then she added, "We have all the time necessary. We'll get your take on this morning, no matter how long it lasts."

He breathed a sigh of relief. "You know Sylvie and I wanted to get married. My parents didn't want us to do it. I was seventeen, so I had to have their consent. Yeah, I was mad as hell. After that, I was mad with Sylvie, because she was flirting with Julius and she was saying it might be better if we waited until we were older to marry.

"Neesie, you know I've got a hot temper. It gets away from me. I started being angry all the time when they wouldn't let me marry Sylvie. Then when she said she didn't want to marry right away, I struck out at her with that anger." He paused. "I wish I could say I didn't kill her, but she was flirting with Julius, and I was mad enough to kill her."

She had begun to ask him a question when he began to talk faster. "Now, Carole," he said. "She kept rattling my cage. I was beginning to like her more and more. Then I loved her. She played me and Julius for fools. I didn't care about that, but I wanted her—bad. She reminded me of Sylvie. I got scared when I wanted to slap her one day. I don't want to be like Julius. She told me she was going to cut him out of her life and I was happy. Then she changed her mind. . . ."

"And?"

His body tensed. "I don't know what happened. Maybe I killed her." The room was hushed as he told her. "I kill every one I love."

"That may not be true. You certainly didn't kill your parents."

"I may have. I told them I hated them before they left, that I wished they were dead."

"Did you tell Sylvie and Carole you wished they were dead?"

"Sylvie, yes, once, a while before she died. Not Carole, but I would have with a few more times of her spinning me around."

Annice sat up straight. "Marlon, listen to me, please. Our angry thoughts don't and can't kill. You wanted these people dead at the moment, but you're not omnipotent. Your parents certainly didn't die because you wished them dead. And I don't think you killed Sylvie or Carole. Forgive yourself for wanting them dead, and forgive them for the pain they caused you. Ask God's forgiveness; it's always there for you."

Marlon hung his head.

"I hear you, but I don't feel it. I'm going to go now, Neesie. Both of us have done the best we could. Maybe I'll never remember."

They got up then and she saw him to the door where she paused, touched his shoulder and said to him, "I'm with you all the way, all the time. Let God be your anchor."

Annice leaned back in her chair. It hurt when she couldn't help someone the way she wanted to. Marlon had looked so woebegone. She was making her mark in the psychological treatment field. With Will Casey as a mentor, how could she not? Marlon had seemed to change before her eyes when she had mentioned fear that one's anger would kill. He had seemed livelier. There had been understanding and hope on his countenance. Then in a few minutes he had slipped into a well of despair, seeming to nearly drown.

She studied her notes carefully, trying to distill information that could heal a broken heart and psyche. A knock sounded and she got up to answer her door. Marlon stood on the threshold.

"I . . . ah . . . thought you might let me walk you home," he said.

She patted his arm. "That's sweet of you, but I'm going to work a little while longer, then I'll hook up with Luke to go to my place or his." She wanted to tell him the news about Luke's decision to blend their lives again, but Marlon looked too down.

"Well, Luke's kind of tied up now," he said. "He's busy."

"In that case, I probably won't bother him, but I have a few things to do here before I leave. Go home. Get some rest and later, stop by Luke's place or mine. I'll call you when I get to one place or the other."

He left reluctantly and she watched him go down the hall, his dejected stance making her heart hurt for him. As if he knew she watched him, he turned midway in the hall and waved at her. She waved back. In the little time she had practiced as a psychologist, she had never wanted more fiercely to help someone heal.

Going back over her notes told her a lot as she studied them. Marlon was not a killer; she was sure of that. But mental health workers had been wrong, had let patients go home from hospitals against advice, only to have them kill as others said they would.

After an hour or so, she shook her head and stood up. Luke should be less busy now. He was studying his proposal to the Sunderlin Foundation and she didn't want to bother him, but she needed to talk.

The secretarial and waiting area to Luke's office was empty and she thought she heard voices. She hesitated and went toward the partially open door. In brilliant sunlight she could see Luke with his back to her. Claire was in his arms and she smiled into Annice's eyes with malice and triumph. Then Claire moved her head away from Luke's shoulder to his face. They had to be kissing. She stroked his back as Annice had stroked it the night before and he murmured something Annice couldn't hear.

Annice fled back to her office, took time to put her notes away, collected her bags and set out for home. The walk was good for her; it cleared her head. Had she seen what she thought she saw? Her legs felt like lead. Luke had known she might still be in the building. Hadn't he cared? Had Marlon seen them earlier in this embrace? Had they stood there all this time?

"You bastard," she grated. "After last night, how could you do this to me?" Quieting as the wind whipped her face, she gained some measure of composure. Luke was an honorable man. He would explain and they would be together again.

Luke came around two o'clock as she paced her house restlessly. She answered the door and avoided his kiss. He looked puzzled.

"What do you say," he suggested immediately, "that we fix a few sandwiches and a thermos of something hot and walk in the woods?" He stood there, still in his overcoat. "How'd it go with Marlon?"

"Not as well as I'd hoped."

He was silent a moment. "Well, I know you're disappointed. So am I. I've always found walking in the woods helps when I feel things are going against me. Say yes."

"Yes." She said it without hesitation. Perhaps he found the woods a good place to explain what was going on with Claire and him. He looked so dear as he stood there, somberly studying her.

He put his outer gear on the sofa and they made grilled cheese and turkey sandwiches in the kitchen.

As they bumped into each other, he said, "Don't let it get you down, Neesie. Marlon and I trust you and we trust Dr. Casey. We think you two are the best."

"Thank you. I haven't doubted myself before. I'm afraid I do now."

"Don't. Is Marlon coming by?"

"I asked him to. I called him, but he didn't answer. He's really down in the dumps. I'm afraid he could hurt himself. Dr. Casey prescribed antidepressants, but I wonder if he's taking them regularly."

They entered the woods behind her house through a big gate that led to a winding wagon road. The holly trees were fabulous at this time of the year and bare-limbed trees, blue-green spruce and other evergreens shot toward the sky.

They found a clearing, sat down and ate the sandwiches and drank hot red clover tea with lemon slices poured from a thermos into paper cups.

She would let him talk, she decided, but he had little to say. She began to get a little angry, then controlled herself. *Give him time.*

Finally he said, "Mel has asked that Claire come with me to New York. We might have to spend the night. There's been a glitch. Two of the board members are suddenly holding back and Mel wants the vote to be unanimous on this one."

"I see."

He seemed distant. They both had so much on their minds.

"About Marlon. I'll never give up on him. Never." Luke's face was set and anguished.

"Nor will I."

He didn't take her hand as he usually did. What was he thinking? Why didn't he tell her why Claire had been in his arms that morning? There were many possible explanations; he voiced none of them.

They walked deep into the woods and she wanted to tell him about the glove she had seen at the edge of the small clearing. Wanted to tell him about the figure dressed in black that had stared at her with hatred in the dark. Or had she imagined he stared at her? It was dark. Surely she couldn't know. But the heart, the spirit has is own knowledge. There had been danger in that stance. Give the figure a scythe and it could have been the symbol of death.

There was a crashing noise in the underbrush and a tall figure dressed in black stood twenty feet or so away, then streaked from them. The figure wore the cloak and the hood and a black ski mask was on his face as he turned to look at them.

"I'm going after him," Luke said. "Go back and report this to the police."

"No," she said stubbornly. "I'm going with you."

"You've got a hurt foot."

"It's barely hurting. I can do it. Let's both go back. I'm not going to leave you. He could have a gun."

"Don't talk. Save your strength if you won't listen to me."

They ran then, but the figure never got any closer. All three crashed through trees and underbrush as the path gave out, then came to another wagon path near the main highway.

Winded, they saw the figure climb through the barbed wire over the block wire and go out to the highway. Luck was with him; he caught the red light and raced across the highway to another fenced woods. Winded, far behind, they stood on the path and saw him go through the fence and disappear into those woods.

There were two men sitting on a culvert bank by the side of the road.

Luke and Annice went up to them, spoke. The men were shabby, but looked intelligent and friendly.

"The man who just passed you," Luke said, "did you get a good look at him?"

The older man laughed. "Wasn't much to look at. He had a mask on."

The younger man spoke up. "Couldn't see nothing but his eyes. He looked at me straight and mean." The man hugged himself. "That dude had eyes from hell. Mad-dog eyes."

Luke and Annice looked at each other. They thanked the men and turned back.

"One of us should have brought a cell phone," Luke said.

"Twenty-twenty hindsight," Annice murmured. "Sometimes I have to get away from our twenty-first–century world."

"We can hurry along and call the sheriff. Something's bothering you, Neesie."

"I'm upset, Luke, about this and everything else. Marlon. Carole. I'm scared and my world is closing in on me."

He touched her then and love for him flooded her heart. *Tell him. Make him give you some answers,* her mind screamed, but she held her peace. He would tell her in his own time. And did she want to know?

It was nearly midnight in a small clearing in the deep woods behind Annice's house. He held a ballpoint pen poised over a black-covered diary, and he wrote by the bright moonlight in a clearing.

I did it and I still feel wonderful.

It was getting harder and harder to be clear about what he wanted to do next. But never mind, there was one more female to rid the world of. He was proud of what he'd done. He had evened the score. A loss for a loss. He had taken two lives for the life she took from him, and he would soon take another.

He chewed on the ballpoint pen. His modus operandi was always the same. Shoot them through the heart the way the first bitch had broken his heart. He hadn't killed the first one who'd broken his heart because . . . He'd never know why. But he'd killed the other two. Then beat their wicked bodies with all the rage he felt. Leave the faces untouched. Their faces were pure, showed no malice. They were angel faces on devil bodies, and those bodies lured men to betray the heavens, everything.

The man and the woman had been nowhere near to catching him this afternoon, he thought, laughing at their failure. He could run like the wind. Funny the confidence his temporary rages had brought into his life. He was powerful. He was a powerful god like the ones he read about. But most important, he could take a life in punishment when the pain in him got too bad.

Chapter 28

"Neesie!"

Annice burrowed deeper into the covers, on the edge of sleep.

"Neesie!" The doorbell rang and someone pounded on the door. Marlon was calling her. She sprang up and grabbed her robe, rushing through the house. But the voice had been joyful, not frightened or angry.

She looked out the viewfinder as she opened the door with nervous hands and almost fell into Marlon's arms. He hugged her tightly, laughing, crying at the same time. For a moment he couldn't seem to speak.

"Marlon, what is it?" she asked gently.

He let her go. "I remembered," he said urgently. "I *remembered.*"

This time she hugged him tightly. "Oh, Marlon, that's wonderful! Now let's sit down and tell me about it. But first let's call Luke and tell him."

She got Luke on the line and he responded with a loud and happy shout. "Hold tight," he said. "I'll be right there."

Going back to Marlon, she demanded, "Now tell me everything!"

They sat on the couch close together. He leaned forward, his hands hanging between his knees. "I can't get my breath, I'm so shocked," he told her.

"I don't wonder. You don't have to start at the beginning. Start anywhere. Just tell me."

"Well," he began, "you know the mood I was in when I left you yesterday?"

"Yes."

"Hopeless. I took two of the antidepressants you gave me and I went to sleep. I didn't wake up until around five-thirty this morning."

She listened intently as he raced on.

"I know I said I wouldn't go back to the cave even if I felt I had to go back to Ellisville where Sylvie died. But I put on my clothes and walked the floor. I felt I had to go back. I argued with myself. What if one of the sheriff's people caught me there? It could be my goose cooking. But I knew I had to go.

"I dressed and went out into the dark. At the cave, I turned on the lights, unlocked my lockbox and looked at my paintings then I locked them back up and walked around. I wanted to go back to the spot where I had found Carole, but I couldn't. What if I had killed her? Are you following me now, Neesie?"

"Yes. Go on."

"I was beginning to love Carole the way I had loved Sylvie and my heart was tearing up as I made up my mind that I was going to look at the spot where I found her, see if I could remember. Neesie, if I didn't already believe in God, I'd believe now. I felt someone powerful was with me as I walked through that archway and looked at the floor of the cave where I had found her. In that dim light, I saw light like none I've ever seen surround me. . . ."

He paused and she urged him, "Go on."

"I remembered walking back to the room where I found

her and knew I hadn't done it. I was plenty mad at her for spinning me around, but I hadn't killed her.''

He paused for a long while, and this time she didn't say anything.

Finally, he spoke on a deep sigh. ''Almost immediately, I remembered coming back to the garden house in Ellisville and finding Sylvie's body. Both times, then and now, I remembered trying to get a pulse, bending to put the side of my face to first Sylvie's and later Carole's chest and trying to make there be a heartbeat.''

He put his head on her shoulder and wept like a small child. ''I didn't do it, Neesie. I haven't killed anybody. Oh God, you don't know how that makes me feel.''

She stroked his shoulder slowly, held him and in a few minutes she heard a car door slam, then Luke let himself in with his key. Rushing to the sofa, Luke sat on the other side of Marlon and hugged him tightly. He and Annice and Marlon cried as Marlon repeated his story of seeing the unearthly light to Luke.

''You know,'' Marlon said, ''I began to feel different this morning when I woke up after sleeping so long. I was so mad with my parents, I couldn't use what I'd learned from them about God. Yesterday, when I talked with you, Neesie, you said they lived on in me. That meant Carole and Sylvie lived on in me too, and I didn't have to die from misery and hurt.

''You said I felt my *anger* had killed them all.'' He shuddered a bit, then he turned tear-blinded eyes to her. ''Thank you, Neesie. Thank you so much.''

''Yes,'' Luke said quietly. ''Thank God and thank you.'' He leaned over and kissed her gently on the lips.

They sat in companionable silence for a few minutes before Annice asked, ''Who'd like waffles and blueberry syrup?''

Marlon laughed, his breath catching, ''Better make a heap. I'm one hungry man.''

"With Canadian bacon, I could be tempted," Luke teased her.

"Everybody gets to help," Annice said, laughing. "I'm not doing this rap alone."

As they went into the kitchen, another car door slammed and Luke looked out the window. "That's Sheriff Keyes and Mac Townsend."

Annice answered the doorbell and let the men in. A thoughtful Sheriff Keyes shook Marlon's hand. "Good news, son, but I'm afraid that's not the end of it."

"What do you mean?" Luke asked.

Mac Townsend spoke up. "I was at the sheriff's office getting the scuttlebutt when you called and we talked about this latest news. I believe my client, but a girl is dead. Another girl died by someone's hand a year ago and Marlon was at the scene both times. His story is that he put his head to their chest to get a heartbeat, but there was blood on his hands and his face. That's evidence. His DNA was there in Louisiana. His fingerprints there and here. I've got the reputation of freeing sinners from hell, but it won't be easy. And this isn't over."

The sheriff nodded as he looked at Marlon. "I'm afraid he's right."

"Hearing this new information, you think they'll still indict?" Annice asked.

"There's no telling what a grand jury will do. We don't have many murders in this neck of the woods. Attorney Townsend here's a crackerjack lawyer, and if anybody can prove you innocent, he can."

Marlon looked scared again now. "I don't want to be *proven* innocent. I *am* innocent. Don't you believe me?"

Both the sheriff and Attorney Townsend nodded and said they did. Then the sheriff turned to Marlon. "Son, I've seen men swear they didn't kill or commit other crimes, only to confess later. It's not that we don't trust you, it's just that we have to make every effort to punish whoever did this deed. And first, we've got to find whoever did it."

"And me," Mac Townsend said, "I've had men who've killed and confessed in the end. They had choirboy faces and butter wouldn't melt in their mouths. But they killed and some went on killing until they were caught redhanded. We may need more than what you've just told us." Mac turned to Annice. "He doesn't have limbic rage, you told me. That's a blessing. I'm sorry things can't be clearer here, but there's a lot of hope now where there was little before."

By then, Annice and Marlon had prepared breakfast and it was ready. Mac Townsend and the sheriff decided to stay. The sheriff laughed and sniffed the air. "When I smell waffles and blueberry syrup and Canadian bacon, I know there's a heaven somewhere."

Annice served as the men sat at the big table in the kitchen, sipping coffee. Marlon helped her. Annice turned to him. "Two waffles, honey? Three?"

Marlon drew a deep breath. "Just one," he said sadly. "I'm not very hungry after all."

After the sheriff and Mac Townsend had gone, Annice, Luke and Marlon sat in the living room listening to music. A quiet, thoughtful Marlon listened to their choice of classical music and they listened to his Toni Braxton and Snoop Doggy Dog CDs.

What the sheriff had said about the case not being over hung in their minds, saddening them.

After a while, Luke told them, "I have to go put the finishing touches on my—our—proposal changes. I've spent more time on this one than on all my proposals combined."

"Why do you say 'our'?" Annice asked.

"Just giving credit where credit is due. Claire helped me a lot with this one. She's brilliant with language." Did his face light with pride? Annice wondered. Was there a distance between Luke and her now? He had had plenty of time and had offered no explanation for the kiss between him and Claire. She could have screamed with frustration and hurt.

"I'm going back to the cave this afternoon," Marlon said

slowly. "I want to sort my paintings, but I won't be working there for a while, maybe not ever again."

Annice looked up. "Any idea what time you'll be going?"

"I'm not sure. Just sometime today. It's not something I look forward to. I'll ask one of the guys to help me move my stuff."

"Feel free to stay here as long as you want to. We can talk further later on. Talk through what this wonderful new happening means to you, to all of us."

"Could we do it now? Walk over with Luke? I'm full of things I want to tell you. Not even the sheriff's news washes that away. Neesie, even if I still have a hard row to hoe, I thank you from the bottom of my heart for helping me."

"And I thank you, too" Luke said heartily. "I've got to be moving on."

It was early afternoon when Annice left the administration building. Luke and Claire were together. Claire had been waiting for him and they had shut themselves up in his office. His secretary, Lisa, wasn't there. In Annice's office, Marlon had talked his heart out, getting up and walking around, smiling a lot, then looking sad.

"It's like someone took a big stone off my back," he had said. "If the world belonged to me, I'd give it all to you."

"Marlon, you did the heavy work. Give yourself most of the credit. I could only winnow through the material you gave me—freely gave me. You trusted me, and most of all, you trusted yourself. Always do that."

In a short while she was on the sidewalk, headed home. She had not said good-bye to Luke. Did he want to be bothered? It nettled her that Marlon hadn't said the definite time he would go to the cave or how long he would stay. And now, more than ever she wanted to find the letter Carole had written to him, because that letter could help clear him, or contribute to his doom. The sheriff had been right. He wasn't out of the woods yet. She wished Jon Ryson had had more to say; he was so sharply aware of what went on, had so many answers, but he had been mostly silent, listening.

As she started to pass the Johnsons' house, Velma hailed her. "I've been calling you for the last hour," Velma said. "Do come in for a few minutes."

"I'll be delighted to. I've got good news, not completely out of the woods yet, but good."

Velma threw her head back, laughing. "And I've got good news for you, completely out-of-the-woods good. You're going to love this—I hope. Arnold and I hope."

Inside, Arnold greeted and hugged her. "Imagine your passing by at such a great time. We were coming over."

"We can still go to my place if you're going stir crazy during the holidays."

"No, this can't wait any longer. I'm bursting to do it, but I give the honors to Arnold."

"Not much honor," Arnold grumbled, "and I go down on my knees to you in apology, Neesie. Let's sit down."

Velma and Arnold sat close together on the couch while Annice sat on a giant hassock near them.

Arnold cleared his throat as Velma beamed. "What's happened lately, and seeing you suffer so has nearly broken my heart," he said. "I wanted to tell you, but I just couldn't bring myself to do it. I can be a consummate coward."

"Stop knocking yourself, honey," Velma said softly. "Just tell her. You're doing it now and that's what's important."

Arnold looked at Annice, his eyes wide, his breathing shallow. "You always wanted to know who your parents are. . . ."

Annice tried to agree that she had always wanted to know, but she couldn't speak she was so tense.

Arnold patted his wife's knee as he said, "This woman here is your mother, your birth mother."

"Velma?" Annice whispered. "But how? Are you my father?"

He shook his head. "There's a story here. Frank Steele is your natural father."

"But. . ." Annice began as Arnold raised his hand.

"Hear me out. I want to say this now while I can. Who knows? I may go back into my coward's shell once more and never be able to speak again. My pride has been the cause of all this. My damned pride. Do you want to tell her, honey?"

Velma patted her husband's hand. "No. You're doing an excellent job."

Arnold paused for a long time before he began. "My wife and I split up about the same time your adoptive mother and real father split up. After a while, my wife and Frank began seeing each other. But they found they loved the mates they'd left, and both asked for a reconciliation." He swallowed hard. "After we'd been back together for a while, Velma found she was pregnant, and it was not of a timeframe to be mine. It was Frank's child. Had to be."

Annice put her hands to her face. "How wonderful," she said, beaming. She got up and hugged them both.

"You're mighty forgiving," Arnold said. "And hold on. I want to tell you. I want you to know that only my pride stood in the way of your knowing from the beginning. Velma wanted to tell you. Frank and Caroline wanted to tell you. I was the skunk at the picnic."

"Hush," Annice told him. "You're a wonderful man. You didn't have to tell me now."

"Well, you may forgive me, but I'll be a long time forgiving myself. I've been going crazy lately thinking you always wanted to know from the time you were a teenager. You needed to know. I only thought about what people would say. My wife pregnant by another man. Oh, I know it happens, but I had my pride to consider. Well, pride can choke you sometimes, leave you empty. The question is, Neesie, can you forgive me?"

"Wholly," Annice said. "The answer is that you've got to forgive yourself. We make mistakes, Arnold, terrible mistakes, and this is one I can understand. You love your wife and you were jealous. . . ."

"We never had another child," he said as a few tears gathered in his eyes. "Maybe that was God's punishment to me."

"No." Annice shook her head. "Forgive yourself as I forgive you. I'm sure God does. Arnold, I love you and Velma, always have, always will. Do you want me to call you mother and daddy as I call Frank and Caroline Mama and Dad?"

"No," Velma said. "*Velma* and *Arnold* is fine with us. You'll want to phone Frank and Caroline. I told her this morning we were going to tell you. I'm sure she's waiting for your call."

Annice went to the telephone, dialed, and Caroline picked up on the first ring.

"Mama," Annice said excitedly, "they just told me. I love you all. I think I'm the luckiest woman in the world."

"We're the ones who're lucky," Frank chimed in from the extension.

They had talked a while when Caroline asked, "Have they found whoever killed that poor girl?"

"Not yet," Annice said, "but Marlon's got his memory back. Isn't that wonderful?"

"What a blessing!" both Frank and Caroline said.

"We didn't get over there Christmas, and you and Luke didn't come. How is he?"

"He's fine," Annice said with a heartiness she didn't feel. It didn't fool Caroline.

"Honey, what's wrong?"

"Nothing," Annice answered with tears in her voice. "This thing with Carole has just worn me out."

"Anymore news from the person who was giving you trouble, maybe stalking you, killing your cat, leaving sheets of paper in your desk?"

Annice hesitated and said no. She didn't tell them about chasing the man in the woods or about tripping over the wire in the cave. They'd be there in a heartbeat. And she certainly didn't tell them she was going back to the cave to look for the letter that could possibly help Marlon. They would forbid it. Luke would forbid it. But then, none of them was going to know.

"You're happy about this?" Frank said. "You're sure? You forgive us for not telling you all these years?"

Annice was so delighted, she would have forgiven them anything. "I forgive you," she told them, "and I love the four of you and my beloved sister and brother very, very much."

"And sweetheart," Frank said, "we're so happy you and Luke are altogether back together again." Caroline said softly, "How happy you must be." But Annice felt sad. She needed to know what lay between Claire and Luke.

On the way home, Annice felt lightheaded with success at Marlon's breakthrough. To know you could help someone put their life in order, that you could help them to heal. That was what her work was all about.

"Darn it," she said suddenly. Why couldn't Marlon have set a specific time for going to the cave? She didn't think he would think to look for a letter from Carole, since he wasn't expecting one, but he might. She had asked Mac Townsend not to tell him about the letter just yet and he had agreed. "Now don't go withholding evidence," he'd said, and she had flinched at remembering the manila envelope she held with the letter to Bill Sullivan.

Her head hurt with wanting this to be over. She had the most wonderful news in the world and she gloried in it. But life never ran smoothly. There was Luke, too closely bound to Claire just now. And there was Marlon—not out of danger yet.

Chapter 29

The next morning, Annice set out for the cave. She was skittish about going and she wouldn't stay long, but she had to do this for Marlon. Bundled against the sharp December winds, she hurried along when she struck the side of her gloved hand to her forehead. She had told Della she would be by that morning.

Slowing her pace, she looked from the cave to Della's place in the distance. She should have driven, but she wouldn't go back now. She would go to Della's first.

Luke and Claire would be driving to New York about now. He had said he'd call her when they arrived. Her heart constricted as she wondered about the new distance between them. But he was still sweet, thoughtful.

Walking briskly then, she made her mind a blank. She reached the house in record time and found a note on the door addressed to her. Taking out the thumbtack and opening it, she read:

Neesie, love, I had an urgent call to go to D.C.
Make yourself at home. I'll be

*back shortly. Calvin will entertain
you.*

D.

She put the note in her tote bag and knocked. There was no answer. She knocked louder. Still no answer. Trying the lock gave no results. Drawing herself up in her heavy coat, she went around the side of the house to the round house where Della served summer meals to guests. Calvin must be back here. As she passed a clump of evergreens next to the round house, she heard guttural sounds inside and stopped. When the sounds continued, she listened harder and heard violent cursing. Creeping closer to the house, she looked in a window.

Calvin was inside with his back to her. He blindly turned once and his face was a study in rage. Limbic rage? Her breath nearly stopped. As she watched, he screamed an epithet. To her amazement, he picked up a big, heavy oak rocker and threw it across the room as if it were a folding chair. The chair mostly struck a wall, but part of it struck a window, breaking it. Limbic rage sufferers had unusual strength.

She was lightheaded with surprise, and every instinct told her to leave. She couldn't help him now. Pressing her tote bag close to her body, she turned and walked swiftly away from the house, toward the cave, then moved into a jogging stance.

As she neared the cave, Annice slowed, her thoughts overwhelming her. Calvin almost certainly had limbic rage. The two girls had been badly beaten; had he used the devilish strength the malady gave him? You didn't necessarily kill with the affliction, but you might. The knowledge disoriented her a little.

Slowing as she reached the cave, she dug into her tote bag for the flashlight and found only the smaller one. Damn it! She had meant to put the more powerful flashlight in her bag last night but had left it on the kitchen table. She shook her head. She would pick up the flashlight and come back. She felt winded and tense but it took her only a short span of time to accomplish this errand.

The yellow police tape was on the ground now and she stepped over it, only to come face to face with another shock. A painting of her sat on an easel near the doorway. So Marlon had been here. Was he still around?

She shook her head to clear the fog from her mind. She had come looking for a letter to Marlon from Carole. She would get it and come out quickly, and if she couldn't find it, she wouldn't stay too long.

Walking swiftly, she felt herself developing sight all over, like eyes in the back of her head. She paused at the place where she had tripped over the wire and went into the room where Carole had been killed. She didn't look at the chalk outline of Carole's dead body. Shuddering, she found she couldn't stop looking. Then she turned and went to the opposite room. Going directly to the ledge with the slots in it, she got the powerful flashlight from her bag, searched each of three rough rock slots and found nothing. She couldn't give up now. Feeling frustrated, her eyes fell on the body outline across the way and her heart thumped wildly.

Wait! There was the edge of a white envelope that had slid behind the ledge, and she slipped her hand in and pulled it out. Only the word *Marlon* was on the envelope. Quickly shoving it into her tote bag, she turned to leave when a crowlike croaking, a shrill whistle followed by low and crazy cackling laughter, filled the room. She had stayed too long.

"Turn around," the familiar voice demanded.

She turned and was eight or more feet from the figure dressed in black with a black ski mask on his face.

Throwing his head back, laughing fiendishly, he held the gun in his hand steady. He waved her across to the other room and her legs threatened to buckle under her. "Sit down in the place I killed Carole," he commanded.

A blanket of fear nearly smothered her, making it almost impossible to breathe.

"Don't do this," she whimpered.

"*Shut up!* Sit down, I said."

He waved the gun about as she sought some advantage and found none. She had been trained in karate when she studied in New York. She wouldn't go down without a fight. She sat down quietly. "Let me introduce myself," he said, chuckling, "but then I believe you know me." Throwing back his hood, he snatched off the ski mask and she gasped with horror.

"Calvin!"

"Yeah. *Good little Calvin.* I can tell you the whole story. You won't be telling anyone."

"Please. I can get you help and I can help you."

"Shut up, bitch!" he roared. "I don't want to have to tell you again."

She thought it best to be silent then and wait for an opening to strike. Her body seemed to be encased in ice and ice water slush took the place of blood. Fear seemed to come from the ground, racing up her body until she was nearly unnerved.

"I'll give you something before I kill you," he said. "I'm sure you want to know why I killed Sylvie Love and Carole and why you'll be next, then God only knows how many more."

They were both silent before he began. "I spied on Sylvie and Marlon in the garden house when they made love. I listened to them talk and knew he'd be gone for a while. I knocked after he left. I wanted to have sex with her. They'd turned me on. She slapped me hard when I asked her, and when I tried to grab her wrists, she scratched me. It didn't matter. I knew I was going to kill her before she did anything. I got my gun out of my jacket and moved in. I knocked her down and jammed my gun to her chest as she fought me. I shot her twice in the heart. When she fell, I fell onto her and I beat her, really beat her. Then I raped her. I was having a spell like the ones I started getting when my Dad left us. Sylvie reminded me of the woman who took him away from Mom and me. Independent. Knowing men wanted her. I wasn't going to let her play with me that way . . . leading me on.''

But nothing he had said showed that Sylvie had led him on in any way.

"There was a stream in the woods near by. I washed off the blood from my hands and clothes. I nearly froze my ass off, but I was happy.''

He laughed then, a hyenalike sound. "I was there only a day or so after, and I came home. I was visiting a cousin of my Mom's. I left and no one ever questioned me. I knew Sylvie from other summers I'd visited. So I knew what she was. Marlon went to her head. She shouldn't have led me on.''

Sylvie hadn't led him on. She died because she was like the woman Calvin's father had left Calvin and his mother for. And Carole? She couldn't bear to think of her now as she sat in the space where Carole had been killed. Annice was crying inside that Sylvie and Carole were lovely, lovely girls who never should have died.

He cocked his head to one side. "And Carole? You want to know about Carole? She and Marlon were fooling around. Not sex, but she liked him enough to do it. They turned me on like Sylvie and Marlon had when I sneaked up on them. I knew she was supposed to meet Marlon the morning I killed her, so I hid in the back of the cave. I called to her and she came back. I tried to kiss her, but she knew what I wanted. She laughed at me. Laughed at me, said she wouldn't want me if I was the last boy on earth. . . . I went into a rage. I carry my gun all the time, so I made her lie down and I shot her, beat her. You know the rest. I was too scared to stay and rape her.''

"You were going to kill them anyway, even if Sylvie hadn't slapped you and Carole hadn't laughed. . . .'' This was a bad dream, a nightmare, she thought, but her mind refused to back away. This was the deepest reality.

His malevolent eyes were like coals of fire in the dimly lit room. She remembered the man by the culvert had called them "mad dog eyes." "Now," he said, "it's your turn."

In spite of his commands not to, she had to speak. "Why would you kill me? What have I done to you?"

He didn't hesitate, as if it were a question he'd waited for. "You're like my Dad's wife, Julie, the one he left Mom and me for. I wanted to stay with him and he agreed, but *she* didn't want me with him. I started to have spells after she wouldn't let him take me. But I don't need a spell to kill. I think when I killed Sylvie, I was in a spell. But with Carole, I don't know."

He held the gun back, softly chuckling. "I saw you as you walked away today and knew you knew about my 'spells,' but I would have killed you anyway.

"I saw you stop in front of the cave and dig into your bag, then leave. I thought you had forgotten something and you'd be back. I kept my cloak and other stuff hidden in the cave.

"I knew I was going to kill you from the start. Before you got the damned security, I used to watch you sleep. I followed you in the woods as you walked on the sidewalk. It was me you and Doc Jones chased through the woods.

"And I put the papers by Sylvie and Carole and in your desk. *Angel face. Devil body.* I've got another one ready for you in that bag." He pointed to his knapsack on the ground.

His voice seemed tired now as he said, "I killed your cat. I hate cats. Julie has three cats.

"Sylvie and Carole were like her, too. Leading men on. Teasing. Throwing it up to us, then backing down. And you act like you own the world and all the men in it. I won't let you treat me like that." He stopped as his face contorted. "Bitches! All of you! I'm gonna rid the world of all of you!"

"Calvin!"

"I told you to shut up! I left a painting of you outside this morning that I stole from Marlon sometime ago. Marlon set up the painting and the sketch of Carole before and after I killed her. He'd already left the ones of Sylvie."

"This is wrong," she said firmly. She could only die once.

"I love my Dad and *she* took him away," he said, his voice catching in his throat. "I'm going to make every woman pay who reminds me of her. Be happy in hell, Doc!"

He bent above her then and got to his knees, his gun pointed at her heart. He was only a couple of inches from her chest when she held her breath and lunged, digging her fairly long fingernails into his eyes, making him scream with pain. Her move startled and enraged him, throwing him temporarily off balance. Then she took the outside ridge of her right hand and struck him just under the nose, a violent clout, and he screamed again.

But he managed to pull the trigger, and her heart stopped. Blessedly, there was only an empty click. Beyond fury now, he flung the gun from him as the cave was filled with a bellowing Luke calling "Neesie!"

In a panic, Calvin went toward the gun, then changed his mind. He was getting the hell out of here. It would be her word against his, and there was always a later time. He swore he'd get her. He bounded toward the cave back opening. Then, feet flying, he headed toward the highway.

Scrambling up, Annice met Luke in the doorway. "We've got to stop him!" she cried.

"Are you all right?"

"Yes. Let's go, Luke. Let's go!"

But Calvin had a good head start on them. They were no match for his crazed feet. They followed him as he streaked across the clearing. He was powered by youth and the fury of his illness and his anger at his father and his father's second wife. Then Calvin was slowed a bit as he vaulted the fence and went onto the highway. Déjà vu. Only a few days before, they had followed him and the red light had proved him lucky; he had escaped. This time, they watched in horror as a sports utility vehicle struck him, throwing him up in the air at least fifteen feet.

Three cars ran over his body before the drivers could brake, and then it was chaos on the highway.

Chapter 30

"Thank you for coming in. We won't keep you long."

Annice and Luke seated themselves with the sheriff and Jon Ryson at the pockmarked table in the interrogation room of the sheriff's office.

"Just tell me slowly what happened," Sheriff Keyes said.

Annice recounted the incidents of the just past hours, shuddering in memory as she did so.

When she had finished, Luke reached over and squeezed her hand. "You've been through hell," Jon Ryson said.

She reached down and picked up her tote bag and took out the larger manila envelope that held Bill Sullivan's letter and the bracelet. She put it on the table, then took out the envelope addressed to Marlon and put it beside the first envelope.

"I found these in the cave," she said, "a couple of days back and today. They were well hidden. Bill Sullivan told you the contents of the letter in the manila envelope and how he left it in the cave, intending to pick it up later. The white envelope holds a letter to Marlon. I went back to look for it because I thought there might be some incriminating evidence against Marlon. He's been through so much; I wanted to help him.''

The sheriff looked at her sharply. "Well, we won't charge you for withholding evidence. You were just trying to make it better for Marlon."

The sheriff reached into a drawer of the table, took out a letter opener and slid it toward Annice. "You open it. Read it to us."

Annice opened the envelope, took out the letter and stared at it blindly for a minute or so before she began to read:

Dear Marlon,

I will tell you tomorrow where I have hidden this letter for you. I'm turning over a new leaf and I won't be teasing you anymore.

Talking to Dr. Steele has made me know that I'm not acting the way I should. She feels I deserve respect and honor, and I'm beginning to feel that way, too. So I've got to respect and honor myself.

Marlon, I really love you. I'm giving Julius his ring back. He's going to be mad, but what can he do?

I'm going to wait for you and work hard to become the woman you deserve.

> *My very best love,*
> *Carole*

With brimming eyes, Annice passed the letter to Luke. A sob escaped her throat as Luke held her hand.

The sheriff's and Jon Ryson's eyes on her were vividly sympathetic.

"We'll be able to tie this one up," the sheriff said. "We'll get DNA and fingerprints from the murder scene in Ellisville and compare them to what we get from Calvin's body. They found DNA they've never been able to match. I'll want to talk with you two again tomorrow. There're lots of questions I'll need the answers to."

An officer stuck his head in the door. "There's a Mrs. Curtis here to see you, sir. I told her you were busy...."

"This can't wait." A stricken Della came into the room as Luke and Annice looked up with surprise. Della held a book with a black cover in her hands.

The three men stood up. Annice went to Della, hugged her tightly for long minutes. Finally the sheriff said, "Sit down, Mrs. Curtis. You're welcome to talk with me, but can it wait a few minutes?"

Della shook her head. "I want to talk with them in the room." Her outflung hands indicated Luke and Annice.

"Very well," the sheriff said. Della sat at the table and passed the black-covered book to the sheriff.

"Read the last page," she said, crying. "It tells you everything."

The sheriff opened the book and leafed through the pages until he came to the last double page. He read slowly:

2 down and 1 to go for right now.
I have killed Sylvie Love and Carole. What a thrill.
Now for the prime act, to press a loaded gun to Dr.
Steele's chest and pull the trigger. To beat her as
I beat Sylvie and Carole.
My Dad broke my Mom's and my heart when he
left us for another woman, Julie. This is the first time
I've ever written her name. Dr. Steele reminds me so
much of Julie. She thinks she owns the world.

I feel like I own the world as I plan her death. She
will never suspect until the end. Then she will know
when it's too late.

Della's eyes had dried as the sheriff finished reading. The room was silent when her thin prolonged wail rent the air, then she was silent again.

Della looked at Annice a long while. "I knew my son was sick. I spoke with him about getting treatment for his *spells,* which was what we called his loss of temper. He told me, 'No, Mom, they're *fun.*' He said if I made him see a doctor, he'd run away.''

She lifted her tear-stained face to the heavens. ''I'd lost my husband. I couldn't lose my son. Now I have lost him forever.''

Annice got up and squatted beside Della's chair, hugging her. ''Come home with me,'' she said. ''You don't need to be alone.''

''No,'' Della moaned. ''I've got to go home and be with his spirit. He kept the diary and asked me not to open it. I never did. He trusted me not to open it, and I trusted him to do no wrong. Then tonight when I got home from the accident, I broke it open and read some of it. Dear God, what did I do wrong?''

''Don't blame yourself,'' Annice said gently. ''Losing his father affected his brain. He developed an illness. He blames his father's wife for not accepting him. He was at an age when a boy needs his father.''

Della listened to Annice's words and seemed comforted. She stood up. ''I'm going to go now,'' she said. ''His spirit will need me to be with it. He changed so much after his dad left. It was like witnessing an angel change into a devil.''

A swift look passed among Luke and Annice, the sheriff and Jon Ryson as they remembered the words on the sheets of paper: *Angel face. Devil body.*

''I should have tried harder,'' Della cried. ''There must have been something I could have done. My boy stayed out until all hours of the night, and when I threatened to put a stop to it, he said I'd never see him again if I made him stop. He said he needed to be free. He said he hurt a lot and he had to deal with it, in *his* way. What was he running from today when he got hit?'' She flung the question out.

The sheriff licked dry lips. ''Calvin tried to kill Dr. Steele in the cave,'' the sheriff said sadly. ''Dr. Jones caught him. He was running from them.''

Shock lined Della's face. "Oh no! Neesie, forgive me. I can't ask you to forgive him. Why would he try to kill you?"

"He said I reminded him of his stepmother whom he hated and he said he wanted to kill, had wanted to kill since his dad left."

"Oh Lord, forgive me," Della whispered. "Can you ever forgive me?"

"You must forgive yourself," Annice said. "And I certainly forgive you. We all make terrible mistakes and we have to live beyond them."

Standing up, Annice held Della and rocked her. "Luke and I will be here for you. Depend on it."

Della nodded. "I'm going home now to be with my son's spirit. I have many prayers to pray and I will talk with God as Calvin couldn't seem to talk with Him. I drove over so I'm OK. Thank you all for helping me."

"I'm not sure you should drive," the sheriff said. "I can have someone take you home and I can send your car home tomorrow."

Della shook her head. "I've been crazy with worry. I knew Calvin couldn't go on the way he was headed. I had one bad dream after another. Now, he's at peace." She looked at them fiercely. "I'm all right, I tell you. I'm all right."

The sheriff stood up. "Tomorrow, I'll need to talk with you again, Mrs. Curtis. There'll be questions you'll want to ask me and questions I'll want to ask you. I'm so sorry about what has happened. God help us all."

Chapter 31

At home that night, Annice and Luke sipped mulled cider.
Luke massaged Annice's shoulders; then she massaged his.
They sat on the sofa and listened to Christmas carols, humming "O Holy Night" as the CD played the song. It was
nearly New Year's, but the carols were so soothing.

Annice was thoughtful as she lay back. "I'm really worried about Della, and I'll call her later. She should stay with
me."

"It's the shock of a lifetime." Luke was suddenly still.
"Perhaps she'll come later on."

Suddenly Annice sat up. She would wait no longer. "Are
you growing away from me?" she asked quietly. "You've
seemed so preoccupied."

Luke hugged her, kissed her fiercely, then asked her,
"Does that kiss come from someone who's growing away
from you?"

Annice blushed. "I've wondered. I saw you kiss Claire
a few days back. Then you've seemed bothered, preoccupied," she said again.

He looked at her with his eyes half closed. "You saw

Claire kiss *me*. Let me get to what's happened today, love, then we'll cover that day.''

"Yes, today. I was so frightened. I thought you and Claire were on your way to New York."

Luke rubbed the side of his face with his forefinger. "It's the damnedest thing," he said. "We were out on the Washington-Baltimore Parkway, and I suddenly felt you were in danger, that you were calling me. Did you?"

"Not aloud," she said, "but I was screaming inside, especially when Calvin made me sit, then lie down."

Luke's eyes flashed fire. "It makes me crazy to even think of it. We stopped at a rest stop and I told Claire to drive on to New York. I was lucky enough to get a taxi back here. I went to your house, to Della's. The Johnsons hadn't seen you. It didn't take me long to figure out the cave—and I heard voices and shouted for you. . . ."

"The loudest, most welcome shout I've ever heard."

Luke stroked her back. "As for Claire, the day you must have seen us, she was morbidly upset, having a hard time. Honey, Claire suffers from deep depressions, has ever since we were children. She's lucky to be alive."

"She's so beautiful."

"Physically perhaps, but she's never grown up. She's spoiled and doesn't seem to want to get away from being spoiled. You're the one who's beautiful and just what I need to fill my cup."

Annice looked at him, her eyes shining. "And you're not in love with her?"

"I'm in love with you. Fallen-off-the-cliff in love with you."

"You're a nut."

"Oh?"

"A sweet, wonderful nut."

"And you're the most desirable woman I've ever known."

She smiled widely then and her eyes were dreamy. "I'm glad. I'd hate to feel all this surging desire by myself."

She touched his face. "Let's give Marlon a call. Give Della a call. And the Johnsons."

"Yes. Claire's got my cell phone number. I forgot to tell you she's taking your erstwhile boyfriend away."

"My erst . . . ?"

"Mel Sunderlin. They seem to be developing a sudden thing."

Annice smiled. "I'm happy for them."

Luke tipped her chin up. "You're not jealous?"

Annice touched her tongue to the corner of his mouth as he hugged her tightly. "I've got you. That's all I've ever needed. Spend the night."

"Try and drive me away."

Chapter 32

March of that same year

By the first days of March, things had settled down at Casey's School. There was still a certain sadness at Carole's death, but young minds often heal swiftly. Luke and Annice had asked Carole's mother and received permission to put the statue of an angel above her grave. Now things were beginning to settle down.

Riding into Alexandria in Luke's new Infiniti, Annice felt happy. They would choose a ring today to replace the one she had thrown away. Luke reached over and touched her thigh under the heavy coat she wore.

"Penny for your thoughts," he told her.

She shook her head and said slowly, "I was thinking about the first ring you gave me. Luke, I'm so sorry."

"Stop it! You were hurt and alone. I wouldn't blame you if you came after me. I won't say I forgive you because there's nothing to forgive. We're back together. That's all that matters."

Inside Kismet Jewelry, which was partially owned by a

friend of Luke's, they were immediately greeted by the solicitous friend who took their outer garments. The group of banana glove leather chairs and the big glass coffee table lent an air of luxury as they settled in.

Shortly after, an assistant returned with a cart carrying trays of platinum, white gold, and yellow gold mountings on the bottom shelves and trays of splendid unmounted diamonds on top of a black velvet bed. Annice held her breath. Could she find another diamond like the first?

She was disappointed with the first half tray of diamonds. Splendid, but not what she wanted. But ah-h-h, the second half.

Breathing faster now, she pinpointed a diamond setting that was so like the first diamond Luke had given her. A large emerald-cut diamond, with two smaller emeralds flanking it, set in platinum. The diamonds flashed fire and were beautiful to behold. With a happy cry, she pointed out to the manager the diamonds she chose, and he beamed.

"Your ring will be ready for you tomorrow," the manager said. "You have chosen well. It is one of our most beautiful rings."

Luke's eyes on her were warm, dancing. He loved to give her presents, as she loved giving him presents. Luke and the friend shook hands. Then he and Annice walked out in a haze of joy.

In the car she said laughingly, "Let's go home, so I can give you the present of myself."

"Uh-uh," he told her. "We've got one more stop."

"Oh? Where?"

"You'll know when you get there."

Shortly after, they pulled up in front of Best of the Lot Pet Shop. Luke parked and squeezed her hard after helping her out.

The shop was crowded, but a salesman Luke knew came to them. He and Luke exchanged conspiratorial looks. "The package you ordered is ready," the salesman said. "I'll get it for you."

Facing him, Annice tapped Luke's chest with her fists. "This can only mean you're getting me another cat."

"My lips are sealed."

They strolled the aisles looking at the pleasing display of pet supplies and the birds and animals. An African gray parrot whistled loudly and jauntily as Annice passed. A nearby salesman chortled, "He does have an eye for lovely women."

Luke waggled his finger at the parrot who reared back on his perch. "You're aching for a black eye, buddy." The parrot scrunched up his neck, then croaked, "Pretty girl! Pretty girl!"

The salesman came back with a gold foil-covered box with several holes in it, topped by a big, red satin ribbon bow. Luke took off the lid, and huddled in a corner was the most darling kitten. Annice picked up the animal, examined it, stroked it. Luke put the box on the floor.

"It's like Calico." Her eyes filled with happy tears. "Oh, thank you, sweetheart. You even got me a female, like Calico."

"It wasn't easy. Calico had a certain aplomb, wouldn't you say?"

"Definitely."

The salesman looked at them approvingly. "Now look around, and if there's anything else you need I'll be right with you."

"We'll need food for it," Annice said. "Supplies."

"We've got the best."

Luke looked at her and grinned. "Making you happy is making me horny. Put the cat back in the box. *Now* we can go home."

Annice put the cat in the box. "Not until we get cat supplies."

"*Now*. I'll stand still for one bag of cat food."

"You're hopeless."

"No, I'm very hopeful at the moment."

"Stop it. I'm beginning to laugh, and I don't want to get hysterical."

"It's OK. The whole world is our friend right now. All the world loves a lover, and I'm taking you home and making love to you until your toes curl with rapture."

"How poetic. How enthralling." Annice flashed him with her eyes. "Promises. Promises. I've got a few promises of my own."

Luke took her in his arms and kissed her then, long and hard, as she struggled a bit at first, then relaxed and loved.

In a little while, the people in the store were laughing, then they clapped and whistled, enjoying the lovers. When they finally came apart, the clapping accelerated as Luke said, "I'll grab the cat food and you get the boxed cat. We're heading for home."

In the car, she sat smiling.

"What are you thinking?" he asked.

Without hesitation she told him, "I was thinking about how long my heart was haunted with wanting you, needing you. Now I've got you for my own."

He reached for her hand and squeezed it. "I was haunted too. Now we've got each other," he said softly. "No more haunted hearts."

She felt the joy of heaven surge in her breast as she echoed him. "No more haunted hearts."

Epilogue

One year and a half later

"Comfortable?" Luke stroked Annice's long, slender fingers, then kissed them one by one.

Annice lay propped up in a high white hospital bed, beaming at him. Any time now, their child would be born.

Annice blew a stream of air at him. "Am I comfortable? Well, I guess I'm as comfortable as I can be with this huge kid not being able to make up his mind if he wants to join us or not."

"He's like you, stubborn."

"I hope he's more like you. I have names for him. Luke, for you, Frank, for my father, and William for Dr. Casey."

"They'll all be really proud. I know I am."

The doctor stuck his head in the door. "May I speak with you a few moments, Dr. Jones?" He asked Annice, "Can you spare him? This won't take long."

"Of course," Annice told him.

Luke would be watching as she gave birth and the thought thrilled her. Frank and Caroline were in the waiting area, with Velma Johnson. She couldn't wait to e-mail photos of the baby to her sister and brother, Ashley and Whitley, who were both traveling out of the country.

As happy as she felt, she sighed. It was April now and it had been over a year since Carole's death. She and Luke had had a white marble angel placed at the head of Carole's grave. Her mother had wept. "I never told her I loved her," she'd said.

So much had happened, and she mulled it over quickly. She and Luke had been married over a year.

Julius had come to her. "I'm sorry, Doc, that I've been such a fool. I apologize. I knew how you felt about Carole. I loved her. Still do. My Dad would have had a fit, but I was going to start college, then marry her. Marlon and I got so close I think because we both wanted to marry early." Julius was now in college in New Orleans.

Dr. Will had decided to retire, leaving the school to Luke and Annice to run.

Marlon was studying on scholarship in a prestigious New England art institute. He seemed to have completely recovered. Ah, the resilience of youth, she thought.

Annice and the Johnsons were closer than ever, but the Steeles had a permanent place in her heart. Finding that Velma was her mother had brought her such joy, but it in no way intruded on her love for Caroline and Frank Steele.

Belle was graduating from D.C.'s famed Ellington School for the Performing Arts, with a scholarship to Juilliard.

Claire and Mel Sunderlin were married now, and Claire seemed happier. Mel had found it necessary to tell Annice that she would always hold a place in his heart, but he'd decided to move on. Smiling, she had murmured, "Wise man. Wise move."

Sylvie Love's parents had apologized profusely to Marlon and Luke for insisting Marlon had killed her. Both Marlon and Luke said they understood.

And Della, the friend she had first thought of now was the one she focused on last because it was still so painful.

Della was healing slowly with maximum help from Luke and Annice. She still blamed herself for Calvin's madness and death and was in therapy with Dr. Casey.

As the doctor and Luke came back into the room with a nurse, Annice grimaced with a flash of ripping pain and cried out.

A medical team was soon around her, positioning her for birth. Everybody was in masks. She had been in the hospital earlier that day because the doctor thought the baby was ready, but he had not been ready.

"Go on, yell," the doctor said to Annice, laughing. "This is hard and we all know it." Her whole body seemed to be tearing apart and pain flashed around her in lightning waves.

"Dear God," she cried, with tears raining down her face.

"Bear down, hard," the doctor said. "And scream your head off. I chose a sound-dampened room for you."

Annice shook a bit with laughter in the midst of all her tears. If Luke wanted more children as he said he did, he could share in the birthing. She'd tell him that as soon as she could, but just now she was focused on bearing down. "Down and out," she murmured. "Come on, kid. Show your precious face."

A wondrous kind of pain held her in its grip—a pain like no other. The exalted pain of birth, promising a depth of life like no other.

"Bear down, hard!" the doctor kept saying as if it were a chant, a mantra.

Luke squeezed first one then the other of her hands, stroked her fingers. Then she clutched his hands, her fingernails digging mercilessly into his flesh. "Help me," she cried inside, but she didn't want to scare him by crying the words out. Finally she did say it and his tears dropped on their intertwined hands.

"Oh, my darling, if only I could."

"It's a first birth, but it's going really well," the doctor reassured him. "In a few minutes now. . . . We've done all the right things."

Annice opened her eyes that she had shut against pain and saw the earnest masked brown faces of the doctor and the nurses delivering her baby, but more, she saw Luke whom she loved more than life itself. She had a precious world.

With one last pain of protest, the baby's head appeared, and it was all pleasure from then on. The doctor held the infant aloft and lightly slapped its bottom. A shrill scream of anger rent the room and the baby was here. The child she had so long wanted was here!

As they cleaned the infant and laid it on her bare stomach, Luke seemed about to burst with joy. She was bonded from the beginning with this small bundle of flesh that was utterly dependent on her, and she held him and Luke in the circle of her arms, her heart, her soul.

Luke's eyes on her were warm with pride and love. "Congratulations, my beloved," he said gently, his eyes wet with tears. "Welcome to our own special heaven."

Dear Readers,

Thank you so much for your many gracious and generous letters comenting on my books and inquiring about the ones to come.

I enjoy your comments. They're helpful to me in plotting future stories. Let me know what you don't like as well as what you like.

I fervently wish for you a long, happy, healthy and prosperous life. May you thrive and thoroughly enjoy a romantic future.

Best of everything,
Francine Craft

ABOUT THE AUTHOR

Francine Craft is the pen name of a Washington, D.C.-based writer who has enjoyed writing for many years. A native Mississippian, she has also lived in New Orleans and found it fascinating.

She has been a research assistant for a large nonprofit organization, an elementary school teacher, a business school instructor, and a federal government legal secretary. Her books have been highly praised by readers and reviewers.

Francine's hobbies are prodigious reading, photography, and songwriting. She has a significant other and presently lives with a family of friends and many goldfish.

More Sizzling Romances From
Gwynne Forster

__Obsession	1-58314-092-1	**$5.99**US/**$7.99**CAN
__Fools Rush In	1-58314-037-9	**$4.99**US/**$6.99**CAN
__Ecstasy	1-58314-177-4	**$5.99**US/**$7.99**CAN
__Swept Away	1-58314-098-0	**$5.99**US/**$7.99**CAN
__Beyond Desire	1-58314-201-0	**$5.99**US/**$7.99**CAN
__Secret Desire	1-58314-124-3	**$5.99**US/**$7.99**CAN
__Against All Odds	1-58314-247-9	**$5.99**US/**$7.99**CAN
__Sealed With A Kiss	1-58314-313-0	**$5.99**US/**$7.99**CAN
__Scarlet Woman	1-58314-192-8	**$5.99**US/**$7.99**CAN

Call tool free **1-888-345-BOOK** to order by phone or use this coupon
to order by mail.

Name_____

Address _____

City_____ State _____ Zip _____

Please send me the books I have checked above.

I am enclosing	$_____
Plus postage and handling*	$_____
Sales tax (in NY, TN, and DC)	$_____
Total amount enclosed	$_____

*Add $2.50 for the first book and $.50 for each additional book.

Send check or money order (no cash or CODs) to: **Arabesque Books, Dept.
C.O., 850 Third Avenue, 16th Floor, New York, NY 10022**

Prices and numbers subject to change without notice.

All orders subject to availability.

Visit our website at **www.arabesquebooks.com.**